ONLY THE QUIET

A Death Gate Grim Reapers Thriller Book Two

AMANDA M. LEE

WinchesterShaw Publications

One

"Did you hang out with them?"

"Sometimes."

"Did they know what you are?"

"Yes."

"Did you guys ever talk about anything important?"

"Once we had an illuminating discussion on why your mother wouldn't eat oranges."

I furrowed my brow, confused, and stared hard at Oliver Samuelson. I was relatively new on the job, so I'd yet to become comfortable with my co-worker's moods. We'd been working together for only two and a half weeks and we'd already undergone a tense situation that resulted in another of our co-workers dying at my magical hands — she had it coming, don't worry — so I'd taken to endlessly questioning him the past ten days thanks to the information he let slip during that encounter.

He wasn't taking it well.

"My mother didn't eat oranges?" I racked my memory for any hint that I knew that. I remembered very little about my mother. Mostly images gathered from the terrifying night something came through the death gate and killed her and my father, but seemingly sparing me for no particular reason. I was back at the death gate now in an official capacity. I was the Belle Isle gatekeeper. And Oliver, apparently a vampire, was a fixture in this location as far back as when my father served as gatekeeper ... and he was tightlipped when it came to sharing information about my parents. I found it irritating.

"You have to tell me something," I prodded, frustration bubbling up. "You can't drop a bomb — like you knew my parents before they died — and not say a single thing ever again. That's not fair."

Oliver, attractive in a classic Hollywood Cary Grant sort of way, let loose an exaggerated sigh. "Has anyone ever told you how annoying you are?"

"Yes." I saw no reason to lie. I, Isabella "Izzy" Sage, had been called annoying more times than I could count. Frankly, I was over it. "Before you get all high and mighty, you're annoying, too. In fact, I think you're more annoying than I am."

Oliver arched an eyebrow, amused. "Then I must *really* be annoying."

"You have no idea. You're also kind of mean." I didn't enjoy tossing around the word "mean" willy-nilly. It was very teen movie, and I liked to think I was above that. Still, I couldn't shake the suspicion that Oliver was purposely keeping information from me ... and I hated it.

"I'm mean?" Oliver checked an intake sheet and shook his head. "The Grimlocks are missing a delivery from last night."

He acted as if he was concerned about work — we serve as the ferrying system for souls after death, the last stop in this world before they move over to the next — but I knew better. He was bringing up the Grimlocks, a local reaper family I'd met upon moving back to the Detroit area, because he wanted to distract me with thoughts of dark hair, purple eyes and lean muscles. Well, I had news for him: I wasn't going to be easily distracted. "You have to tell me at least one thing."

He slowly slid his eyes to me and I could read the conflict in them. "Izzy ... ."

"You have to." I was firm. "I barely remember them. I want to know something important. Like ... did you know me when I was a kid?"

He slowly nodded. "You were around the gate all the time," he acknowledged. "They set up a spot for you right over there." He pointed toward an empty corner. "You always had the same blanket. It was purple and had some sort of cartoon character on it. You would sit there and draw for hours."

Well, that was something. I didn't know what to make of the tidbit, but it was something. "I still draw. I mean ... I haven't since I got here. We've been kind of busy. But I still draw."

"You had quite the imagination, as I recall." Oliver watched me with contemplative eyes. "You know, dwelling on the past won't help anyone. You should look forward, not back."

I appreciated the sentiment – not really but I liked to pretend I did – but I wasn't about to let him opt for an easy escape when he was finally opening up about the past. "Did you ever talk to me?"

"Of course I talked to you. I worked here for years with your parents. They weren't always gatekeepers. For a time, they ran the boathouse and served as assistants at the gate. Were you aware of that?"

I wasn't aware of much when it came to my parents' tenure on Belle Isle, a small island in the Detroit River between Michigan's automotive capital and Windsor. The island was essentially a 982-acre park that featured a yacht club, aquarium, casino, boathouse, nature center and conservatory. It's connected to Detroit by a bridge. It's not too large or special ... and yet I found it magical. Of course, that could have something to do with the death gate located beneath the aquarium, an opening between worlds that occasionally whispered to me. I rarely admitted that to anyone.

"I didn't know they were assistants," I admitted after a beat. "I don't remember them very well." And that right there was a big rip in the fabric of my very makeup. My parents died while protecting me — that's what the few memory shards I can recall tell me — and yet I barely remember them. They died when I was seven, and I was raised by my grandfather in New Orleans after that. I joined the reaper academy fresh out of high school and set my sights on returning here as soon as possible. Why? Even I wasn't sure. I felt I needed to be here. As an overachiever, that meant becoming one of the youngest gatekeepers ever … and taking an assignment absolutely nobody wanted.

"I'm sorry you don't remember them." Oliver appeared sincere. "They were good people and they loved you a great deal. They wouldn't want you fixating on their deaths this way. That's not who they were."

"You can say that because you knew them. I don't remember them."

"Which doesn't seem fair."

"It's definitely not fair," I agreed. "I'm not asking you to spill their secrets or anything." Not yet, I silently added. "I just want to know … something."

He pursed his lips. "Fine. Your sixth birthday party was held in the aquarium. There weren't a lot of kids around, but all the workers came and brought you presents. I gave you a stuffed dog that you carried around until … it happened. Your parents thought it was funny because you immediately fell in love with the dog and tried to walk it on a leash. Your father actually bought a leash for the stuffed dog because you insisted that dogs weren't allowed on the island if they weren't restrained and you didn't want him taken away."

"Max," I murmured, surprised. "You gave me Max."

He arched an eyebrow. "You remember the dog?"

"I still have him. He's in my room right now. He's one of the few things I still have from my childhood. Everything else was … destroyed." That included the house I'd shared with my parents. It was no longer in existence and no one had bothered to rebuild, which is why I lived in an apartment on the second floor of the boathouse instead of in a regular house. Of course, that was a relief. I didn't want to return to the abode where my parents died.

"You still have him?" Oliver's eyes lit with amusement. "That's fairly funny. I'm glad you still have him, though. For some reason it makes me happy."

He cracked a smile and then shook his head. "We need to focus on work. With Renee gone, we're down a body."

Renee was another sore spot between us. She'd been his co-worker for a long time. I'd killed her almost two weeks ago — using the Bruja magic passed down to me by my mother and grandfather — and we'd barely talked about it since. Oliver stood with me in that fight, and I had no doubt he would've killed Renee himself if it came to it, but he never mentioned her or what I'd done. It was as if he was avoiding the subject.

"I'm going to talk to the home office about getting someone else in here," I offered, uncomfortable. "I'm not sure when that'll happen. I'm sorry if you're working too many hours."

"I'm fine with the hours."

"Yeah, but ... ."

"I'm fine with the hours ... for now," he repeated. "We do need to get another person in here in case of an emergency. The two of us cannot handle everything ourselves. There's a reason this has always been a three-person job."

"I'll make a call this afternoon," I promised. "I meant to do it sooner, but ... well ... it seems weird to request a replacement for the woman I killed."

Oliver snorted. "It was her or you. You did what you had to do."

"Yeah, but ... she's still dead. She was also your friend."

"I don't know that I would consider her a friend," he hedged. "We were acquaintances. We had a few good times. It doesn't matter now. She's gone and we need to move forward."

That was a fairly brutal opinion. "It's not always that easy."

"It should be." He forced a smile that didn't make it all the way to his eyes. "Tell me about what's going on with you. Are you and Braden Grimlock officially an item?"

My mouth dropped open at the ridiculous question. "Um ... no! Why would you think that?"

"I've seen you two together."

Oh, well, that was simply ... absurd. Braden was handsome, sarcastic and completely full of himself. During my first few days on the job, when a rogue wraith had traveled through the gate and enhanced itself to the point it became a legitimate threat to all of us, we'd been forced to work together. A brief flirtation grew out of that interaction, but it had since died ... and I wasn't bitter about it at all.

"You haven't seen us together lately," I pointed out.

Oliver furrowed his brow. "No, but I thought he was sent to that conference in Florida."

I frowned. What conference in Florida? I didn't know anything about a conference in Florida. Of course, I didn't want to know about that conference ... or what else he did in his free time. I told myself over and over that was true. I almost believed it.

"I don't know what you're talking about." I made a big show of averting my eyes. "He hasn't been around. That's all that's important."

"But ... he's been emailing."

My cheeks colored under his intense gaze. How could he possibly know that? "We should focus on our work," I said crisply, gesturing toward the computer monitor. "You said the Grimlocks were down one delivery. Perhaps you should call them."

"Perhaps *you* should call them," he shot back. "You're the boss."

"Yes, but I think it would be better for everyone if you called."

"I could do that," he offered, the corners of his mouth tipping up. "But if I call them, you have to go up to the main floor and help with the tour."

I stilled, legitimately confused. "What tour?"

"The one Tara is running in the aquarium," Oliver replied without hesitation. "Renee was supposed to help her, but ... ."

Renee was dead, I silently finished. I'd burned her alive in front of witnesses and felt almost no remorse. She was evil and intended to hurt as many people as possible before fleeing the island, enhancing herself like the wraiths she'd employed. I stopped her, which was the right thing to do. That didn't mean she didn't occasionally invade my dreams.

"The tour with the kids from the deaf school," I remembered, my stomach twisting. "I forgot that was today."

"I believe they're up there now," Oliver prodded. "One of us has to go up and help Tara. The other has to remain down here ... and call the Grimlocks about their failed delivery."

Oh, well, that was just great. I had two choices, and both filled me with dread. "I kind of think you planned it this way," I complained as I stood, smoothing down my basic black shirt as I straightened my frame. "I'm not sure how you planned it — perhaps you're in cahoots with the Grimlocks, I don't know — but I'm positive you planned it."

He snickered. "Yes. I often find myself in cahoots with reapers. That's a fun word, by the way."

"My grandfather always uses it." I turned wistful for a moment. My grandfather had been distant since I joined the reaper academy, but he kept in touch despite his passive-aggressive attitude. He'd been downright chilly since he found out I was returning to Detroit, however. We'd taken to emailing each other about the weather and nothing else, which was difficult because we'd always been close. I refused to kowtow to him, though. When he wanted to make up, he would call me ... but not before. "I guess I picked it up from him."

"Yes, well ... I'm guessing you're heading up to help with the tour."

"You guess right. You can call the Grimlocks."

"Uh-huh." His expression was full of mirth, which agitated me to no end. "If I talk to Braden, is there a message you would like me to share with him?"

"Nope. I have nothing to say to him."

"Well ... then have fun with the kids."

"It'll be fun." That was a lie, but I didn't want him to know he'd gotten to me. Instead, I pasted a fake smile on my face and strolled out of the room, not letting it slip until I was at the stairs and could really think about what I was about to do.

It's not that I hate kids. I don't particularly like them, but I don't outright hate them. I hate being the center of attention. Plus, well, these kids are deaf. I wasn't sure how to communicate with them. Once, when I was in fifth grade, I checked out a book on sign language from the library. I was determined to learn another language and that seemed a good one. After the first few chapters, I lost interest. All I remembered was the alphabet and a few basic words ... like "hello" and "how are you." Those might come in handy now.

Tara, the woman who worked in the aquarium and served as something of a liaison between departments, was already in the main room when I exited through the private door that led to the gate room. I made sure to latch it so none of the kids could accidentally discover our biggest secret — explaining to a parent why a gate that separated different veils was located in the basement of the aquarium would be a nightmare — and smiled at the kids as I moved to join Tara. She looked relieved when she saw me, but I didn't miss the flash of irritation that lurked in her eyes.

"You're late," she muttered under her breath as the children's teacher, a pretty woman with busy hands communicated with them in front of one of the tropical fish aquariums. "You were supposed to be up here ten minutes ago."

"We're dealing with a late delivery. I had to take care of that. I'm sorry." That was a bit of an exaggeration. I'd forgotten about the tour until Oliver reminded me. Still, Tara didn't need to know that. "How many kids?"

"Only fifteen of them, which is a relief."

"They don't look so bad." I grinned broadly at a dark-haired boy as he moved closer to the glass enclosure. He cast me the occasional look, as if he didn't trust me or was trying to feel me out, but didn't say anything. Of course, I had no idea if he could say anything.

I decided now was the time to dust off my rusty sign language.

How are you?

I signed the question slowly to make sure the hand gestures were correct.

The boy didn't look impressed. He merely stared at me as if I'd sprouted another head.

"She asked you a question, Granger," the teacher spoke as she signed, which was apparently for our benefit. "You should answer her."

The boy narrowed his eyes, suspicion evident as he looked me up and down.

"It's okay," I said hurriedly. "He doesn't have to answer. I'm a stranger to him. Perhaps his parents taught him not to speak to strangers."

"Yes, but you're here in an official capacity." She kept signing and speaking at the same time. "Manners are important, aren't they, Granger?"

The boy looked at her for a long time. Instead of raising his hands to talk back, he opened his mouth ... and took me by surprise.

"They're coming," he announced.

The teacher — I hadn't gotten her name — made a face. "What ... and when did you start speaking that clearly? That's amazing. I knew you'd been working with a speech therapist, but that was completely clear. Good job."

"They're coming," he repeated.

"Everyone is already here," the teacher countered. "No one was absent today."

"They're here," the boy insisted, turning shrill. "They're here! They're here! They're here!"

Something buzzed at the back of my brain as I moved closer to him. It wasn't just the panic washing over his features, or the way his voice caused shivers to run up and down my spine. I sensed something approaching ... and I was afraid. "Who's here?"

He didn't look at me. Instead, his eyes went unbelievably wide and he screamed. "They're here!"

The room was plunged into darkness as the power went out and a deafening roar of what could only be described as thunder drowned out the children's screams.

It was utter chaos ... and then something dark and unsavory passed through the room, and I knew things were going to get worse.

Two

"What do we do?"

Tara was breathless as I worked overtime to recover from the feeling of dread that cascaded over me like a relentless waterfall. The panic lacing her voice was enough to force me back to reality.

"We calm everyone down," I instructed, raising my hands and clapping them to get the panicking students' attention. "Listen ... ."

They didn't stop screaming and I could hear them scattering across the floor, as if they were running from something. The ominous presence I felt was on the wind, not the ground. I very much doubted there was a predator in the room ... and yet I couldn't entirely shake the feeling that something terrible was either about to happen or had already occurred.

"Hey!" I yelled again.

Not one of the kids stopped screaming.

"They can't hear you," Tara pointed out. "It's a deaf school."

Oh, flaming hell! I bit the inside of my cheek to keep from cursing out loud. Of course they couldn't hear me.

"Seriously, how are we going to calm them down?" Tara asked.

I had no idea. I opened my mouth to exclaim just that when the overhead lights flashed back to life.

I swiveled quickly, my gaze going back to the door that led to the gate room. There, an incredulous look on his handsome face, stood Oliver. "What's going on?" he asked over the din.

I held my hands out and shrugged. "I don't know. The power just died. Maybe there's a storm."

"I don't think so." He shook his head. "I can usually pick up on those things."

He didn't need to explain. I understood exactly what he was saying. As a vampire, his senses were more exaggerated. He would know if it was going to storm hours before one actually hit.

"So, what took out the power?" I asked as Tara attempted to calm the children, who had scattered across the room.

"I don't know. The breaker was thrown. It was an easy fix." He turned to look at the kids. "We should probably collect them, maybe give them some ice cream or something."

That sounded like a good idea. "Sure. We should get their teacher first. I ... ." I lost my train of thought when I started looking for her. Of course, I started in the last place I saw her, which was where she remained. She was no longer on her feet, though. Instead, she lay unmoving on the ground, her eyes open and staring at the ceiling. The fact that her neck was bent at an odd angle made her almost look like a creature from another world.

"Son of a troll," I muttered, starting toward her with some wild notion that I was somehow going to fix her, that the broken neck she obviously suffered was an optical illusion.

Oliver, quick as lightning, raced across the room and grabbed me before I could put my hands on her. "Don't," he hissed. "It's too late."

"But ... ."

"It's too late," he repeated, shaking his head. "I can smell her. She's long gone."

"Not that long," I argued, keeping my voice low. "She was alive a minute ago."

"She's still long gone. She's no longer anywhere near this plane. Trust me. When I say I can smell it, I can smell it."

That was a freaky gift. "So ... what do we do?"

"We call for help." He was grim. "That means the main office first and then the cops."

My heart stuttered. "The cops. But ... ."

"We have no choice." He didn't back down. "Someone is going to be missing her and we have fifteen kids with special needs whose parents will be panicking in a few hours. We need professional help."

"Yeah, but ... how are we going to explain this?"

He shrugged. "Tell the cops the truth. You didn't do this, right?"

"Of course not."

"Then you have nothing to hide."

That didn't stop the fear from grabbing me by the throat and squeezing. "I'll call 911." I was resigned. He was right. It was the only thing we could do.

"I'll call the main office. We need direction."

"That should go over well," I grumbled. "It's basically my third week on the job and we're about to face a second crisis. That has to be some sort of record."

Despite the serious nature of the situation, Oliver smirked. "Perhaps you're gifted."

"I'm ... something."

"AND YOU DON'T KNOW how it happened?" Detective Steve Meeks arrived within ten minutes. By then we'd collected the children and grouped them together in the gift shop. They were sniffling and upset. They were also largely silent, even Granger Downey, who had been screaming "They're here" seconds before the death. I only knew his name now because one of the other students jotted it down on a sheet of paper for us.

"It happened very quickly," I replied, holding myself together as several uniformed officers and a team from the medical examiner's office spread out across the aquarium. "One minute everyone was looking at the fish and the next ... well, the next the power went out."

"And you don't have any idea why the power went out?" Meeks asked.

"No."

"How did you get the power back on?"

"I did it," Oliver replied, drawing the detective's attention. "I was in the storage room when things went dark. I've worked here a long time, so I knew where the breaker is. We have emergency lights in the back hallway, so I followed those to the breaker and threw it. The lights immediately came back on."

"So ... you think the breaker was somehow tripped. Do you know how that could've happened?"

"I don't," Oliver replied. "We have a generator, but it only comes on after the power has been down for a full five minutes. It never got to that point today."

"Well ... what about her?" Meeks tilted his head in the dead woman's direction. "How did that happen?"

"I have no idea," I replied. "I was in this room with her when the power went out. We couldn't see anything, and the kids started screaming."

Meeks turned his attention to the gift shop, where two officers stood with the students. No one was speaking. "They're from a deaf school, right?"

I nodded. "I don't remember the name."

"The Duskin School for the Deaf," Tara interjected. She'd been quiet since events unfolded. I knew she was aware of the gate, our real purpose at the aquarium. She didn't often bring it up. "They contacted us about a month ago and wanted a tour. I thought it would be fine, especially given the time of year.

"Because our facility isn't big, we could lock the front door and the kids could wander without us having to worry about them," she continued. "We thought it was fine because it's not warm enough for many visitors to come to the island. We don't get busy until May."

"Uh-huh." Meeks flicked his eyes to the door as it opened to allow a tall, distinguished man entrance. "Who is that?"

I frowned and stared at the man in question. "Cormack Grimlock. He's technically the boss here."

Instead of reacting with dread, like me, Meeks brightened considerably. "Oh, right. He's Griffin Taylor's father-in-law."

I happened to know Griffin, too. I'd met him through the Grimlocks several weeks ago. He was a new father and prominent face on
the Detroit police force. I wished he was the one on this particular
job. It would make things easier.

"Where is Griffin?" I asked. "I would think he'd jump at the chance
to take this case."

"He's on paternity leave," Meeks replied. "He's with his wife and
daughter."

Of course he was. That made perfect sense. "Oh, well … ." I forced
a smile as Cormack approached. "It's good to see you, although I wish
it was under different circumstances."

Cormack faked a smile and nodded. "Yes, I think we can both say
that," he drawled, his eyes busy as they bounced around the room.
"What do we know?"

"The deceased is Lauren Tate," Meeks replied. "Her neck is broken.
The medical examiner will obviously need to do an in-depth exam, but
for now, that's all we know."

"I see." Cormack pressed the heel of his hand to his forehead. "And
no one knows how this happened?"

I shook my head and ran through the story again. I was quickly
growing tired of relating it, but there was no other choice. When I was
finished, Cormack was befuddled.

"I don't understand." He glanced between Oliver and me. "Are you
sure you didn't hear anyone in the room?"

I thought about the feeling of dread that overwhelmed me right
before it happened, and shook my head. "It was hard to hear anything
over the screaming kids."

"It also happened in a matter of seconds," Tara added. "Like …
thirty seconds. The kids were screaming, Izzy tried to yell at them to
be quiet, which was a wasted effort because they couldn't hear her. I
pointed out they couldn't hear her. Then the lights came back on."

"That fast?" Meeks asked.

Tara nodded. "It was definitely less than a minute."

"Then I don't see how we can explain this," Meeks noted. "I mean
… it was a room full of children and two women." His gaze was heavy
when it landed on me. "I'm assuming everyone here denies killing her."

"Why would we kill her?" Tara was appalled. "We didn't even know her. I mean ... I met her exactly twenty minutes before it happened."

"We don't have motives," I pointed out.

"Sometimes that doesn't matter."

Cormack cleared his throat to get Meeks' attention. He had a commanding presence, one that struck fear in those around him. Sure, his children – all five of them – didn't fear him because they recognized he was a big marshmallow beneath the tough exterior. That didn't mean he wasn't dedicated to his job and willing to play hardball if necessary.

"Should I hire a lawyer for my employees?" Cormack challenged.

Meeks shook his head. "I have no interest in arresting either one of them right now. No, seriously. They're right about a lack of motive. Still, this doesn't look good."

"Then we'll have to find the truth," Cormack said simply.

"Can you think of anything that might lead us to answers, Ms. Sage?" Meeks pressed.

Briefly my eyes flicked to Granger, who stood in the center of things and stared at nothing. He'd turned sullen and mute the moment the lights came back on. I'd wanted to question him myself, get a look in his mind, but Meeks showed up quicker than I'd expected.

"No," I answered, avoiding Tara's probing gaze. I worried she would bring up Granger's outburst, but apparently she decided to defer to me because she remained quiet. "I don't know what happened. Honestly ... I can't fathom what possibly could've gone down in the darkness that resulted in this. I have no idea how to explain it."

"Well, maybe we'll get more from the medical examiner," Meeks suggested after a few seconds. "It's always possible she somehow fell and hit her head. I mean ... that's been known to happen."

He said the words but none of us believed them.

"I guess." I forced a tight-lipped smile. "What about the kids?"

"Their parents have been notified and are on their way. They should be here in the next thirty minutes or so. They're all locals who go to the school during the day and return home at night."

That didn't give me much time to operate. "Well, that's good." I focused on Cormack. I needed him to keep Meeks busy for a few minutes so I could question Granger. Unfortunately, I couldn't convey my needs in front of a witness. "How is Aisling?" I asked, making up my mind on the spot. Cormack enjoyed talking about his youngest child and only daughter. Meeks knew Griffin, so I hoped they would take a conversational detour and allow me to slip away.

"She's well." Cormack offered up a genuine smile. "Tired. The baby isn't much for sleeping, so that's been an adjustment. She was at the house with us for a few nights and then returned home, although I'm not sure how well that's going. She's a cute little thing."

"I've seen her," Meeks volunteered, causing me to inwardly smile. They were both falling into my trap. "She's adorable."

"She looks like her mother." Cormack's smile widened. "Aisling looked exactly the same as a baby."

"Griffin is over the moon," Meeks enthused. "I mean ... he's tired. He brought the baby in for us to see the other day and he had huge circles under his eyes, but he's thrilled with her. She was wearing a shirt that said, 'Melting grandpa's heart is my super power.' I think she charmed the entire squad."

Cormack beamed. "She's my baby girl. She charms everybody."

Once I was certain they were lost in their own conversation, I slipped away to talk to Granger. Oliver followed. Once I hit the gift shop, I ignored the two officers watching the kids and headed immediately to the boy in question.

I knelt in front of him, forced a smile that I didn't feel, and searched the kid's eyes. There was nothing there. He looked dead inside. "Hey, Granger."

He didn't respond.

"Um ... do you remember talking to me?"

Nothing. The boy didn't as much as lift a shoulder or meet my gaze.

"You know he can't hear you, right?" Oliver challenged. "He goes to a school for the deaf. That means he's deaf."

I wanted to strangle him. "He talked to me right before it happened."

Oliver was taken aback. "He did?"

I nodded. "He kept saying, 'They're here' over and over. I don't think that was a coincidence."

Oliver's gaze was thoughtful as it washed over Granger. "Well ... did you sense anything when the lights went out?"

I glanced around to make sure the police officers weren't eaves-dropping and then nodded. "I did."

"Well, don't keep me in suspense."

"I felt ... evil."

"That's it?"

"Yeah. I felt a sense of evil. It was quick. It washed over the room and was gone by the time you turned on the lights."

"Did you see anything?"

"No."

"Hear anything?"

"No."

"You just felt ... evil."

"That's what I said."

"Well, that sounds peachy."

I ignored his tone and focused on Granger, staring hard until the boy's eyes finally locked with mine. "Do you remember what you said?"

The boy's stare was blank.

"Do you remember talking?"

He didn't open his mouth or move his hands to respond.

"Do you know what sort of creature was here?"

Still nothing. Finally, I straightened. I was getting nowhere with the kid and I sensed that would continue. "I don't know what to do," I admitted after a beat. "I have no idea what was in that room ... but whatever it was, a woman is dead because of it."

"Because of what?" Cormack asked, sliding into the spot behind me and causing me to jolt.

I slid a sidelong look to Oliver. "Couldn't you have warned me he was coming?"

"And miss all the fun?" Oliver smirked. "Mr. Grimlock, it's good to see you. I wish it was under different circumstances, of course."

"We both wish that." Cormack was contained. "Tell me the part you didn't tell Meeks. Don't bother denying you're holding something back. I know better than that."

I sighed, resigned, and then told him the story as quickly as possible. I trusted him. He was a good boss. I wasn't particularly thrilled about being drawn into the Grimlock net again, especially so soon after the previous catastrophe, but I didn't really have a choice. When I was finished, he looked more curious than concerned.

"And this is the boy?" he asked.

I nodded.

Cormack bent at the waist and regarded the child with kind eyes. "Hi, buddy." I was surprised when I realized he was signing as he spoke. "Do you want to tell me what happened?"

The child watched his hands for a bit but didn't respond. If anything, he appeared to grow more disinterested the harder Cormack tried to engage him in conversation.

"Well, if he can talk, he's decided to stop for the time being," Cormack said as he straightened. "I don't think it was a coincidence that he began babbling right before it happened."

"You don't think he did it, do you?"

"I don't see how." Cormack was thoughtful as he studied Granger. "He's far too small. It's more likely that he heard something or channeled something. My guess is some sort of creature or malevolent force was in the aquarium with you and it disappeared with the light."

"How did it get in?"

"I have no idea." Cormack mimed stretching so he could look in Meeks' direction without drawing attention. "He's going to be a problem. He obviously suspects we're hiding something. I'll ask Griffin about him, but we're not going to have the usual amount of cover we do with Griffin on leave."

"We'll figure something out," I supplied. "If there's some sort of evil presence hunting on this island, it's only a matter of time before it shows itself again."

"That's why you need to be careful."

"I can take care of myself."

"You still need to be careful." Cormack was grave as he lifted his eyes to Oliver. "That goes for you, too. Watch out for each other ... and start putting some effort into replacing Renee. Having additional backup out here couldn't possibly hurt."

"I'll get right on that. Although ... where do I look?"

"I'll send you files and you can start searching there. We've had several people from inside the organization apply for the position. If you like someone, tell me."

"Okay, I ... okay." I had no idea what else to say to him and felt awkward.

Oliver, perhaps sensing my discomfort, decided to take control of the conversation. "You guys were late with a delivery last night. We still haven't received it."

"It's probably Braden," Cormack said, scowling. "He just got back from Florida and went to bed early. I'll bet he forgot to transfer his souls."

"So, he was out of town, huh?" Oliver gave me a smug look. "Funny. I heard a rumor saying the same thing. I guess he's been busy."

"He wasn't happy about it. He lost the coin toss, though. It was between him and Redmond. He really didn't want to go." Cormack slid his gaze to me, but I refused to meet his somber orbs. "I think he had something else he wanted to do here. He's back now, though, so don't be surprised if he drops in."

"Oh, I won't be surprised." Oliver grinned. "I'm looking forward to seeing him again. You are, too, right?" He looked to me for confirmation but I refused to answer the question.

"If something else pops up, I'll call you," I said to Cormack. "Until then ... I don't know what else to do."

"That makes two of us."

Three

"What about this one?" Hours later, as I sorted through the files Cormack had emailed, I pulled up information on a woman who worked at the main office. It was almost time to call it a day, but I thought I should at least feign interest in hiring someone after Cormack's admonishment.

Oliver slid his gaze from the screen he was watching and looked at the photograph I pulled up. He immediately cringed, which caused me to shift in my chair. "What is it? What's wrong?"

"I ... nothing." He focused on his computer. "The Grimlocks sent their missing load from last night. I'm guessing Cormack got on Braden."

Mention of Braden's name made me grit my teeth. I knew exactly what he was doing ... and I didn't like it. "That's good. What's wrong with this chick? Her name is Annemarie. That's one word. I love it when something that's supposed to be two words is turned into one word. That means she's efficient."

Oliver scowled. "I think you should keep looking."

"Why?"

"Because ... well, actually, I don't want to influence your decision. If you want to hire her, it's completely up to you."

"Really?" He didn't say anything, so I read further into the file. "It says here she's been in the reaper office for ten years. That means she has experience and is probably unlikely to panic under fire. Although ... ." I trailed off as I kept reading.

"Do you think Braden will call you or will he arrange some accidental meet-up so he can romance you that way?" Oliver queried.

I pretended I didn't hear him. "I'm somewhat concerned that she's had six positions in the main office in ten years. That probably indicates she has personality issues, wouldn't you say?"

"You know who has personality issues but still manages to be charming?" Oliver challenged. "Braden Grimlock. I mean ... that guy is all sorts of morose, and yet he makes you smile. I kind of like him."

That did it. I lost my temper and slammed my hand on the desk. "Stop bringing up Braden!"

Oliver's smirk was sly. "I was simply trying to carry on a conversation. Obviously you're not comfortable with that conversation. I apologize. It's hell when a conversation is uncomfortable, isn't it?"

Oh, I had his number. "This is about me questioning you regarding my parents, right?"

"Did I say that?"

"No, but I'm not an idiot."

"You're very far from an idiot," he agreed. "I like that about you. Even as a child you were smart. In fact, one day your father was having a meltdown because there was a computer glitch and you told him to chill out and fixed it within about two minutes. You were five at the time."

I turned to him, surprised. "I did?"

He nodded. "You were always a smart cookie. You were also a pusher. You demanded what you wanted out of life even at a young age. Sometimes it's best to wait."

"I have waited. It's been twenty years. I was taken from this place right after it happened ... and I don't remember. There are flashes here and there, and I know something horrible went down that night, but I can't remember. Do you know how horrible that is?"

Oliver opened his mouth to answer, but I didn't give him a chance to respond.

"I love my grandfather," I continued. "I really do. He was good to me ... and taught me things ... and loved me. It's not the same life I would've lived with my parents, though, and that hurts."

Oliver sighed, the sound long and drawn out. "I'm not trying to hide them from you. It's just ... I don't know that dwelling on the past is good for you. They're your parents and I'm sure your grandfather has filled you with fond memories of them. What if I say something that ruins those memories?"

I knit my eyebrows. "Do you know something that could ruin those memories?"

"I don't know. I don't want to be the person who somehow screws up what you do remember. I mean ... we spent a lot of time together when you were little. Like ... a lot. You don't remember me. For some reason, you've blocked out that part of your life. I have to believe you've done it for a reason."

I watched him for a long beat. "I need to know the truth. Don't you understand that? There's a hole in my heart where they should be and I want to fill it."

"Is that why you're hiding from Braden? Are you afraid he'll fill it before you get your answers?"

The question frustrated me. "Why are you so fixated on Braden?"

"Because you are."

"I am not." My response came out shriller than I expected and I struggled to adjust my tone. "Seriously, he's just a man. We worked together on one case. It's behind me. Nothing happened. I've moved on. I don't see why you can't do the same."

"First, you haven't moved on." Oliver leaned back in his chair, laced his fingers and put them behind his head as he met my challenging gaze. "You like him. You can admit it. It's weird for me because I knew you as a child, but I'm familiar with the Grimlocks. Braden was always the most annoying of the group, but he's matured. I think he might be good for you."

I absolutely hated this conversation. "I didn't come here to get involved with someone. I came here for answers."

"Fair enough." He held his hands up. "The thing is, I believe that you can do more than one thing while you're here. You might not have come for him, but that doesn't mean you can't have him all the same."

"I don't think it's a good idea."

"You know what I find interesting about that statement? You didn't say I was wrong. You said you didn't think it was a good idea. That means you've considered it."

"I haven't."

"I think you're lying."

"Yeah, well ... I don't really care what you think." Suddenly antsy, I hopped to my feet. "I'm done for the day. I'm going to run upstairs and make sure the police crew and medical examiner's team cleared out and didn't leave anything behind. You can be done, too."

"Thanks for that." Oliver's expression was hard to read as he watched me. "Don't you want to finish talking about Annemarie Scofield?"

"No. I've decided against her. I find it suspicious that she's been juggled between departments the way she has."

"That's probably smart because she claims sexual harassment wherever she goes. It doesn't matter if her boss is male or female. Apparently everyone wants to see her naked."

I was appalled. "Why didn't you tell me that?"

He shrugged. "I wanted to see if you would figure it out on your own. You did. There's no reason to be cranky."

"Ugh. You're really starting to grate on me."

"That is one of my better talents."

"Yeah, yeah, yeah." I offered him a half-hearted wave and headed for the door. "You need to help me go through that list Cormack sent me tomorrow. If you have information on these people, I should know it. I don't want to risk getting the wrong person in here ... again."

"Sure."

I slowed my pace and arched an eyebrow. "Just like that? I expected you to fight me on it."

"I have no intention of fighting you ... as long as you make an effort to see Braden."

Shut the front door! He was unbelievably annoying when he wanted to be. "That's not going to happen. He was hanging around because we had an issue that required multiple people to figure out. That's no longer the case."

"Are you sure? We had a woman die in a room full of kids. You felt, but didn't see, a malevolent spirit. If that's not an issue, I don't know what is."

"That doesn't mean it's his issue."

"I get that. Still ... I'm betting he turns up."

"And I'm betting he doesn't." I offered him another wave. "I'm out of here. I'll check the aquarium floor on my way out. You don't have to worry about it."

"I'm not worried ... and Braden will be around."

"If that's what you need to tell yourself."

I heard him grumble something under his breath but made a point not to acknowledge it. His insistence on trying to force the issue with Braden was so annoying I wanted to start shaking him. I understood he thought he was being funny. I felt exactly the opposite.

The aquarium was quiet and deserted. I took time to circle the area where Lauren Tate died in an effort to search for clues, but it was completely clean. I even used my magic, but there was nothing there. Whatever force blew through the room was seemingly gone ... and I was alone.

I walked to the front door to check the locks, taking a moment to stare out the window and gauge the encroaching darkness. It was staying light later these days — which was welcome — but the darkness still came early. I looked forward to the summer months when the sun wouldn't set until after nine.

As far as I could tell, the parking lot was empty ... except for a lone vehicle near the front. It looked familiar, but I couldn't get a clear view of it from where I stood. I thought about exiting the building to circle the car, but my inner danger alarm sparked in such a way that I immediately thought better of it.

Behind you.

We're here.

We've arrived.

Look behind you.

The voices caused a shiver to course down my spine. I swiveled quickly, the hair standing up on the back of my neck. There, grouped together, hovered a variety of ghosts. Honestly, I don't know how else to describe them. They were definitely ghosts, ethereal and almost glowing in the limited light. They stared at me. There had to be at least twenty of them. They whispered. Some knew my name, and they raised their hands in unison as if reaching for me.

I took an involuntary step back when I recognized Lauren. She stood on the far side of the group, her expression morose. Like the others, she whispered words I had trouble making out and reached toward me.

On instinct I fumbled with the lock and threw open the front door. I had every intention of racing through the opening and not stopping until I was certain I'd left the ghosts behind. That was impossible, though, because a dark figure cut off my avenue of escape. I smacked into him hard, bouncing backward with enough force that I assumed I would topple over.

The shadow, however, caught me before I could lose my balance ... and then began to laugh.

"Falling for me so soon?"

I recognized the voice and slapped at the hands, frustration bubbling up. "Braden! That's not funny."

"I thought it was a little funny." He stepped into the dim lights, his handsome features practically glowing. "Miss me?"

He had to be joking. "No. I absolutely did not miss you." I smoothed my clothes in an effort to look anywhere but his face. Then I remembered the ghosts and turned back in that direction, breathing a sigh of relief when I realized they were gone.

"You didn't miss me even a little?" Braden challenged, his tone lazy.

When I turned back to him, I found his flirty gaze on me. He was seemingly oblivious to the terror of moments before, for which I was grateful. "No. I didn't miss you."

He snagged my wrist and made a face as he pressed his fingers to my pulse point. "I don't know. Your heart is racing. I think that means you missed me."

"And I think I was running from ghosts when I smacked into you," I shot back. "That's why my heart is racing." Seriously, the nerve on him. As if my heart would race because of his proximity. Although ... it was still going relatively well given the fact that I'd started to calm down. Still, I blamed the ghosts. It had nothing to do with him.

"Ghosts?" Braden arched an eyebrow. "What ghosts?"

"I ... they were in there." I gestured toward the aquarium. "I don't know what they were doing there. Heck, I haven't seen ghosts since I got here. They're a little more prevalent in the French Quarter than they are in this area."

"There shouldn't be ghosts if the reapers are doing their jobs."

"Nobody is infallible."

"Yeah, well ... ." He moved his hand to my back and started rubbing. "Are you okay?"

"I'm fine. I was simply caught off guard."

"Hmm." I couldn't quite decide how he meant the sound he was making as he walked into the aquarium. His gaze was keen as he searched the room, but after a few minutes he turned back to me. I didn't miss the question in his eyes. "Do you think it has something to do with the death this afternoon?"

That was a good question. "I don't know. But ... one of the ghosts did look a lot like the dead teacher. I didn't get close enough to ask her any questions or anything because it was weird how they were beckoning to me, but I'm pretty sure it was her."

He frowned. "Beckoning to you?"

I reenacted how they moved their arms and gestured for me to join them. "They did it in unison, and it was creepy. I freaked out ... and that's why I was going out the front door."

"So, you're saying you really weren't excited to see me." He almost looked sad at the prospect.

"I was happy not to be alone, if that helps."

He chuckled. "I guess it's better than nothing." He sidled closer to me. "I missed you, if that counts for anything."

I wanted to rip out my traitorous heart when it rolled. "Huh. I would think that if you missed someone you would call." I hadn't meant to say that ... and definitely not in that tone. It came out a bit too passive-aggressive and obnoxious for my liking. Still, my mouth had a mind of its own and said whatever it wanted from time to time.

"I wanted to call," he hedged. "I felt kind of weird, though."

"Well, there's no reason to feel weird." I clapped his arm as hard as I could, as if we were buddies at the bar watching a football game. "No hard feelings here. I'm perfectly fine."

He tilted his head to the side, considering. "Yeah. I'm getting a different vibe. Still ... I emailed."

"Oh, that's the same as a phone call."

He grinned. "You *did* miss me. That's why you're so annoyed. It's okay. You can admit it."

"No." I folded my arms over my chest. "I didn't miss you. I barely know you. I mean ... we worked together and I would be sad if someone killed you or something, but I didn't miss you.

"Like, for example, I would totally be sad if you were the one who died during the blackout today," I continued. I realized I was babbling, but I couldn't stop myself. "That would be heartbreaking, but only because you were a human being and not for any other reason."

Braden's grin was back, and it caused me to go warm all over. "Has anyone ever told you what a terrible liar you are?"

"No ... and I'm not lying."

"You're totally lying."

"I am not!"

He met my gaze for a long moment and then slowly raised his hand to brush my dark hair from my face. "I'm sorry. I don't usually go out of town. I lost the coin toss."

"So your father told me."

"I won't have to leave town anytime soon, but next time I'll be sure to call."

"I don't need a call."

"I'll be sure to call," he repeated. "What do you have planned for the rest of the night?"

"I'm going to the boathouse and ... reading." I didn't have any plans. That was the first thing that came to mind. It sounded lame, but I didn't care. "It's a really good book."

His eyes lit with mirth. "What book?"

"Um ... it's about witches and stuff. I like reading about witches. Heck, I like witches, period."

"I like them, too." He winked at me. "I was thinking — and I know this will be difficult because you were obviously attached to your plans — but I was thinking that maybe you might want to go out to dinner with me."

That was a horrible idea. He already had butterflies dancing in my stomach, which I was mortified to admit even to myself. "No. I'm not dating you. We've been over this."

"It wouldn't be a date."

"What would it be?"

"Dinner."

"That's a date."

"No. See ... I figured I would take you to Grimlock Manor. We could tell Dad what you saw, grab dinner there and then see where the night takes us. That's not a date because my family will be there and no sane man would take a woman on a date with his family."

He had a point. "I don't know."

"Have you eaten?"

"No."

"Were you planning to tell my father what you saw?"

"Yes."

"Then this solves both problems ... and ensures that it's not a date at the same time."

I hated to admit it but he had a point. "Fine." I heaved out a sigh. "Just dinner with your family, though. I'm not letting you turn this into a thing."

"I would never turn this into a thing."

I didn't believe him. Still, I wanted to put distance between the aquarium and me. I was still shaken by the visions. "I hope your father is having something good."

"I believe there's a Mexican bar tonight."

"I love Mexican food."

"Then this should be right up your alley."

Four

G rimlock Manor was exactly as I remembered it.

I still wasn't over the fact that the Grimlocks named their house — it looked more like a castle — and found the entire thing hilarious. The house I shared with my grandfather growing up was a two-bedroom shack compared to the glorious abode Braden parked in front of.

"It still looks the same," I noted.

He cast me a sideways glance. "Did you think it grew in your time away?"

"No. It's just ... it's beautiful." I knew I sounded wistful, but I couldn't stop myself from being a little jealous. "You must've had the best time growing up here."

"It certainly wasn't a bad time. We had a lot of fun, but it wasn't all easy."

"I know you lost your mother. That had to be hard. You were already an adult, though. Your childhood must have been amazing."

Instead of immediately agreeing, he shrugged. "Money doesn't buy happiness. My mother told me that at a young age. I was whining because I wanted some toy and my father told me no. I didn't understand because it was obvious Dad had the money for it. She explained that money made things easier, but it would never make us happy."

That was interesting. "We didn't have a lot of money growing up. I never went hungry or anything, but there wasn't much to spare. My grandfather taught me how to catch frogs in the bayou so I could sell them to local brujas and make extra money if I needed anything."

"You caught frogs for money?"

I nodded. "Why? What did you do?"

"We had chores around the house, but in retrospect that sounds lame. It certainly wasn't much work for the allowance we received."

"Still, you all seem to have good work ethics."

"We appreciate a job well done." He hopped out of the car and hurried to my side. I was already halfway out before he arrived. "I was trying to open the door for you," he groused, making a face.

Puzzled, I met his serious gaze. His eyes were a ridiculous shade of purple that made me want to dive into them. "Why?"

"It's the gentlemanly thing to do."

I was sincerely amused. "Did your father teach you that?"

"No. My mother did."

He didn't cringe when he mentioned her this time. The sadness that often permeated his being when he talked about her was absent. I hoped that was a good thing. No one deserved to be as sad as he often looked.

"Well, this isn't a date," I reminded him.

"Oh, it's a date." He chuckled when I glared. "Oh, don't give me that look. We both know it's a date. You're not ready for a formal date yet, but this is a half date."

"I already told you ... ."

He cut me off with a shake of his head. "You don't want to date me. I know. I'm going to change your mind."

"I'm not big on the alpha male tendency to club a woman over the head and carry her to his cave until she agrees to his demands."

"I have no intention of clubbing you."

"Oh, no?"

"Nope. I'm going to walk into that house and wow you with food and family. After an hour with the rest of the Grimlocks you'll be begging me to take you someplace quiet where we can be alone."

He was full of himself. Still, there was something appealing about the glint in his eyes. "Let's just eat," I suggested. "You're right about me wanting to talk to your father. After that, you can take me home and we'll forget the rest of this ... nonsense."

"Sure. That sounds exactly how I pictured things in my head."

I couldn't stop myself from chuckling. "I'm sure things will work out for both of us."

"Oh, I'm sure they will, too."

ONE STEP INTO GRIMLOCK Manor told me he was right about the noise level. We were barely inside the door when I heard an infant wailing as if she was about to die. There was only one baby in the house, so I didn't need to ask who was making the noise.

"Lily doesn't sound happy," I noted as I shrugged out of my coat.

Braden shook his head as he collected it. "I'm starting to think she's possessed."

I pursed my lips as I followed him through the house. "What's wrong with her?"

"She's already spoiled rotten, that's what's wrong with her. Just prepare yourself. She's even louder up close and personal. She was staying here, but then Aisling got self-conscious and went back home. That doesn't stop her from visiting constantly, though, and she brings the noise with her." Braden held open the door that led to the parlor and I cringed when I walked inside and found Aisling pacing the floor with the squalling infant.

"Hello," I offered, my eyes going wide when I saw the circles under Aisling's eyes. She looked like death warmed over ... and then run over ... and perhaps set on fire after that. "How are you?"

Aisling, never one for pleasantries, was more caustic than ever. "How do you think?"

I recoiled when the baby screeched at the top of her lungs. "She doesn't sound ... happy."

"She's never happy."

"Give her to me," Griffin instructed, appearing from behind me. He had a fresh bottle in his hand and a spit blanket on his shoulder. "Just ... take a walk around the house, baby. I'll take care of Lily."

Aisling happily handed over her only child. She did not, however, leave the room. "I think I'm going to drink instead."

I spoke before I thought better of it. "Can you do that and breastfeed?"

The look she shot me was withering. "I'm not breastfeeding. Apparently I'm bad at it."

I looked to Braden for help. "Um ... ."

He merely shrugged. "She has a low supply of breast milk. The doctor says it's rare, but happens. None of us like talking about it."

"That's because it's gross," the oldest Grimlock child, Redmond, said as he scooted past us. "We should not be talking about our sister's breast milk. Hello, Izzy." He beamed at me, the full Grimlock charm on display. "I'm glad to see you're back to visiting. I thought about stopping in to see you and make sure you were okay after the big hoopla a few weeks ago, but I was warned to keep away." His gaze was heavy on Braden, whose cheeks flushed. " I'm a good brother, so I decided to do as I was told."

"Oh, really?" I pinned Braden with a dark look. "You warned your brother to stay away?"

"He's a pervert. I did what was necessary." Braden gestured for me to move to one of the settees. "What would you like to drink?"

The baby's shrieks as Griffin tried to feed her made me wonder if they were handing out fifths of whiskey to cut through the noise. "Um ... a Jack and Coke is fine." I focused on Griffin as he bounced the baby. He looked as tired as Aisling, which wasn't good. "Do you mind if I hold her?"

Griffin cast me a surprised look. "What? Why would you possibly want to hold her? She won't shut up."

"She definitely won't shut up," Aidan agreed, skirting into the room with his fiancé Jerry right behind him. "We share a wall with her at the townhouses and had to move into the guest room to get any sleep."

"Try living with her," Aisling muttered, rubbing her forehead. She'd looked healthier when she was nine months pregnant. Now her hair was dull and listless, and she was unbelievably pale.

"Please. Let me hold her."

Griffin arched an eyebrow but willingly handed Lily over. "She never stops screaming unless she's asleep ... and she doesn't sleep anywhere near as much as the doctor told us she would. She's up the entire night ... and the morning ... and the afternoon."

"And you've had her checked out?" I smiled at the baby as she continued to wail in my arms, adjusting her so I could rest her against my lap with one arm and press my free hand to her forehead.

"The doctor says there's nothing wrong with her," Aisling said dully. "He says some babies simply need to cry and she'll settle down when she's ready." She accepted the drink Redmond brought her and downed half of it in one gulp. I wasn't sure how healthy that was given her current state, but now was not the time to question her decision-making skills.

"When was the last time you slept?" I asked, adjusting the baby so I could feed her. Lily automatically took the bottle and started vigorously sucking.

"I don't even remember what sleep is," Aisling said. "That's a thing, right?" She looked to Griffin for confirmation as he sat next to her. Together, they looked like the walking dead. "I don't think we're ever going to be able to sleep again."

She was in a bad place mentally, that much was certain. I turned back to the baby, who seemed perfectly fine sucking her bottle. "Is she quiet only when she eats and sleeps?" I asked.

Griffin nodded. "Yup. Otherwise she's constantly screaming."

I turned my attention to Cormack as he walked through the door. Compared to his children, he didn't seem bothered by Lily in the least. "Have you considered hiring a nanny for them?" It was a pointed question, but I couldn't stand seeing Griffin and Aisling so run down.

"I have," Cormack confirmed. "The first thing I offered was a baby nurse. Aisling said she wanted to do it herself."

"It doesn't matter," she noted. "The townhouse is so small that we'd be able to hear her no matter what. Even if someone else was with her all night, we would hear her. She'd make sure of that."

"Yeah, but you could stay here," I suggested. "I know you have your own home, but you need sleep. In fact ... your aura is way too yellow. It was magenta before. The change is ... jarring. You can't keep on like this."

Cormack tilted his head toward me, his eyes alert. "What do you mean? Is she sick?"

"You can't tell that by looking at her?" I challenged. Lily had finished her bottle so I shifted her to my shoulder to burp her. Griffin wordlessly handed me the spit blanket and Braden helped slide it in place. "Lack of sleep can hurt someone more than almost anything. In fact, twenty-four hours without sleep is enough to affect cognition, memory and bodily function."

Cormack slid his eyes to Aisling. "We have a nursery here. Why don't you guys move in for a bit like we talked about before ... and you ultimately decided against? We'll all get her through this tough stretch together. I'm sure she'll calm down soon."

"That doesn't seem fair," Aisling argued, annoyance flashing. "I'm supposed to take care of her. It's my job."

"Yes, well, I'm your father. I'm supposed to take care of you."

"Not once I'm an adult."

"It never ends." He flashed her a fond smile. "You'll stay here and we'll take turns watching Lily. You need to get some sleep."

Aisling looked so relieved that for a moment I thought she would start weeping. "Maybe just a few nights," she conceded.

Cormack smiled as he rubbed her shoulder. "It'll be fine. Just ... have another drink. I'll send the cleaning staff up to get the nursery ready, including buying anything we might need. We'll set up a schedule and I'll get a night nurse in if we need help."

"Thank the maker," Jerry enthused. "If Lily is here, that means we can sleep in our bed again. I thought I was going to have to redecorate the guest room to our tastes."

"Yes, that's the important thing," Griffin drawled.

"Hey. I need my beauty sleep. No one wants to see me with bags under my eyes. It's unseemly."

"That's exactly what I was thinking."

· · ·

CORMACK MET ME BY THE FOYER WHEN Braden and I
were getting ready to leave.

"Thank you for stopping by," he offered. "I appreciate you telling
me what you saw at the aquarium. I don't know what to make of it, but
it's ... interesting."

"I find it more interesting that I never thought to look for Lauren's
soul," I admitted sheepishly. "She should've been there when the lights
came back ... but she wasn't."

"I should've considered that, too. I don't know what to make of it,
but I plan to put the research team on it tomorrow."

"He means he's going to make Cillian start digging into it," Braden
offered, handing me my coat.

"Cillian is the most important member of my research team,"
Cormack admitted. He grabbed my wrist before I could walk out the
door Braden held open. "Wait. I also want to thank you for what you
did for Aisling."

"I didn't do anything for her. I mean ... I fed the baby. That seems
pretty small compared to everything else."

"Yes, but ... I didn't see. I mean, I did. She looks rundown. I didn't
see how close she was to the edge. The fact that she agreed to stay
here without a whisper of lip tells me that she needed more help than I
realized."

"I'll be around now," Braden noted. "I'll help with Lily. Put me on
the schedule. Aisling really does look like death. She needs a good
night's sleep."

"She needs more than one night," I corrected. "You guys can't be
expected to fill in constantly, but she's at her limit."

"What I don't understand," Cormack said, "is why Lily refuses to
calm down?"

That was an interesting question. Unfortunately for him, I had no
answers. "I don't know. Eventually she'll cry herself out. You guys need
to help Aisling until that happens."

"That's the plan."

"Well ... just keep me informed. I'll try to think of something
to help."

"You fixed her feet," Braden noted. "Maybe you can fix Lily, too. If you could make it so she never cries and doesn't crap ten times a day that would be great."

I shot him a look. "She's a baby. Those things are normal."

"I'm starting to think nothing that kid does is normal."

Something was definitely abnormal about the situation, but for now I'd done all I could. "I'll think about it. I'm sure there's an answer we've overlooked."

"I certainly hope so," Cormack said. "If that baby doesn't stop crying we're all going to join her ... and then things will really fall apart."

"WELL, THANKS FOR DINNER."

Braden insisted on walking me to my apartment when we returned to Belle Isle. He made a big show of searching the boathouse for errant ghosts, even going so far to look behind the Welcome Center bulletin board, which was full of classified ads and missing person reports, before stopping in front of my bedroom.

"It was my pleasure. You did more for my family than we did for you."

"I don't know. I thought the taco bar was amazing. I can't remember the last time I've had guacamole that good."

He smirked. "Yeah, well, my father is big on theme bars."

"Your father is a good man." I meant it. "I feel sorry for him that he didn't see how badly Aisling was struggling. He'll carry that guilt with him."

"They all will. I wasn't home, so I get a pass. Still, I saw her on a few video calls. She was mostly in the background. I should've realized something was seriously wrong."

"It's not that there's something seriously wrong," I cautioned. "It's just ... she's exhausted. That baby is two weeks old and I don't think she's slept more than an hour straight since giving birth. In case you haven't noticed, she's pretty much lost all of her baby weight already ...and she's not breastfeeding. That's not a sign of good health."

Braden's handsome features twisted. "Can we not talk about my sister breastfeeding? It's gross."

"It's natural."

"No, it's gross. She's my sister."

"And you're going to go home and take first watch with the baby," I surmised, grinning. "You act as if she annoys you — and I have no doubt she does — but you love her."

"She's ... a piece of work. That doesn't mean I want to see her run off the rails. Lily is a part of our lives now. Apparently she's going to be a really annoying part. She must get that from Aisling."

I had other ideas, but I didn't want to give them voice. Er, well, at least not yet. "You love your niece. I saw the way you were looking at her when I was holding her. You were making faces, trying to get her to smile."

"That shows what you know. Babies don't really start smiling until they're, like, six weeks old. Some don't start until they're three months old."

I was officially impressed. "You've been doing research on infant development?"

"I ... no. I ... maybe a little." His cheeks flushed with embarrassment. "She's our first baby. We're going to spoil her rotten. I'll blame my father for it, but I'm sure I'll be equally responsible. I can admit that."

His moment of candor had me leaning forward. I surprised myself when I pushed his hair away from his face. "You're going to be an amazing uncle."

He stared hard into my eyes, his lips inches from mine. He didn't move forward, though, and it took effort to tamp down the hot rush of disappointment that caused my skin to burn when he didn't close the distance to plant his lips on mine.

"I'm not going to kiss you," he announced, ending the moment.

"What?" I took an involuntary step back, thankful for the whoosh of air that blew between us. "I didn't ask you to kiss me. In fact, I told you we're not going to date. I said it first."

His lips curved. "You don't mean that. I'm not going to kiss you until you ask me to. I just thought I should make you aware of that."

"Ask you?" I thought my eyebrows would fly off my forehead. "I'm

AMANDA M. LEE

never going to ask you to kiss me. I just ... you're dreaming if you think that's going to happen."

"Oh, it'll happen." He was smug as he took a step away from me. "I think it'll happen sooner than you realize. I want you to be the one to ask me, though. I insist on that."

I couldn't stop myself from asking the obvious question. "I'm not saying it's ever going to happen. In fact, it's not going to happen. I'm putting my foot down ... and hard. But out of curiosity, why would you possibly want me to ask you?"

"Because I want to make sure you want it. I'm pretty sure you do, but you need to put a little effort in. It can't be all about me pursuing you. You need to want me as much as I want you."

I chewed my bottom lip and kept silent. Honestly, I had no idea what to say.

"You're going to ask." He grinned as he waved. "I can't wait until it happens, by the way. I'll be in touch tomorrow. I'll make sure to call if something comes up."

"That's really not necessary," I called after him.

"I'll do it all the same. You asked for it."

Sadly, I worried that was true. It wouldn't be the first time my big mouth got me into trouble. I very much doubted it would be the last.

Five

I tossed and turned for an hour before I fell asleep. Braden's cocky attitude haunted me, and not simply because I thought he was wrong. There was a very good chance he was right ... and that irritated me.

When sleep finally claimed me, I dreamt about the baby. That was weird in a different way, and frustrating because trying to ascertain what an infant is thinking isn't easy. Still, I woke with a clear idea how to make the situation better ... and that's what I set out to do.

"What's in the conservatory?" I asked Collin O'Reilly, the man who ran the only eatery on the island. It happened to be located in the aquarium, which meant it was convenient for breakfast.

"What do you mean?" Collin was the odd sort. He was a merrow, which meant he was a man of the sea, but he had a cranky temper and reportedly hated his wife to distraction. I'd met both of them, and her feelings for him were equally complicated. I didn't pretend to understand their issues, but they were expedient sources of information for an island I was still reacquainting myself with.

"The conservatory," I repeated, shoveling oatmeal in as I sucked down coffee. "There are plants inside, right? Herbs?"

"It's a greenhouse."

I fought to control my temper. "I know that, but what sort of things are inside? I mean ... what sort of plants?"

"Oh." He shook his head. "Everything is divided and looked after by volunteers. There're five areas. There's the palm house, which is the domed center. There's also a tropical house in the south wing, a cactus house and fernery in the north wing and a show house in the east wing. That's on top of the lily pond, which is just opening for the season."

I ran the information through my head. "What's in the show house?"

"It varies. They do a lot of shows in there."

Well, duh. I pretty much figured that out myself. "I'm betting they have a lot of different plants in there."

Collin shrugged, seemingly disinterested in the conversation. "I don't particularly like the building. I'm a water guy, not a plant guy. Plus, Claire spends her time there." He scowled at mention of his wife. "She's a volunteer and helps take care of the plants. Apparently she's spending more time than usual there because some of the seasonal volunteers just stopped showing up without warning. I try to stay away from her as much as possible."

I was new to the island and still learning about the inhabitants. Collin and Claire were among the few who actually lived on the island, along with Oliver and his boyfriend Brett Soloman, who lived in the casino, and me. I couldn't understand why Collin and Claire didn't divorce if they truly hated each other as much as they claimed, but whenever I asked they would only say that it was impossible. It really was none of my business, so I pushed their marital problems to the back of my mind and focused on Lily Taylor's rather obvious distress.

"Do I need special permission to go in there?" I asked, cleaning my bowl.

"No. This time of year the volunteers are around, but if you have your lanyard with you they won't give you any grief. Why?"

I merely smiled. "I need some herbs. Plus, well, I figure it's about time I learned more about my surroundings. I've been distracted."

"That's what happens when wraiths supercharge themselves by crossing over and returning."

I wasn't sure how much of the previous story he knew, but he didn't seem all that invested in the tale. "Yeah, well, that's over and done with." Something occurred to me as I wiped the corners of my mouth with a napkin. "Have you ever seen ghosts here?"

He arched an eyebrow. "Should I be seeing ghosts?"

"No, but I'm wondering if there's a contingent of them hanging around, perhaps hiding, because of the proximity to the gate. Maybe ... I mean, is it possible that they're drawn to the gate?"

The look on Collin's face had me wishing I'd kept the question to myself. "How should I know? I'm responsible for the food, not the gate."

"I ... you're right." I forced a smile for his benefit. "It was a stupid question."

He didn't look convinced.

"Really stupid," I added, getting to my feet. "It was the stupidest question ever. Forget I asked it."

Collin watched me with suspicious eyes until I vacated the eatery. If he wasn't on the fence about me before, he definitely was now. But that was the least of my worries. I had a baby to calm and ghosts to track. I didn't have time for him ... thankfully.

I FOUND THE CONSERVATORY largely empty, which was a relief. I caught sight of Claire in the fern room as I pointed myself toward the palm room. I felt out of place, as if I was encroaching on her territory, so I offered up a lame wave so she wouldn't think I was avoiding her. She didn't return it.

I opted to ignore her after that, losing myself in the majestic foliage. The building was absolutely beautiful, and the plants inside were exactly what I needed. I spent a good hour searching for the ingredients I needed. When I'd found everything on my list — except for one specific item — I headed out to the lily pond. That's where I found the final ingredient ... and where Cormack Grimlock found me.

"I don't want to judge," he hedged when he realized my shoes were off and I was wading in the cold water.

"You can judge." I smiled at him as I rummaged in the water, coming back with a plant that I managed to yank from beneath the surface while maintaining the important root ball I sought. "Finally!"

"What is that?"

I smiled at him. "Sweet flag. I'm making a salve for you to rub on Lily's chest. It should help to calm her."

Cormack was taken aback. "I ... that's why you're out here so early? You're trying to help Lily?"

"She's a very high-strung baby." I almost tripped coming out of the pond. He grabbed my arm and gripped hard before I could topple to the ground face first. "You've probably noticed that she has a few issues."

"Oh, I've noticed."

Up close I realized he had circles under his eyes. The man was always together, dressed in an expensive suit without a hair out of place, but he looked tired today.

"I'm guessing that Lily ran you ragged last night?" I carried the sweet flag to the pile of herbs I'd collected and then motioned for him to follow me to the golf cart parked in the lot.

"Lily is ... a very loud child." Cormack was obviously choosing his words carefully. He didn't want to disparage his only grandchild. His restlessness was palpable, though. "Where are we going?"

"Back to the boathouse," I replied without hesitation. "I need the kitchen to make the salve."

"I ... well ... okay." He didn't protest when I handed him the herbs and hopped in the driver's seat. My feet were still bare because they were cold and drying. I didn't want to ruin my shoes by putting them on too early, so I simply tossed them in the basket at the back of the cart.

"Did you get any sleep last night?" I asked as we sped toward the boathouse. "Were you up by yourself the entire time?"

"No. Everyone pitched in. Braden and Redmond were with me the entire time. We panicked at one point and called Maya, which meant Cillian showed up, too. They ended up spending the night in Cillian's old room."

I smiled. "So ... it was a group effort."

"Aidan didn't help." Cormack's gaze turned dark when he

mentioned his youngest son and Aisling's twin. "One would think he'd want to help his sister."

"I'm willing to bet he has been helping," I offered. "He lives next door to Aisling and Griffin, right? I'm sure he's been taking Lily as often as possible. Ignoring the way Aisling is fading wouldn't be in his wheelhouse."

Cormack's eyes were sharp when he looked toward me. "She's not fading. She's just ... struggling."

"You're all struggling." I stopped in front of the boathouse and collected the herbs from him. "Come on. You can help."

"Help what?" He looked lost as he trailed behind me. "You said you're making a salve. I don't understand. Can't you just wave your hands and make this better? For that matter, can't you just wave your hands and make the baby sleep?"

"I probably could, but that won't make things better for you over the long haul. It's a temporary fix at best."

"Yes, but ... even a temporary fix is better than nothing at this point."

I wasn't sure that was true. "We need to get to the root of Lily's issues," I countered, leading him into the kitchen and dropping the herbs on the counter. I searched through the cupboards until I found a huge pot, to which I added water and put on the stove. "We need to chop the herbs," I instructed. "You can help with that."

I retrieved two knives from the drawer and handed him a cutting board. "Start with the sweet flag. We want the roots."

"I don't know what that is." He looked helpless but game to try.

I pointed out the herb in question. "Wash the roots first and then chop them into tiny pieces."

He didn't offer up any complaint as he started to work. "Did you learn how to do this from your grandfather?"

"Yes."

"He's a Bruja like you, correct?"

"He's ... kind of like me," I hedged. "The thing is, I got a double dose of it. My father was a reaper, something he inherited from his mother. My grandfather is my father's father, which means my father was half Bruja and half reaper. My mother was a different sort of Bruja

— more air than earth, which is not necessary information in regards to this conversation. She was trying to teach me a different way of life when she died."

"Ah." Understanding dawned on his handsome features. "So, you're really only one-quarter reaper."

"Does that bother you?"

"No. My son-in-law has no reaper in him. I'm not one of those fanatical purists who think reapers should mate only with other reapers. My wife wasn't a born reaper. She was absorbed into the family fold and had enough magic in her that she could serve as a reaper after we wed, but she was hardly a pureblood."

"That means your children are only fifty-percent reaper and fifty-percent something else."

"I suppose so. I never really thought about it." He rubbed his forehead with the back of his hand. "I stopped here because I wanted to talk to you. I didn't get much of a chance last night given everything that's going on with Lily.

"First, I really am thankful that you noticed Aisling's distress and said something," he continued. "I thought she was just tired ... like a normal new mother would be tired. She complains so much that I didn't notice the signs that she was truly spiraling."

"It's not as if she was going to do anything drastic," I said hurriedly. "I mean ... she often acts out and does things without thinking them through. She wasn't going to hurt herself or the baby, though. I would've seen that."

"I don't want my children to suffer." He spoke from the heart. "I'll do what is necessary to help her. If that means hiring a full-time nurse to ease her burden so she and Griffin can get some sleep, I'm fine with that. Money is good only if you can use it to help those most important to you."

I smiled. He had a ridiculously sweet heart, something I figured he passed on to his children ... even though some of them would rather cut off their own arms than admit it. "This should help. The baby only has an issue because Aisling has an issue, and she's not going to shake her issue until she manages to get some sleep and regroup."

"What issue?"

I dropped some of the herbs I'd been cutting into the pot, buying myself time to consider how I wanted to respond. Finally, I decided telling the truth was the best option. "Aisling is afraid she's going to be a bad mother. Lily can feel that worry. She picks up on the fear, and it unsettles her."

Cormack stilled. "Why would Aisling think that?"

"I don't know. The answers I got were from Lily's brain. She obviously doesn't understand what's going on. She only knows it upsets her."

"But ... Aisling is going to be fine." Cormack sounded sure of himself. "She won't be perfect, but no one is. Her mother wasn't perfect. Although ... perhaps I built my wife up to be more perfect than she was after the fact."

"You turned her into a martyr," I surmised. "I'm guessing that's normal when a parent dies. You turn the dead partner into a perfect example so memories are never tarnished."

"Did your grandfather do that with you?" he asked, curiosity etched across his handsome face. "Your parents died and he was left to pick up the pieces. Did he paint them as perfect?"

"No." I smiled at the notion. "My grandfather is a bit more ... persnickety. He was angry with my parents for failing to escape. He was also angry because he didn't want my father to join the reaper profession. He blamed my father for what happened."

"I'm sure that was a cover for what he really felt," Cormack said hurriedly. "Grief makes people act out in peculiar ways."

"I know. He didn't mean the things he said."

"I saw it in my children when they lost their mother a second time." Cormack appeared mired in deep thoughts, but he continued to cut herbs. "Seeing the real Lily — my wife, I mean — was difficult for all of us. It brought peace in some ways and angst in others.

"Aisling was the one who got the most peace out of seeing her," he continued. "Knowing that the thing that came back wasn't the mother she loved allowed her to let go of some of the anger she carried. She was better after losing her mother a second time. Braden, on the other hand, was worse."

Mention of Braden made me uncomfortable. "He seems fine. I

mean ... I don't know him well, but he's not being a royal pain or anything."

Cormack chuckled, the sound low and throaty. "You're funny. You have all this insight into other people but can't point it inward."

That felt like an insult. "I see things clearly."

"Not where Braden is concerned," he countered. "You think you do, but you're wearing sunglasses indoors when it comes to him. It's all right. Don't get defensive. I learned my lesson with Aisling and Griffin. I'm going to allow you and Braden to figure things out on your own."

"There's nothing to figure out."

"Of course not."

"I'm serious."

"I can tell." He grinned as he handed me some herbs. "I really did come here for two reasons. One was to thank you, which I've already done. I got distracted by our discussion. The other is to tell you that the home office is starting to make noise. You need to fill the open position under your purview. You can't let it drag much longer."

"I haven't purposely been letting it drag," I protested, annoyance coming out to play. "It's just ... I'm still getting used to the job. Today was the first day I'd ever been in the conservatory, for crying out loud. How am I supposed to know who to hire when I'm not even sure where I fit in yet?"

"You don't have to carve out a space for yourself in this facility. Your space is already set."

"Yeah, but ... ."

"Renee is gone," he reminded me. "She was trying to mold things to her liking. Oliver has been here for a long time. He goes with the flow ... and is more than happy to pick up the slack."

"Even though he's tightlipped on things from the past," I muttered, pressing the heel of my hand to my forehead. "I'll find someone to hire. I promise. I'm not putting it off. I simply thought helping Lily was more important."

"Helping Lily is important to all of us. Making sure you're safe here, that things are running smoothly, is also important.

"You've gone out of your way to help my family," he continued. "Whether you realize it or not, that means you're part of it. I expect things to progress with you and Braden. Don't give me any lip. You might be fighting the effort, but you know how things are going to go. You're too sensitive to look past the obvious."

The irritation I thought tabled bubbled up again. "I think you're seeing things that aren't there."

"And I think you only see clearly when you're not looking at yourself," he countered. "It doesn't matter. I meant what I said. I learned my lesson about poking my nose into my children's relationships when it backfired on me several times with Aisling and Griffin. You and Braden are on your own in that department."

"Well, great."

His grin broadened at my reaction. "You're funny. I genuinely like you ... and not only because you're trying to help calm a very cranky baby so we can all get some sleep."

"That baby is nervous because her mother is nervous. Once Aisling calms down, Lily will calm down. For that to happen, though, Aisling needs the occasional break. She might be Lily's mother, but she had a vibrant life before giving birth. You can't completely strip that away from her."

Cormack was back to being thoughtful. "I didn't really think about that. I will going forward. You've been a great help."

"Well, once this salve is finished, you might want to double the accolades. Until then, we need to talk about the ghosts. I don't know what to make of them ... and I'm starting to wonder if they're really there or I somehow made them appear for a different reason."

"What reason would that be?"

"I have no idea."

"Well ... let's run through the timeline again. We didn't really get a chance to talk because we had an audience. I want to hear everything, from the beginning."

"Okay. You asked for it, though."

Six

Oliver was in the gate room when I finally made my way there. He didn't greet me as I entered, instead remaining fixated on his computer screen. The lack of acknowledgment grated even though I was the one who was late.

"Good morning to you, too," I called out.

He lifted his eyes and, if I wasn't mistaken, there was a hint of mirth lurking in the dark depths. "Good morning," he said. "It's nice you finally showed up for work."

"I got distracted," I admitted, dropping my coat on the table at the back of the room before moving toward my desk. "Cormack Grimlock stopped by and we had a discussion."

"Really?" Oliver suddenly appeared interested. "Does he have any information on what went down yesterday?"

"No, and he's as worried as we are. He won't come right out and say it, but the fact that I saw ghosts up there last night is making everyone nervous."

Oliver abandoned his computer and focused completely on me. "What ghosts?"

Oh, right. He was out of the loop on that one. I'd forgotten to tell him. "So, when I went upstairs yesterday to make sure everything was locked up tight I saw about twenty ghosts in the aquarium. Lauren Tate, the dead teacher, was one of them. They started whispering and raising their hands, which was really creepy. I was going to run, but Braden showed up ... and then the ghosts disappeared."

"I see." Oliver's expression was hard to read. "So ... why didn't you call me for help?"

The thought had never entered my head. "I don't often call out for help. I can take care of myself."

"I get that. You're strong. I've seen you in action. Still, what you described is beyond anything I've ever seen here. Ghosts shouldn't be a thing in our world — especially here — because of the overabundance of reapers on the property. The gate is another issue entirely. If we really had ghosts, they would be drawn to the gate."

"Are you sure?"

He nodded. "I've seen it happen. I don't know if you remember what happened with Edgar right after he died. You were in your own little world because you'd just killed Renee and she didn't have a soul. Edgar, however, had one. The moment he died and his soul emerged it headed straight for the gate and disappeared."

Oddly, I didn't remember that at all. Edgar Mason was a famous face in reaper circles and he was on the premises to help with our previous problem. Unbeknownst to us, he was the cause of that problem ... and died at his own partner's hand during the final battle. "Huh. I just assumed one of the Grimlocks absorbed him."

"They were busy fighting the wraiths."

"Well, that's interesting." I rolled my neck and leaned back in my chair. "I can't be sure what I saw. I mean ... maybe I imagined it. Maybe my subconscious created them for a specific reason."

"Has that ever happened before?"

"Not to my knowledge."

"Well, then it seems to me we're dealing with something else."

"And what would that be?"

"Your guess is as good as mine. The thing is, you still should've called me. We're a team. That means we work together on everything ... not just the soul transfers."

"Even though you rarely want to talk to me," I groused under my breath.

"I heard that."

"I know. You're a vampire. You have terrific hearing. I met a few vampires in New Orleans, although I was told after the fact that the only vampires drawn to the city are wannabes."

"Because of *Interview with a Vampire?*"

I nodded. "And those Charlaine Harris books about Sookie Stackhouse."

"I'm not familiar with those, but I'll take your word for it."

"Yeah, well ... ." I decided to change the subject. "How do you get here without getting toasted by the sun? I mean, you don't burn to a crisp daily, so I'm assuming you have a secret way into the building."

"There's a tunnel that runs under the entire length of the property. Sometimes I use that. Sometimes I simply come here before the sun rises. In the winter, it's constantly cloudy so I rarely have to face the sun. Why else do you think I settled in Michigan?"

"Yeah, but that doesn't explain what you do when you leave before the sun sets and there's no way to avoid it."

"I wear a hoodie."

I frowned. "And that works?"

"Most of the time. I also have special glass in my car. When none of those options are available, I use the sewer."

"How does that smell?"

"Pretty much as you imagine."

"Well, now I'm going to have a different sort of nightmare." I rubbed my forehead. "Anyway, I don't know what to make of the ghosts. I told Cormack about them last night — and again this morning — but he seems equally flummoxed. I'm not sure what's going to happen there."

"And you saw him at his house last night, right?"

I sensed trouble. "I ... well ... Braden thought it best I tell Cormack what I saw right away."

"Uh-huh." He was clearly dubious. "How late were you out with Braden?"

"Not very. That house may be the size of a castle, but you can hear the baby screaming from one end to the other. I had dinner, told my story, held the baby and called it a night."

"You purposely held a screaming baby?" He shuddered. "That sounds like the worst idea ever."

"Yes, well ... I wanted to get a reading on her."

"And what did your reading tell you?"

"That Lily Taylor is a complicated baby ... and she has a whole gaggle of people willing to dote on her. Cormack was up all night with her. From what he said, I'm guessing Braden and Redmond were with him. They were determined to give Aisling a good night's sleep."

"That's nice of them. Although ... do you think there's something wrong with the baby?" He looked legitimately concerned. "I thought infants were supposed to sleep for, like, twenty hours a day."

"I believe that's cats, but Lily definitely isn't sleeping as much as she should. Hopefully the salve I cooked up this morning will help that."

"Salve?"

I told him about the herbs and working with Cormack. When I was finished, all he could do was shake his head.

"I guess you've had a busier morning than I realized. Do you think your ointment will help the baby?"

I shrugged. "It can't hurt."

"True enough." He turned back to his computer screen. "We're on schedule. Both of us don't need to be down here. If you have other things to do, don't let me stop you."

Instead of taking advantage of the situation and fleeing, I scowled as I turned to my computer. "Cormack didn't visit simply because he wanted to thank me. He also reminded me that I need to pick a replacement for Renee ... and soon."

"Ah." Oliver's grin was back. "It sucks to be the boss, huh? I'll happily handle the workload while you go through endless reams of paperwork to find our new co-worker."

"Oh, no." I made a tsking sound with my tongue as I shook my finger. "You're totally helping."

"I would prefer you handle that particular job."

"Yeah, well, get used to disappointment. You're the one familiar with some of these names. We'll work quicker if we do it together."

"What makes you think faster is better?"

"In this particular case, I'm guessing that's the only answer I'm allowed."

Instead of continuing to fight, he shook his head. "Fine. I'll help. I'm not making the final decision, though. That's on you."

"Fair enough."

WE WORKED TIRELESSLY FOR two hours. After that, we headed to the eatery for lunch. Oliver didn't eat, but apparently Collin kept chilled blood on hand for him, cracking it open only when no one else was around.

"That's ... lovely," I intoned as I watched Oliver drink his blood through a straw. It was in a bottle, which I found odd, but I couldn't look away. "Where do you get it from?"

"The butcher," Oliver replied, wiping his mouth. "I believe it's the same place your meal came from, so don't get dainty." He inclined his chin toward my burger. "Now, I believe we're down to ten files remaining. We should get through those before we finish lunch."

"Right." I dragged my eyes from the bottle and focused on the tablet I'd brought to lunch. "Leslie Faraday. She's forty, works in the main library and says she's passionate about helping souls cross over. She says her best trait is that she's a giving soul and thinks she'll be beneficial for the transition of those most tortured by their new lot in life. Those are her words, not mine."

"Pass," Oliver said derisively. "She clearly doesn't understand how the process works if she believes that she's going to have time to waste talking to souls. I'm betting she's one of those people who want to learn about the other side because she figures she can find a way to keep from visiting if she digs deep enough."

I hadn't considered that. "Yeah. You're right. I wonder why she would assume we talk to the souls before we transport them."

"Because she's an idiot. Who's next?"

"Um ... Mike Baxter. He's thirty-three and says he grew up in a reaper family in the middle of the state. He says he's always been fascinated by the science of the gate and his dream is to be around it twenty-four hours a day."

"Pass." Oliver was quickly losing interest in the conversation. "There's no science to be learned. It's not as if he can take the gate apart and look at the mechanical guts to determine how it works. He's dreaming if he thinks he can replicate the process. That's above his paygrade. Once he realizes that, he'll stop caring about his work. Then we'll have to hire someone else right away ... and nobody wants that because the training process for this gig is a pain in the keister."

"Wow. You're good at this." I grabbed my burger. "You think of things I never would. Maybe you should be in charge."

"If I wanted to be in charge, I would've taken over the job a long time ago."

"Why didn't you?"

He shrugged. "Being the boss has never been important to me. I'm dedicated to making sure the process runs smoothly, but I don't need to be in charge to do it."

It seemed like an evasive answer, but he was helping me so I decided to let it slide. "Okay, well ... let's move on to the next person. But ... something is bugging me about what happened yesterday."

"What's that?" Oliver asked, smiling at Collin as the merrow appeared at the edge of the table to start clearing dishes. The taciturn cook returned the smile, which made me think the two had a much chummier relationship than I would ever share with either of them.

"The boy. Granger Downey. He was talking right before it happened and Lauren seemed surprised. Apparently that wasn't his normal reaction. Right after it happened, he went back to being silent and surly."

"Okay. What do you think that means?"

"I don't know. I can't help but wonder if one of those ghosts I saw — the ones I'm convinced might be in my head — managed to possess him right before the incident. Perhaps his chatter was a warning."

"How do you suggest figuring out if your hunch is correct?"

That was a very good question. "I don't know." I shrugged. Maybe I can go back in a vision and get a better look at the moments leading up to his outburst."

Collin let loose a derisive snort. "Oh, geez. You Bruja are all the same. Magic is always your answer. Sometimes you need to look at modern technology and leave the old ways behind."

That was rich coming from a guy who reportedly stayed married to his wife because she stole his hat, some old fairytale that still plagued his people ... even though it made zero sense to me. "And how can modern technology help us?" I asked, biting back my temper.

"The security cameras."

I was confused. "What cameras?"

"The ones in the aquarium." Collin rolled his eyes. "Some leader. She doesn't even realize there are cameras in the aquarium."

"They're hidden," Oliver reminded the grouchy merrow. "Only those who are in the know are aware of their existence."

"She's the gatekeeper. She should know."

He had a point, which irritated me beyond measure. "Why didn't anyone tell me about the cameras?"

Oliver merely shrugged. "I thought you knew." He wiped the corners of his mouth with a napkin and stood. "Come on. He's right. If you want to see what went down yesterday, the best place to do it is in the security office."

That made sense, which only served to infuriate me more. "Why didn't you mention the cameras before?"

"I couldn't fathom why you would be interested in the footage. They're not night vision, so you won't be able to see what happened after the lights went out." He led me down the main hallway before splitting off into a branch I'd never used. "It never occurred to me that you would want to see what happened in the moments leading up to the tragedy. I guess that makes sense."

"Oh, you think?" I refused to rein in my temper. "I can't believe we wasted twenty-four hours. We could already know what sort of enemy we're facing."

"I very much doubt that."

"Why?"

"Because the lights were killed for a reason," he replied, matter-of-fact. "That means whoever murdered the teacher didn't care about the crowd and was most likely aware of the cameras."

"How did you come to that conclusion?"

"Why else kill the lights?"

"Maybe whatever it was thought that it could hide its identity handling things the way it did."

"It still makes no sense. Why go after the teacher?" Oliver waved his security badge in front of a door I'd never seen before and the sound of a lock clicking echoed throughout the hallway. "If this creature — and I happen to agree we're dealing with something other than a human — but if this creature wanted to remain hidden, why go for such a public kill? Why not wait until Tara was alone on the main floor to go after her? Why not try to take you out when you were closing down shop in the evening?"

He'd obviously given this more thought than me, which was humbling. "Well ... I don't know."

I watched as Oliver moved to the computer banks at the far side of the room. There were cameras pointed at various parts of the island. "Is this ... everything?"

He shook his head. "We obviously can't watch everything," he replied. "There are cameras pointed at the main buildings, although most of the time we have only one angle. There are three cameras on the main floor of the aquarium. It's important we keep people from crossing through the door that leads to the basement."

"For obvious reasons," I murmured as Oliver sat at the desk and started tapping away. He clearly knew what he was doing, because before I realized what was happening, he'd pulled up the footage we were looking for. "This is when the children arrived."

I watched without comment as Tara greeted the teacher and the excited students traversed the open space. Lauren looked to be an attentive instructor. She took the time to focus on each child when he or she asked a question. She smiled often and encouraged the children to look around. For her part, she appeared to be innocent and without guile, which made her death even more senseless.

"Her name never showed up on a list," I noted as I watched the footage. "Cormack double checked. No one was expecting her soul to pass over, which meant no one was here to collect it."

"And yet her soul is not running around unattended," Oliver mused. "I mean ... I guess it could be. It's possible the gate called her even through several floors and she immediately headed in that direction. We don't know what happened in the darkness."

"No," I agreed. "I don't think that's what happened. She was one of the ghosts I saw yesterday. She's either still hanging around and we can't see her or ... ."

"Something else absorbed her," Oliver mused, thoughtful. "That's an interesting notion. Perhaps whatever creature is haunting us is a soul eater."

"How many creatures eat souls?"

"More than you would be comfortable with. That's the child, right?" He pointed at the screen, to where Granger stood next to his teacher and stared at a tank full of seahorses.

"That's him," I confirmed as I leaned forward to get a better look at the boy. "He looks like a normal kid."

"He's not talking," Oliver noted. "He's interested in the animals, but he's not talking."

"No, I ... ." A shadow flitted across the screen, causing me to straighten. "Did you see that?"

"What?"

"Rewind a little bit and go back."

Oliver did as I instructed.

"There!" I pointed at the shadow again. "I can't make out any features. I ... do you know what that is?"

Oliver shook his head. "No, but look at the child after the shadow passes."

On the screen, within seconds of the shadow crossing through the frame, Granger turns in my direction and starts babbling. I couldn't hear what he was saying through the footage, but I already knew because I'd witnessed it the previous afternoon.

"He was definitely possessed," I muttered.

"Or propelled by a magical force," Oliver countered. "We can't be sure. That didn't look like a normal possession to me."

"Have you seen a possession before?"

"I have."

"Other than in *The Exorcist?*"

He scowled. "I don't live my life by things I've seen in movies."

"You don't know what you're missing." I flashed a smile before sighing. "Show it to me again."

After watching the footage a third time, I could do nothing but shake my head.

"I think I need to talk to Granger."

"He might not remember anything."

"I know, but he's still our best shot. If we can't get him to explain what happened ... well, at least we'll know where to start looking."

"I guess there's no harm in trying."

Seven

Braden was waiting in the aquarium when we made our way out of the security office. His attention was solely focused on a snake, one of the few reptiles we housed in the facility — he was busy tapping on the window to get the serpent's attention — and obviously didn't hear us approaching because he didn't look in our direction.

"Don't you know a watched snake never hisses?" I challenged.

He swiveled quickly, sheepish. "Hey. I ... um ... Tara said she was going to track you down. She went that way." He pointed toward the door that led to the basement.

"We were in the security office watching footage of yesterday's event."

He straightened. "Anything good?"

"I guess that depends on how deeply you value the image of what looks to be a shadow swooping across the screen," Oliver replied, striding forward and shaking Braden's hand. "Izzy is far more excited about it than I am."

"Yes, well, she's an odd duck." He winked at me to emphasize he was teasing and then planted his hands on his hips. "So ... I finished up my work early today and thought maybe you could use some help here."

"Really?" I managed to keep my tone even, but just barely. His sudden appearance threw me. Of course, I figured that's what he was going for. "Isn't there a baby at your house that needs tending?"

His flirty smile slipped. "That's another reason I had to get out of there. Lily's lungs are apparently the sort that never grow tired of screaming."

My heart sank. "What about the salve I sent with your father? He's supposed to rub that on her chest. It will calm her."

"Believe it or not, it's already starting to work. Lily is no longer auditioning to be a banshee later in life. The screaming has stopped, which is why I escaped when I did. I had no inclination to be present when she decides the silence isn't to her liking."

"The salve should prevent that."

"Yeah, well, she's Aisling's daughter. I happen to believe her mind will eventually overcome whatever woo-woo you did with the potion you concocted."

"It's not a potion. It's a magical remedy."

"Is there a difference?" His gaze was challenging.

"Well ... yes."

"Great. I can't wait to hear about it. You can tell me while I'm helping you with ... well ... whatever you've got going today."

I recognized his game. He was trying to get me to invite him on my afternoon trek. I had no intention of doing so. "I have nothing going on today," I smoothly lied.

"She's going to the deaf school," Oliver volunteered. "We saw something on the security footage. It looked like a possession ... only not. Whatever it was, the kid was acting normally before it happened. He went back to normal after the lights came back on. We need to figure out what happened to him that caused his brief outburst."

My mouth dropped open as I lobbed my most hateful glare in Oliver's direction. "Wow! And I thought you were the tight-lipped sort."

"That's what you get for assuming." His smile was smug. "One of us has to stay here and monitor the soul transfers. We've yet to bring anybody else on — even though it's overdue — since Renee's death.

That means Izzy was going to the school alone, Braden, which I wasn't keen on. You're here now, so you can go with her."

Braden's eyes twinkled with delight. "That's a happy coincidence, huh?"

I could think of a few other words to describe it. "It's ... something," I muttered, shaking my head as I narrowed my eyes at Oliver. "Actually, I think it's a fine idea." I brightened considerably. "Someone needs to question Granger. He knows me ... well, kind of. He should recognize me at least, which means he won't be thrown by our visit.

"You know a lot of the people in the home office so you can finish sorting through the files that were sent our way and narrow down the list of people applying for the job to five," I continued. "We both agreed that I would make the final decision on our new co-worker, but you can narrow the list so my decision will be easier."

Now it was Oliver's turn to frown. "I don't believe I agreed to that."

"Yes, well, we're both dealing with things we didn't agree to, aren't we? I guess you'll simply have to suck it up ... just like me."

We stared at each other for a long beat. It was a standoff of sorts. Finally, he heaved a sigh and relented.

"Fine. I'll cull the entrants to five. You're still in charge of the final decision."

"I can't wait." I shot him a sunny smile. "Have fun with your files."

"Have fun with your Grimlock."

The corners of my lips turned down as I turned my gaze to the left and found Braden watching me with the smuggest expression I'd ever seen outside of a George Clooney flick. "This is a work trip," I stressed, not for Oliver's benefit but Braden's. "We'll be doing work things and nothing else."

Oliver snorted as Braden's grin widened. "Right. Have fun with your 'work things.' Make sure to call if you don't intend to return. I don't want to worry about you."

"Yeah, yeah, yeah." I graced him with an absent wave as I pinned Braden with a pointed look. "We're working together. Nothing more."

"Did I mention anything else?" His smile never dimmed, which I found frustrating. He was unbelievably full of himself. "I think you're the one who has dirty thoughts on her mind. You should probably wash your brain out with soap. I'm a good boy."

I wanted to strangle him. It should be impossible to be that smug. "I don't have dirty thoughts."

"Really?" He leaned closer, so close in fact, that his lips were extremely close to mine. "I can see inside your head. You're having a dirty thought right now."

Sadly, he wasn't wrong. I was having a dirty thought ... and it made me want to smack both of us. "I am not."

"You are."

"No."

"Yes."

"You like to hear yourself talk, don't you?" It took all my strength, but I took a step away from him. "We should probably get going. I don't have a vehicle so you drive."

"I'm happy to drive." He spun his keys around his finger. "I've always wanted to serve as the personal chauffeur of a beautiful woman. I'm so glad I get to mark that off my bucket list."

I growled without realizing it. It reminded me of a bear ... or an angry cat. "We should get moving. We don't have all day."

"I do. My father cleared my schedule to help you. He said you'd earned it after shutting Lily up."

"Lily is a baby. She'll straighten herself out eventually."

"I certainly hope so. I don't know how long my sister can hang on if things stay this way."

"Your sister is stronger than you think," I said as I strode through the doors that led to the parking lot. "She's a freaking Amazon."

"Oh, I know." Briefly, he took on a far-off expression. "She's stronger than the rest of us combined, I think. Er, well, sometimes I think that. Right now she seems fragile. I'm not used to it."

Even though he agitated me — which was obviously his plan — I felt sympathetic toward his plight. His relationship with his sister seemed an ongoing project, one that he was willing to work on even though he clearly wasn't sure what his next step involved. "She's fine. She'll find her footing."

"I hope so."

"I *know* so. Now ... let's get going. We need to come up with a convincing lie if we expect the administrators of the school to allow us to talk to Granger."

"Why can't you just do your thing?" He waved his hands in such a way that I knew he was indicating my magic.

"Because I'm not adept at mind control."

"Have you ever tried?"

"Actually, I have."

"Oh, well ... how did that go?"

"Not well."

"You don't strike me as a quitter. Maybe you should try again."

"And maybe we should think of another way to get access to the kid. I think I'm going to put you in charge of that on the drive to the school."

"That sounds reasonable."

"I thought so."

BRADEN'S IDEA of schmoozing our way into the school was to flirt with the administrative assistant. At first I thought it was the dumbest idea ever. But five minutes in, I realized he was really good at it. His skills were on full display when Kelly Martin — she of the blond hair and covetous eyes — called for Granger to be brought to the front office so we could question him away from prying eyes. All the while, she kept batting her lashes at Braden ... and he let her.

"It's so nice that you're taking such an interest in Granger," Kelly cooed as we waited for the boy to make his way to the front office. "So few people actually care about the psychological needs of children after a trying event. You must have children at home to be this ... in tune ... to the needs of a frightened little boy."

I knew exactly what she was doing, though I managed to keep from snorting directly in her face by sheer force of will. That didn't stop me from rolling my eyes at her back, something Braden found hilarious as he tried to keep a straight face.

"I don't have children of my own," he replied, allowing a charming grin to flit across his open features as Kelly sighed in relief. "I'm not married ... yet. Eventually I would like a child or two of my own. I think fatherhood is a noble calling."

I almost choked on the bile that threatened to bubble up. "So noble," I intoned, earning a playful look from him.

"Right now I'm just an uncle," he continued. "My sister gave birth to my first niece a few weeks ago. We're all staying under the same roof to help her with the transition to motherhood, so I feel like a surrogate father of sorts."

That was freaking ludicrous. "Weren't you out of town until two days ago?" I challenged.

Braden's smile slipped. "I was still with my niece on a spiritual level."

I thought about gagging to show my opinion of his "spiritual" beliefs, but the idea fled when I looked to the door and found Granger walking through it.

He was a small boy — at least two inches shorter than he should be for his age, I surmised — and he had dark eyes. He was paler than most of the other kids, which told me he didn't spend much time outside. I could practically sense the fear wafting off him as he stepped into the office.

"Hello, Granger." Kelly immediately started signing when she saw him. "This is Braden and ... I'm sorry, but I forgot your name." She acted contrite as she met my gaze, but I knew better.

"Izzy." I signed my own name to him. "I was at the aquarium with you yesterday. Do you remember?"

Kelly served as interpreter and signed the question. The boy opened his mouth, and for a moment I thought he would actually speak, but instead he started signing.

Kelly translated the boy's hand gestures. "I remember you," she said. "You came in right before Mrs. Tate fell down."

Fell down? That was a nice way of putting it. I glanced to Kelly for reassurance. "Do they know what happened?"

Kelly nodded. "They know that something bad happened and Mrs. Tate fell down and couldn't get up," she replied, signing again. "They're well aware that she's not coming back and they're sad. They also know that she's in a better place."

"Is this a religious school?" I asked, glancing around to see if I'd missed the signs.

"No, but it's always better to talk about a happy place on the other side with young children."

I exchanged a quick look with Braden, who seemed to understand my agitation, because he smoothly led Kelly away from Granger and toward the front window. "I just love the view here. It's a beautiful piece of land. How long has the school been located here?"

Obvious confusion etched its way over Kelly's face. "Oh, well ... it's been years. Close to twenty, I think. Doesn't your co-worker need me to translate for her?"

"I believe she has everything under control." Braden cast a final look over his shoulder before drawing Kelly's attention to something on the other side of the window. "You must spend a lot of time sitting and dreaming while you're here. That fountain is wonderful. Do you throw coins in and make wishes? I know I would if I were in your position."

Kelly's eyes widened to comical proportions. "How did you know I did that?"

"Just a guess. You look the sort."

I tuned out the rest of their conversation and focused on Granger. I was in a precarious situation because I couldn't sign — other than the basic alphabet — and he was obviously in no mood to communicate. That meant we would have to come to a meeting of the minds if we wanted to interact. Still, this was better. I didn't want Kelly involving herself in the conversation we needed to have.

"I think you saw something yesterday," I supplied, keeping my voice low as I drew the boy to a set of chairs and a bench on the other side of the office. "Can you read lips? I just ... I need to know if you saw something."

Granger stared at me without response.

"Can you read lips?" I repeated.

Slowly, he nodded. "Good. I wish I'd paid better attention to that book when I was a kid so I knew more than the alphabet. I can't go back in time and fix that, so we're going to have to move forward. That means I need you to tell me what you saw. Anything. Just tell me one thing."

Granger carefully held his hands out and shook his head. It was a universal response that told me he either didn't understand what I wanted him to do or couldn't comply.

"Do you remember what happened yesterday?" I asked, desperate.

There was a flash of something dark in his eyes, something that took me by surprise and forced me to lean closer.

"You do, don't you?" My voice was barely a whisper as I searched for a hint of recognition in his dark orbs. "Was something else there? Someone who looked and sounded different, perhaps? Did you hear something? How about a whisper?"

Granger didn't answer. I caught a hint of something in his head, though. A quick flicker of darkness that practically beckoned for me to follow.

I spared a glance for Kelly and found her completely entranced with Braden, and took advantage of the situation by grabbing both sides of Granger's head before he could pull away.

I didn't have much time, so I shoved my consciousness inside his head and immediately went for his memory. I was hopeful I would be able to catch a glimpse of what happened, even if the boy was unsure what he saw. Instead, I ran into a roadblock in the form of an ethereal figure.

It wasn't solid, and yet it stymied me, glowing green as it shook its head. I tried to move around it, but the figure cut me off at every turn when I tried to access Granger's memories.

"What are you?" I asked, confused. I'd never encountered anything remotely like what was happening now. "What are you doing here?" I wasn't sure if I spoke out loud or simply in Granger's head. Ultimately, it didn't matter.

"Get out." The specter glowed brighter, reminding me of the shadows I'd witnessed in the aquarium the previous day.

"Just tell me what's going on," I prodded.

"Get out."

I refused to back down. "I need to know."

The phantasm lost its patience. "Get out!" It screamed so loudly it blew me backward, forcing me away from Granger and nearly knocking me off the bench.

The noise I made as I struggled to maintain my seat was enough to draw Kelly's attention. She was full of annoyance when she strode in our direction.

"What happened? What's going on?"

"Nothing." My voice sounded raspy as I collected myself. "We were simply having a nice conversation."

Kelly obviously didn't believe me. She hurried to Granger's side and pulled him to a standing position. "I think that's enough for the day. Perhaps you should be going."

I was so shaken, all I could do was agree. "I think that's a fabulous idea."

Eight

"What just happened?"

Braden was hot on my trail once we hit the parking lot, Kelly and her flirty eyes all but forgotten.

I glanced over my shoulder and frowned when I saw the look of concern on his face. "You could've stayed with your new girlfriend."

"Oh, stuff it." He clearly wasn't in the mood to play passive-aggressive games. "What happened? Did you get a look inside that kid's head?"

I nodded, glancing back at the office and finding Kelly watching us from the window. "We should probably get out of here."

"Tell me."

"As soon as we're away from this place." I was firm. "I need some air."

He looked as if he wanted to argue further, but instead nodded. "Okay. Come on." He opened the passenger door for me, something I found intriguingly dated, and then crossed to the driver's door. "Where to next? Do you just want to get away or do you have a destination in mind?"

That was a very good question. "Just drive for now."

"You've got it." He pulled out onto the nearest road without further comment, occasionally checking the rearview mirror as he put distance between the school and us. He waited until he was on the freeway to speak again. "You're okay, right? I mean ... I shouldn't be driving you to the emergency room or anything, should I?"

"That's the last thing I want." I rubbed my forehead as I attempted to organize my thoughts. "That little boy isn't alone in there." I blurted, even though I wasn't certain what I was saying.

"What do you mean?" He didn't adjust his speed. "Are you saying he's possessed?"

"No. I've seen possessed people before, inside their minds. He's not possessed ... or, at least not possessed in the traditional manner. I guess that's a better way of putting it."

"That's good, right?"

"On a normal day I would say it's good. Now I'm not so sure. I don't know how to explain what I saw in there."

"Try me."

"Well, for starters, there's a barrier."

"Like ... a magical barrier?" He made a face when I shot him a dirty look. "Hey, don't get snarky with me, missy. I'm not used to the magic thing."

"You grew up and work in the paranormal world," I reminded him.

"Yeah, but it's not the same as dealing with a magical individual. I'm a reaper. My only gift is that I can see souls when they separate from a body."

"That's kind of like seeing a ghost." I rested my temple against the cool glass of the window. "I think that's almost like what I saw ... only different."

He pulled off the freeway. I didn't think to ask where we were going. Even when he pulled into a park, which was quiet given the time of day, I didn't ask why he'd picked this location. He seemed to know where he was going, though, which was good enough.

"Izzy, you're starting to worry me," he offered, flashing a smile that didn't make it all the way to his eyes. "You're a little scattered. Now, don't get me wrong, I like a woman who is goofy at times ... mostly because that means she's less likely to laugh at me because I'm goofy. Still, you're all over the place, and I don't like it."

I didn't know what to say so I simply met his gaze and shrugged.

"That's it?" he demanded "That's all you're going to say? Heck, you didn't even say anything. I don't like that either. I would vastly prefer you punch me or something."

I found my voice. "Is that what you like? Are the women in your life supposed to punch you?"

"I only have one woman in my life with any regularity. That's Aisling ... and she definitely likes to punch me. When we were kids, I told her she looked fat from behind and she hit me with a baseball bat. I lost three teeth and had a black eye for weeks."

"You probably deserved it," I muttered.

"I definitely deserved it. Still, I prefer you hit me rather than sit there and say nothing."

"I was taught that hitting boys was wrong unless they did something that earned a punch," I offered. "I'm not keen on the idea of punching you."

"Great." He flashed an enthusiastic thumbs-up. "Go ahead and kiss me if that's what you're after. You don't even have to ask ... at least this time."

"Ugh." I made a disgusted sound in my throat. "Do you think that's funny?"

His smile was back, which gave me my answer. "I think I feel a little better than I did. Still, I would feel better if you told me what happened."

"I already told you. There's something in that kid's head."

"What? A ghost? Are you telling me that little boy has a ghost in his head? If so, we've got to find a way to get it out of there."

"Oh, really?" I rolled my eyes. "I never would've figured that out."

"At least the sarcasm is back." He gently reached over and snagged my hand, giving it a good squeeze before prodding me further. "Tell me what you saw and we'll figure it out."

"I've been trying to tell you." It took everything I had not to snap at him. I knew he was attempting to help, but I wasn't sure he could. He wasn't magical. He said it himself. He was a player in the paranormal world, but he wasn't a magical participant in *The Game of Life*, at least not in a manner that would be of any immediate benefit.

"There's something taking up residence in his head. I think it's a man ... or at least was a man."

"So ... a ghost?"

"Maybe. It's definitely a displaced soul, but I don't think it feels like a ghost."

"So, it's something else. I don't suppose it said anything of interest to you."

"Just to get out, but I did hear something in another voice. It sounded like a child's voice."

"Granger's voice?"

"I don't know. I guess that makes the most sense. If he's trapped in there with this thing taking charge, perhaps he's trying to figure out a way to escape."

"What did he say to you? I mean ... you said he whispered something. What was it?"

"I can't be sure." I licked my lips, nervous.

"Then tell me what you think you heard."

"A name. Ryan Carroll."

"Does that name mean anything to you?"

"No. Does it mean anything to you?"

He shook his head. "No, but I know someone who might be able to help us."

"Let me guess, he looks a lot like you — only with long hair — and has the same purple eyes."

"That would be the guy." Braden released my hand and put the car into drive. "We need to head downtown."

"I thought we were going to see Cillian," I argued. "Doesn't that mean heading back to Grimlock Manor?"

"No. He's conducting research at the main library today. No one can concentrate with Lily around."

I felt bad for the baby. She was getting a reputation before she even realized she had a nose. "Lily will be okay," I stressed. "She's just upset because Aisling is upset."

He cast me a sidelong look as he navigated back toward the freeway. "Why is Aisling upset?"

"She's afraid she's going to be a terrible mother. I already told your father this."

"Yes, well, Dad won't spread information like that ... especially if he thinks it will upset Aisling. I don't understand why she thinks she'll be a bad mother. That's ... ridiculous."

"Maybe it's because your mother tried to kill her and she's afraid she has that inside her."

His eyes went momentarily dark against his pale skin and then he recovered. "Our mother didn't try to kill her," he said finally. "That wasn't our mother."

I knew the story. Lily Grimlock died when Braden was just out of his teens and starting out as a reaper. She went to collect a soul at a fire and never returned. He was haunted by it. Several years later, a woman popped up wearing her face and claiming to be his mother ... but she was different.

To hear Aisling tell the story, she knew from the start that the woman who returned wasn't her mother. I tended to believe her, but I had my doubts about whether it was as easy to discard the woman as she pretended. The one thing all the Grimlocks agreed on was that Braden was crushed by the loss of his mother a second time. I probably should've kept my mouth shut while I was ahead. Of course he was annoyed by the mention of his mother trying to kill his sister.

"I shouldn't have said that," I offered hurriedly. "That was uncalled for."

"No, it wasn't. Aisling is clearly struggling. I'm glad to know why so we can fix it. The sooner Lily stops screaming, the better."

"I didn't mean what I said about your mother." My stomach filled with a sick sort of dread. "It's not fair. She's your mother. I wouldn't react well to anyone saying anything bad about my mother, and I barely remember her."

"It's okay," he repeated, his voice lower. "That wasn't my mother. My mother would never try to kill Aisling. I understand why you're concerned. I'm concerned, too."

I felt like a bit of an idiot. "Well ... I'm still sorry."

His smirk was back. "Don't worry. I'll come up with a way for you to make me feel better later."

"Geez!" I didn't want to laugh. It would only encourage him. But I couldn't stop myself. "You're kind of a pervert, aren't you?"

"I'm totally a pervert, although I prefer it when people call me a connoisseur of all things perverted. You'll get used to it."

"Good to know."

BRADEN KNEW HIS WAY around the main office, so he was in the lead when we arrived. This was only my second visit — my employment interviews were conducted online — so I was still unsure of where we were going until I recognized a beautiful marble hallway that led to a set of double doors.

"I remember where we're going now. I came here before ... with Cillian."

"My brother has never met a library he doesn't love," Braden agreed, grinning. "He especially likes this one. He visits at least once a week."

"I thought your father had a full library. I mean ... I know you said Cillian doesn't want to be around the baby. He could close the door and pretend he doesn't hear her."

"Cillian wouldn't purposely walk away from Lily no matter how loudly she's crying. He's like the rest of us. She's family and we'll deal with her no matter what it takes. He doesn't live at Grimlock Manor any longer. Ever since he moved into an apartment with Maya, he comes here more often. It's more convenient and he loves the room."

"Well, it is a spectacular room." I let loose a long sigh as we entered, grinning when I caught sight of Cillian sitting on a couch near a fireplace. He had an absolutely huge book resting on his abdomen and his feet propped on a pillow. "He likes to make himself at home, huh?"

Braden chuckled. "He does, especially if there are books around. Come on."

I fell into step behind him, watching Cillian for a hint of movement to suggest he realized he was no longer alone. We were almost on top of him before the long-haired Grimlock finally looked in our direction.

"Do I even want to know what went wrong?" he asked with a grimace, immediately reaching for his phone. "Did I forget to turn it on again?"

"We're not here because you missed a call," Braden replied. "We're here because we need your help."

Cillian's gaze spent a long time roaming over me before returning to his brother. "The last time you needed help you slept with a woman after meeting her at the bar and you couldn't get her out of the house without help because she refused to leave. It took two of us to carry her. Please tell me this isn't a repeat."

Braden's eyes burned bright with embarrassment. "That is not exactly how I remember that story ... and thank you so much for bringing it up."

Cillian's grin widened. "You're welcome."

"We're here for another reason," Braden supplied. "It's kind of a long story. I'll try to keep it neat and tidy for you." He launched into the tale, leaving nothing out. Oddly enough, he managed to be more succinct than I'd imagined. When he was finished, Cillian stroked his chin as he absorbed the new information.

"Well, that's weird," he said finally.

"You guys have a way with words," I groused, shaking my head as I sank into the oversized armchair across from him.

Cillian barked out a laugh as Braden took the other open chair. "You remind me of my sister sometimes. But you're easier to get along with."

"Don't compare her to Aisling." Braden made a face. "It creeps me out."

"Yes, well ... from your perspective, I can understand that. Tell me more about the ghost thing in the kid's head. Did it look like a soul that someone forgot to absorb?"

That was a good question. "Not really. I mean ... I guess. The figure was ethereal. It was complete, though. Usually when I hop in some-one's head the only resistance I run into is their conscious mind, which doesn't have a form. This had a freaking form."

"You're saying it looked like a man."

"It definitely looked like a man."

"And you heard the little boy whispering a name."

I nodded. "Ryan Carroll. The name doesn't mean anything to me. I'm sure that's what he was saying. I got out of there as fast as I could because it was so weird."

"I would think taking up residence in anyone's head is weird," Cillian mused, rolling to a sitting position. "We need to find out who Ryan Carroll is, but I have no idea where we even start looking for that information."

"I do," a new voice announced, causing me to practically jump out of my skin as I turned to my left. There, sitting on the floor in all his glory, was the gargoyle Bub. I'd met him upon my previous visit. He seemed to have a history with the Grimlocks that included an injury, maybe some betrayal and some weird in-joke about his tail. I couldn't quite keep up on all of that.

"You know, I should make you start wearing a bell," Cillian shook his head. "You barely make any noise and you frighten people when they finally remember you're here."

"I'm the librarian," Bub pointed out soberly. "This is where I'm scheduled to hang out from nine to five, Monday through Friday. Also, you're supposed to be quiet in a library. I'm sure that's not how things work in your family — I've spent extensive time with your sister, after all, so I know better — but in polite circles you don't yell your presence in a library."

"Oh, you're an absolute delight," Braden drawled. "I can't tell you how much I've missed hanging out with you. Oh, wait, that's totally not true."

"I see you got your wit from your father." Bub was blasé as he flicked his eyes to me. "And who did you get your wit from? Was it your mother or father? I knew them both. Your father was much funnier."

I was surprised by the conversation shift. "You knew my parents?"

"I did. I used to spend a lot of time on Belle Isle. I also knew you, but you probably don't remember me. You tried to throw a ball and get me to chase it when you were three or so. I believe you thought I was a dog. I'll try not to hold that against you."

Braden let loose a low chuckle. "Aisling kept calling you a dog-owl for days after she first met you. That's kind of funny."

"You weren't expected to fetch a ball." Bub's gaze was heavy on me before he turned to Cillian. "You mentioned the name Ryan Carroll. I'm familiar with that, too. I'm actually surprised you're not."

Cillian arched an eyebrow. "Am I supposed to know that name?"

"You should. He was a big reaper back in the day. We're talking fifty years ago or so, but I'm positive he was renowned in some circles. I believe he used to throw rather extravagant parties."

"Wait." I held up my hand to quiet him, flustered. "Are you saying the guy taking over Granger's head is a former reaper?"

Bub gave an approximation of a shrug. It was the best a gargoyle could do. "I have no idea who Granger is. I'm merely telling you who Ryan Carroll is."

"Well, son of a troll," I muttered. "This keeps getting creepier."

"And here I thought it couldn't get worse after you told me the ghost ordered you to get out of Granger's head," Braden said. "I guess I was wrong. There's a first time for everything."

Cillian made a face. "Yeah. A first time. Whatever." He flicked his eyes to me. "What do you think this means?"

Why was he asking me? "I don't know. I'm guessing it means we should do some research ... and talk to your father."

Braden heaved out a sigh. "I figured you were going to say that."

"Do you have a better idea?" I challenged.

He shook his head. "No, but Dad won't like this."

"When does he like any of the stuff we fall into?" Cillian queried. "I think there's a book here that keeps track of all the old reapers from the area. I'll try to find it. Other than that, I don't know where to start looking."

"Do that." I nodded. "I need answers. I'm not sure what to make of any of this."

Nine

Cillian couldn't find the book he was looking for and it frustrated him no end. He stomped around the library, ignoring the way Bub admonished him to be quiet, and pored through the reaper history books looking for Carroll's name.

He came up empty.

His distraction, however, gave me an opening to talk to Bub.

"So ... you really knew my parents?"

Up close, the gargoyle was weathered and scarred. I had no idea how long gargoyles lived, but Bub looked as if he'd already led an interesting and full life. He almost died protecting Aisling from her mother. I was aware of the story, and that she went above and beyond to make sure Bub was taken care of after the fact ... even if he didn't like eating cat food, which she assumed was his delicacy of choice for some reason.

Bub tilted his head to the side and regarded me with unblinking eyes. He reminded me of an owl. Of course, it was a giant featherless owl straight from a nightmare, but an owl all the same. "I knew them," he said finally. "Your mother was a big fan of the library."

"She was?" I wished I could remember our day-to-day life. That was a big, black hole in my memory that I was desperate to fill. "What kind of books?"

"She liked research books, but those were for daylight hours. She also liked mysteries ... and dirty romance novels she would read aloud to your father."

I smirked at the tidbit. "That's kind of funny. I ... ." I trailed off, something occurring to me. "Wait a second. I was under the impression you've only had this job for a short time. How can you possibly know what books she liked to check out?"

"I was stationed on Belle Isle back then," he replied without hesitation. "I was supposed to act as a guardian statue during the day and patrol the island at night. That was before gargoyles fell completely out of use."

I didn't know the history of gargoyles very well. I felt slightly guilty, as if I had perpetuated harm on Bub's kind. "I'm sorry."

"You needn't worry about it. You're not to blame."

"Still, though ... did you hang out with my parents a lot?"

He watched me with unguarded eyes that made me feel self-conscious and I shifted in my chair and pretended interest in Braden as he tried to calm an annoyed Cillian. "They should be done soon," I offered lamely.

"Especially because I don't believe the information the long-haired Grimlock seeks is here," Bub said. "Like all of them, he has a fiery temper. He needs to vent before he cedes defeat."

"You know them well?"

"Better than most," he clarified. "I know the youngest the best. She's ... obnoxious."

I chuckled. "She's tired right now. She just had a baby."

"I've heard. I remain close with the guardian gargoyle circuit. They perform rounds by Grimlock Manor and the townhouses to keep the family safe. Apparently the baby never sleeps, which means it's sick."

"She's not sick," I said hurriedly, my eyes flashing when Braden worriedly glanced toward us. Had he heard that? I hoped not. He had enough on his plate without worrying about a sick baby. "She's just disgruntled right now," I added, lowering my voice. "The baby is full of anxiety because Aisling is full of anxiety. It will pass."

"That sounds like she's sick."

"Well, she's not sick." I wanted to gag him ... or at least point him in another conversational direction. "She'll be fine. In fact, before it's all said and done she'll be the most spoiled little girl in the land. She has five uncles who dote on her, a grandfather who believes she'll eventually walk on water, and dedicated parents. She'll be fine."

"You sound awfully sure of yourself."

"Yeah, well, I am sure of myself. I've seen her. She's not sick ... just a ball of nerves."

"I guess I will have to defer to you then." He turned his full attention to me as Cillian viciously swore under his breath and moved to another aisle. "You were always a nurturing child. I remember when you used to sit on the lawn outside the aquarium and put bandages on your stuffed dog."

"Max." I mustered a genuine smile. "I still have him. Apparently he was a gift from Oliver, though I don't remember that. He's one of the few things I got to carry with me from my childhood."

"Oliver doted on you."

I stilled. "What?"

Bub nodded. "He spent a lot of time with you. I remember the night your family fell. No one could find you right away. He went into blood-stalker mode to seek you out. When he found you hidden in the rubble, he was so relieved that he cried.

"Vampire tears are made of blood," he continued. "You were borderline catatonic and yet you awoke at the sight of his tears and told him everything would be okay. I remember it as if it happened yesterday. You wiped away his tears and he handed you to Brett while he returned to the rubble to find your dog. You were desperate for the dog.

"When he finally found it, you spent hours bandaging it," he said. "There was confusion about what you remembered. Everyone was afraid to ask what you saw. Still, the reaper council arrived and questioned you until you were exhausted. Oliver insisted you be allowed to sleep. He said he would keep you safe, take care of you.

"They allowed it for the first night, but your grandfather arrived the next day to take you," he explained. "Oliver was broken-hearted when they took you. He wept again, tears of blood, and you cried as you were dragged away. It was a terrible time ... but you appear to have come out of it okay."

I was flabbergasted by the story. "I don't remember any of that."

"Probably because your mind isn't capable of absorbing the horror. You saw something that night, more than just the death of your parents. You saw something evil cross over from the gate. It marked you, which in turn made you forget."

That sounded too simple. "Well, let me ask you this." I leaned closer so my voice wouldn't carry. "If something came through the gate that night, where did it go? Why is there no mention of it anywhere else? Did it escape? Is it still here? What happened to it?"

Bub merely shrugged. "I have no idea. I never saw it. I don't know that anyone did. Two gargoyles were slaughtered that night, too. They're never brought up when the tale is told, though."

"I'm sorry for that. I still want to know what happened."

"I think everyone would like to know what happened. Those who were present to explain are gone. Well, except for one person." His gaze was pointed when it landed on me, causing me to balk.

"I can't remember. I've tried a million times. Don't you think I'd remember if I could?"

"I think you will remember when it's time," he replied. "You simply might not be ready yet."

His cryptic answer set my teeth on edge. I didn't get a chance to question him further, though, because Braden suddenly appeared and started gesturing toward the door. "Come on," he prodded. "Cillian wants to head back to Grimlock Manor. He insists we have better books there ... and he's totally melting down."

"I noticed." I slowly got to my feet and slid a look to Bub. "We'll talk again."

"Maybe."

"Definitely." I was firm as I stepped toward Braden. "You know things I need to know."

"I don't know nearly as much as you think I do. In fact, the only thing I know with absolute truth is that you were a big fan of *Where the Wild Things Are* and made your mother read it to you every night. I could hear her soothing voice through the window of your house when I made my rounds after dark."

My heart gave a painful roll. I'd always loved that book. "Well ... that's something."

"I guess that depends on how you look at things. You know where to find me. Until then, have faith in the Grimlocks. They're mouthy pains in the behind, but they're loyal and lucky. They always figure things out in the end and somehow manage to stay alive. I'm not sure you can do much better than that."

"WHAT WERE YOU AND Bub talking about while I was helping Cillian?" Braden asked as he opened the door of his car to help me out after arriving at Grimlock Manor. He'd been largely silent during the drive, which was fine by me because I had plenty to think about. Apparently quiet time was over.

"He ran security on Belle Isle when I was a kid," I replied. "He remembers me ... and my parents. I asked him about the night they died, but he didn't know what killed them."

"No one knows," Braden stressed as he put his hand to the small of my back and prodded me toward the door. "I asked my father, and he swears up and down it's a huge mystery. I checked for myself after the fact just to be sure. We don't know what happened to your parents."

"Someone knows."

"Who?"

"Me. I was there."

He grimaced. "I thought you couldn't remember."

"I can't, but the memories have to be in there somewhere. They're simply locked away. I need to find a way to access them."

"Or you could wait until you remember on your own. I don't know that memories are something you should try to force."

"Why do you care?"

He shrugged as he held open the door for me. "Perhaps I don't want to see anything bad happen to you. Did you ever consider that?"

"Not really."

"Well, you should. I will happily help you track information from that time in your life. I don't necessarily think the memory of a trau-matized seven-year-old is where you should be looking, though. There's a reason you blacked all that out."

"I'm an adult now. I can handle it."

"If you say so." Braden tilted his head when we reached the foyer. The normal sounds of family I expected when entering Grimlock Manor were missing and the house was unnaturally quiet.

"What's going on?" I asked, instantly alert. "Has something happened?"

He slid me an amused look. "I don't know. Let's check, shall we?" He held out his hand for me to take. It was an easy gesture, and my initial instinct was to link my fingers with his.

I fought the urge. We were treading on dangerous territory as it was. If I encouraged him, it would be so easy to fall ... and then, when it came time, how would I ever get up without help? I didn't want to think about that. It was too much to bear.

"Where are we going?" I asked, shoving my hands in my pockets.

He looked momentarily disappointed. He dropped his hand and inclined his head toward the west side of the house. "This way. We're earlier than expected. I'm guessing everyone is in my father's office."

I'd spent time in his father's office the first day I'd visited the house, when my energy level was waning thanks to a wraith attack and Braden brought me here to recuperate. I hadn't been in the office since.

Braden didn't bother to knock, instead throwing open the door and striding into the room. He was right about most of his family being there. Redmond sat in a chair across from his father's desk and held a conversation with the elder Grimlock. Aidan sat in another chair. And there, at the back of the room, Griffin slept on a couch in front of the fireplace, Lily asleep on his chest, tightly swaddled, looking comfort-able as she slumbered.

"Lily," Braden muttered automatically, stepping in that direction.

"Don't you dare," Cormack warned, shaking a finger. "She's been quiet for most of the day. The only times she's cried is when she needed her diaper changed or was hungry."

"In other words, she's been acting like a normal baby," Redmond offered, grinning. "Perhaps the demon possessing her has been exorcized."

"That's not funny." Cormack glared at his oldest son. "That baby has exhausted herself with the crying. She's slept most of the day. Can you imagine how much effort she expended in the past few days? She barely weighs ten pounds, for crying out loud."

"I'm sorry." Redmond held up his hands in surrender. "I wasn't casting aspersions on your favorite granddaughter. Chill out."

"Oh, don't play coy," Braden admonished, moving closer to Griffin and Lily so he could get a better look at his niece. When he returned to my side, he was grinning. "She's kind of cute when she's not all red-faced and screaming."

The strength of his smile momentarily turned me gooey. He was clearly as enamored with the baby as the rest of his family. He probably didn't want anyone to know that, but it was broadly advertised all over his face, which made him even more handsome than normal and was all sorts of distracting.

"She's definitely cute," Cormack agreed, tilting his head as he stared at the sleeping father and daughter. "Griffin took her all afternoon. It wasn't really a hardship, because she was much better than she has been."

"Does that mean Aisling got some sleep?" I asked hopefully.

Cormack nodded. "She slept all day, which she desperately needed. I thought she would be perkier afterward, but she's had attitude."

That didn't surprise me. "Doesn't she always have attitude?" I asked.

Cormack snickered. "She's ... feisty."

"She's spoiled rotten," Braden corrected, gesturing toward a small couch at the side of the room. "Take a load off," he instructed. "We actually have some news to share with you, Dad."

"Does this have something to do with the cryptic text I received from Cillian?" Cormack asked. "He was complaining about the library at the main office falling woefully short for the research he has to conduct."

"It has something to do with it," Braden hedged, quickly glancing at me. "Do you want to tell the story? You're the star of it."

I felt put on the spot, but I nodded. It would be easier for me to describe what happened. In quick order, I led Cormack through my day. It had been only a few hours since I saw him, but it felt much longer. When I got to the part where I found the being inside Granger's head, Cormack looked as if he had questions. He stifled them until I was finished.

"You've had quite the day." He rubbed his chin. "Not only did you miraculously quiet my granddaughter so she could finally get the sleep she so desperately needs, you also found a ghost living inside a young boy's head. I don't know how many people can say that."

"I've never come across anything like it," I admitted. "It's ... weird. I've seen ghosts before. They're much more prevalent in New Orleans."

"The reaper circuit there is lazy," Cormack muttered, his expression darkening. "They have a much more lackadaisical attitude than we do."

"Yes, well ... chicory and beignets will do that to you." When no one laughed at my lame joke, I sobered. "What I'm trying to say is that I'm not sure it was a ghost. It had qualities of a ghost, if that makes sense, but it didn't look or act like a ghost. It was something else."

"What?"

"I have no idea."

"Hmm." Cormack rubbed his chin and watched as Griffin shifted slightly, keeping a firm hold on Lily as he went back to sleep. It was a heartwarming sight, and I didn't miss the way Cormack's expression softened as he watched them. The man liked to talk big. Aisling told me he used to threaten Griffin when they first started dating. He was obviously more bark, though, because he was genuinely fond of his son-in-law ... and he loved his granddaughter to distraction.

"You said you heard a name," Aidan prodded, his expression thoughtful. "What was the name again?"

"Ryan Carroll," I answered automatically.

"That sounds familiar, although I can't remember where I've heard it."

"I know where," Cormack said. "He used to be a reaper a long time ago. He's from before my time. He was active during your grandfather's era."

"Really?" Aidan arched an eyebrow. "Is he famous or something?"

"Well, I guess that's a matter of debate." Cormack rolled his neck. "I suppose you want to hear the story."

That was an understatement. "I think it would be best."

"Then we need to get the others in here. I want to tell it only once."

Ten

Cillian and Aisling joined the action in the office within ten minutes, Aisling immediately shuffling toward the back of the room to study her sleeping husband and baby with unreadable eyes.

Perhaps sensing that something unfortunate was about to happen, Cillian slid an arm around her shoulders and directed her toward one of the couches near Cormack's desk.

"Let sleeping babies be," he whispered to her, poking her side as he led her to the couch. "Mom always said that about you and Aidan when you were little. We would stand over your cribs and try to get you to wake up and she would always yell at us."

"Oh, yeah?" Aisling arched an eyebrow as she settled. She had more color in her cheeks than the previous day, but that wasn't saying much. "I don't remember her saying that."

"That's because you were the baby we all wanted to sleep."

"You and Aidan were definitely loud," Redmond agreed, grinning. "I was used to babies at that point — even though I tried to convince Dad I would be better off as an only child — but you guys were especially loud."

"And smelly," Braden added, grinning when his sister scowled at him. "You two could fill more diapers than any ten babies twice your size."

"I'm pretty sure he's insulting us, Ais," Aidan noted. "Get him."

She merely shook her head and rubbed her forehead. "Maybe when I'm feeling more like myself."

Concern washed over me as I regarded her. "I thought you got some sleep."

"I did ... and thank you for making that happen." She was earnest. "I don't know what I would've done if the crying hadn't stopped."

"You would've been fine," Cormack reassured her. "You already look better."

"You do," Braden agreed. "Although ... you're ridiculously thin. I can't remember you ever being that thin."

"I remember," Aidan said darkly. "She was trying to get into a specific dress for homecoming so she would look better than Angelina. Dad had a fit and made her eat three burgers in one sitting because he said no daughter of his was ever going to diet. By the time the dance rolled around, Angelina had the dress Aisling wanted and had starved herself for weeks to get into it. She made a big deal of lording it over Aisling."

I'd met Angelina Davenport, the woman Aisling referred to as her "arch nemesis," during a shopping excursion several weeks ago. I didn't know the woman well, but it was easy to see she was unpleasant, and I could imagine her doing that and much worse during her teenage years.

"I would rather wear a bigger dress than worry about looking like Angelina," I offered helpfully.

Aisling's smile was wan. "Too bad I haven't run into her the last few days, huh? She would foam at the mouth over the fact that I can fit into jeans I wore when I was fourteen."

Cormack frowned as he studied his youngest child. "Yes, well, we're having an ice cream bar for dinner tonight ... along with grilled scallops, your favorite garlic mashed potatoes, and all the other fattening fixings you so enjoy. I expect you to eat three helpings."

"I'll do my best," she said dryly.

Cormack's eyes shifted to me. "That goes for you, too. You look a little pale for my liking. You had much more color this morning when you were ordering me around the kitchen."

For the first time since I'd entered the house, Aisling cracked a smile. "I would've paid money to see that. He reenacted it a bit when he brought back the jar of magic ointment — I can never thank you enough for that, by the way. We were all on pins and needles to see if it would work."

"Obviously it did." I cast a look toward Griffin. "She seems comfortable now."

"She's comfortable with her daddy." Aisling's smile slipped. "She still cries when I'm holding her."

"Oh, that's not true," Cormack protested, his eyes flashing with impatience. "She settled down when you were holding her. We barely got the salve on her chest like Izzy told us to do before Griffin took her so you could have a rest. She's quiet for everybody now ... except when she fills a diaper."

"Which happens a lot," Aidan complained.

"A heck of a lot," Redmond agreed, earning a stern look from his father. "What? The kid is a poop factory. Don't tell me you haven't noticed. Whenever anything goes in one end, something comes out the other. It's as if she has only so much room inside her and she's reached her limit or something."

"That is a delightful visual," Cormack drawled, shaking his head. "That won't give me nightmares or anything."

I grinned as I shook my head, sparing a glance for Griffin and the still-slumbering Lily. "I'll make more of the salve now that I know it works," I offered Aisling. "That way you won't run out."

She looked so grateful I momentarily worried she would burst into tears. Then I reminded myself that was allowed. It had been only two weeks since she gave birth. Her hormones were still out of whack, which was probably why she was so sensitive regarding the baby. Well ... that and a few other things that I knew better than to bring up in front of a crowd.

"Thank you," Cormack offered with heartfelt emotion. "We really appreciate it."

"We do," Redmond agreed. "We're actually going to be able to get some sleep tonight. At least I hope that's true."

"We need to talk about serious things for a few minutes," Cillian prodded, sober. "The big one is Ryan Carroll. You said you knew him and only wanted to tell the story once, so spill."

Cormack shook his head. "I didn't really *know* him. I mean ... I knew him as one of my father's co-workers. I didn't know him beyond that."

"I kind of forgot that Grandpa was a reaper," Aisling noted, rubbing her forehead. Her color was back but she was obviously still struggling. "He retired before we all came along."

"He was working in the main office when you were born. He was there a few years before retiring."

"I kind of remember that," Redmond noted. "I think you took me to visit him there once or twice. I think Cillian and Braden went, too."

"Probably," Cormack confirmed. "Your mother often wanted me to get you three older boys out of the house when Aisling and Aidan were infants. That was a lot of noise to absorb and she sometimes needed a break."

"See." Cillian poked Aisling's side. "It's normal for mothers to need breaks."

The look she shot him was withering. "Mom had five kids below the age of six. I have one baby who should be sleeping twenty hours a day. It's different."

"And you're doing the best you can, Aisling, so I don't want to hear another self-deprecating word come from your mouth," Cormack warned. "We're here for you. Everything will be fine. Don't I always take care of you?"

She nodded, sheepish.

"Then trust me to continue taking care of you," he ordered. "Right now, we need to talk about Ryan Carroll. He didn't have the best reputation, as I recall. Cillian, you should probably pull up his personnel record to confirm that."

"I've tried," Cillian replied. "The basics are in there. His date of birth, when he was hired, when he was no longer active. You know the drill. There aren't many specifics. Also, he has several sealed files."

Cormack's eyebrows rose up his forehead. "Sealed?"

Redmond shifted on his chair as Cillian nodded. "What does that mean?" he asked. "I've never heard of reapers having sealed files."

"It means some sort of disciplinary action," Cormack answered, his expression thoughtful. "You're allowed only so many strikes before you're kicked out of the order."

"How many strikes do I have?" Aisling asked. "It has to be a lot. I've gotten us in trouble a good five times in the past two years alone."

Cormack winked at her. "Believe it or not, you only have two black marks in your file. You also have six gold stars for going above and beyond to solve certain issues. I know, because I was worried and checked your file. You're a reaper in high standing. In fact, you're in higher standing than three of your brothers."

The room fell into silence ... and then all four Grimlock brothers started talking at once.

"Excuse me? I better be the one higher than her," Redmond complained.

"I'm definitely higher than her," Braden argued. "I never get in trouble and always follow the rules."

Cillian snorted derisively. "Please. I do all the heavy research we need ... and I always come through no matter how many hours I've worked. I'm definitely higher than her."

"It has to be me," Aidan argued. "I've saved her from trouble at least three times that I can recall off the top of my head. That has to count for something."

For her part, Aisling looked smug. "I'm coming for whatever brother is ahead of me," she warned, dramatically jabbing a finger in the direction of her siblings one at a time. "I will be victorious."

Instead of admonishing his daughter, Cormack smiled. He clearly enjoyed seeing the spark return to her eyes. So did I. She looked so much better I almost forgot what she was going through.

Almost.

Then her expression fell when Griffin shifted and opened an eye. He kept Lily pressed against his chest, the baby's head over his heartbeat, and glanced around the room as he got his bearings. "Was I snoring?" he asked finally.

Aisling shook her head and got to her feet. Her footsteps were heavy as she trudged to the sofa and knelt next to her husband. She looked genuinely happy to see him, but it was obvious the baby made her wary ... which hurt to witness.

"You were fine." She pressed a quick kiss to his cheek, causing him to smile. Her fingers were shaky as she briefly reached out to touch the baby's head, which was covered with a mat of dark hair. "She's been quiet all afternoon."

"She has," Griffin agreed, grabbing Aisling's fingers when she pulled them away from Lily and pressing a kiss to the tips. "It's okay. She's settling. Izzy gave us a miracle and things are going to be better now." He winked at me, causing me to smile in return even as I watched Aisling stare at the baby. "You know what you need? You need some dinner."

"She definitely does," Cormack agreed. "We'll move things into the dining room. The night nurse should be here shortly. She'll take care of Lily while everyone eats. Then we'll discuss the Ryan Carroll situation further."

Griffin blinked several times in rapid succession. "Who is Ryan Carroll?"

That was the question of the evening. It didn't sound like we had an answer.

"I ONLY KNOW WHAT I already told you," Cormack stressed an hour later, waiting until everyone was settled around the table and the night nurse took charge of Lily. The baby wasn't squawking and complaining — at least as far as I could tell – which I took as a sign that things were turning around on that front.

"Carroll worked with my father," he continued. "He had a poor reputation, was known for carousing and cheating on his wife. He also was known as something of a brawler. He enjoyed going out to the bar every night, and it was commonplace for him to get into a physical confrontation during those outings."

"I'm surprised he was allowed to remain with the company," I noted as I cut into my prime rib. It was like butter and made my mouth water just looking at it. Cormack clearly knew how to plan a dinner, and his children obviously agreed, because they were shoveling food into their mouths rather than talking. "I thought you had to stay out of trouble to remain with the outfit."

"That's a rule now," Cormack conceded. "Back then, it wasn't enforced. You have to remember, this was a good sixty years ago. During that time, there was a general 'boys will be boys' attitude around the office."

"What about the women?" Aisling asked, slathering a dinner roll with butter. "How did they feel about that?"

Cormack cleared his throat, discomfort rolling off him in waves. "Well ... ."

"There were no women in the general reaper ranks back then, Ais," Cillian offered, smiling indulgently at his girlfriend Maya as she enthusiastically dug into her food. She'd arrived following a shift at the hospital not long before dinner started and she hadn't said much, seemingly happy just to listen to the conversation as it swirled around her.

"What do you mean?" Aisling was instantly suspicious. "There had to be women. I mean ... it couldn't have been all men."

"There were women performing clerical work," Cormack explained. "The filing ... answering calls ... busywork. Women didn't start working in the field until almost forty years ago. Even then there were very few of them. It's only been in the past twenty years that female reapers have started equaling their male counterparts."

Aisling furrowed her brow. "That's a bunch of sexist crap."

"Totally," Griffin agreed, tapping the side of her plate. "Eat your dinner. I want to see you clean two plates." He was serious and didn't as much as cringe when she glared at him. "Baby, you're too thin. I need you to eat."

"I said she had to clean three plates," Cormack interjected. "I stand by that. She's so skinny she looks as if a stiff breeze could blow her over."

"Which is the opposite of how she's supposed to look," Aidan noted. "Jerry did a lot of research on losing baby weight when Aisling was pregnant — he was worried she would never reclaim her girlish figure and be forced to wear muumuus the rest of her life — and he says it should take months to lose all the weight. Aisling has lost it in two weeks ... and she's even thinner now than when she got pregnant."

"Thank you so much for paying so much attention to my body, Aidan," she drawled. "That's not weird at all."

"You're too thin," Cormack stressed. "We're going to fatten you up whether you like it or not."

"We are," Griffin agreed. "Starting right now. Eat."

Aisling narrowed her eyes to dangerous lavender slits. "And what if I don't want to eat?"

"Then I'll hold you on my lap and let your father feed you. You'll be mad and it will be undignified, but I'm not allowing you to lose another ounce."

"Well ... I'm so glad I'm living with a bunch of Neanderthals," she muttered as she stabbed a piece of prime rib and shoved it in her mouth. She vigorously chewed, and then spoke without swallowing. "Happy?"

Griffin grinned at her. "I'm ecstatic."

"So am I," Cormack noted. "In fact, I'm so ecstatic, I'm arranging for you to have a spa day with Jerry tomorrow. I'm paying for the works, so you can get a massage ... and a pedicure ... and a haircut ...and whatever your heart desires. I've already talked to the owner. I was going to surprise you at breakfast tomorrow, but I think now is as good a time as any."

Aisling was taken aback. "But ... I can't leave."

"Why not?"

"I have a baby." She was matter-of-fact. "Lily needs me here. New mothers don't just take off to the spa and abandon their babies for a day."

"Who says?" Cormack refused to back down. "Lily needs her mother to be at the top of her game. You're still exhausted. You need a few hours away to regroup."

"I have to watch the baby," Aisling persisted. "That's my job."

"I'll watch her," Griffin interjected quickly. "I'm on paternity leave for a reason, remember? I'll take her all day. A spa outing is a great idea. You and Jerry can be buffed, powdered and pampered. You need to get your mind off things for a little bit."

Aisling didn't look convinced. "I don't know."

Braden ultimately sold her on the idea. "I think you should take Izzy with you," he suggested. "She made the salve. She also had a trying day seeing the ghost in the kid's head. She's as fried as you are."

I shot him a dirty look. "Thanks for that."

He ignored me. "You'd really be doing her a favor. She won't agree to go unless you make her. She needs a day off, too."

Aisling pursed her lips and turned her thoughtful eyes to me. "You do look kind of rundown."

I was fairly certain that wasn't a compliment. "Yes, well ... ."

"Okay, we'll do it." Aisling bobbed her head decisively. "We'll spend the day at the spa. I'll text Griffin every so often to make sure everything is okay. Maybe you're right; I might feel better if I get a massage."

"More than that, you've been locked away in the townhouse and here since you gave birth," Cormack noted. "It will be good for you to get out. In fact, I'll arrange for that Lebanese place you love so much to deliver lunch there for you.

"It will be a great way for you and Izzy to talk about things," he continued, his gaze pointed when it landed on me. "She's very wise, and if you have anything you're worrying about, anything at all, she's the one to talk to."

I understood what he was saying. He wasn't exactly subtle. I told him Aisling was anxious about being a mother and he wanted me to fix it so she was no longer anxious, as if I could magically somehow make that happen. Now that I'd fixed one thing — er, well, two things if you included her swollen pregnancy feet — he expected me to fix everything.

That was a real kick in the pants.

"This is going to be great," Aisling announced, brightening. "I bet I'll feel loads better after a day at the spa."

Cormack smiled at her. "I bet you will, too." The look he cast me was pleading. "You're going, right?"

I felt put on the spot but didn't see where I had a choice. "I'm going," I confirmed. "I can't wait. I've never had a spa day."

"You're in for a treat." Aisling was almost bubbly as she attacked her mashed potatoes. "We'll get hot stone massages. Those are relaxing ... and pedicures ... oh, and I haven't had my hair trimmed in months. It's going to be good."

I could only hope she was right.

Eleven

Braden was waiting for me when I left the restroom after dinner. I was absolutely stuffed — two servings of prime rib and a trip to the ice cream bar managed to make me consider buying larger jeans — and all I could think about was taking a walk to burn off some of the excess calories.

"Thanks for doing this," Braden announced, taking me by surprise when he swooped in. "You have no idea how important it is to my father to get Aisling acting like her old self."

Obviously Cormack wasn't the only one eager for Aisling to return to normal. "It's not a big deal." I rubbed the back of my neck and forced a smile. "I've never been to a spa, but I've seen plenty of television shows depicting the ritual. I'm sure I'll be fine."

"It's fun. They'll tell you what to do, show you how to lay and even pick out an oil you like."

I knit my eyebrows. "I ... you've been to the spa?"

"It's a family activity," he said defensively. "Aisling and Jerry forced it on us."

I wanted to laugh ... except it sounded like an interesting bonding exercise. "Well, I'm looking forward to it. Is your father going to send a car for me in the morning? I still don't have my own vehicle. I should probably get on that."

"Um ... I can pick you up."

He didn't sound as if that was something he wanted to undertake. "Or I can get an Uber," I offered. "Just get me the address of the spa and a time and I promise to meet Aisling and Jerry there. Where is Jerry? I haven't spent any time with him. I only met him the night the baby was born, and after that, well, things changed."

Braden's expression was sheepish. "They didn't change," he stressed. "It was work. My father apologized for having to send someone, but these things sometimes happen. Obviously Aisling couldn't go. Cillian and Aidan had other things going on, too. It came down to Redmond and me, and I lost the coin toss. I didn't want to leave."

I bit back a sigh. He was trying. Really hard. He was trying so hard, in fact, he was wearing me down. At one point I was adamant our interaction would lead nowhere and was a waste of time. Now I wasn't so sure.

I was still wary. He had the potential to steal my heart, and I wasn't certain that was the smart move to make.

"I'm not blaming you. In fact, maybe it was meant to be. I mean ... perhaps that was the universe's way of telling us we should just be friends."

Braden immediately started shaking his head. "No. I don't believe that."

"No?" I cocked a challenging eyebrow. "You don't believe in signs?"

"Oh, I believe in signs. I just think you're reading this one incorrectly. It wasn't a sign that I got sent to Florida for ten days to attend a workshop. It's a sign that all I could do was think about you until I got back."

Ugh. That was a disgustingly sweet thing to say ... and it melted my resolve faster than gelato at a New Orleans stand in the middle of summer. "Listen ... ."

"No, you listen." He waved a hand to cut me off. "I'm attracted to you. I've already told you that, more than once. I think you're attracted to me." He waited for me to respond.

I could've lied, said there was no spark, but my heart wouldn't have been in it. "I like you," I admitted. "I simply don't know that we can make this work. I didn't come here for this," I reminded him. "I have priorities, and a relationship is not one of them."

"I know why you came here. You want to know the truth about your parents, what killed them, what came through that gate. I get it. I can help you with that ... just as soon as we figure out what's haunting the aquarium and living in that little boy's head."

I let loose an exasperated sigh. It was almost impossible to argue with him. "I'll think about it. That's the best I can do."

"I'm fine with that." He held up his hands in surrender. "I have no interest in pushing you. I've seen firsthand how that backfires on people. Griffin tried to push Aisling a few times and it turned her into a sweating and spitting mess."

I narrowed my eyes. "I think you have a warped view of your sister. She's not nearly as bad as you make her out to be."

"Maybe. It's still good you're going to the spa with her. You're an outsider, but I look for that to change." He winked in such a manner that it caused my cheeks to flush. "You can read my sister better than we can in some respects because you don't see what you expect to see when you look at her.

"You were the one who noticed how rundown she was while the rest of us assumed she was dealing with normal stress," he continued. "You made things better before they could get really bad. We're thankful for that."

"You don't have to pursue me because you're thankful."

"Oh, that's not why I'm pursuing you." His eyes twinkled as he moved closer, chewing up the space between us until there was almost nothing left. "I'm pursuing you for purely personal reasons. I can't wait until you finally fold and admit you want to kiss me."

I scowled at him. "Listen ... ."

"No, you listen." He pressed his finger to my lips to quiet me. "I feel something when you look at me." He was deadly serious. "I don't know what that something is, but I'm guessing it's the same thing Griffin felt when my sister first started looking at him. It kind of makes me want to punch him because she's my sister, but that ship has long since sailed."

I blew out a sigh. "You are one of the most infuriating people I know. Somehow, you manage to be egotistical and charming at the same time. It's an interesting feat."

"Yeah, well, I had a good teacher." His grin was so wide it almost swallowed his entire face. Then he sobered. "Thank you for doing this. I'm serious. My sister needs to get out of the house for a few hours, breathe some fresh air and get some perspective. I think you can help her with that."

"I have no problem helping her. I like her. I find her funny. Even though ... she's not exactly putting on a comedy show these days."

"Which is why I'm glad you're going with her. She needs it."

"She does."

"I think you need it, too."

"I'm fine." I bumped against him as I folded my arms over my chest. "There's nothing wrong with me. I'm good at taking care of myself."

"I have no doubt about that. I'm still going to worry. You're seeing ghosts. That's worrisome."

He had a point, which was ridiculously annoying. "I'm fine," I repeated. "I'll make sure your sister has a good time tomorrow and everything will work out."

"Oh, I have no doubt about that."

"Great." We lapsed into uncomfortable silence for a moment, his proximity causing my skin to heat to the point I worried I might combust. I had to say something to ease the silence. Ultimately, I went for the mundane. "So ... I'm going to Uber to the spa tomorrow, I guess."

"Actually, I thought you might spend the night here."

"You did not," I sputtered, horrified. "I am not spending the night with you."

He chuckled and shook his head. "I didn't say with me. There are more rooms in this house than we can ever use. I thought you might sleep in one of those."

"Oh." I was mortified that I'd jumped to the wrong conclusion. "I don't know," I said after a beat. "I don't have any of my stuff ... or pajamas."

"My sister keeps all those things here. She'll share."

"Have you asked? She doesn't strike me as a sharer."

"You would be surprised. She's extremely grateful, too."

I blew out a sigh, if only to clear the hot air building between us. "Fine. I'll spend the night ... in a guest room."

His eyes gleamed with wicked delight. "That's great. Maybe we'll run into each other when sneaking around for a midnight snack."

"I sincerely doubt that."

"Never say never."

EVERYONE STAYED the night. That included Aidan and Jerry, the latter stumbling in late. He was exhausted because he was working on an important wedding, though he seemed excited to see me. That lasted only until he disappeared into the kitchen to eat leftovers and tell Aidan about his day.

Maya and Cillian retired to his old room, which Braden explained was basically a shrine because Cormack refused to change any of his children's bedrooms should they need to return home. Braden and Redmond still lived with their father, which would've been a red flag in the dating department if Grimlock Manor wasn't the size of a castle. Cormack was in no hurry to push his brood from the nest because he enjoyed having them close ... and the boys didn't want to leave because the maids and cooks handled their every need.

I understood the arrangement, but it still felt weird to sleep in Aisling's pajamas, on a king-sized bed, under what was essentially the biggest roof I'd ever seen. Despite all that, I fell asleep right away. It simply didn't last. I woke shortly before midnight and found myself restless. With nothing better to do, I decided to find my way downstairs for a bottle of water.

That's when I heard voices in the hallway.

"You're doing it wrong," Redmond barked, causing me to slow my pace. I was under the impression his room was in a different wing of the house. This was Aisling's wing ... and the open door down the hallway belonged to her room.

"I'm not doing it wrong," she fired back. "You're doing it wrong. I don't understand how you could've forgotten. You're supposed to give it a little tug before reeling."

Confused, I increased my pace until I was standing outside the room. When I peered inside, I found several faces awash with the glow of electric blue on Aisling's huge sleigh bed, all of them focused on the television on her nightstand.

"Good evening," Braden offered, grinning when he saw me. "Do you want to join us?" He wore a simple T-shirt and boxer shorts, and was clearly ready for bed. That only served to confuse me more because I couldn't understand why he was in his sister's bedroom.

"I ... um ... ."

"Don't worry," Griffin offered. He rested with his back against a mountain of pillows. He was also ready for bed, though he didn't seem bothered by the number of bodies in his bedroom. "This is normal in the Grimlock house. In fact, this is how I was introduced to the normal twilight shenanigans the first night I spent under this roof."

I was still confused. "I don't understand." I flicked my eyes to the television, to where a video game was playing. That's when I realized Redmond had a controller in his hand and he was desperately trying to reel in a graphically-generated fish. "You're playing a fishing game?"

Aisling bobbed her head and grinned. "We always do this when we're all under the same roof."

"Not always," Braden countered. "We haven't done it in a long time. In fact, I think that first time with Griffin was one of the last times we played."

"Untrue," Griffin countered, his hands automatically going to Aisling's shoulders and pulling her back against him. If he was bothered by the crowd interrupting his sleep cycle he didn't show it. In fact, he seemed perfectly at ease allowing the game to continue uninterrupted. "We played the day before the wedding."

Braden furrowed his brow. "I forgot about that," he admitted after a beat. "We were all restless and looking for a distraction. Dad said sock hockey was out of the question because he didn't want anything broken before the reception."

"He also banned Frisbee golf from the yard because we can't play without breaking windows," Redmond added. "That's why we settled on Shark Attack."

I stilled, confused. "I thought you were playing a fishing game."

"We are," Braden replied. "The thing is ... if you don't win the fishing round you get tossed in the ocean to survive the sharks."

His explanation did little to ease my befuddlement. To buy myself time, I glanced at the floor and realized there were several stuffed sharks — all of them looked old and well-loved — scattered around the floor. "Where did these come from?" I bent over to pick one up and immediately received a memory flash of a shrieking child with black hair and purple eyes. It was Aisling, and she was laughing like a maniac as Cormack threatened to toss her in the "water" that was her carpet. A young boy who looked a lot like Jerry jumped on her bed and clapped during the action.

"My dad bought them for me when I was a kid," Aisling explained, content as she leaned against Griffin. "That's when we invented this game."

"That's why the rules don't make sense," Redmond offered. "In fact ... got him!" His yell was triumphant as he reeled in a huge fish I couldn't identify. "Ha. Beat that!" He handed the controller to Braden, who merely rolled his eyes.

"I will definitely beat that," Braden said, casting me a sidelong look. "Come on. Join us. You can play, too."

That seemed like a bad idea. "Oh, well, the bed is full."

"It's about to get fuller," Aidan announced, causing me to jolt as he moved past my back, Jerry in tow. "I can't believe you didn't send out a group text."

"And I can't believe you started without me, Bug." Jerry's gaze was incriminating as it fell on Aisling. He was marrying into the family — and soon, if the bridal magazines that littered the tables were any indication — but he was Aisling's best friend first. He always deferred to her, which probably wasn't easy on Aidan but was somehow considered normal in this very loud family.

"I didn't want to bother you," Aisling supplied. "I wasn't sure you wanted to play given the mood you were in when you arrived."

"Yes, but that's the real world," Jerry noted, crawling onto the bed next to Aisling and crowding Griffin as he snuggled with his best friend. Griffin didn't offer a single word of objection, which made me realize that he was open to this game, and which meant Aisling would have a better chance of returning to normal if she played. "This is the shark world. You can't play in this world without me. It's simply not allowed."

"Good point." Aisling grinned at him.

"Will you look at this?" Cillian complained, appearing in the doorway. "I knew the second I realized Redmond wasn't in his room that you guys were playing without me. I can't believe you would cut me out like this."

"Hey, Maya had a double shift," Redmond countered. "We didn't want to wake her."

"She's dead to the world," Cillian admitted. "I just passed the baby nursery, too, and Lily is down for the count. The nurse is watching her, so you don't need to worry about that, Ais."

Aisling smiled in thanks and then held up a baby monitor, which she had apparently hidden near the pillows. "I know. I'm monitoring."

"We're not going to play long," Braden warned. "Aisling needs a good night's sleep."

"That's because we have a spa day tomorrow," Jerry said, winking at me. "We're going to use our time wisely and learn everything there is to know about Izzy. I can't wait."

I felt out of place in the room, and yet I also felt love zinging from every corner. Whatever the game, the family members acknowledged it was ridiculous ... and perhaps the rules didn't need to make sense. That didn't mean they weren't willing to play simply because they knew it would make their sister laugh.

"Okay. Teach me how to play," I said, resigned. "I'm not sure I'm familiar with the rules."

"Come over here and I'll teach you." Braden suggestively patted the open spot nearest him on the bed and grinned. "It won't take you long to catch up."

"I figured." I glanced over my shoulder and found Cormack standing in the doorway, smiling. He looked thrilled at the game ... even though it was bound to get loud. "Do you want to play?" I asked.

He shook his head. "I'm just going to watch. I've been watching this particular game for decades. It's like a favorite television show coming back in reruns."

He looked happy, so I merely smiled and waved. "Okay. I'm climbing aboard so I can learn the rules."

"You certainly are." Cormack winked at me as he leaned against the door jamb. "Just remember, my children play to win. They'll do whatever it takes to get what they want."

There was a double meaning to his words that wasn't lost on me. "I play to win, too."

"I know. That's why this adventure is going to be entertaining."

I had no doubt he was right.

Twelve

Apparently spa visits were big deals in the Grimlock house, because my outfit had to be checked over by Jerry — and Braden, for some reason — before I left Grimlock Manor the next morning.

"You look adorable," Jerry announced in the foyer, beaming.

I didn't feel adorable. The yoga pants he insisted on dressing me in had wide legs and showed off my calves. They were pastel ... and I didn't wear many pastels. Apparently they were a favorite of Aisling's, because she wore a similar pair, although hers were lavender, as she stood next to Griffin and waved at Lily.

"Are you going to be good?" she asked hopefully, contorting her face in an attempt to get the baby to smile.

"I told you she's too young to do that," Braden offered helpfully. "I read about it on the internet. She's weeks away from doing that."

"You don't know," Aisling challenged. "She could be gifted or something."

"Of course she's gifted," Cormack said, gliding into the room. He had a black credit card in his hand, which he deftly slid away from Jerry and handed to me. "You have been cleared for everything at the spa. Don't let Jerry have the credit card because he likes to online shop during facials."

I accepted the card with a furrowed brow. "Um ... okay."

"I think you're casting aspersions," Jerry sniffed, folding his arms over his chest. "Just because I'm gay doesn't mean I'm addicted to shopping."

"I know. You're addicted to shopping because you're you." Cormack rested his hand on Aisling's shoulder. "Lily is definitely gifted. She won't smile just yet, though, so you don't have to worry about leaving the house and missing it."

Aisling, clearly uncertain, shifted from one foot to the other. "Maybe I shouldn't leave. She's only two weeks old."

"She'll be fine," Griffin insisted, shifting the baby to his other arm. "I'm here. Your father is here. Your brothers are here, though I doubt they'll be any help."

"I'm tons of help," Braden shot back. "I'm going to be her favorite uncle."

Jerry's expression was withering. "Puh-leez. I'm going to be her favorite uncle. There's not even competition for that spot."

"You're right," Cillian agreed, striding into the room and handing his father a sheet of paper. "She's going to love me best. I'm the hand-somest ... and I'm going to be able to help her with her homework."

Redmond snorted. He had an apple in his hand and some added swagger in his step. "Yeah, because that's important to a toddler. We all know I'm going to be her favorite. I'll take her to the park and get her all sugared up on ice cream and then use her to snag women. I have many festive outings planned ... especially now that she's stopped crying."

"You're all out of luck," Cormack said, plucking his granddaughter from her father's arms and beaming at her as he pressed her to his chest. "I'll be her favorite because I'm going to spoil her rotten."

"Yes, because that worked out so well with her mother," Braden said dryly.

"I think it worked out well," Cormack countered, leaning closer so Aisling could kiss the baby's cheek. "We've got her. I swear we will have cameras ready to snap photos and video if she does anything interesting. It's the perfect time for you to take a day away."

"I know that in my head." Aisling was rueful. "It's just ... I don't think she likes me. I feel as if I should be hanging around and trying to make her like me."

Griffin frowned. "Of course she likes you. Why would you say that?"

"She cries whenever I hold her."

"Hey, she cried whenever any of us held her until Izzy made the magic salve," Braden pointed out. "She's fine now. You were holding her at breakfast and she didn't let out a peep. I bet it will be the same when you get back this afternoon. Try not to worry about things like that."

"That's easy for you to say," Aisling groused, slipping into a hoodie. "You don't have a kid who hates you."

Braden let loose a sigh. "No, but I have a sister who gives me heartburn. Besides, Lily doesn't hate you. She's simply disgruntled." He chucked his niece under the chin and made a face when he got drool on his finger. "That's how we know she's a true Grimlock. She's going to be a pain to deal with even on her good days."

"That's definitely the truth." Griffin moved in and gave Aisling a long hug. "Call if you need to check in. Otherwise, try to enjoy yourself."

Aisling still looked doubtful as she moved toward the door. "Okay. We're going."

Braden offered me a wave and a wink. "I really like how you look in those yoga pants," he called out. "I think you should consider adding more color to your wardrobe. I've only ever seen you in black."

"I'm totally on that," Jerry said, snagging the credit card from my hand and grinning at Cormack. "We'll see you in a few hours. By then, we'll be so refreshed you'll hardly recognize us."

"That will be a nice change of pace," Cormack said, shaking his head.

I'D NEVER BEEN TO a spa, so I was perfectly happy letting

Aisling and Jerry lead the way. I thought Aisling would be morose once we were away from the baby, but she was fine ... and chatty.

"So, what's going on with you and my brother?" she asked as soon as we were in the facial chairs located in the heart of the day spa.

"I don't know what you mean," I hedged, avoiding her probing gaze as a technician approached with a bowl full of goo. "What is that?"

"It's a cleansing mask," she replied in a voice straight out of a phone sex commercial. "It will clean out all the impurities in your skin and leave you looking ten years younger."

"So ... basically you're saying this will make me look like a child?" I wasn't sure that was something to strive for.

"You'll like it," Aisling supplied. "I didn't use to be big on spa days either, so I get that you're nervous. Jerry made me see the light, though, and now I live for them. Your face will be so smooth by the time you leave here you'll swear your cheeks are made of satin. No joke."

"You should get it put on your butt, too," Jerry suggested, causing my mouth to drop open. "Aisling managed to get away with murder for an entire month when she did that and allowed Griffin to get a good feel."

"That was an overshare," I chided.

Jerry merely shrugged. "That's how we roll."

"It really is," Avery agreed, sighing as her technician started applying a lavender mixture to her face. "He's not just talking about him and me either. He's talking about my entire family. We're all up in each other's business."

"Geez. I never would've noticed." I eyed my technician suspiciously as she instructed me to lie back in the chair and relax. "I thought you guys were docile and demure. My bad."

Aisling chuckled. "I love how sarcastic you are. You fit right in with us."

"Just for the record, every family has cliques. We're the cool clique." Jerry gestured between Aisling and himself. "You should join our group if you want to have the most fun."

"I didn't realize that was limited by who you hung around with," I replied. "I'll give it some thought."

"You should definitely do that."

I could feel Aisling's eyes on me but opted not to meet her gaze. "I don't want to tell you your business, but the baby doesn't hate you."

"Oh, no? Did she tell you that?" Aisling was dubious. "I can tell she hates me. She's always eager for Griffin or my father to hold her. Heck, she even likes it when Braden holds her. She's stiff and uncomfortable for me."

"I think the problem is that you're stiff and uncomfortable when you hold her and the baby picks up on that."

"I told you, Bug," Jerry said. "You're worked up, so the baby is worked up. You need to chill so she chills."

Aisling balked. "I am not worked up!" She sounded unbelievably shrill.

"Obviously not," Jerry said dryly. "You're completely normal."

"I am." Aisling was insistent as she looked to me. "I'm not nervous. I mean ... I don't get nervous."

I had a choice. I could agree with her, say I'd been mistaken and let things go. Or, I could tell her the truth and perhaps shove her a bit in an effort to keep her from becoming mired in her own head.

"You're not nervous about most things," I clarified, making up my mind on the spot. "Lily is different. I think it's because of your mother. In your head, you know that the woman who died and the one who initially came back were not the same person. But you still can't seem to shake the fact that one of them tried to kill you."

"Multiple times," Jerry muttered. "I mean ... seriously. Mrs. Grimlock — the *real* Mrs. Grimlock — would never hurt her children. You need to get with the program, Bug."

Aisling made a protesting sound deep in her throat. "You were the one who insisted I hang out with her ... and allow her to help prep for the wedding ... and go shopping with her."

Jerry suddenly found something of interest to study on the wall. "I don't exactly remember things going that way."

"Oh, they went that way." Aisling's eyes filled with fire as her technician darted to her other side and tried to pretend she wasn't listening to the conversation. "You made me spend time with her even though I knew she was evil. Heck, I told Griffin from the beginning that she was evil. He was the only one who didn't give me grief about it."

"I didn't give you grief," Jerry argued. "I just ... thought you should give her a chance. That was before I knew she was eating people. It was definitely before I knew she wanted to take over your body and live forever."

My technician made a face but continued working on my mask. "He means that metaphorically," I offered lamely. "She *metaphorically* wanted to take over Aisling's body."

"And yet she was literally eating people," Aisling lamented, grinning when I frowned. "Don't worry. We'll tip so well they won't even care what they overheard. This is hardly the first time they've dealt with us."

I wasn't convinced the women would simply ignore what they heard, but there was nothing I could do about it because the wraith was already out of the cloak, so to speak. I decided to direct the conversation back to something healthier. "I believe we were talking about Lily. The sooner you relax around her, the sooner she'll relax. You're her mother. She loves you. She's just confused about why you're so tense. She's sensitive, so she picks up on it.

"Eventually you won't be tense at all," I continued. "Er, well, at least not about the little things. I'm sure you'll still get tense about the big things. When that happens, you'll look back on this and laugh."

"I hope so." Aisling rolled her neck and closed her eyes. "Tell me about Ryan Carroll. Do we know anything about him?"

I was surprised by the question. "I didn't think you were interested in work stuff right now."

"I'm interested in anything that takes my mind off my troubles. Focusing on your troubles would be an example of that."

"Oh, well ... we don't know much," I admitted, being careful when choosing my words. "I've never heard about anyone in our line of work having a sealed file. I mean ... that seems counterproductive, right?"

"I think it sounds counterproductive now," Aisling replied. "The thing is, this was fifty-some years ago. We're talking about a time when men were allowed to beat their wives and the women had no recourse

AMANDA M. LEE

because they were basically considered property simply because they signed a marriage license."

"Wow," I said dryly. "Tell me how you really feel."

"I feel as if we're going to find some really gross stuff about this guy in those sealed files," Aisling replied without hesitation. "I'm guessing Carroll was a complete and total loser and he has more than skeletons in his closet. I bet there are bodies there ... and maybe the remains of dead wives. Oh, maybe there're some dead pets, too."

I made a face as my technician pointed toward the wall and mouthed the words "fifteen minutes." I understood. I was supposed to remain in my spot, motionless, for fifteen minutes so the mask could do its thing.

"I think you watch too many movies," I countered, closing my eyes and getting comfortable in the massage chair. The vibrations were so comforting I thought I might fall asleep. "I'm guessing this guy was a rule breaker, don't get me wrong, but I don't know that we can jump to saying he's a murderer. We need more information."

"I'm more interested in what he was doing in that kid's head," Aisling admitted. "I mean ... that's not normal. This started at the aquarium, which is right above the gate. That seems to indicate that he's been hanging around that area for some reason ... or someone called him to that location."

"What about the other ghosts I saw?" I asked, thankful the technicians had excused themselves to the back of the building so I could talk freely. "What do you think is up with them?"

"I don't know. How many did you see again?"

"I didn't count, but I would estimate around twenty. One of them was definitely the dead teacher, Lauren Tate."

"Did you run her?"

The question caught me off guard. "Well ... no. Do you think I should?"

"I would. We can have Griffin run her when we get back to Grimlock Manor. He has his work computer so he can check his email. That means he has access to the search system. He might be able to tell us a few things about her we don't already know."

110

In truth, I hadn't considered tracking information on her because I assumed she was a victim of convenience.

"I think that's a good idea," I said after a beat. "I didn't really think about it before, but maybe she has ties to some group we're not aware of. Like ... maybe she was a witch and had visions of doing something to the gate. Perhaps the ghosts I saw were sent to protect it."

"That sounds like a bit of a stretch," Aisling countered. "I mean ... if that were true, I think we would've heard more reports of ghosts hanging around by the gate. This is hardly the first time there has been trouble near it."

"I want to see the gate," Jerry offered. "I think it sounds magical. I mean ... is it like Harry Potter? You know the scene in the movie when Sirius Black gets killed and drifts through the gate? Does it look like that?"

"Kind of," I hedged, my skin starting to prickle. The mask was clearly doing something. "It's shimmery. You can't really see through it, and it hurts if you brush up against it."

"What happens if you go through it?"

"I don't know. Cormack claims you die. He said there were people who ran experiments back in the day."

"Have you ever wondered how the gate came to be?" Aisling asked. "I mean ... did it appear right there? Was it created? Did someone try to make it and harness its power for another reason?"

I shifted in the chair, uncomfortable. I felt as if a bevy of eyes were focused on me, which was ridiculous given our location. "It was created by early reapers," I automatically replied. I knew the basic history of the gates because I'd spent years researching them in an effort to find answers about what happened to my parents. "The reapers worked together to create the gates. Originally they sent demons through. Then they started handling others, like the recently deceased."

"I think there used to be a lot more ghosts around than there are now," Jerry noted. "If they didn't decide to move souls to the other side when they did, the world would be more crowded."

"Definitely," I agreed, fighting the urge to scratch the side of my

AMANDA M. LEE

nose. I was ridiculously uncomfortable. The mask itself felt good. Something else was going on. "I ... ."

Whatever I was going to say died on my lips, because when I opened my eyes I found at least eight ghosts surrounding me. I recognized several of the faces from my earlier interaction in the aquarium. Lauren was one of the faces, in fact.

"What the ... !"

"What's wrong?" Aisling asked, opening her eyes. The second she saw the new faces in the room she bolted into a sitting position. "You've got to be kidding me!"

"Oh, you're ruining my quiet time," Jerry complained, opening his eyes. "I ... wait. Are those ghosts?"

The fact that he was human and could see them was interesting. It was something to think about later, though, because we had a situation on our hands.

"What the heck are we going to do?" Aisling asked, her eyes widening as Lauren's ghost moved closer to her. "I don't like this one bit."

"Join the club," Jerry muttered. "That makes two of us."

"Three," I corrected, gripping the arms of the chair. "This is so not good."

"Oh, really?" Aisling's sarcasm was on full display. "What was your first clue?"

112

Thirteen

My heart hammered as I slowly looked around the room, counting in my head as I went. Nine. There were nine ghosts. That meant three for each of us. Even if Aisling and I could somehow fight off those surrounding us — which was doubtful, because she was underweight and exhausted — that still left the three eyeing Jerry with overt interest. He had no special powers other than snark, as far as I could ascertain, which meant he was the most vulnerable.

"Hold still," I instructed, rolling to a sitting position. "I just need a second to ... ." I trailed off when Lauren appeared directly in front of me. She moved her mouth, as if trying to speak, but no sound came out. Worse than that, it looked as if someone had tried to sew her mouth shut. She was a ghost, so I guessed that had to be accomplished on another plane of existence ... although how they were even here was beyond me.

"They're not regular souls," Aisling announced, taking me by surprise when she whipped her scepter from her pocket and tried absorbing the closest entity. "This isn't working."

Jerry furrowed his brow. "Why did you bring that?"

"I've been stuck in the real world several times now when I

could've used it. I've taken to carrying it with me everywhere. That includes the movie theater, hair salon and gynecologist."

Jerry made a horrified expression. "You take it with you to the gynecologist? Do you think a soul is going to crawl up ... well ... there?"

If looks could kill, Jerry would be dead. Aisling made a disgusted sound deep in her throat. "No. I don't think a soul is going to crawl up my vagina, Jerry. I have enough going on up there these days. You have no idea what it's like to give birth. Everything is stretched and broken already. I just don't want to be caught without it. You know what happened on my honeymoon because I was without a scepter."

I was fascinated enough by the discussion that I decided to engage, even as I moved from my chair and circled the room. I needed to figure a way to scatter the ghosts — or whatever they were — without drawing too much attention. Thankfully the three facial technicians remained in the back room.

"What happened on your honeymoon?" I asked absently, cocking my head to the side so I could better study Lauren. She looked ragged, even for a dead woman. To me, that seemed to indicate her soul had undergone some sort of trauma ... other than the horrific death, of course.

"My father surprised us with a trip to Moonstone Bay," Aisling replied, her eyes on me as I circled. "It's an island off the coast of Florida. Almost everyone there is paranormal."

"Really?" I was intrigued. "What kind of paranormal people are we talking about?"

"Witches and shifters, of course. I met a cupid. Oh, and there's this nifty half-demon who can make fire swords. It's all kinds of interesting. They also have a cursed cemetery where all the bodies get up and walk around at night."

I jerked my head in her direction. "Zombies?"

"Yup. They keep it locked so the tourists don't accidentally wander in and get bitten. They have no idea how to fix the problem, but they don't want to destroy the bodies because they're loved ones of the residents."

"That's pretty interesting. I've never really gotten the chance to see zombies. I mean ... they're rumored to be rampant in the French Quarter, but that's simply not true, at least as far as I can tell. Most of the time people report the walking dead it's a hoax, though I've heard of a few bad brujas who wanted to resurrect an army to take over during Mardi Gras because of the noise."

"Ooh, Mardi Gras!" Jerry's eyes sparkled. "I've always wanted to go."

"Maybe you should head there for your honeymoon," Aisling suggested, using her finger to poke at one of the specters. "You said you wanted someplace cool rather than trendy. Hmm. The air surrounding these things is cold, like 'January in the middle of an arctic freeze' cold."

"You probably shouldn't touch them," I pointed out. "They don't look friendly."

"Aisling doesn't care about doing the smart thing," Jerry said. "She always leaps before she looks, which is only one reason she spent an entire year grounded when we were teenagers. Her father almost had a conniption fit, although he allowed me to visit because it was the only way to shut Bug up."

I smiled at the image Jerry painted. "A whole year, huh?"

"At a certain point it became a challenge to see if I could accomplish it," Aisling replied, pointing her scepter at another ghost and pressing the button. The scepters were meant to absorb the souls and hold them until they could be uploaded into a regional transportation device — which Cormack kept in his office — and then transferred to us. "These are definitely not normal souls."

"What was your first clue?" I challenged. "For me, the green color was a dead giveaway."

"They're more of a teal," Jerry corrected. "I'm thinking of making the vests and bow ties that color for the wedding, Bug. What do you think?" He leaned his head and posed in front of one of the ghosts. "But now I'm starting to shy away from the color because it might be a bit too garish."

"I definitely don't like the color," Aisling complained. "I would go back to the lavender. It looks better with my brothers' eyes, and Griffin looks good in it, too. You and Aidan are essentially splitting the wedding party, so that makes sense."

"No." Jerry vigorously shook his head when I held out my hand for him. "Wait ... what are you doing?"

I stilled. "Are you saying no to me or her?"

He pointed toward Aisling. "I'm just curious about what you're doing."

"I'm trying to get the three of us in the same area so I can do something about these ghosts."

"Oh, well ... that sounds like a good idea." He readily grabbed my hand so I could help him off the chair, and turned back to Aisling. "You're going to be my best woman. We already talked about this."

"I thought we agreed that we were going to have one wedding party and share all the attendants," Aisling argued, hopping off her chair and shooting the nearest ghost a look that promised mayhem if it dared touch her. "Aidan wants me to stand up for him, too."

"Yes, well, I come before Aidan."

"I know you don't like to be reminded of this, but we shared a womb. Technically, I think he has dibs over you."

Jerry's mouth dropped open as incredulity washed over his features. "Are you kidding me? We've been best friends since kindergarten."

"Yeah, but Aidan and I were embryos together."

"I can't even." Jerry folded his arms over his chest as I gave him a little shove toward the hallway. "You've broken my heart, Bug. I hope you know that."

"Oh, don't be that way, Jerry." Aisling made a face as she moved toward us, pulling back slightly when the nearest ghost — he looked to be a teenager with an eyebrow ring and a bad attitude — made a threatening lunge in her direction. "You know I love you. I have responsibilities to Aidan, too. Why can't we just go back to the way things were supposed to be and share one big wedding party?"

"Because I want designated grooms people ... and you were supposed to be the lead one."

"Oh, geez. I ... ." Aisling's reflexes were in full gear as she hopped back at the exact instant the overzealous ghost tried to jump on her.

I reacted on instinct, lashing out with my magic and slamming a bolt of power into the ill-mannered ghost. The boy instantly shredded into a million pieces and dissolved in front of us.

He never made a sound.

"That was interesting," Aisling noted as she fought to regain her breath.

"It was just a spell my grandfather taught me. He wanted to make sure I was safe no matter what area I happened to walk in. After Katrina ... well ... there were some rough months."

"Oh, the spell was impressive," she said. "But that's not what I'm talking about. I'm talking about what just happened with your face. You kind of looked like a Catrina."

I was taken aback. I'd seen the transformation before, mostly in mirrors and window panels. It generally only happened when I expended a lot of energy funneling my magic, which I did not do today. "Oh, well ... ."

"What's a Catrina?" Jerry asked from the hallway. He still sounded petulant.

"It's a Hispanic icon of the dead, usually a female skeleton," Aisling replied, her eyes still on the spot where the teenage ghost had been standing. "Did you destroy him?"

That was a very good question. "I don't know." I looked to the other ghosts, who were watching me with wary eyes. "You need to go," I ordered. "I don't want to shred you, but I will. You're not supposed to be here."

Lauren met my gaze with a mournful one of her own. She looked wretched, as if she was being dragged through the very depths of Hell and had no recourse.

"I'm sorry." I felt helpless. "I'll try to do what I can for you ... but now is not the time. You need to go." I made little walking motions with my fingers. "If the technicians see you ... well, I can't let that happen. You're too hard to explain. You have to go. Right now."

"Definitely go," Jerry agreed. "You're ruining our spa day and that's just rude. Come back when we're not paying hundreds of dollars to be buffed and pampered."

Aisling rolled her eyes. "I don't think they care about that, Jerry."

"Well, I care. I want to go back to you choosing Aidan over me."

"That's not what I said."

"It's exactly what you said."

I only half listened to the argument as the ghosts slowly dissolved. I had no doubt most of them were still around, but they'd made themselves invisible and that was the most important thing. I wasn't sure about the teenager, who seemed angry about pretty much everything, but for now things were back to normal.

"That was pretty good," Aisling offered, smiling. "You got them to go away."

"Yeah, but for how long?"

She shrugged. "Long enough for us to finish our spa day."

"That's what we need to focus on above all else," Jerry agreed.

I wasn't sure, but I was outnumbered so I merely nodded. What the heck was going on with the ghosts?

"WAIT ... YOU'RE SAYING YOU sat back down in the chairs and pretended nothing happened after a ghostly mob tried to attack?"

Braden was positively apoplectic when we returned to Grimlock Manor and told the story that afternoon.

"Hey, nobody gets between me and my massage," Jerry barked, holding out his arm as he sat on the couch in Cormack's office. Aidan, who looked as if he had zero interest in "oohing" and "aahing" over Jerry's soft skin, forced a smile and nodded as he made a big show of running his fingers up and down his fiancé's forearm.

"They didn't come back," Aisling offered helpfully as she slid closer to Griffin, who sat with Lily on his lap on the couch closest to the fireplace. The baby was awake and alert — well, as alert as a two-week-old infant could be — and hadn't as much as made a peep as she happily rested in her father's arms.

Griffin watched Aisling with speculative eyes and then tipped his head in the direction of the open seat next to him. "Do you want to hold her?"

The look on Aisling's face clearly told me she thought that was a trick question. "I don't want her to start crying."

Griffin smirked. "Just ... try. If she starts crying, I'll take her back. You need to get over the fear."

Aisling swallowed hard, but did as he asked, holding her breath as he shifted the baby to her. Once Lily was settled in her mother's arms, she merely switched her gaze from Griffin's face to Aisling's and continued doing whatever she was doing before. As far as I could tell, that was nothing.

When I glanced at Cormack, I found him watching the scene with a certain measure of trepidation. He relaxed when he realized the baby wasn't going to start squalling and turned to me.

"It sounds like you fought off the ghosts the best way possible," he offered after a beat.

"There wasn't much fighting. I only took out the one and then ordered the others to leave."

"That was smart. Now we know they can understand and even follow instructions. We also know they can't be absorbed. It's a good thing Aisling took her scepter with her."

The look Aisling shot Jerry was triumphant. Jerry merely rolled his eyes and went back to stroking his own skin.

"We need to figure out what's going on," I insisted. "They're not normal ghosts. They're green ... and I swear that Lauren's mouth looks as if it's been sewn shut. I'm pretty sure that's not normal ghost behavior."

"Agreed," Cormack nodded. "We need answers. We managed to come up with some interesting information while you were out, but piecing it together remains a chore."

"What information?" I asked, straightening.

"Ryan Carroll," Cillian volunteered, grabbing his tablet from a nearby end table. He'd been engrossed in his work when we entered, something he shuffled to the side as we started telling our thrilling tale. "We managed to get some files that we didn't have access to previously."

"The sealed files?" I was officially intrigued. "What do they say?"

"We still haven't been able to access the sealed files." Cormack grimaced, his distaste for the bureaucracy of the home office evident. "The file we did manage to open came from one of Carroll's co-workers. He filed a complaint because there were rumors abounding about Carroll, saying that he stole a book that detailed harnessing the power of the dead."

"Stole a book from where?" I asked.

"The library." Cillian made a disgusted face. "I mean ... who steals books from a library?"

Braden snickered and patted his brother's shoulder in a form of solace. "I'm sorry you had to read about that. I know it's going to give you nightmares."

Cillian shrugged off the teasing. "Shut up. You know what I mean. No one should ever steal books from the main office library. They've been collected for a reason, so everyone can use them for research."

"Yes, it's a travesty," Braden agreed, his eyes lighting with amusement.

"What did the complaint say?" I asked. "I mean ... other than that."

"Apparently Carroll was talking long and loud to anyone who would listen about enslaving ghosts," Cormack replied, his expression twisting into something dark. "He's hardly the first one who thought souls could be used for nefarious means. Reapers have always existed, but the organization involved in the process of collecting souls has steadily grown and evolved."

I never really thought about that. "Were there reapers back in days of the Neanderthal?" The question popped out, causing Braden to snicker. However, he sobered quickly.

"Wait, were there Neanderthal reapers?"

Cormack shrugged. "I have no idea. Neanderthals lacked the brain power to develop writing and keep journals."

"And do anything other than point sharp sticks at each other," Aisling noted. She looked ridiculously relaxed as she held the baby and rested her head on Griffin's shoulder. For his part, Griffin looked like a blessed man. Their little family appeared as comfortable as I'd ever seen.

"I'll ask about Neanderthal reapers during the next conference call," Cormack said. "I don't have an answer right now ... and I don't think it's important given everything we're dealing with."

"Is there any more information on Carroll?" I pressed. "I mean ... all we have on him right now is a rumor reported by another co-worker. That's hardly concrete."

"That's all the information we've been able to dig up," Cormack replied. "We did find one other interesting tidbit, though."

"What's that?"

"It seems Ryan Carroll was Angelina Davenport's paternal great-grandfather. I didn't know that until I looked into his personnel file, which is missing several important pages. One child is listed, and it's Angelina's grandmother."

Aisling was officially paying attention now as she leaned forward. "Are you serious? Are you saying Angelina's great-grandfather was a nut who believed in enslaving ghosts?"

"I don't believe I used the word 'nut,' but it's surprisingly accurate."

"I guess that explains why Angelina's mother was so freaking crazy, too." Aisling appeared lost in thought. "I wonder if Angelina knows anything about her great-grandfather."

"Wait." I held up a hand to silence everyone. "Angelina is the woman you had the weird fight with in the mall, right?" I racked my brain as I thought through the confrontation. "She's the one who you kept teasing about being a slut."

"Prostitute," Aisling corrected. "And that wasn't teasing, that was the truth. She's a complete and total prostitute. Her pimp thinks she's lazy so he often slaps her around, but she's not really lazy. She often gives it away for free when he's not looking."

I knit my eyebrows. "I'm not sure that makes sense."

"It doesn't have to make sense," Braden offered. "Aisling only cares that it's mean."

"Oh, well, it's definitely mean." I focused on Cormack. "Does this mean we need to track down this Angelina and question her?"

Aisling's hand shot in the air as she clutched Lily to her chest with her other arm. "I would like to volunteer for that assignment."

Cormack let loose a weary sigh and shook his head. "I'm not sure what it means yet. All I know is that we have a predicament I have no idea how to resolve."

Fourteen

I thought I should return to Belle Isle and relieve Oliver — he'd been covering every shift for almost twenty-four hours — but when I called he seemed fine. In fact, if I didn't know better, I would almost call him cheery.

"I narrowed down your list of possible employees to five," he announced. "I emailed the files. The rest is up to you."

"Are you sure you don't want me to head back so we can discuss their merits?" I pressed.

"Absolutely not. It's been quiet here for a full day. I've enjoyed it. Besides, things are light today. I only have two more intakes before calling it a day. I'll be done before you can get here."

"Oh, well ... ." I felt like a slacker. "I'll be back to help with things tomorrow."

"Just call," he suggested. "It sounds to me as if you're getting important information. We need that if we're going to make sure no more teachers drop dead in the middle of tours at the aquarium."

"But ... ."

"Just keep doing what you're doing," he insisted. "Spend another night at Grimlock Manor if it becomes necessary. I'm sure Braden will be happy to have you there."

I narrowed my eyes and glanced around suspiciously. I was alone in the parlor, but I almost expected Braden to jump out of nowhere and yell "a-ha" and perform a smug little dance. "I am sleeping in a guest room," I announced. "I am not sleeping in his room, so don't you dare start spreading that rumor."

"I'm here alone," he noted. "Who would I spread that rumor to?"

"Oh, well ... there's Collin ... and his wife ... and your boyfriend."

"I've already told Brett that you and Braden are hot for each other. He says he can see it because you're both so pretty. As for Collin and Claire, I haven't seen them all day. Apparently they're not speaking to each other."

"When do they ever speak to each other?"

"That's a fair point. I still haven't seen them."

"Well ... ." I trailed off, uncertain. I thought for sure he would insist I come back and relieve his work burden. Once he did the opposite, I found myself at a loss. "I'm not sure what I'm supposed to do here," I admitted. "I mean ... I went to the spa today. I've never been to the spa before."

Oliver chuckled. "You're making friends with Aisling. That's ... entertaining."

"I like her."

"I'm sure you do. You have a lot in common."

"Is that an insult?"

"No." Oliver was matter-of-fact. "Aisling may be full of herself, but she's a survivor. Also, she's charming ... in her own way. I find her delightful, especially when she's giving her father and brothers a hard time. They're all alphas who basically bow down to her, which is interesting to watch because that makes her the ultimate alpha."

"You're talking about them as if they're a psych experiment," I admonished.

"Yes, well, there's a reason I find them interesting. I was a psychologist at one time."

"Really?" That was news to me. "When was this?"

"Almost a hundred years ago. My, how time flies when you're having fun."

The more I thought about how old he was, the more my brain

hurt. "We'll talk about that fascinating topic later. Just be careful when you're leaving ... and if you see anything, don't hesitate to call. I'm still not sure if these ghosts can do any real damage, but I'd rather not find out the hard way."

"I've got it under control. I can take care of myself. I've been doing it a very long time."

"Yeah? Well, I'm not done pulling information out of you regarding my parents. For example, I'm dying for you to tell me about the time you rescued me from the rubble of a house right after my parents died. I'm pretty sure you never told me that."

His silence stretched a little too long.

"Oliver?"

"We'll talk about things when the time is right," he stressed, his tone grim. "I don't know who told you that ... ."

"Does it matter? It's the truth, isn't it?"

"It is. But I wanted to wait before talking about that. You're not ready."

Who was he to tell me if I was ready? "You know what?"

"I have to be going." Oliver cut me off with smart efficiency. "I have a load of souls coming in. I'm almost done for the day. You should have fun and take a break, perhaps dig into the research more. Don't worry about me."

"This isn't over, Oliver," I growled. It was too late. He'd already hung up. "Oh, bite me."

Braden lifted an eyebrow as he strolled into the room. "Are you talking to me?"

I shook my head. "Oliver says he's fine. He doesn't need me this afternoon. I still want to head back to Belle Isle tonight. I don't want to spend another night here."

His expression didn't shift, but I was almost positive I scented a hint of disappointment wafting off him. "I can make sure that happens. You don't have to go right now, though."

"I guess. What did you have in mind? If it's another meal with your family, no offense, I think I'll pass. Aisling and Jerry are busy going at each other over the wedding party fiasco and Cillian is still griping about stealing books from the library. I don't think I can take three more hours of either."

He snorted, genuine amusement rolling off him. "How about I take you out for a simple dinner? There's a good place right around the corner."

That sounded a lot like a date. "I'm not sure that's a good idea."

He didn't back down. "It's also a bar. We can get a few drinks and then I can get one of my father's drivers to take you back to the island."

That was better than him driving me back. At least this way there would be no awkward goodbye in front of my bedroom door ... again. "I guess I can live with that," I supplied. "What kind of food are we talking about?"

"Typical bar fare. Burgers. Fish and chips. Stuff like that."

"Actually, that sounds really good. I haven't had good fish and chips in quite a while."

"Then I think we have a plan." He held out a hand. "Shall we?"

I sighed as I watched his wiggling fingers. He seemed to be having a good time at my expense. The problem was his charms were getting harder to resist.

"Definitely." I sucked up every ounce of strength I had and bypassed his hand as I strolled toward the door. "Who doesn't love fish and chips?"

"I'm a big fan."

"That makes two of us."

WOODY'S BAR WAS WITHIN walking distance of Grimlock Manor. The second I entered I felt as if I'd stepped into a familiar watering hole. Sure, the bars in New Orleans were fancier — and usually came with a theme — but Woody's was a welcome respite after a long day.

"This place is great," I announced.

Braden bobbed is head as he waved to an older man behind the counter. "We've been coming here for years. Heck, we came here before it was legal for us to come here."

"Really? Did you get served?"

"Nope. Woody and my father go way back. He thought it was funny whenever we tried. We would wait until he had a new bartender in place and then come sauntering in with our fake IDs. It never worked."

"And that's Woody?" I inclined my chin toward the grinning man Braden had waved at.

"That's him."

Braden led us to an intimate circular booth. It was far too big for just the two of us, but he snagged it anyway. Because of its design, there was no reason we couldn't sit reasonably close to one another. In a regular booth it looked idiotic for people to sit next to one another if there were only two bodies at the table. This booth erased that problem.

"Cozy," I muttered, grabbing a menu from the display at the center of the table.

Braden's lips quirked. "It is cozy," he agreed. "This is my family's regular booth. Oh, and look. Here comes the man of the hour right now." He straightened his shoulders as the owner approached. "Woody, it's good to see you."

"And you, Braden." Woody's eyes were on me as he shook Braden's hand. "Who is your friend?"

"This is Izzy. She's new to the area."

"And you fell in with this reprobate?" He made a tsking sound with his tongue. "Just let me know if he gets fresh. I'll be more than happy to send security over here to sort him out."

I smiled at the good-natured offer. Woody was clearly a friendly guy who had a long past with the Grimlocks. Braden didn't look worried in the least that he would make good on his threat.

"I'll let you know ... I can take care of myself. You don't have to worry about that."

"You look the sort who can take care of herself," Woody agreed. "Deep-fried mushrooms are on special for appetizers tonight. I ordered a round the second I saw you come through the door because I know they're a favorite for Braden and Aisling."

Braden slid his eyes to me. "Do you like mushrooms?"

"I do. That sounds good." I smiled at Woody. "I think I'm going for the fish and chips, too."

"That's what I'm having," Braden agreed. He hadn't even opened a menu, which told me he ate at Woody's often. "I'll have a Jack and Coke to drink, too."

"How about you?" Woody asked me. "Do you want something heavy or light with your dinner?"

The last thing I wanted was to lose my head now that I was alone with Braden. If I had something alcoholic to drink, I was more likely to let my defenses down ... which was probably a very bad idea given the circumstances. "I'll have an iced tea."

"Sweetened or unsweetened?"

I was surprised by the question. "I thought all the tea up here was unsweetened."

"Mostly, but Woody likes to cater to an eclectic clientele," Braden teased.

"I serve your family," Woody shot back. "It doesn't get more eclectic than that."

"Sweet tea," I announced to Woody's nod.

"No problem. Speaking of your family, how is your sister? I haven't seen her in a really long time."

"She's good." Braden's lips curved. "She had a baby a couple of weeks ago. Lily Taylor. She looks like Aisling."

"Oh, that means she's cute." Woody beamed. "Hopefully, once she's settled, she'll come back to see me."

"I guarantee that will happen," Braden said. "I don't think it's imminent, because Lily is loud and demanding, but once she's in a routine, I'm positive Aisling will be back."

"Good enough." Woody left with our orders, leaving Braden and me to keep up the conversation on our own. I didn't want to turn to romantic subjects, so I grappled for issues that we could talk about that would quench the spark that continuously seemed to be igniting whenever we were close.

"So ... how long do you think you'll be living with your father?"

Braden barked out a laugh at the brazen question. "I don't know. I haven't given it much thought."

"That came out a lot more judgmental than I thought it would," I admitted, mortified. "I didn't mean that the way it sounded."

"No, it's fine. I haven't decided how long I'm going to stay at Grimlock Manor. I know I'm not leaving anytime soon."

"Because you like having servants wait on you?"

"Honestly? That's only part of the draw. The house is big enough that we can all live together without stumbling over one another or feeling penned in. My father has never been one to ask us about our every move. And except when it came to Aisling, he never complained about overnight guests."

"Your father didn't like it when Jerry spent the night?" That surprised me. "I thought he loved Jerry."

"Oh, my father loves Jerry to distraction. Jerry is like another child where my father is concerned. He's allowed to spend the night whenever he wants. I meant overnight guests of a romantic sort."

"Oh." My cheeks burned as realization washed over me. "Like Griffin."

"Yes. The first time Griffin spent the night, my father walked the halls with a baseball bat grumbling to himself the entire evening. He swore up and down he was going to make us hide a body."

I laughed because I could picture it. "Wow. Poor Griffin."

"Griffin was afraid of my father at the start, but it didn't last long. Now my father dreams of the days when Griffin was terrified of him."

"Your father obviously loves Griffin."

"He does. More importantly, my father recognizes that Griffin loves my sister ... and would die for her. I'm not sure Aisling could've found a better husband."

The words were simple, and yet they warmed me. "They seemed better tonight. I mean ... I'm not imagining that, am I?"

"They seemed loads better. I'm guessing that means you talked to Aisling at the spa."

"Maybe a little," I hedged. "I just let her know that she was on edge and the baby was picking up on it. She seemed surprised, and I wasn't even sure she was listening until we got back and she made a concerted effort to hold the baby and relax at the same time."

"Was this before or after the ghosts attacked?"

"Before. After, all we could talk about was Jerry's bitter disappointment in Aisling's insistence on a communal wedding party so she could be there for both him and Aidan."

Braden snorted. "That sounds just like him."

"Yeah, well ... ." I didn't want to circle back in the conversation because I was afraid of how it would make me look, but I couldn't stop myself. "So ... how many women are we talking about?"

He furrowed his brow, confusion evident. "What do you mean? In Jerry's wedding party? Just Aisling."

"Not in the wedding party. As overnight guests. You said your father only had a problem when Aisling tried to have overnight guests. I'm curious how many women you've had stay the night in your father's house."

"Oh." Braden pressed his lips together as his cheeks flooded with color. "Um ... I don't think that's important."

"No? It must be quite a few to garner that sort of reaction from you."

"I didn't say that. I ... not a lot. Only a few. And it was a very long time ago."

"I don't think I believe you. In fact, I'm almost positive you're lying."

"I'm not lying." He turned serious. "I brought a few girls home after high school. We weren't allowed to bring anyone in who was underage, and my mother had strict rules about overnight guests. My father was the one who relaxed them after her death.

"I guess, in the first few years after she passed, I might've been sowing my oats a bit," he admitted. "In recent years I haven't brought anyone home."

"Why?"

"We had wraiths attacking at every turn and my mother came back from the dead. I guess dating took a backseat. Plus, well, I wasn't sure I wanted to risk my heart given what my father was going through. He was gutted when my mother came back. He'd finally started dating a woman from the office and he actually brought her around. All that ended when my mother decided she wanted to reclaim her family."

I'd never heard this part of the story, so I was understandably curious. "What happened to the woman he was dating?"

"She took a step back because she thought we needed time as a family to deal with things. She was nice enough, though I'm not sure she revved my father's motors, so to speak. I've come to the conclusion that my mother — my *real* mother — was the only one for him."

"It's still sad that he's alone," I offered. "Is that another reason you haven't moved out?"

He nodded without hesitation. "The house is big. It's just Redmond, Dad and me now. We're not tripping over each other."

"You don't want to leave your father alone."

"I don't want to be alone either." He was earnest as he met my gaze. "Cillian was in the house until he and Maya decided it was time to strike out on their own. The same with Aidan. He left when it was time to move in with Jerry.

"Aisling left much earlier, but I'm pretty sure that's because my father had a different set of rules for her," he continued. "She and Jerry moved into the townhouse together and ate meals at Grimlock Manor several times a week. It's not as if they weren't around."

"Your father had five children. He's used to noise ... and people. You don't want to leave him. I find that commendable."

Braden's smile was easy. "I'm a commendable guy. In fact ... ." He didn't get a chance to finish what he was saying because a whirlwind of motion plowed into the booth at his left and momentarily left him breathless. When he realized the figure taking up space in his world wasn't of the dangerous or paranormal variety, he frowned ... and then he outright glared.

"Hello, Angelina," he gritted out as the pretty brunette tilted her head and smiled. "What a lovely surprise."

He didn't mean it, but I was intrigued. Here was the woman who played into our mystery, even though she didn't yet know it. Cormack said he didn't want to seek her out, but she'd just fallen into our laps. I could hardly let the opportunity slide.

Fifteen

"Are you the only ones here?" Angelina, who appeared tipsy, couldn't hide her disappointment as she glanced around. "No one else but you?"

"There are plenty of people here," Braden countered. "Look over there. There's, like, ten people over there. You should bother them."

I put my hand on his wrist to still him, earning an incredulous look. "She's fine," I supplied. "In fact, I'm happy to see her."

A drink clutched firmly in her hand, Angelina slanted her eyes in my direction. "I recognize you," she said after a bit. "But I can't exactly remember why I recognize you. You're not Griffin's sister. I know that ... harlot."

Braden shot her a quelling look. "Maya is a good woman. You're just jealous because she and Cillian are living together."

Angelina couldn't hide her surprise — or the brief moment of sadness that washed over her features — although she managed to cover relatively quickly. She was a good actress when she wanted to be, and apparently she was in the mood to put on a show. "I didn't know Cillian had moved out of Grimlock Manor."

"Is that why you drive by twice a day?" Braden's tone was biting. I got it. He didn't like Angelina. There was a lot of history between her and his family, most of it bad. Now was not the time for him to rehash it, though.

"I happen to live around the corner from you guys," Angelina snapped. "Your house is on my way to work. Should I go out of my way so I don't drive by your house?"

"That would be nice."

"Ignore him," I said hurriedly, drawing Angelina's attention. "He's in a bad mood. You'll have to forgive him."

"He's always in a bad mood," Angelina grumbled. "He's the head sourpuss in the Grimlock clan. You should know that if you plan to date him.

"Redmond is the friendliest, but he'll sleep with just about anyone," she continued. "Everyone knows he's not ready to settle down. He likes playing the field."

"He won't sleep with you," Braden muttered.

Angelina ignored him. "Cillian is the smartest ... and the most charming. We dated."

"I heard." I searched for the right words. "I'm sorry that didn't work out."

"I screwed it up. I wasn't ready. You know ... afraid and stuff." She looked morose.

"And a total whore," Braden added.

It took everything I had not to wrap my fingers around his neck and start squeezing until he stopped talking. I thought Aisling was the one who picked the absolute worst time to talk. Apparently she wasn't the only one in the family with that particular gift.

"Braden is crabby like Aisling," Angelina continued, apparently lost in her own world. "They're two peas in a pod. They're both jerks, so if you're thinking of dating him you should start running now. Look how badly things worked out for that poor Griffin guy. He fell for Aisling — I still don't know how that happened — and she ruined his life."

Braden opened his mouth to spew something that I was certain was hateful and would end up ruining everything. I slapped my hand over his mouth to quiet him, earning a dark look for my efforts.

"I think Griffin and Aisling are very happy. They're tired right now because they have a newborn baby, but when I saw them a few hours ago they were sharing a blanket next to the fire and holding their little girl. I think that makes for a happy family."

Angelina rolled her eyes so hard I thought she might fall out of the booth. "Please. He only pretends to be happy because he's afraid of Cormack and all of Aisling's brothers. They'll kill him if he tries to leave her."

"She's not wrong," Braden admitted, pushing my hand away. "But Griffin doesn't want to leave. He loves my sister. I've often struggled with why they mesh so well together, but Griffin loves her."

"See." Angelina extended a knowing finger toward Braden. "He understands. His sister is the devil. Of course, he's the devil, too."

"How much have you had to drink?" Braden challenged. "I'm guessing quite a bit."

"I like coming here," Angelina replied. "I can walk."

"Yes, we're all happy you're not getting behind the wheel."

I squeezed Braden's wrist as hard as I could. "You know what's weird, Angelina? We were just talking about you earlier," I offered. "You were the star in a Grimlock family conversation."

Angelina snorted and took a huge gulp of her drink. "I can imagine the sort of things that were said."

"They were all complimentary," I lied.

"Oh, puh-leez! I guarantee the word 'pimp' was said. I know, because you already told me Aisling was there."

"Yes, well, motherhood has softened Aisling," I offered.

"Yes, she's a total marshmallow now," Braden drawled. "Kind of like that huge one that wanted to eat New York in *Ghostbusters*."

I continued as if I hadn't heard him. "The reason your name came up was because of your grandfather. Ryan Carroll was your grandfather, right?"

She nodded, seemingly disinterested. "My great-grandfather, not my grandfather. Although ... both of them were kind of jerks."

"Great-grandfather," I corrected. "We were talking about him."

"I don't know why." Angelina was almost slurring now. "He left my great-grandmother not long after my grandmother was born. Then, my grandfather left my grandmother not long after my mother was born. My grandmother was abandoned twice.

"I didn't know either of them very well. There are a lot of stories about my great-grandfather," she continued. "My mother said he was nuttier than a Baby Ruth candy bar." She laughed at her own joke, which was beyond annoying.

"Did you know him?"

"Me? No. He died before I was born."

Braden shifted in his seat, finally engaged in the conversation. "Do you know how he died? There's no record of it in any of the files we found."

"Files? What files?" Her forehead wrinkled as she swirled her straw in her glass. "Why would you be looking at files on my great-grandfather?"

"He worked in the same office as our grandfather," Braden replied.

"You mean he was one of you?" Angelina's disdain was evident. "That is ... all kinds of depressing. You guys are freaks. I don't want to be descended from freaks. Of course, that could explain why I'm alone ... if I'm descended from freaks, I mean.

"Aisling and Cillian aren't alone and they're descended from freaks," she continued. It was often difficult to understand her thanks to the slurring. "I wonder why they got so lucky."

"It's probably because they're not drinking away their lives in the bar every night," Braden noted.

"I am not drinking away my life." As if to prove it, she drained her glass. "I am having a great time now that my mother is gone. In fact ... I'm having an awesome time. I can't remember when I ever had a better time."

I shifted my eyes to Braden, surprised.

He slowly nodded. "I was sorry to hear about your mother, Angelina," he offered, almost sounding sincere. "I didn't know her well — mostly because she threatened to spray me with a hose whenever she saw me running around the neighborhood as a kid — but it's still sad when a parent dies."

"She sprayed all you guys. She thought you were dirty ... and she hated your mother. Your mother came back from the dead." Her gaze sharpened. "How did you manage that?"

"We didn't manage that, and that wasn't our mother." Braden was firm as he glanced around the bar to make sure nobody was listening. Thankfully, nobody cared how drunk Angelina was or what weird tales she spewed. "You can't dwell on this stuff, Angelina. It's wrecking you ... and you don't have far to fall before rock bottom because you're already the lowest of the low."

I elbowed him. Hard.

"What?" He rubbed his side. "You can't give me grief about this. She's been horrible her entire life. I'm not going to suddenly pretend I like her simply because her mother died. Besides, her mother was a terrible person."

"My mother *was* a terrible person," Angelina agreed, turning whimsical. "She spoiled me rotten. She got off on pitting me against Aisling. She always wanted to win the competition, though I was never sure what the competition was. I just knew I had to beat Aisling."

"Which you never did," Braden muttered.

"Oh, there's still time." Angelina tried to take a drink from the glass and frowned when she realized it was empty. "I need another."

"I think you should stop," Braden argued, collecting the glass. "You've had more than enough for tonight."

"You're a spoilsport." She made a face. "I still want another."

"Maybe after you finish telling us about your great-grandfather," I suggested. "We're dying to hear about him."

"There's nothing to tell," Angelina shot back. "He left his family because he didn't want to be a father. He ran off with some floozy — I think her name was Irene Wagner or something. I swear that's what my grandmother said, because she blamed Irene Wagner for most of her woes — and he never looked back."

"You must know something about him," Braden pressed. "Even if you didn't meet him, every family has stories that are passed down. What have you heard about your great-grandfather?"

"Just that he was a nut. He thought there was a way for him to live forever. Apparently he was obsessed with dying. He wouldn't even cross the road unless there were no vehicles in sight. I mean ... like, none. He thought for sure he was going to die a horrible death. He even hired someone to taste his food at some point so he wasn't poisoned."

"He sounds paranoid," Braden mused, sliding his eyes to me. "I don't know that matters either way, but I'm guessing he was delusional."

"Oh, he was totally delusional," Angelina agreed. "He said that there was a gate that separated this world from the next and that he was going to find a way to cross over and back because he was convinced that was the way to fool death ... as if death was a person."

She fell silent for a moment and then turned to Braden. "Your family is kind of like death, isn't it?" Suddenly, she sounded clearer than she had when she sat down. "You're kind of like walking grim reapers. If he was right about that, maybe he was right about the gate."

"There is no gate," Braden lied. "I'm more interested in why your great-grandfather thought he could fight death. Was he ever diagnosed with anything?"

"No. He was a hypochondriac, but everyone in my family is. I heard he went to the doctor once a month for a battery of tests to make sure it would be caught early if he was sick."

That was interesting. "What did he die of?" I asked. "If he was determined to stave off death, it must've come as a shock when he finally lost the war. What claimed him?"

She shrugged. "I don't know. He was long gone by the time he died. No one kept in contact with him because he was afraid the government was going to tap his phone and send a deadly disease through it."

"He definitely sounds paranoid," Braden commented.

"Which means we need to figure out where he went after he abandoned his family," I said. "Whatever he did in the time after that plays into what's happening now."

"How can you be sure?"

"I don't know ... but I'm sure. He was terrified of death, which means he wanted to control it. Something is controlling those ghosts. I think we're definitely onto something."

"Okay. I guess that means we need to track down more information on Carroll. There must be records somewhere."

"Yeah. I ... ." I forgot what I was going to say when Angelina slouched in the booth and rested her head on Braden's shoulder. She was truly drunk, and the picture she painted was beyond sad. She was clearly a woman mired in difficulty and having trouble finding her way out of the sadness that plagued her.

"At least tell me Aisling's baby is ugly," Angelina whispered. "I'm betting she looks like a freaky monster or something."

"Lily is the prettiest baby ever," Braden snapped, his temper coming out to play. "She's absolutely perfect."

I had to bite my lip to keep from laughing at his protective uncle act. No matter how tough he pretended to be, he resembled a marshmallow when it came to his family.

"Well, that sucks." Angelina got to shaky feet. "I think I'm going to have another drink. We'll toast Aisling's not-ugly baby. How does that sound?"

"I think you should call it a night," I said gently. "You're going to regret it if you keep drinking."

"Oh, you have no idea the regrets I have. Why do you think I'm here?"

"WELL, HERE WE ARE AGAIN."

Angelina's drunken appearance was enough to have Braden switch to iced tea during dinner so he was sober enough to drive me home and it was unnecessary for one of Cormack's drivers to handle the situation. That meant another awkward encounter as he walked me from the parking lot to the boathouse. I was desperate to avoid it.

"Listen, you don't have to walk me all the way up," I insisted. "The building is safe. I mean ... totally safe."

"Except for the ghosts who might come calling."

"Yeah, well, there's nothing you can do about them," I reminded him. "We're not sure where they're coming from and we're not sure how to destroy them. Heck, we're not sure if we want to destroy them at all. I mean ... it's not their fault they're ghosts. At least I don't think it is. I don't know all of them personally, of course, but I get the feeling that this was something thrust upon them rather than something they chose."

Braden slowed his pace and stared at me. "Wow. That was a mouthful, huh?"

I smoothed the front of my shirt, which was really Aisling's shirt that I'd borrowed. "I don't know what you mean," I lied.

"You blather on and on when you're nervous," Braden noted. "I find it rather adorable. I don't want you to be nervous around me, though. That I don't like."

"I'm not nervous."

"No? It seems to me you are."

"Yes, well ... ." I desperately needed to change the subject. "What do you think about what Angelina said?"

"I think the baby is adorable and I'm going to break my father's rule about hitting girls if she says otherwise again."

I viciously pinched his flank. "Not that. You need to stop letting things like that get to you. She's a sad woman mourning the death of her mother and questioning her place in the world. She has nothing of her own. You should feel sorry for her, not hate her for the stupid things she says."

"Do you know the horrible things she did to Aisling and Jerry when they were kids? Heck, she still does horrible things to them."

"I don't doubt that." I refused to back down. "The thing is, you're not asking the important question. Why did she do those things? You heard her. Her mother pitted her against Aisling her entire life. Angelina only followed along because she wanted her mother's approval."

"She was still a jerk."

"I get that, but she's spiraling now. She'll kill herself at this rate if she doesn't get it together."

"Maybe the world would be better off without her."

Disappointment reared up and grabbed me by the throat. "You don't mean that."

"I do."

"You don't."

"If you're asking if I want her dead, I don't. I won't miss her when she's gone, though. She tortured my sister."

I let loose a long sigh. "Braden, I'm too tired to have this discussion right now. We were up late playing the shark game ... and then there were ghosts at the spa. I really need some sleep. Can we table this discussion until tomorrow?"

"Sure." He didn't miss a beat. "I'll bring you lunch and we'll pick it up then."

I wanted to argue with him, but weariness was quickly overtaking me. "Fine. We'll talk at lunch."

"Great." He took me by surprise when he leaned forward and pressed a kiss to my cheek. "I'll save you from the awkward walk to your door because I don't want you begging me to kiss you tonight," he whispered. "You're too tired for that."

My strength rushed back with a vengeance. "I totally want to punch you."

He chuckled as he moved to his car. "You can do that at lunch tomorrow, too."

I didn't watch him drive away. It was a point of pride to keep myself from staring. Instead, I pointed myself straight for the building and headed inside. I locked the door, being careful to set the security system before climbing the stairs. When I reached my room, the lights were off, but I saw a soft glow through the window. Briefly wondering if there were outdoor water lights I didn't know about, I moved to the window.

Standing on top of the water and spread out so they covered a huge expanse were at least twenty ghosts. They perched on top of the rippling water, all staring at the building, and they raised their hands toward me.

This time I realized they weren't beckoning for me to join them. They were begging me for help. Somehow they were trapped, and it was my job to help them ... if I could.

Sixteen

The ghosts never moved. I watched them for an hour, my fingers poised over my phone should I need to call for help. They didn't encroach on my territory, so I finally retired, leaving them to haunt the water ... and my dreams.

Ever since I was little, my dreams served as a portal of sorts. I asked my grandfather about them when I was in middle school. He said they weren't prophetic when I asked. In fact, I came home from seventh grade in a tizzy because the night before I'd dreamt that Hildie Brant had lost her ability to talk, and the next day we heard she had laryngitis and would be out of school for at least a week. I thought I caused it ... or perhaps somehow figured out it was going to happen before the fact.

My grandfather disabused me of that notion quickly. He explained that dreams were very real, and only those capable of dreamwalking could boast prophetic dreams. That didn't mean there was no meaning to my dreams, he stressed. It simply meant that I wasn't powerful enough to curse my schoolmates while slumbering.

I was disappointed, but I grew to understand why that was a good thing. Tonight was a different story. My dreams this night were convoluted ... and full of faces I was starting to grow familiar with.

"What are you doing here?" I asked Lauren when I woke in my dreams. I was on the island, near the conservatory, and she seemed to be entranced with something near the building only she could see.

"I live here now," she responded, her mouth no longer sewn shut. "I used to live over there." She pointed toward Detroit. "Now I live here."

"On the island?"

"No. *Here*." She tapped the side of my head. "I can't ever escape."

That sounded frightening. "I didn't do this to you," I offered quickly. "I mean ... this isn't because of me."

"Isn't it?" She didn't look convinced. "You're the keeper of the gate. You say who can cross over. I'm stuck here because of you."

Her response frustrated me. "That's not true." Arguing with a ghost was a waste of time, but dream logic is often suspect so even though I knew it was a bad idea I continued pressing the issue. "I didn't do this to you." I was firm. "Whatever force blew through the building the other day did this to you. It wasn't me."

"If you say so."

I folded my arms over my chest, petulant. "I mean ... why would I hurt you? I have no reason to hurt you. I didn't even know you. Plus, well, kids frighten me most of the time. Especially when there are so many of them. There's no way I'd want to kill you so that I had to watch them."

"Of course. I believe you." Lauren absently patted my arm. "Oh, look, the king is here."

"King?" I made a face and swiveled, frowning when I caught sight of Carroll. He stood next to the pond, regal in crown and cape. I was certain I'd dressed him that way in my subconscious for a reason, but I couldn't figure out why. "Well, if it isn't the jackass in chief," I said. "I'm glad you're here. I have some questions for you."

Outside, Carroll didn't glow like the other ghosts. He was shiny, almost translucent, but there was no green hue setting him off. He almost looked human ... except for his clothing and the occasional skull I saw peeking through his human suit. "What are you?" The question escaped before I thought better of it.

"I'm just a man," he replied, smiling. "That was my problem in life. I was just a man and I wanted to be more."

He looked normal again, but I couldn't forget the brief glimpse of horror I saw seconds before. "No, you're something else. You might've started out as human — or a reaper, which is close to human — but you turned into something else. I saw you in Granger's mind. You've taken up residence there, though I have no idea why."

"Perhaps the boy is making me stay."

"I seriously doubt that. You crawled into him ... or a part of you." I thought hard about what I'd seen on the video feed. "Have you been here all this time? I mean, did you die on Belle Isle? Is that where you took your last breath?"

He made a big show of sucking in oxygen. "I'm still breathing."

"No. That's not possible. You're dead."

"Am I? There are different ways to live. Some say they're living." He gestured toward the water. This time, instead of the ghosts, it was wraiths I saw standing on the water. They caused me to jolt, my heart rate to speed. "Are they living?"

"I guess they think they are," I replied, swallowing my distaste. "I'm not sure that's how I view it."

"Probably not," he agreed. "You live life by the standards you set for yourself. Or, rather, the standards your grandfather set for you. In your head, you assume that you're living the life you always wanted. Ultimately, it doesn't matter. You are who you are ... and you live how you want to live.

"They, however, cling to life because they were afraid to let it go," he continued. "I saw plenty of them during my time as a reaper. I didn't want to end up like them, but I also didn't want to die. There is no living if you don't have a soul, and yet there's no joy in dying."

"You don't know," I countered. "How do you know there's nothing on the other side? Perhaps there's joy there. Just because we're not privy to what goes on beyond the veil doesn't mean it's not a happy place."

"It's too much of a gamble."

"Is that the reason you were so desperate to stay?" I wanted an honest answer. Yes, inherently I knew that the Carroll in my dreams was a manifestation of my busy brain. That didn't mean I wasn't keen for him to break things down for me. "Was it mental illness? Was it a mixture of fear and doubt that drove you to be unbalanced? There has to be something you're not telling me."

"I can't tell you anything." His smile was serene. "You must learn for yourself if you truly want answers."

"Where? We don't know where to look. Even your family can't help us."

"Answers are closer than you think. Where does one always go when in need of information?" He waved his hand and the conservatory disappeared. In its place stood the basement, the gate shimmering to my right as he looked to his left. "The answers are here if you take the time to look for them."

I was confused as I glanced between the gate and the gaping opening that was an old library, only recently discovered. "Are you talking about books? Is the answer in books?"

"Perhaps. Or perhaps the answer is someplace else." His eyes traveled to the gate. "Either way, you will find the answers you're looking for if you simply open yourself to new possibilities."

I frowned at the gate. "I can't cross over and get answers. There's no way back."

"Are you sure?"

Actually, I wasn't. Cormack said early reapers took expeditions to the other side and none came back. These were men with wives and children, families left mourning, so it was assumed they died. I wasn't sure they simply didn't choose to stay on the other side. Perhaps it was that glorious.

Of course, I wanted to believe that for my parents' benefit. I truly had no idea what was beyond the gate.

"I guess that means you're not going to answer my questions?" I was rueful. "I can't say I'm not disappointed."

"I can't answer them." He was calm. "You must find the answers ... and it's time to get up."

"What?"

"It's time to get up." His voice was drowned out by the sound of my alarm and I jerked awake, rubbing my forehead as the early morning light filtered through the window.

"Well, that was weird," I muttered.

"Definitely," he echoed in my head. "Get up. Your answers await."

OLIVER WAS ALREADY AT HIS COMPUTER station when I entered the gate room an hour later. I was feeling sluggish, fresh coffee and a banana clutched in hand, and I couldn't muster a smile when he greeted me with an arched eyebrow.

"What?"

"I didn't say anything." He shifted in his chair and watched as I sat. "Are you feeling okay? You look a little pale."

"I had a long night."

"Braden?"

I wanted to slap the smug smile off his face. "No. Braden dropped me off around nine. Nothing happened. I wish you would let that go."

"I'll let it go when you admit you like him."

"Well, then you'll be waiting for a long time."

"I very much doubt that." His eyes never left my face. "Seriously, are you okay? You look as if you're about to boot."

Confused, I glanced at my feet. "Boot what? Do you mean kick someone? I don't have the energy for that ... at least not yet."

He chuckled loudly. "That's not what I was referring to. If you feel the need to kick someone, I would like to point you elsewhere. I simply meant that you look sick to your stomach."

"Oh, boot. You mean like throw up."

"I do, although I'm not a fan of talking about it."

That made two of us. "I don't think I'm going to throw up, although my stomach is a little iffy. I had the weirdest dream last night, and that's after all the ghosts lined up on the water to beg me to help them."

Oliver's body was stiff as he swiveled and faced me head on. "Excuse me?"

I told him about the previous night, leaving nothing out — except some of the flirting Braden and I had shared, because that was opening a topic I didn't want to deal with — and when I was finished he was thoughtful.

"Do you think it was really him?"

"In my dreams? No. I think it was me trying to work out all the crap in my head. I don't get the ghosts. I mean ... they shouldn't be here. I don't understand why they are. Why did Lauren drop dead on the aquarium floor without a soul? I mean ... her soul was already gone. I should've realized that at the time, but I was in such shock I didn't think about it."

"I didn't think about it either," Oliver admitted. "It's not our job to absorb souls, so I can see why we overlooked what should've been obvious. Still, ... tell me about Ryan Carroll. What have you learned about him?"

"Not much. He was an enigma. I'm pretty sure he was mentally ill. From what his drunken great-granddaughter told me, he abandoned his family and was paranoid people wanted to kill him. He was terrified of death and wanted to fight it off."

"Most people in that situation become wraiths."

"They do, but Carroll was a reaper. He had to know that wasn't a true life. I'm sure most of the other people who decided to become wraiths to stave off death thought for sure it would be different for them, that they would somehow be able to control things and essentially have the same life they did before.

"Carroll knew better," I continued. "He understood that he wasn't going to be able to make that work. So, if he wanted to live, he had to find another way. We know he apparently was going through books at the main office library — and not returning some, which has Cillian cursing his very existence — but I can't think of another way to extend your life that doesn't involve fracturing your soul. Can you?"

"Actually, I can. I'm a vampire, which means I will live forever unless something happens to end my life. And I still have a soul."

"Huh." I hadn't considered that. "How long have you been a vampire?"

"My whole life."

"You were bitten as a baby?"

"Not all vampires are bitten. Some are born. The stronger ones, in fact, are born. There are very few lines left, though, who manage to procreate that way."

"Why? Were they killed?"

"Some," he acknowledged. "Some simply chose not to procreate. Others still haven't decided either way about procreating. When you live forever, there's often no reason to hurry things along."

"What about you? I mean ... I know you're gay, so the basics of child creation are probably the same. You can't have a baby with another male vampire. Can't you get, like, a vampire surrogate or something?"

He snorted. "I've never really considered it. I thought I didn't like children ... until I spent some time with you back then. Even then, while I enjoyed your boundless energy, I was always happy to retreat to my home, which was quiet and devoid of toys."

"So ... no kids for you," I mused. "You bring up a good point, though. If Carroll really wanted to live forever, why not track down a vampire and make a deal? He could never become a born vampire, but a bitten one ... those vampires can live forever, too, right?"

"Yes." He nodded. "They're often mentally unstable after a few hundred years and willingly greet the sun when they get despondent, but that's still a possibility."

"But he didn't want to do it." I rubbed the back of my neck. "That means he chose another way, because I'm certain that he at least tried to enact some sort of spell. That's why this is happening. That's why the ghosts are here. The question is: Have they always been here?"

"I can't answer that, but I'm leaning toward no," Oliver replied. "I think I would've seen them if that were the case."

"So why are they here now?"

"I don't know. As for Carroll, I knew him – a little."

My stomach somersaulted. Every time I thought Oliver was done surprising me, he proved me wrong. "You're kidding. You were around back then?"

"I was. The gate has always fascinated me. I uprooted my life so I could always be in close proximity."

"Did Carroll visit often during his tenure?"

"Not at first. Back in those days, reapers almost never visited the gate. There was no reason and the office bigwigs thought it best to keep the departments separate. Still, at one point he was forced to drop something off ... and I'll never forget his face the first time he saw the gate."

"Was he entranced?"

"To say the least."

"So, what happened?"

"He started making excuses for why he had to visit more often. He would voluntarily bring us souls rather than utilizing the provided runners from the front office, say he was in the neighborhood. Each time he showed up, he spent hours simply staring at the gate. I thought perhaps he saw something that the rest of us couldn't, but then I realized that wasn't why he stared. He only saw possibilities.

"After that, he started making noise about the library," he continued. "He spent a lot of time researching things in there. You should know that library was the main library for a long time. It was only after it was closed that the big library, the one you know now, took center stage."

I was confused. "Why did they close the library here?" The hole from the library, which had only been rediscovered weeks before, remained. I hadn't heard what was going to happen to the space and I'd almost managed to push it out of my mind.

"I wasn't in on the decision-making about the library," Oliver answered, averting his gaze.

"But you know, don't you?"

"I have my suspicions. That's not the same as knowing."

"Yeah, well ... I want to know. Did it have something to do with Carroll?"

"It had something to do with the gatekeeper at the time," he clarified. "Peter Washington. That was his name. He was the amiable sort, although a little goofy if you spent too much time talking to him. I thought he had the perfect personality to serve as gatekeeper ... until he started spending a lot of time with Carroll."

Ah, we were finally getting somewhere. "Did they hatch a plan together? Did they decide to cast a spell so they could live forever?"

"I don't know. I was only part-time back then. I spent twenty hours a week at the gate and another twenty at the conservatory. In those days, the conservatory was the big draw on the island. It's fallen into some disarray since, especially because a lot of the more popular flowers that were kept inside were wiped out by a weird fungus years ago."

"No offense, but I don't really care about fungus right now," I said. "I care about Washington and Carroll. You said they became friends and that somehow that led to the library closing. I need to know how ... and why."

"All I know is that they had a big fight ... and then Peter disappeared. Carroll was banned from the property weeks before the big blowout, but he refused to stay away. He was caught trespassing one evening. I was not here and don't know the specifics. Two days later, the library was walled off and we were instructed to never ask about it again."

Oh, well, that was weird. "That can't be right."

"And yet that's what happened."

"There has to be more."

"I have nothing to give you. If you want answers, you'll have to climb the reaper food chain or find them someplace else. I honestly can't help you."

Well, that was a bummer.

Seventeen

I'd almost forgotten Braden promised he was going to show up for lunch ... until Aidan appeared with takeout.

"I don't understand." I glanced around, searching the spot over his shoulder for his mischievous older brother. "Not that I'm not happy to see you or anything, but what are you doing here?"

Aidan's smile was enigmatic. "Braden got called away on a job. He was angry, fought really hard to force one of us to do it, but he lost. As payback, he made me agree to bring you lunch."

The explanation did little to ease my confusion. "I still don't understand." When I opened the bag he handed me, a heavenly scent wafted through the room. "Gumbo," I said on an exhale, my mouth instantly watering. "Where did he get gumbo?"

"There's a place in Macomb County," Aidan replied, his lips twitching as he watched me. "He made me drive out of my way to pick it up for you."

"Oh, well ... ." I had no idea what to say. Despite my best efforts, my heart was melting.

"There's a note inside, too," Aidan offered helpfully, slanting his eyes to the left at the sound of a noise and frowning when he realized

Jerry, who he had brought with him, was trying to climb over the caution tape to check out the library. "What are you doing?"

"There's a room over here," Jerry replied simply.

"I know there's a room over there. It's the library I was telling you about."

"I want to see it."

"I don't think you're supposed to see it. They haven't decided what they're going to do with it yet."

"I still want to see it." Jerry wasn't the type to be dissuaded — he had a lot of natural energy — and he disappeared behind the hanging plastic curtain at the back of the room. "Oh, it's dirty."

Aidan shook his head and shot me an embarrassed smile. "I'm sorry. He's enthusiastic about stuff."

I waved off the apology and dug in the bag. "It's fine. As far as I can tell, there's nothing that can hurt him over there. Although ... I did just learn that Carroll was one of the reasons the library was closed, so there could be a ghost or two hanging around I don't know about."

Aidan was taken aback. "What?"

I jerked a thumb toward Oliver, who was steadfastly studying his computer screen as names of the recently departed scrolled by and he marked them off a list. "He was here back in the day. He knew Ryan Carroll a little. I just found this out."

"Interesting." Aidan rested his hip on the corner of the desk and smiled. "Don't forget the note. He agonized over writing it for a full ten minutes."

My cheeks burned as Oliver's gaze slowly slid to me. I pretended I didn't notice I was suddenly the focal point in the room and rummaged in the bag until I came up with a small notecard. The message inside was simple, and it was egotistic enough to make me laugh out loud.

"What does it say?" Aidan asked, curiosity etching its way across his handsome face. "He wouldn't tell me."

"It's nothing." I moved to tuck the card away, but Aidan snagged it before I could.

"Sorry, but it's the little brother's prerogative to torture an older brother." He furrowed his brow when he read the lone line aloud.

"'You're definitely going to ask me.'" His lavender eyes flicked to me. "What does that mean?"

I shrugged and grabbed back the card. Sentimentality ruled when I tucked it in my pocket, although I was starting to get beyond the point of caring. "It's a private joke."

Oliver snorted, which I pretended I didn't hear, as I focused on opening the gumbo container. It obviously wasn't authentic — nothing can match New Orleans gumbo, after all — but whoever made it put in a good effort; it was the closest thing to home I'd managed to smell since landing in Michigan.

"This was really sweet of him," I admitted after a beat. I was mostly talking to myself, but I said the words out loud. "I can't believe he thought to do this."

"You're telling me." Aidan was blasé. "Braden was always the brother I could count on to be self-absorbed. If he's starting to care about others more than himself, that means I'll have to start paying more attention to the things he says."

As far as I could tell, the Grimlocks were all about big boasts and bravado. I had no doubt Aidan loved all his siblings, including Braden, but he felt exposed on his brother's behalf having to be the one to deliver the gumbo. He wanted to make sure things didn't get too poignant on his watch. I didn't blame him.

"Don't worry. Braden's secret is safe with me." I slipped the provided spoon into the gumbo and carefully tested it, grinning at the strong roux flavor that assailed my senses. "It's good. It's not perfect — maybe I will make some authentic gumbo for you guys one day — but it's pretty good."

Aidan grinned. "Yeah, well ... apparently my brother knows the way to your heart."

I stilled. "Oh, well ... ."

"Don't get all weird," Aidan admonished, straightening. "I was just making an observation. There's nothing wrong with it. Obviously you and Braden have been spending a lot of time together."

"A great deal of time," Oliver agreed, his lips curving. "I believe she spent the night at his house the other evening."

"Oh, I already knew that," Aidan said. "We were all there. Braden still lives with my father, and because the baby has been a screaming wreck, Aisling and Griffin have essentially moved in for the short haul so they can have help at the ready. My father is tickled they're there. If he could find a way to get them to move in full time, he would totally ignore the perverted things he believes Griffin says to my sister on a daily basis and spoil Lily rotten."

"Wait ... Braden still lives with his father?" Oliver appeared troubled at the news and his opinion was obvious when he glanced at me. "I take it back. Perhaps you should start looking elsewhere for a paramour."

"It's fine." I continued eating as I talked, not caring in the least that it might be considered rude. "Cormack has a freaking castle — no, I'm not joking, it's huge — and Redmond lives there, too. They're like roommates with servants."

"It's honestly fine," Aidan offered. "I lived there until I moved in with Jerry about a year and a half ago. Cillian has been out for only a few months. He actually tried to move Maya in because it would save them both money — and he loves my father's library — but Maya wanted a place closer to the hospital. They still spend nights there all the time when Maya isn't on call."

"And now your sister, her husband and a baby have moved in." Oliver's distaste was obvious. "How very *Brady Bunch* of you."

Aidan snickered. "We're co-dependent. There's no getting around that." He craned his head as he stared at the opening Jerry disappeared through. "You're sure there's nothing he can hurt himself with back there?"

"I don't see how," I replied. "It's just dusty old books."

"And it was closed off because of Carroll?" Aidan met Oliver's even gaze. "Why?"

"I don't know. There were rumors ... but I can't answer that question no matter how many different people ask me. Even back then Carroll had a terrible reputation."

"Meaning?"

"People knew he was trying to find a way to extend his life. His paranoia was legendary. People had started whispering about the way he was hanging around the gate in his spare time, to the detriment of his family. He was a womanizer who stopped worrying about women and focused on the hereafter. He was considered a bit of a loon, if you want to know the truth."

"We've already heard the loon stories," I acknowledged. "Braden and I ran into Angelina last night at the bar. She said that she barely knew him and that his claim to fame was essentially rampant paranoia. It sounds to me like he was mentally ill.

"That said, he apparently made friends with one of the former gatekeepers," I continued. "They spent a lot of time here, in the library, and the gatekeeper disappeared at some point."

"Was this before or after Carroll disappeared?" Aidan asked.

"Before."

"And they spent a lot of time in the library?" Aidan's expression was hard to read when he turned back in that direction. "Have you spent much time in there since it was opened?"

I shook my head. "I mean ... I did in the initial days. I was there with Cillian. We were trying to figure out what was going on with the books, and that idiot Edgar was going on and on about them being in ancient Sumerian, which Cillian denied. After the big event, I didn't see a reason to go in there. I've been waiting for word from the home office to see what they were going to do with the space."

"Well, there's no time like the present to look around," he suggested. "I mean ... I'll have to pry Jerry out of there with a crowbar as it is. Perhaps we should take another look around."

Oliver nodded when I looked to him for an opinion. "It couldn't hurt. I didn't get a chance to really look around when it first opened because I didn't want to tangle with the reaper council members. It's empty now. We might find answers to questions we didn't even know to ask."

I was definitely open for answers. "Why not? It can't hurt."

JERRY WAS HAPPY TO LOSE himself in the library for a few hours. He wasn't thrilled with the grime — apparently he was deathly allergic to dust but was willing to take one for the team if he thought he could help — but the books themselves were a big draw and he couldn't stop himself from "oohing" and "aahing" over the old illustrations as he worked next to Oliver.

"These are great," he announced, holding up a book so I could see what looked to be a charcoal drawing of a naked man with a bull head perched on his shoulders. "I wonder if all bull men are hung like this." He turned the book sideways so he could look from a different angle.

"It's a Minotaur," I corrected absently, a much larger book resting on my lap as I sat on the floor with my back to one of the shelves. "In mythical times the Minotaur lived in the center of a labyrinth."

"Like the movie?" Jerry looked intrigued.

"Not quite like the movie."

"That's a bummer. David Bowie had the best outfits in that. I would totally live in a labyrinth if it was like the movie."

Aidan chuckled as he tapped away at his tablet. He'd given up looking at books and was instead communicating with his father in an effort to find out more information about the previous gatekeeper. "You would look good in those outfits."

"Who wouldn't?" Jerry slid his eyes to Oliver. "Are you a reaper?"

"I work for the reapers," Oliver replied. "I am not technically a reaper."

"I thought you had to be a reaper to work here."

Oliver glanced at me, his expression troubled. "Well ... ." It was obvious he didn't want to come out as a vampire to Jerry, who had missed the previous excitement. The Grimlocks accepted his true nature without asking questions. Heck, for all I knew, they already knew he was a vampire ... something I hadn't considered when I discovered the news weeks before. The fact that he didn't want to spread the information was understandable. Jerry, while sweet and fun, had an absolutely huge mouth. I was surprised he hadn't blabbed the Grimlocks' secrets starting in kindergarten.

"Not always," I interjected quickly. "Oliver doesn't collect souls. He only helps transport them. He doesn't have to be a reaper for that."

"Oh. I guess that makes sense."

Oliver sent me a gracious look of thanks. "I hear you two are getting married." He smoothly changed the subject. "You must be excited. When is the big day?"

"Two months," Aidan replied, his eyes never leaving the tablet. "I can't wait for it to be over with."

Jerry growled, his eyes flashing. "I think you mean you can't wait to marry me."

"That's what I said," Aidan supplied, shifting to face me. "My father says that Peter Washington was before his time. He doesn't know much about him, but he's going to contact Renley to see if he can find any good information."

Renley Hatfield headed the Michigan reaper office. He was the only person higher in the food chain than Cormack.

"Do you think he'll help?" I'd met the man once and hadn't been impressed. I was much happier dealing with Cormack.

"I don't know." Aidan shrugged. "I'm just now realizing how woefully inadequate our records are when it comes to former reapers and gatekeepers. Maybe Dad will have more luck tracking down information on Washington than he did with Carroll."

"I still don't understand that," I admitted. "Do you think information on Carroll was lacking because he wasn't from a reaping family?"

Aidan's face was blank. "What do you mean?"

"Your family is clearly a dynasty. Your father is a reaper. All his children are reapers. It sounds like his father was a reaper. Does it go back longer than that?"

Aidan nodded. "Yeah. It goes back seven generations."

"See. That's exactly what I'm talking about. Carroll was a lone wolf in reaping circles. I'm not even sure how that happens."

Aidan slowly got to his feet, his expression hard to read. "You know what? You have a very good point. How did Carroll get into the reaping business in the first place? I mean ... it's a secret world," he continued, his mind clearly busy. "We're not allowed to share our business with outsiders. How did he find out?"

Jerry said, "I'm not a reaper and I know what you do."

"Only because Aisling told you when we were kids."

"I think I would've found out between then and now anyway," Jerry said dryly. "I'm smarter than I look."

"You're a genius," Aidan automatically responded. "You're also a family friend. There was a time my parents treated you like their sixth child."

"Your father still does in some respects."

"He does," Aidan agreed. "Carroll is different. Izzy nailed it. He's a lone wolf who managed to worm his way into the reaping world. How did he make that happen?"

"That's definitely something we need to know," Oliver agreed soberly. "We also need to know what happened to Washington. My recollection of the event is that he simply disappeared. I know there was an investigation, but back then I kept my nose to the grindstone and didn't intervene. I was too nervous to ask the questions I would readily ask now."

"Back then?" Jerry wrinkled his nose. "Wait ... what do you mean?"

I exchanged a quick look with Aidan, who seemed to realize we were treading in dangerous waters and a shark was circling. "It's a figure of speech," he said hurriedly, getting to his feet. "Come on, Jerry. I think I know where to go to ask a few questions. I need to drop you at home before heading there. Only people with certain credentials are allowed inside."

"What are you talking about?" I was officially intrigued. "Should I go with you?"

"I don't know that you have the proper credentials." Aidan was sheepish. "Besides, it might be a dead end. I'll let you know later this afternoon after I do some digging. Come on, Jerry, we need to go."

"I don't want to go," Jerry protested. "I'm having fun hanging out with Izzy and Ollie. Why can't I just stay here? You can pick me up on your way back."

Aidan showed infinite patience when he answered. "I'm pretty sure that they don't want you here. They have work to do."

"And don't call me Ollie," Oliver said darkly.

Jerry made a dismissive motion with his hand. "The name fits you. In fact, you should get monogrammed shirts made up. People would fall all over you."

"I don't want people to fall all over me." Oliver's brow furrowed. "Seriously, why would I want people falling all over me?"

"It's awesome," Jerry replied. "I love being the center of attention."

"I never would've guessed."

I bit back a laugh as I latched gazes with Aidan. The idea of playing witness to the Jerry and Ollie show over the course of the afternoon held some appeal. It would surely chase away the doldrums.

"He's more than welcome to stay," I offered, avoiding the hateful glare Oliver shot in my direction. That would teach him to withhold information from me. "You can pick him up on your way back. He can help us with research."

"I'm awesome at research," Jerry agreed. "Although ... do you have a vacuum? This room could use a real spruce before we delve into research. Maybe I could clean while you guys research. I'm a big fan of multi-tasking."

I avoided Oliver's pointed glare and enthusiastically nodded. "That sounds like a great idea. We should totally do that."

Eighteen

Following an afternoon with Jerry, I understood why the Grimlocks loved him beyond reason. He was fun, said wacky things without giving much thought to how they might be taken, and completely ran me ragged. I felt as if I needed a nap once he'd finished cleaning ... and I was never one for taking naps.

"Isn't this much better?" he asked as he pulled out a dust cloth — I had no idea where he'd found the rag — and started attacking the shelves. "A clean workspace is a pleasant workspace."

"Yes, it's delightful," Oliver muttered around a sneeze. He'd shot me so many dirty looks the past few hours I couldn't remember what his normal face looked like. "I can't tell you how much our afternoon has been enriched thanks to your presence."

If Jerry picked up on the sarcasm he didn't show it. Instead, he moved to the next shelf and continued wiping at dust that was likely older than him. "You live on the island, right?"

I wasn't sure if he was talking to me or Oliver, but I nodded. "Yeah. I live in the boathouse. I have the entire second floor as an apartment. Er, well, mostly. There's some storage up there."

"The boathouse used to be a place for actual boats," Jerry offered. "A lot of people have weddings here. I considered it for my wedding, in fact, but then we decided to have the ceremony in the backyard at Grimlock Manor instead. If the weather doesn't cooperate, we'll go inside."

"You don't want a church wedding?"

"The family church doesn't condone same-sex ceremonies."

I stilled, annoyance creeping over me when I realized how insensitive the remark had been. "I'm sorry. I didn't even think about that. I ... that's awful."

He shrugged, seemingly unbothered. "I'm used to it. Cormack has been great, going above and beyond trying to bend wills in that arena. He even offered to give a big donation to the church ... but I didn't want that."

"Why?" Oliver asked, his eyes keen on Jerry's face. It was the first time the gregarious man had been solemn since he arrived. "If he's willing to help ... ."

"That's just it. I think the church elders should want to do it. If they don't, well, then they're missing out. I can't make them see things from my perspective, and I'll never see things from their perspective. It's kind of like we're at a stalemate."

"That is depressing." I meant it. "In New Orleans we have a lot of Catholic churches. That's essentially the primary religion."

"I thought the primary religion was voodoo." Jerry was serious as he stopped dusting. "I swear I saw that on television."

"Well, then it must be true," Oliver deadpanned.

I shushed him with a look and kept talking. "I believe kind of like you do. If a church doesn't want to perform the ceremony, I don't see the point in forcing it. People should want to celebrate love, and you and Aidan clearly love each other."

"Yeah." Jerry remained quiet for a beat and then shook himself, as if to dislodge the melancholy. "I'm going to torture Aisling until the end of time for not being my best person. We promised to do this for each other as kids and she's totally backing out. I don't like it ... and this is after I was her best person."

I felt bad for him. "Maybe if you explain how you feel she'll change her mind."

"She won't change her mind," Oliver interjected, taking me by surprise with his participation in a conversation that obviously bored him. "She's stuck. She promised to stand as your matron of honor — or groomswoman, however you want to refer to her — but I think her brother wants her to stand with him. They are twins, right?"

"Yeah, but ... we're best friends."

"I get that, but she's the one in the tight spot. May I ask who stood up for her during her wedding?"

"I did," Jerry snapped. "I just told you that."

"You did, but were you the only one?"

"Well ... no." His expression was measured as he looked back at a ceremony only nine months in the past. "I guess they kind of had a communal wedding party now that I think about it. Maya had a nice dress, but she stood on Griffin's side as his best person. I was on Aisling's side."

"And all her brothers?"

"Well, they just kind of split up between both of them. Aidan was definitely on Aisling's side. I ... hmm." Jerry was lost in thought. "Maybe I need to talk to Aisling again."

"I think that would be a good idea," I said, biting back a laugh as I flipped open another book. "I don't think she's trying to slight you."

"Definitely not," Oliver agreed. "She wants to do right by both of you. It probably won't be easy for her no matter what you decide."

"I guess." Jerry turned whimsical. "She still has to throw me the bachelor party to end all bachelor parties."

"I think we're all looking forward to that," I muttered, furrowing my brow. "I think I found something."

Slowly, Oliver turned his face to me. "Are you just saying that to change the subject?"

"No." I shook my head. "I'm serious. This is a journal ... and the name on the first page is Peter Washington. That's our missing gatekeeper."

Oliver arched an eyebrow. "Well, that *is* interesting. Hold on." He tipped the portable lantern we'd brought with us so he could better read the journal. The library had natural light from some windows, but the electricity in the room was long dead and if the home office wanted to start utilizing the space it would require an upgrade. "Hmm. It's been a long time, but that looks like Peter's writing."

"Does it say anything good?" Jerry abandoned his dusting project and joined me on the floor. It was much cleaner after he'd vacuumed, forcing us to move several times to make sure he attacked all the grime equally.

"It seems to be a diary of sorts," I mused. "Like ... a teenager's diary. It's basically a record of his everyday activities."

"Turn to the back," Oliver suggested.

I did, knitting my eyebrows as I struggled to read his handwriting. It looked to be much shakier than the earlier pages. "'I need to get out of here,'" I read aloud. "'I thought we were on to something, that we'd come up with a proper solution to our problem. Now I realize he doesn't want to solve the problem. Things can't go on like they have been. If he won't change his mind, I will have to go to the front office. They will definitely change his mind.'"

Oliver pursed his lips. "Do you think he's talking about Carroll?"

"That would be my assumption. That could be wishful thinking, though."

"Is there anything else that describes what they were doing?"

I flipped a few pages earlier in the journal and shook my head. "I don't see any specifics. I need to sit down with this thing and read it cover to cover." I glanced at my phone screen to check the time and frowned. "It's almost six. I thought Aidan was coming back for you, Jerry."

"Oh, he texted two hours ago," Jerry replied. He was back to dusting, seemingly over the discovery of the journal. "I told him we were still having fun and you volunteered to take me home."

"You did?" Oliver's shoulders shook with silent laughter, and now it was my turn to glare. "Don't you think you should've asked me if I wanted to take you?"

"Why wouldn't you? I've been cleaning your workspace all day. It's the least you can do."

"Yeah, but ... I don't have a car."

"What?" Jerry was absolutely flabbergasted. "How can you not have a car?"

"I didn't need one in New Orleans. Everything I cared about was within walking distance ... or streetcar distance."

"Well, you're in the Motor City now." He was matter-of-fact. "I guess we'll have to Uber."

"We have to Uber? You're the one who lost your ride."

"I can't Uber alone. It's not safe."

"And what happens when I have to Uber back? Are you going to come back with me then?"

"Don't be silly. Braden will take you."

That sounded like a bad idea. "Listen ... ."

"No, you listen. There's prime rib tonight ... and prime rib is my favorite night at Grimlock Manor. It's the only night I let myself eat complex carbohydrates and fat."

I didn't believe that for a second. I'd seen him eat his weight in cake, and it most certainly wasn't on prime rib night. "But ... ."

"We're going." Jerry was firm. "You can bring the journal and show it to Cormack. He'll want to see it. He might be able to pick out details you're not familiar with."

Loath as I was to admit it, he had a point. "Fine," I snapped, letting my anger out to play. I wanted him to understand how agitated I was with his actions. "I'll take you to Grimlock Manor. This won't happen again, though."

Instead of nodding, or perhaps offering an apology, he grinned and patted my shoulder. "You're funny. If you weren't ready to do the mattress mambo with Braden I'd think you were separated from the family at birth."

"There will be no talk of the mattress mambo."

"I can get behind that. You're clearly a funky monkey girl. I will adjust my vocabulary accordingly."

"Oh, geez!" I slapped my hand to my forehead and glared at Oliver, who was suddenly having the time of his life. "This isn't funny."

"He's really starting to grow on me."

"Of course he is. You're not the target of his overactive imagination."

. . .

GRIMLOCK MANOR WAS BUZZING with activity. Redmond and Aidan were sliding across the foyer floor in socks, getting a running start and having a grand time as they skidded into the twin stairwells that bookended each side.

"What are you doing?" I asked, stepping around Redmond so he didn't accidentally plow into me.

"Sock hockey," Jerry volunteered, kicking off his shoes on the front mat and taking a small slide of his own. "It's the Grimlock family's official sport."

"Sock hockey?" I arched a dubious eyebrow. "Do I even want to know?"

"You'll get used to it." Jerry headed straight for Aidan and gave him a hug.

"You seem in a good mood." Aidan beamed at him. "I take it you had a good time helping Oliver and Izzy conduct research."

"Ollie."

Aidan's forehead wrinkled. "Did he okay that nickname? He doesn't strike me as the sort who would be okay with that."

There was the understatement of the year. "He's not exactly happy with it," I offered.

"I can see that. Well ... luckily Jerry won't be hanging around the gate very often." Aidan's expression brightened as Redmond lightly hip-checked his fiancé into the stair railing. "Thanks for volunteering to bring Jerry back. That was nice of you."

I stilled. "What?"

"Volunteering," Aidan replied, seemingly unaware of the change in my demeanor. "It was actually a big help because I was at the main office much longer than I'd planned. It turned out I had to put in a formal request to get a full file on Washington. I did — and they warned it might take a few days — but I followed protocol. I think they should just hand over the files we need, but they like their bureaucracy."

"Uh-huh." Annoyance, bitter and rough, returned with a vengeance as Jerry made his way over to us.

"What's going on?" he asked, laughing as Aidan slid their feet together. "Other than everyone enjoying the freshly-waxed floor, that is."

"Aidan was just thanking me for volunteering to bring you here," I replied pointedly. "He was very grateful."

"Isn't she a peach?" Jerry cooed without missing a beat.

I wanted to grab his arm and shake him. I understood exactly what he was doing, and I didn't like it. "Yes, I'm a peach. Hey, speaking of peaches, do you want to go with me to the kitchen and look at the fruit? I'm starving."

"I'm good." Jerry refused to make eye contact. "It's prime rib night. You'll want to save as much room as possible."

"Yes, but ... ." I didn't get a chance to finish because Aisling picked that moment to stroll into the room. She looked markedly better, as if having two nights in a row of solid sleep had allowed her to return to the person she was meant to be. Her long black hair was back to being lustrous and there was a sparkle in her eyes.

She also had a baby in her arms, which didn't seem like a good idea given the men sliding across the floor.

"How are things?" Aisling beamed as she bounced Lily, who looked almost happy as her eyes moved from uncle to uncle. She clearly didn't understand what was happening, but she liked the movement. There were practically happy thought bubbles floating over her head.

"They're fine." I forced myself to shove Jerry's machinations out of my head and focus on the good things in life. Aisling's rebound was one of those good things. "How are you?"

"Better. Lily only cried a few times today, and she stopped whenever we fed her ... or changed her diaper ... or made Cillian stop singing."

"I heard that." The long-haired Grimlock brother smoothly slid into the room, slamming his shoulder into Aidan as he chewed up the distance between the parlor and front door. "The floor feels pretty good. I think we need to put together a game."

I was still behind when it came to what game they thought they were playing. "I don't think beating up your brothers while sliding across the floor in socks is a real game."

"You just haven't played with us yet," he admonished. "Sock hockey is the best game ever."

"Your sister is standing in the middle of what could be a huge mess, holding your infant niece," I pointed out. "That's not safe."

"Oh, you're a rule follower." Cillian chuckled as Braden made his way into the room. Instantly our eyes met and I felt warmth creeping through my chest. The look he shot me was flirty, which only served to make me angrier with Jerry's manipulative effort.

"Hey." I felt awkward greeting him. "I ... um ... wasn't sure you were here." I shoved my hands in my pockets and wished I'd forced Jerry into an Uber alone so I wouldn't have to feel like such a dolt.

"It's prime rib night," Braden explained. "I would never miss prime rib night."

"Yeah, um, speaking of food ... thanks a lot for the gumbo. It was really good. I almost cried it was so good. You'll have to tell me where that place is."

"I'll take you there."

He was getting harder and harder to resist, something I believe he recognized, because his eyes crinkled at the corners and told me that he was fighting off a smirk.

"Um ... I guess we'll see." I felt like an absolute idiot, which meant I needed to change the subject. "You guys really shouldn't be doing that with a baby in the room," I admonished as Cillian and Redmond barreled into each other at full force. "Seriously. You could kill that baby."

"Wow. Who knew you were such a worrier?" Redmond teased as he zipped behind his sister, slowing enough to grin at Lily over Aisling's shoulder. "She does have a point, though. If Lily is going to play, we need to come up with specific rules."

I was horrified. "Lily can't play. She can't even hold up her own head."

Redmond ignored me. "What if we make the person who is holding Lily untouchable? He or she can score, but no one can check that individual into the boards. Possession of Lily changes when someone not magically imbued with untouchable status manages to score."

He couldn't be serious. "You cannot keep that baby out here. I just

... no!" I knew I sounded shrill, but I couldn't help myself. I hadn't toiled for hours to make a salve so she would stop crying and bond with her family just so they could risk banging her head into a wall. "I am putting my foot down."

"Oh, she's putting her foot down," Cillian teased. "That's kind of cute."

"It's totally cute," Braden agreed, smirking as his father joined the fray. "Izzy is very upset that we're going to use Lily as a 'no-hitting' totem in our match, Dad. How do you feel about the subject?"

Finally someone was going to take my side.

"I feel we should wrap a towel around her head just to be on the safe side," Cormack offered, grinning at the baby as her serious gaze found him. "That way there won't be any accidents." He cooed the last line in baby talk. "Isn't that right? We don't want her brains to fall out."

I felt as if I was talking to seven different walls ... and they were all moving and hip-checking one another. "I don't get this family," I lamented.

"You will," Griffin offered, coming in from the opposite side of the room and swooping toward Lily. "They're not nearly as complicated as they pretend to be." He claimed the infant from her mother and then cast a stern look toward the Grimlock boys. "Light contact with Aisling only. She's only two weeks out from giving birth. If you hurt her, I'll hurt you."

Redmond offered him a saucy salute as Griffin trundled toward the parlor with the baby. "Yes, sir. We'll treat her as if she's one of our own."

"She is one of your own."

"Then we'll own up to that," Braden offered, lifting his chin in defiance as he faced off with Redmond. "Let's pick teams. I'll take Izzy. She'll be a detriment because she doesn't understand the game. You take Aisling. She has to go slow because of her lady parts problem."

Aisling was incensed. "I don't have a lady parts problem!"

"And I'm not a detriment," I added. "You're playing a game in your socks. How hard can it possibly be?"

Braden's eyes lit with mirth. "Ah, famous last words. Let the games begin."

Nineteen

Sock hockey was strangely invigorating.

Even when we finished — Redmond's team claiming victory despite fervent protests from Braden — I wasn't sure about the scoring rules. As far as I could tell, the only rule that seemed to stick was that you got five points for checking a sibling into a wall ... or a statue ... or into the stairwell railing. You got extra points if that sibling started bleeding. And if you managed to kick a sock into a net at the end of the room, you got a shot of something that made you warm all over.

Jerry didn't play, which I found interesting. He stood on the sidelines and cheered for Aisling and Aidan, who were on different teams. If either was offended by his divided allegiance, they didn't show it.

And, despite a lot of big talk, Aisling's brothers were ridiculously gentle with her. They simply didn't make it obvious. They slammed into her with alarming frequency, though they often pulled back at the last second and made sure she was kept far from any sharp edges.

By the time Cormack called for dinner, everyone was sweaty and Braden and Redmond were throwing so many sports euphemisms at one another I'd lost count.

"I still don't understand why anyone won," I admitted as I followed Aisling into the parlor, swiping my forehead with the back of my hand.

"It's not about the ending," she explained. "It's about the journey." She stopped next to Griffin and Lily, the baby quietly snoozing in a small basket with handles.

"What's that?" I asked, curious.

"They're carrying her around like a dog," Redmond replied, strolling into the room. He snagged a bottle of whiskey from the drink cart and started pouring the amber liquid into glasses as Cillian added ice. "By the way, we all have to toast the legend of the sock monster after playing sock hockey. It's a family tradition."

That sounded like a lot of nonsense. "I don't drink whiskey."

Redmond looked horrified. "What do you drink?"

"I prefer absinthe, although I'll drink the occasional glass of wine, or sometimes vodka."

"Ugh." Redmond screwed up his face. "I think we finally found your flaw. I would rethink your crush on her, Braden. You can't trust a woman who doesn't drink whiskey."

A quick glance at Braden told me his cheeks were burning, but he didn't challenge his brother. Instead he merely accepted the glass Cillian passed him and raised it above his head. "May the sock monster be forever sated."

Suspicious, I glanced around the room. Redmond, Cillian and Aidan all saluted in time with Braden. Aisling was focused on the baby in the basket. Jerry was busy flipping through a wedding magazine. Cormack was reading the journal I'd brought from the library. Those paying attention seemed to be sincere ... which made me doubly sure they were messing with my mind.

"I'm not saluting a sock monster," I said finally. "You guys like to screw with people. I get it. I draw the line at a sock monster."

"You might not say that when you have no matching socks in the morning," Braden teased, his attention drifting to Aisling when she smoothed the ruffles that surrounded the basket. "Seriously, that's like a pet carrier. I can't believe you're transporting my niece from room to room in a pet carrier."

Aisling was haughty. "Do you have any other suggestions?"

"Why don't we just put a bassinet in every room?" Redmond challenged. "I mean ... she's tiny. We can carry her around and then have handy bassinets when we need them."

"First, she's only in a bassinet for about three months," Aisling countered. "Once she starts rolling around, she'll need to be in a crib."

"So?"

"So, bassinets are expensive."

"Make Dad buy them." Redmond flashed his father a friendly wink when Cormack tore his eyes from the magazine. "You'll do that for your only grandchild, right? I mean ... it is what's best for her."

"I don't even know what you're talking about," Cormack admitted. "What's the problem?"

"Aisling is carrying your only granddaughter around in a pet carrier," Aidan supplied. "Redmond is offended by it."

"I'm offended by it, too," Braden admitted. "Next thing you know, the kid will be wearing a collar and barking instead of talking. Although ... if she has her mother's mouth, which seems to be a given, we might prefer barking. We always did want a family pet."

Aisling murdered Braden with a hostile glare. "I'll show you how to bark," she muttered, starting in his direction. Griffin grabbed her hand to tug her back before things could get out of hand, whispering something only she could hear and eliciting a small smile from her.

"I don't know what you just said to her, but I take offense to that remark," Braden said. "Seriously, though, a pet carrier sends the wrong message."

"It's not a pet carrier," Griffin countered. "It's a portable bassinet, and it allows us to carry her between the townhouse and here without making things difficult for her. Isn't that the most important thing?" He looked to Jerry for backup.

"Oh, I can see where you'd think I would be your best bet because I am a huge fan of ruffles," Jerry said. "I mean ... it's like a giant purse, and who doesn't love a nice purse? The thing is, that's an ugly purse. I might have to side with Braden and Redmond on this one."

"Which is exactly why I'm standing with Aidan at the wedding," Aisling muttered.

"I heard that." Jerry extended a warning finger. "Do you want to start a war, missy? I'll totally fire the first cannonball if you do."

"No one is firing cannonballs," Cormack warned, lowering the journal to the table at his left. "We're going to plan this wedding like adults. I'm not dealing with nonstop arguing as we did last time."

"That was Aisling's wedding," Jerry pointed out. "She's to blame for those fights."

"Oh, please." Cormack rolled his expressive eyes. "You planned that wedding. Aisling had other things going on."

"Like being pregnant before being wed."

"Thanks, Jerry," Aisling called out. "We haven't had a good fight about that in a few months. I'm so glad you brought it up."

"That's what you get for breaking my heart, Bug."

She heaved a sigh. "I'm not trying to break your heart. It's just ... I want to be there for you and Aidan. I don't understand why that's not allowed."

"It's not allowed because this is my wedding," Jerry snapped. "I'm the center of attention for this one, which is a massive change, I know. Still, I should get what I want."

Braden snickered. "Yes, because you're never the center of attention."

"You're definitely standing with Aidan," Jerry groused, glaring at Braden. "I mean ... definitely."

"You know, Jerry, it's my wedding, too." Aidan appeared to be choosing his words carefully as he downed his whiskey. "Why don't I have any say in how things go?"

"Because you're the groom."

"And?"

"Well, we're both men, so I'm a groom, too. I'm also the bride. You don't want to be the bride. It's a thankless position."

"I hear that," Aisling muttered.

"Oh, please. You weren't the bride. I did all the work for you. You were basically a groom in a dress." Jerry shot her a derisive look. "I know what I want for my wedding. I've known for a very long time. If you want to be difficult about it ... well ... then maybe we'll just have the ceremony at a pizza parlor or something."

"Ooh. Chuck E. Cheese." Redmond's eyes lit with delight. "That would be awesome. We could have Skee-Ball tournaments ... and totally pants that animatronic mouse. Is that an option?"

Jerry narrowed his eyes to dangerous slits. "I'll pretend you didn't say that."

"Whatever floats your boat. Now I want pizza. Can we have pizza with the prime rib?"

Cormack sighed. "No. You're going to eat your dinner like a good boy and then go to bed. There will be no Shark Attack tonight either. I want to go through that journal and I can't if you guys are rowdy. I believe Izzy brought us an important piece of the puzzle and I want to give it the attention it deserves."

"Have you found anything yet?" I asked hopefully. All the hijinks had almost made me forget that we had a serious situation on our hands. "I mean ... we have to help those ghosts. I'm pretty sure they're desperate for us to do something to free their souls."

"Then we'll help them." Cormack sounded sure of himself. "For now, we'll eat dinner and then go from there. We'll hand Lily and her dog carrier over to the night nurse and be on our way."

Aisling scowled. "Oh, I see how it is," she groused. "Now you're on their side."

"Well, you didn't win sock hockey by an acceptable margin." Cormack grinned at her. "When you're dominating again, I'll consider taking your side."

DINNER TURNED INTO A DRINKING affair. I wasn't even sure how it happened. One minute I was sipping from a perfectly acceptable glass of wine. The next minute I was sucking down my third glass of absinthe and laughing so hard I thought I might throw it up. That's when I decided I needed to sober up.

"Give me a tour of the house," I suggested to Braden as we left the parlor. "I mean ... I've been here a few times now and seen several rooms. I've never seen all of them, though. I bet the house has a lot of secrets."

"It certainly does," Braden agreed, pointing toward a hallway that led to the back of the house. "When she was a teenager, Aisling found five secret ways to sneak out of the house that Dad didn't know. Three of them led to the garage so she could steal one of his cars along the way."

I fell into step with him, laughing at his expression. "I can't believe she stole your father's car. Did she get grounded?"

"She was always grounded. She didn't seem to care. Besides, my father would talk big when he first grounded her, say there was no way she was going to get off early, that he didn't care how much she begged and pleaded. It never failed, though. Three days later she would be free and clear and he would conveniently forget that he'd sworn up and down that he wouldn't let her off punishment early."

"I bet you guys had a great time living here," I said as I followed him to the back patio, my eyes going wide at the lovely courtyard that was completely decked out in cobblestone and a bevy of empty planters. "Wow! It looks like something big is going down back here." I pointed toward the huge pile of dirt. "Is your father having some gardening done?"

Braden nodded as he stared at the mess. "Yeah. He has a regular gardener who does the planting every spring and fall. He wanted to add something permanent this year, so they're going to start working on that in the next few weeks. They want to make sure we don't get a late freeze that ruins the plants."

"What plants?"

"Lilies."

I slowed my pace and swallowed hard. "Oh. That's ... kind of sweet. It's a memorial to your mother."

"We have that at the family mausoleum. Her body is finally there, where it should be. Her soul has been far removed for a long time."

My heart went out to him. "At least you got a chance to say goodbye the second time around."

"Not really. She was here. We saw her. Aisling got to talk to her the most. She had very limited time. Your aunt ... well, she had only so much power to give."

Not much had been said to me regarding Aunt Maxine. She was my mother's sister, a powerful Bruja in her own right. She wanted custody of me after the death of my parents, but my grandfather won and moved me to New Orleans. We remained close, talking at least once a week by phone. Now that I was in Michigan we could see each other regularly, but it had been days since we'd talked and she was behind on reaper gossip.

"I'm sure she did what she could," I hedged. "If she had the power to give your mother back completely, she would've done it."

"I know." Braden flashed a tight smile. "It's still difficult. Perhaps we shouldn't talk about Madame Maxine."

That was probably a good idea. "Tell me about the lilies. What type did you choose?"

"Oh, we picked six different kinds." Braden's smile was back. "Dad picked white because they're the standard for memorials and he likes to follow rules."

That made sense. "White lilies are gorgeous."

"They are," he agreed, bobbing his head. "Redmond picked orange because they mean respect and honor. Aidan picked pink because they mean admiration ... and that's Jerry's favorite color."

I bit the inside of my cheek to keep from laughing.

"Cillian picked red for love. Aisling picked some sort of paisley hybrid — at least that's what she called it — because she said our mother was more than one thing ... and that's okay."

The expression on his face made my heart hurt. "What did you pick?"

"I picked yellow for happiness, because no matter who came back, we were happy years ago and that's what I want to remember."

Instinctively, I reached out and grabbed his hand. "I didn't know your mother, but I think she would've liked that. It sounds like you guys are going to turn this area into a lily extravaganza, which is probably the best way to honor her."

"Yeah." He squeezed my hand and slowly turned to me. "I heard you found a journal or something."

"In the library," I acknowledged, struggling to look away from the naked emotion in his eyes. He was laid bare right now, the warmth of his body radiating over me as we stood with our chests almost touching. "I don't know why I forget about that room. It's right there all the time."

"Did you find anything interesting in it?"

"No, but I only had a few minutes to look. I got distracted by Jerry, who insisted Aidan couldn't pick him up and was too frightened to Uber by himself."

Braden arched an eyebrow. "Well ... that doesn't make much sense. He Ubers by himself all the time."

"I figured."

"Why do you think he played you like that?"

The answer was simple. "To get me here."

"Here? Because of the prime rib?"

"I think the prime rib was low on the list."

Realization dawned on his handsome features. "Oh. He wanted to force you to spend time with me." He chuckled, the sound warm and content. "In case you haven't noticed, my family has taken it upon themselves to make sure we have no choice but to mash ourselves together at every turn."

"Is that what you want?" I couldn't stop myself from asking the question. "Is that it? Do you want to have a night and then let it go?"

"No." He vehemently shook his head. "I like you. I've already told you that. It's up to you what happens next."

I wasn't sure that was true. I was beginning to wonder if I ever had a choice in what was going to happen from the second I'd met him. My heart seemed to yearn from the moment our eyes met ... and ever since it felt as if I was fighting a losing battle.

"That's not enough for me," I said. "What do you want?"

He moved closer, even though I was already struggling to find oxygen to breathe. "I can't stop thinking about you." His voice was barely a whisper. "I want to be close to you all the time. I have to stop myself from showing up on the island because I don't want to crowd you."

My mouth was dry. "How do you know I don't like being crowded?"

"I can tell." His fingers were gentle when they brushed a strand of hair behind my ear. "You're an only child. You don't get the loudness associated with this house, and yet you enjoy yourself when you're here. It's a brave new world … and you have fun.

"You know, I get that you're here for a reason," he continued, barely taking a breath. It was as if he worried I would suddenly break in and make an excuse to leave if he didn't fill the silence. "You want to find out what happened to your parents. I can help you. That doesn't mean we can't be together at the same time."

I wanted to give in.

"How do you know we're compatible?" I asked, giving myself time to overcome the fuzziness in my brain.

"How does anybody know? They date and try to figure it out."

I sighed. I so wanted to give in.

"Fine." I exhaled heavily. I was done fighting it. "Go ahead and kiss me."

His eyebrows migrated so far north they almost melded with his hairline. "That's not exactly what I had in mind. I need you to tell me you want it. That's the only way this will work. You're the one holding back."

He wasn't wrong. For the first time in a very long time, I was afraid. He recognized that about me and still he didn't back down.

I wanted to give in, and that's exactly what I did. "I want you to kiss me." I meant it with my whole heart as he leaned his head closer. "I want to try."

"Everything?" He was breathless.

"Everything."

His mouth descended on mine and we engaged in a kiss that was so sweet, so painfully loving, and completely hot at the same time that I thought steam would start shooting out of my ears. I lost my head … and probably my heart.

For the first time in my life, I allowed myself to fall. He was there to catch me.

Twenty

I was confused upon waking.

The room was dark, other than a smattering of light that shone through the window blinds. There was a warm body beside me, which seemed out of place.

Oh, there was also a hand on my butt.

I jolted to a sitting position, my mind going a million miles a second. Then, as if in slow motion, I remembered the night before and how I ended up in Braden's bed.

"Flipping frogs," I muttered, dragging a hand through my messy hair.

Braden cocked an eye and regarded me with an unreadable look.

"Aren't you freaking out?" I blurted out.

He shook his head. "No. It's not even seven yet. Go back to bed and I'll flip out in an hour if you want." He slid his hand around my waist and pulled me closer. "We don't get up with the sun in Grimlock Manor. Okay, maybe my father does. That's only because he likes the quiet before we start bugging him with inane questions and petty bickering. And, yes, he actually told us that, which is why I used those particular words."

I was dumbfounded. "I can't go back to sleep. I have to sneak out of here."

"Oh, really?" He didn't move his hand from my hip. "May I ask why you're sneaking out before the crack of dawn?"

"First, dawn has already come and gone." I inclined my chin toward the window. "You might not be an early bird, but that doesn't mean the day hasn't started without you."

He smirked. "You're cute." He pushed my hair away from my face. "By the way, you do that shifting into a Bruja thing when you get excited for more than fighting an enemy. It freaked me out the first time last night. Now I kind of like it."

I was mortified. "What? Are you saying I ... when I ... you know?"

His grin was so wide it almost swallowed his face. "Three times."

"Oh, geez!" I slapped my hand to my forehead and rolled away from him to bury my face in the pillows. "I can't believe this is happening."

Apparently agitated, Braden rolled to his back and finger-combed his hair. "I don't see why you're being so weird about this. We're both consenting adults. Unless ... did you change your mind?"

He looked so horrified at the prospect when I risked a glance in his direction I had to take pity on him. "No." I wrapped my fingers around his wrist and squeezed. "I didn't change my mind. Don't think that. Last night was ... great."

His smile was back.

"Don't get a full head," I chided. "I'm sure you can do even better than you did last night if you practiced a bit."

"Very funny." He poked my side and rolled on top of me so he could tickle my ribs unimpeded. "You're just making me want to try harder right now," he warned.

That was a very bad idea. "Stop it," I instructed, gasping when his fingers caused me to squirm. "I hate being tickled."

"Get used to it." He gave me another tickle before lifting his head and staring into my eyes. "Do you admit defeat?"

That was a weird thing to say. "I'm not one of your siblings. You don't have to win at all costs."

His eyes filled with mirth as I realized the double meaning of what I'd said.

"I mean ... you know what I mean." I lightly pinched his flank. "Not everything in life is a competition. You might've believed that before because of the way you interact with your siblings, but it's simply not true. You don't have to beat me."

He sobered. "I didn't mean it like that. I just ... well, maybe I did." He propped himself on an elbow and rubbed his stubbled chin. Oddly enough, he looked even more handsome in the milky morning light. That should've been impossible, yet he effortlessly pulled it off, which I found distracting. "Fine. I won't try to win at all costs," he said finally. "Does that make you happy?"

I shrugged. "I'm happy regardless ... although that's something we'll need to discuss later. I think I should be going. I need to call an Uber or something."

He furrowed his brow. "What do you mean? Where do you have to go? Do you need to be back at the gate?"

"Oliver is handling the gate this morning. That's not it."

"Then ... what is it?"

"This."

"This what?" He looked around, confused. "Do you not like my room? I guess it could use a spruce. You should be thankful that I finally took down all my posters of scantily-clad women from my teenage years. Things could be worse."

I shot him a withering look. "Not that ... but why you felt the need to tell me that is beyond me. I need to get out of here before your family figures out what we did last night."

Realization dawned on his face and he clamped his mouth shut, pressing his lips together as he made a face I'd never seen before.

"It's not the end of the world," I said hurriedly, resting my hand on his forearm. "I'm sure we can figure out a way to get me out of here without them knowing so you won't be subject to their teasing."

When he finally opened his mouth, it was to let loose a chuckle rather than agree with me.

"How can you think this is funny?" Annoyance came out to play as

I dragged my fingers through my hair. "Your family will know that I spent the night if you're not careful."

"So what?" He managed to stop laughing, but just barely. "What do you think they're going to do to us with this new information? Tar and feathers? The rack? Pear of Anguish? Brazen Bull?"

I had to ask the obvious question. "What is the Pear of Anguish? Actually, while you're at it, what is the Brazen Bull?"

He smirked. "You don't want to know. Let's just say I spent a lot of time as a kid looking up antiquated torture methods because my brothers and sister gave me endless headaches."

That was a horrifying thought. "You were a weird kid, huh?"

He shrugged. "I think I was a fairly normal kid. I was a sullen teenager, though."

"Who wasn't?" I continued combing my hair to smooth it as I rested my chin on his chest. He was well muscled, though not so compact he looked like a bodybuilder. His frame was long and lanky, and I couldn't help giving him an extra look now that we had natural light to lead the way. "You don't want me to sneak out so your father doesn't know what we were doing?"

Braden's lips curved with amusement. "No. My father is well aware that I've had sex."

"Yeah, but ... this is his house."

"And he's fine with overnight guests. Heck, he got so used to Griffin spending the night when he was dating Aisling that he started stocking the refrigerator with his favorite midnight snacks."

Oddly, that made me feel better. "They're going to tease you mercilessly."

"Listen, my little witch, what makes you think they haven't been teasing me since the moment they picked up on the fact that I liked you? We're Grimlocks. Teasing each other is what we do.

"It's going to be fine," he reassured me, burying his face in my neck and exhaling deeply enough to send shivers down my spine when his hot breath washed over my skin. "They'll be jerks, but they'll get over it. After this morning, they'll pretty much work everything out of their systems."

That was a relief. At least I thought so. Still ... . "What do you think they'll say?"

"I ... ." He didn't get a chance to finish because his bedroom door swung open to allow Redmond entrance. The oldest Grimlock sibling swaggered into the room, barely lifting an eyebrow when I scrambled to make sure I was covered.

"Do you knock?" Braden barked, tugging the covers tighter around me as he wrapped his arm around my back.

"Hey, Izzy." Redmond was blasé, his hair messy. He'd clearly just gotten up. "I am out of clean shirts because I forgot to drop my laundry with the maids this week. I need to borrow something."

"Get out," Braden ordered.

"It's just for today." Redmond's grin was sly as he glanced between us. "I'll have it laundered and returned tomorrow."

"Get out!" Braden's voice was a deafening roar as Redmond chuckled and turned on his heel.

"You're right, Ais," he called out. "She spent the night. You win the pool because they very obviously did it. That should make you happy."

My cheeks burned as the bedroom door closed and Braden flopped back on his pillow to stare at the ceiling. "Your family sucks sometimes," I said finally.

"What was your first clue?"

BY THE TIME WE MADE IT downstairs for breakfast I'd managed to calm myself, though only marginally. I wore the same jeans from the previous day and Braden loaned me a simple black T-shirt. I'd showered in Braden's private bathroom and now smelled of his shower gel, which wasn't necessarily a bad thing, but my stomach was full of butterflies as we made our way to the dining room.

"Don't let this freak you out," he whispered outside the door, his lips brushing the ridge of my ear and sending chills down my spine. "They're going to give us grief — me more than you — but then it'll be over. I mean ... Maya and Griffin managed to survive it. You will, too."

That did very little to ease the nerves fluttering through my stomach. "I don't know if I can do this." I felt helpless when I uttered the words, weak. I'd faced countless monsters over the years, fought off bullies in middle school and overenthusiastic dates when I was older. I'd once taken on a bayou stink monster completely on my own without any backup. This was something else entirely.

"Oh, you make me laugh." He squeezed my hand and gave me a quick kiss before pushing me through the door.

I almost tripped over my own feet as I careened into the room, my eyes going wide as I realized the table was full of curious faces — including Cillian's girlfriend Maya, who looked ridiculously amused. "Um ... hello." My voice was barely a whisper.

"Good morning, Izzy," Cormack offered from his spot at the head of the table. He held a wide-awake Lily in his arms, making a series of faces for her benefit as everyone else watched with mugs of coffee and glasses of juice in their hands. "Did you sleep well?"

Aidan and Redmond snickered in unison, causing Cormack's expression to darken.

"Are we back in middle school, boys?" he challenged. "I swear, the older you get, the younger you act sometimes. It's absolutely ridiculous."

"We didn't say anything," Redmond protested, his cheeks flushing. "Did you hear us say anything?"

"I heard you laugh like morons," Cormack replied. "Stop making Izzy uncomfortable. If you want to torture your brother later, that's up to you. Izzy is a guest in my house."

I was bolstered by his words, which made me realize I was acting like a timid and immature child. That was not how I saw myself, and it certainly wasn't how I wanted them to see me. "I'm fine." I found I didn't have to force a smile because it readily came. "If they want to torture me, that's fine. I get how this family works."

"I don't," Griffin complained. "Why didn't you yell at all of them the first time I spent the night here?"

"Because you were a filthy pervert who put your hands on my baby," Cormack replied without hesitation. "You were different."

"Uh-huh." Griffin didn't look convinced. "If I hadn't put my filthy hands on your baby, you wouldn't be holding my baby right now."

Cormack shrugged. "Things worked out in the end. You shouldn't question my methods."

"Yeah, yeah, yeah."

I made my way to the omelet bar, my eyes going wide at the various offerings. A chef stood behind the cooking station, a pan in his hand, and patiently waited for me to place an order. "Um ... can I really order an omelet?" I felt as if I'd stumbled into a magical new world.

"That's what he's there for," Aisling said as she made a move to collect Lily. "I can put her in the bassinet," she offered. "That way you can eat."

"I can eat while holding her." Cormack refused to relinquish his grandchild. "There's no reason to get all worked up. She's perfectly fine."

"I'm not getting worked up." Aisling's expression reflected amusement as she joined me at the omelet station. "I was just making sure." I could feel her eyes on me as I perused the breakfast offerings. "You look all ... glow-y," she said finally. "You must've had a good night. Apparently Braden isn't nearly as bad in bed as all those other girls told me."

"Knock it off," Braden warned, flicking Aisling's ear as he moved behind her. "You'll make Izzy feel uncomfortable, and I know that's not what you want after she cured Lily of that demented crying that was threatening to kill us all."

"Oh, I wasn't trying to make Izzy uncomfortable," she shot back. "You're fair game, though."

"Nobody is fair game this morning," Cormack countered. "As much fun as it is to watch you peck at each other like vultures going after a corpse, we actually have a few things to discuss. I spent a few hours going through Peter Washington's journal last night, and I'm concerned."

His tone told me I should pay attention, so I forced my eyes from the omelet station and focused on him. "Do you know what they were doing?"

"No, but whatever it was, Washington was worried. He had a scientific brain and liked the idea of experimenting. He joined forces with

Carroll because he thought they were on the same wavelength. It didn't take him long to realize that Carroll had a different agenda."

"Carroll was obsessed with living forever," Aisling noted as she pointed toward various items for the cook to add to her omelet. "He's hardly the first bad guy to have that as the ultimate goal. Most of the ones we've dealt with before have revolved around soul walking. Why didn't he go that route?"

"Maybe he was smart and realized that he would end up like a wraith if he tried," Cillian suggested. "I mean ... everyone we know who tried the soul-walking route ended up a certain way. A lot of people tried to be the one to beat the curse and failed."

"That's true," she mused. "There has to be a hint in that journal." She pinned her father with a demanding look. "You're supposed to be the smartest man alive. You must have an idea."

Cormack chuckled. "I don't know any specifics," he countered. "I think whatever they were doing revolved around the gate."

I stilled. "Do you think they crossed the threshold?"

"No. You can't survive crossing the threshold."

"You've mentioned that to me before. The thing is ... we don't know what happens when you cross. We only know that no one has come back. That could be a voluntary choice. There could be sentries of sorts prohibiting it. It doesn't necessarily mean that people die when they cross over. The wraith didn't."

"The wraith was already dead," Cormack argued.

"No, it wasn't." I didn't see the point of getting into a huge argument, but I figured now was the best time to lay out my hunch. "The whole point of becoming a wraith is to live forever. That's why people sell their souls to do it. It may only be a half-life, but they're technically alive.

"When that wraith crossed over a few weeks ago, it didn't die," I continued. "In fact, it managed to somehow return ... and was still alive. We killed it on this side. Not only did it come back, but it also came back with enhanced abilities."

Cormack's gaze was thoughtful as he shifted Lily so her head rested against his chest. The baby was out cold, but he still insisted on holding her. "I guess you have a point," he said finally. "I never really thought about it that way. To me, you can't live without a soul. In the basic sense of the word, though, you're right. That wraith was alive."

"And it didn't die when it crossed over," I said. "What if Carroll and Washington figured out that you could cross over? What if that somehow played into their plans?"

"Maybe that explains what happened to Washington, too," Braden added. "He disappeared. No body was ever found. It was assumed something nefarious happened to him, but we don't know what that something was. Maybe he's on the other side of the gate."

"We have no way to check that," Cormack pointed out. "It's not as if we can poke our heads inside and take a look."

"No," I agreed. "But those ghosts are hanging around for a reason. I keep seeing them. I think they want to communicate."

"Can you communicate with them?" Aisling asked. "They don't talk. I saw them and they didn't say a word."

"I think they've been silenced," I replied. "They can't talk because someone is stopping them from doing so. They whispered the first time I saw them. I was simply too afraid to ask them questions and missed out on any information they could've shared. What if I somehow turn things around and make it so they can talk?"

"I'm open to that suggestion," Cormack said. "Do you have any ideas how to pull it off?"

"No, but I will definitely give it some thought." I slid my eyes to the cook, who was handing Aisling an omelet. "After I have a big breakfast, of course. I'm starving."

"That's because Braden probably made you do all the work," Redmond offered. "He's always been lazy."

I smirked as Braden glowered at his brother. In truth, the morning razzing wasn't nearly as bad as I thought it would be. "And here I thought you were the lazy one," I teased. "That's the word on the street."

"Oh, see, she's already fitting in." Redmond snickered as he leaned back in his chair. "I think Izzy is going to be a lot of fun."

Braden slung his arm around my shoulders. "I couldn't agree more."

Twenty-One

Cormack insisted on driving to Belle Isle with Braden and me — which was a bit of a distraction — but he said he wanted to take another look at the library and talk to Oliver. He didn't elaborate, so I didn't press. If he wanted to be more hands-on, I wasn't going to argue with him. It was getting more and more necessary given the dearth of answers at our disposal.

When we opened the door to head out, we found an unwelcome face standing on the other side of the door. Angelina, her expression uncertain, had her hand poised to knock and she let out a small gasp when she saw us.

"Oh, um, hi."

"Angelina." Cormack straightened his shoulders and regarded the woman with a speculative gaze. "I'm almost afraid to ask what you're doing here. If attacking Aisling is on the menu, I really wish you wouldn't. She's not quite up to her normal energy level."

"I'm not here for that ... although I hear the baby is really ugly and I wouldn't mind seeing her. I mean ... who doesn't love an ugly baby?"

Cormack narrowed his eyes until they were nothing more than malevolent slits. I'd never seen him look so menacing. Apparently a fight to the death with wraiths was nothing compared to calling his only grandchild ugly. "Lily is the most beautiful baby in the world."

"Lily." Angelina pursed her lips. "I heard Aisling named her after her mother. I haven't seen Mrs. Grimlock around in a while. How is she?"

Cormack's temper was clearly holding by a thread. "She is no longer with us. She's been gone for quite some time."

"She died in a fire," Braden said pointedly. "She always died in that fire."

For a brief moment, Angelina looked as if she was going to put up a fight. Instead, she merely shook her head. "Whatever. You guys are so weird. Speaking of that, I found this and thought you might want to have it." She handed over a weathered journal, which I took with some trepidation.

"It was my great-grandfather's," she explained. "My great-grand-mother received a box of his things when he disappeared. His bosses sent it to her or something, I can't remember. She shoved it in the attic without looking inside. My mom inherited the house and pretty much ignored the box my entire life. I looked through it after she died, because I was debating about selling the house and I wanted to see what was up there."

I flipped open the journal. It was full of page after page of neat scrawl. "I guess guys didn't find anything wrong with keeping diaries back in the day, huh?"

"I think, as long as they were considered journals and didn't require a small key, it was fine," Braden replied, glancing over my shoulder. "Do you think there's anything good in there?"

"I don't know. It will take a bit of time to go through it." I lifted my eyes to Angelina. "Are you letting us keep this?"

She held out her hands and nodded. "I don't need it. He's never been much of a consideration for me. I barely liked my great-grand-mother, at least what I can remember of her, and my grandmother was no picnic. I never really thought about my great-grandfather until you guys brought him up the other night."

"Your great-grandfather disappeared," Cormack noted. "Was there a police investigation?"

"I don't know. I'm assuming there must've been. That's standard procedure, right?"

"It is now," Cormack clarified. "Back then I think it was more likely for people to voluntarily go missing. That's how so many men managed to keep separate families in different towns. There were no online banking or phone memory apps to check up on people."

"I'm not sure my great-grandmother would've gone that route anyway," Angelina admitted. "By the time my great-grandfather disappeared, she'd pretty much washed her hands of him. That's what my mother said anyway. They were embarrassed by his mental issues."

"That was the times," Cormack mused, watching me flip through the journal without making a move to snag it. "Back then, it was better to hide your crazy relatives than try to get them help ... or embrace them."

"Oh, just think, if we'd been born forty years before, Aisling would've been locked away before I ever met her. Ah, those were the days."

Cormack butchered Angelina with a harsh look. "We're grateful for the journal. Your great-grandfather has come up in an investigation and we need as much information as we can get regarding his actions near the time of his disappearance. That said, you need to leave Aisling alone. She has a lot on her plate. You have no idea how demanding a new baby is."

Angelina's face twisted into something dark. "Right, because no one will ever want to have a baby with me, right? You sound just like my mother. I still hear her all the time, so there's no reason to add to it."

Cormack was taken aback. "I ... you ... ." He looked to Braden for help.

"I don't know what to say to her," he fired back. "I've always found her nutty. I don't want to talk to her any longer than I have to."

"Thank you, Braden," Angelina said dryly. "You've always been my least favorite of Aisling's brothers. Do you want to know why?"

"Not really."

"It's because you're just like her," Angelina continued, not missing a beat. "I even like Aidan and Jerry the Fairy better than you."

"That will be enough of that," Cormack hissed, his icy tone causing me to jolt. He extended a finger directly in front of Angelina's face. "Young lady, I've put up with a lot from you over the years. I told myself you had a terrible role model and no chance of turning out decent because of the way you were raised. That's no excuse for your constant crap, though.

"Jerry is a member of this family and he's no less of a human being because of his sexual orientation," he continued. "The thing is, I think you know that. I think you even accept it. You still say things like that to get attention because you're starved for it. Even negative attention will do."

Angelina's jaw worked, but no sound came out.

"Now, I'm going to suggest you talk to a professional." Cormack brushed the front of his expensive suit, as if wiping away specks of lint only he could see. "You're clearly spiraling. That's why you're drinking ... and even trying to help us despite the fact that you despise us. You know you need help but don't know how to find it."

He dug in his pocket and came back with a business card. "This is a therapist I think you should make an appointment with. She'll help you discuss your issues. We're not equipped to listen to your crap, and I will not put up with another derogatory remark regarding Jerry or Aidan. I've had enough."

Angelina stared at the card. "Why would you possibly give me this?"

"Because you need it."

"Yeah, but ... no way." She vehemently shook her head, although I noticed she slipped the card into her pocket rather than tearing it to shreds and throwing it on the ground. "I'm not crazy."

"You're not. You're often unbalanced, but you're not crazy." Cormack cocked his head to the side. "There's no shame in needing help. You're alone now. You need help dealing with your new reality."

"I don't need help." Angelina petulantly stomped her feet against the pavement as she stormed back to her Range Rover. "I'm not crazy and the fact that you would say otherwise shows me that you're the one who is. I always knew that. Who would have as many kids as you did if you weren't crazy?"

Cormack didn't get a chance to respond because Aisling poked her head through the door. I watched with unveiled interest as she took in each face in turn and absorbed the situation.

"Hey, whore," she called out, causing Angelina to jerk up her head and glare. "Two weeks. Kerry Field. Bring your best insults and make sure your fingernails are clipped so I don't get scabies or something from your nasty scratches."

My mouth dropped open. "What the ... ?"

"Shh." Braden pressed a finger to his lips and grinned as Angelina perked up.

"I'll be there. I just hope you can drag yourself away from that ugly baby long enough to actually hold up your end of the bargain."

"Oh, I'll be there. You don't have to worry about that. I'll probably bring your pimp and his baseball bat, so you should definitely worry about that."

"My pimp is your father, so I think I'll be fine. No offense, Mr. Grimlock." Angelina offered up a haphazard wave as she jerked open her vehicle door. "You'll be crying by the time I'm finished with you."

"That's what your pimp says to you every night." Aisling watched her nemesis escape to the road in front of the house with smug satisfaction. When she finally turned to her father, she merely rolled her eyes at his questioning look. "Hey. I like taking her down. It keeps me young. Sue me." She shut the door, leaving me to dwell on the interaction.

"This family is never dull, is it?"

Cormack grinned. "Welcome to my circus."

WE DROPPED CORMACK AND THE new journal on Belle Isle and opted to return to the Duskin School for the Deaf. The only thing I knew with any certainty was that Granger was tied to what had happened at the aquarium ... and Carroll himself seemed to have latched onto the boy. That meant a second conversation was in order, if I could swing it.

"Do you think your girlfriend will be here?" I asked when we parked in the lot.

Braden slid me a sidelong look. "Isn't she in the passenger seat?"

It was a simple question and yet my cheeks burned all the same. "I ... oh ... ."

"Too soon? If you don't want me to refer to you as my girlfriend I guess I can live with that ... for now. How would you like me to refer to you?"

"Izzy is fine for now," I said, shaking my head. "That's not what I meant anyway. I wasn't trying to get into a deep conversation. I simply wanted to know if you expect to see Kelly again, the secretary who so graciously helped us thanks to your smile."

"Oh, she wasn't looking at my smile." He winked as he collected my hand and stared at the building. "I'm not sure she'll be open to helping us given what happened last time. She clearly didn't understand what was going down ... but she was concerned enough at the end that she couldn't get rid of us fast enough."

"Yeah." I tugged on my bottom lip as my eyes drifted to the playground. "There are a few kids out there. Is there a monitor watching them?"

"Why? You don't plan to kidnap one of them, do you?"

"Ha, ha." That was a ludicrous suggestion. "I just want to see if Granger is with them."

"How do you plan to get close? I mean ... I'm game. I would really prefer not getting arrested for illegally talking to little kids, though. That might look bad on my record."

"Yeah, well, I have a trick for that if you're interested."

Intrigue lit his handsome face. "Lay it on me."

"I can make us invisible."

He blinked several times in rapid succession. "Excuse me?" he said finally, confused. "Did you just say you could make us invisible?"

"That's exactly what I said," I confirmed. "It's something I learned to do when I was in high school. There were times ... well, after Katrina, the crime rate was really high. A lot of people fled and never returned. My grandfather always knew we would return, but some of the people left behind were desperate and it wasn't the safest place to hang out.

"Anyway, when I was walking home from high school one day, these two guys started following me," I continued, my stomach clenching at the memory. That was one of the few times in my life I'd been utterly terrified. "I felt them behind me and knew they didn't have good intentions, but there weren't many places to hide."

Braden reached over and grabbed my hand but otherwise remained silent.

"I just remember thinking at the time that I wished I was invisible," I continued. "The next thing I knew, the guys were blowing past me and talking to themselves. They couldn't figure out where I went. I was still there ... I was just invisible."

"Wow!" He made a face and shook his head. "That's amazing. Can you make both of us invisible?"

"Yeah, but only for a few minutes. We have to get on the playground, find him, and try to talk to him as quickly as possible. I haven't been able to sustain the spell for an extended period of time. At least not yet."

"Hey. I'm game to try. I always wanted to be invisible ... mostly because I wanted to sneak up on my brothers and punch them when they weren't looking."

"I'm never going to understand your family."

"We're not so bad."

ULTIMATELY, BRADEN FELT IT best to move his car one street over. We parked, joined hands, and cut through the woods. I waited until we were at the border of the schoolyard to whisper the spell, and then in a leap of faith, Braden walked with me onto the playground.

He was full of bravado, but I recognized that he wasn't certain the spell would actually work until we breezed past the playground monitor without earning as much as a glance.

"Can she hear us?" he whispered, his face full of awe.

I nodded, never releasing his hand. "There." I inclined my chin toward the swings. "Granger is over there." I picked up my pace and hurried in his direction, being careful to avoid the other students. They couldn't see us, but if one of them accidentally ran into us, there was likely to be a panic, and that's the last thing I wanted to happen.

Granger was listless as he sat on his swing. He didn't pump his legs and enjoy himself like the other kids. He didn't vigorously sign to indicate he was paying attention to the conversations taking place around him. Instead, he stared into nothing.

It made me unbelievably sad.

"Hey, Granger," I murmured as I knelt in front of him. "I know you can't see me. You can't hear me either, which is good. I just need to sit here for a second and get a look inside your head. I wish I could ask permission, but I don't think that would go over well."

"Not at all," Braden agreed, keeping his gaze on the playground monitor. "She's not even looking in this direction."

"Why should she? She has no reason to believe we're here. She also has her hands full with all these kids." I exhaled heavily and flashed a smile for Granger's benefit before I remembered he couldn't see me. "This is kind of weird. It feels invasive."

"Just get it over with," Braden instructed. "We need to talk to Carroll. If he's still hiding in that kid's head ... well, we need to figure out why and see if there's anything we can do about it."

"Yeah." I believed that with my whole heart. "Here we go." I lifted my hand to hold it as close to Granger's head as I could without actually touching him, which I figured would freak him out. My fingers were barely in the air when the boy spoke.

"You don't want to do that," he said calmly, a cold dread gathering in my stomach as the boy's empty eyes latched with mine. "I won't let you out a second time."

I was flabbergasted. "You can see us?"

"I'm stronger than you think. You don't want to continue involving yourself in this. If you do, I'll have no choice but to force you to stay away."

"You're Ryan Carroll."

"I am ... who I am."

"You're Ryan Carroll," I repeated. "I don't understand this, how you got in his head or where you've been all this time. I can't let you stay there. You don't belong. You're taking over a life that's not yours to claim."

"The boy is better off with me." Carroll sounded sure of himself. "You can't save him. It's already too late."

"I have to try."

"You'll fail."

"Maybe."

"You'll regret it."

"I guess that's a risk I'll have to take."

"You'll die," he hissed, fury emanating from him in waves. "I'll crush you, rip the life from you and add you to my collection. Is that what you want?"

"The ghosts. You call them your collection. Why? What did you do to them?"

"It doesn't matter." His voice was full of menace. "You cannot stop this. You can't change things. The only thing you can do is volunteer yourself for annihilation. Is that what you want?"

"You talk big," I countered. "I don't think you have the strength to back it up."

"You're wrong."

"I guess we'll have to wait and see, huh?"

"If you insist. You're running out of time. With every passing minute, I get stronger. You'll lose ... no matter what that crackpot you call a grandfather taught you."

I was caught off guard. He seemed to know more than he should. I found that ... interesting. "We'll be back."

"Go ahead. You can't touch me." His eyes were derisive as they landed on Braden. "Your kind definitely can't touch me. I made sure of that."

"Never say never," Braden countered, gripping my hand tighter. "Come on, Izzy. We're wasting our time here. We'll come back when we're ready to take him down."

"That's never going to happen," Carroll hissed.

"We'll just see about that."

Twenty-Two

I was still shaken when we returned to the aquarium. We barely made it back to the tree line before my magic faltered and we were exposed. Braden managed to drag me into the shadows before the playground monitor saw us and raised an alarm.

"What's wrong?" Cormack asked, instantly on alert. He sat in my work chair, his feet resting on the table, flipping through the journal Angelina had dropped off, while carrying on what looked to be an intense conversation with Oliver. All of that flew by the wayside the minute he saw us.

"We had an incident," Braden replied grimly, leading me to the only empty chair in the room. "You guys really need more furniture in here," he lamented as he forced a smile for my benefit. "Maybe a couch or something."

"I'll get right on that." I rubbed my head, a headache threatening to start pounding away like a construction worker putting on a new roof. "I'm okay. I didn't even expend that much power."

"I don't understand what happened," Cormack started. "I thought you were going to check on the boy."

"We did," Braden explained. "He was on the playground. Izzy has a trick that can make us invisible. We're totally re-instituting Grimlock

Hide and Seek, by the way, because she and I will dominate. He was on the swings, acting as if he didn't care about anything. Then he started talking and it was really creepy because he could see us even though nobody else could."

"You're talking about the boy," Cormack stressed. "He's the one you talked to."

"He is the one we talked to," I agreed. "But Carroll is inside him. He's taken him over. I don't know how ... or why ... but he's not leaving."

"He uttered a lot of vague threats, but almost all of them were aimed at Izzy," Braden supplied. "He recognized I was a reaper. He said 'your kind,' and it was obvious what he was talking about. He was much more worked up about Izzy's presence than mine, though."

"Maybe that means he recognizes her as a threat," Cormack mused, rubbing his chin. "Carroll's journal is extremely detailed. There are a lot of wild proposals in here. Some revolve around the gate."

"Do you find that surprising?" I asked. "I mean ... he was pretty upfront regarding his interest in the gate. We simply need to figure out what happened to him ... and Washington. We're sure Washington disappeared first, right?"

"Actually, we were just discussing that," Cormack hedged, his eyes darting to Oliver. "It's hard for us to put together a timeline because we weren't present for the events. Oliver remembers the council showing up and acting concerned when Washington disappeared."

"*Acting?*" I arched an eyebrow. "Why phrase it like that?"

"You're good at picking up on verbal cues." Cormack grinned. "Much better than my children. I see I'll have to be careful about what I say in front of you."

"You still haven't answered the question."

He let loose a heavy sigh. "Oliver is under the impression that there's a chance — notice I stressed the word 'chance' — that the council only conducted the search for the sake of appearances."

Oh, well, now we were getting somewhere. "I would love to hear the story," I prodded. "That's not exactly how he described things to me."

"I was very careful when describing things to you," Oliver shot back. "I didn't want to lead you down the wrong path. When you started asking questions about Carroll and Peter, I didn't know what to make of it. That was a very long time ago."

"You're a vampire," I pointed out. "You're going to live forever. That's like the blink of an eye to you."

"Not necessarily. But it doesn't matter. I was friendly with Peter, but we didn't spend much time together. Back in those days, it wasn't exactly as ... welcome, I guess would be the right word ... to be gay. I don't think anything of speaking out regarding my life now, but back then I was much more careful.

"I didn't announce my plans to him when I was leaving after my shifts," he continued. "I designed things that way. Therefore, he didn't share any of his personal life with me beyond what was reasonable. We did occasionally talk philosophy. You can't spend hours upon hours with people in front of a gate that leads to another plane of existence without talking about death."

"Did he seem afraid of death?" Braden asked.

"Everyone is afraid of death in their own way, even those who are ready to welcome it. There's always a question at the very end. Peter didn't seem any more afraid of what was to come than a normal person. He did, however, seem intrigued by the mechanics of the afterlife.

"You have to understand," he said, rubbing his hands together. "He was the scientific sort. He didn't really have what I would call a romantic streak. He was married, had a son, but he never talked about his family the way Cormack talks about his children."

"And how does Dad talk about us?" Braden asked, suspicious.

"As if you're the center of his universe and he would occasionally like to drop a bomb on you." Oliver smirked at Braden's amused reaction. "Your father is a professional man who likes things done a certain way. He's also a sentimental man. He's mentioned Lily five times since he arrived."

"Well, she is the prettiest baby in the world," Cormack protested. "She could be the baby on the Gerber package she's so pretty."

"I get what you're saying," Braden noted. "Washington was the detached sort. It wasn't that he necessarily didn't care for his family as much as he simply lost himself in the science and philosophy of the gate."

"Pretty much," he agreed. "He wasn't a bad man."

"Which is why Oliver thinks it's entirely possible that he didn't read Carroll's motivations correctly," Cormack said. "He thinks that Carroll always had a plan for the gate. He thinks Washington always had a thirst for knowledge. Carroll used Washington's thirst until it came to a breaking point."

"So ... what?" Braden tilted his head to the side, considering. "Are we operating under the idea that Carroll killed Washington and fled? That's how he bought himself enough time to disappear and enact whatever crazy plan he had? I don't understand how this all fits together.

"Why would Carroll flee all those years ago and come back now? I mean ... how is he even controlling what's happening? Why did he possess Granger of all people? Why kill the teacher? I don't understand any of it."

"None of us do." I absently patted his hand as I ran my tongue over my teeth. "We really need to break this down and examine every angle. I think we're missing something ... and it's a big something."

"I agree." Cormack nodded. "I'm going to spend the afternoon trying to match dates between Carroll's journal and the one Izzy found in the library. I don't know that it will help but it certainly can't hurt."

"That sounds like a plan," Braden said. "I'm guessing you need me to take you back home to do that."

"I do."

I pursed my lips and continued to rub my forehead. "I'm going to head back into the library. I can't shake the idea that the closing of that part of the building had something to do with what happened to Washington."

"How can you confirm that?" Braden asked.

"I have no idea. I simply don't know where else to look."

"While you're doing that, don't forget you still need to hire a replacement for Renee," Cormack suggested, grinning at my down-trodden expression as he stood. "It's hell being the boss, Izzy. You can't, however, shirk your duties because you find the thrill of the mystery more invigorating. Both problems must be solved."

I groaned but nodded. "Fine. I'll look at those names, too."

"I'll be in touch," Braden said, smoothing the back of my hair as he smiled. "I don't know what I'll be doing yet, but I'm guessing it will be manly and helpful."

I couldn't stop myself from laughing. "That sounds like a plan."

"SO, WHAT'S GOING ON with you and the surliest Grimlock?"

Oliver waited a full hour after Cormack and Braden departed to ask the question that I knew was plaguing him. I did my best to feign interest in the personnel files I, but that didn't stop him from starting the interrogation.

"Oh, geez. I knew you were going to ask that," I muttered, rolling my neck. For some reason, reading employee histories on five people was enough to make me stiff and uncomfortable all over.

"Well, since you saw the question coming, you should have an answer waiting."

"You would think, huh?" I flashed him a smile and then shook my head. "We're ... dating." I figured that was the easiest word to use to describe our new relationship. "That's it."

"Uh-huh." Oliver didn't look convinced. "Did you spend the night at Grimlock Manor again?"

"Maybe." I avoided his gaze. "Why does it matter?"

"I'm simply curious."

"I didn't realize we were at the part of our relationship where we were going to start sharing details of our sex lives. If that's the case, perhaps you should kick things off. What does Brett look like naked?"

Oliver's expression darkened. "Don't change the subject. I get why you're uncomfortable, but it's really not necessary. Everyone with eyes realized where this was going with Braden. He's been panting after you from the start, and you've been mooning over him since five minutes after you were introduced."

I took offense at that remark. "I don't 'moon' over anyone," I argued, frustration bubbling up. "I'm not the sort of girl who moons. That's a dumb word anyway. You should totally pick another word."

"Oh, well, I would be happy to. Um ... ." He put on a big show of tapping his chin and feigning deep thoughts. "You've been crushing on him something fierce. What? I've been alive for a long time. You wouldn't believe the endless stream of movie jargon I've learned over the decades."

I didn't want to encourage him. He didn't deserve it after playing games with information regarding my parents. Still, he was kind of funny. "Did you make me laugh this much when I was a kid?" I asked, choking on a giggle.

He nodded. "I did. I used to talk to you in funny voices and re-enact *Where the Wild Things Are* while reading it to you."

My heart gave a little jolt. "You're the second person to mention that book to me. My grandfather taught me how to read it myself because it's all I wanted to hear when he first took me in. I guess I know why that is ... you and my parents read it to me all the time."

"That was definitely your favorite book," he agreed. "You liked listening to any stories I had to tell, even if there was more truth than fiction associated with them. Your mother made me promise not to tell you anything too bloody. You liked horror stories ... a lot. Some-times I forgot your age and made them a bit too gruesome."

"Well, I still like horror movies. There's nothing better than curling up with a terrible movie during a thunderstorm."

"Yes, well ... ." He trailed off, seemingly lost in thought. After a few minutes, he cleared his throat. "Have you decided on a new worker? I know you've been busy ... well, getting busy ... but you really should make a decision."

"I know. I've had other things on my mind."

"Like?"

"Like a man who should've died decades ago talking through a small child. Like ghosts walking across the water and begging me to free them."

"Like sex with a Grimlock."

"Oh, good grief." I couldn't meet his gaze. "You make me want to smother you with a pillow."

"That won't work. The only way to kill a vampire is direct sunlight, a stake through the chest or beheading. You should pick one of those routes."

"You're being a little too serious."

"Yes, well ... ."

He was quiet for a long time, and when I shifted to look at him I found him staring at the door. "What?"

He inclined his chin. "I was just thinking how you were going to be too busy to fill that open position again."

"I am? Why?" I followed his gaze, my stomach immediately flipping when I saw the figure standing in front of the double doors that led to the hallway.

Braden, a broad smile on his face, had a picnic basket in one hand and a blanket in the other. His grin widened as my cheeks flooded hot, and I had no doubt I was a ridiculous shade of red.

"I thought maybe you might have time for lunch," he offered, shaking the picnic basket.

The gesture was unbelievably sweet. "I can't." I hated myself for having to say the words. "Oliver has gone above and beyond to cover shifts this week while I've been doing other things. I can't abandon him again."

"I wasn't really thinking of it as abandonment," Braden argued. "The aquarium is closed. I thought we might go up a floor, have a quick bite, and then you can go back to being the most diligent worker in all the land."

Oliver chuckled, genuinely amused. "That's a fabulous idea."

I shot him a look. "You're not helping," I hissed. "I'm trying to be a good boss. I can't stick you with the work yet again."

"You're not sticking me with it. I'm volunteering."

"Because he's holding you hostage with the cutest picnic basket I've ever seen. He was supposed to be doing something manly to help with our problem, not ... this. You're only trying to help because he's too adorable to shoot down."

"That and the fact that I don't eat," he acknowledged. "I'm fine. We're not even expected to have a transfer in the next hour. I'm going to play solitaire online, so there's no reason for you to stick around. I hate it when people watch over my shoulder when I'm playing."

I recognized that he was giving me an opening for a romantic afternoon away from everything that had been seemingly plaguing me for days. I should take it. I wanted to take it. But I felt guilty.

"Are you sure?" I gave him one more out.

He bobbed his head. "I'm sure."

"He's sure," Braden prodded. "Come on."

I got to my feet, Oliver's steady gaze burning holes in my back as I moved closer to him. "I just want you to know, the gesture is appreciated but I feel a little weird about this. I thought you were doing something else and I wouldn't see you until later. Maybe you should call next time."

Braden was amused. "What? Don't you like surprises?"

"Surprises are fine. What I hate is the fact that Oliver is watching us ... and laughing."

"Oliver is playing solitaire," Braden corrected. "He doesn't care."

"Oliver definitely doesn't care," the vampire agreed, referring to himself in the third person. "Go. Be young. Have a good time. I'll hold down the fort until you get back."

I didn't have to be told again. Instead, I took the blanket from Braden and followed him up the steps. When we got to the main floor of the aquarium, I found he'd arranged the lights so they only showed around a central location in the middle of the floor. Everything else was dim ... except for the aquarium openings.

"I see you've been futzing around up here."

"I never futz ... mostly because I don't know what the word means."

"Yeah, well ... let me lay out the blanket." I picked a spot in front of the biggest fish tank on the premises, avoiding the creepy-crawlies closer to the front of the space. It wasn't that I was afraid of them as much as I preferred the tranquility of the water.

Braden waited until I'd spread the blanket to place the picnic basket in the center and then he promptly sat. Even though it felt a bit strange to be eating lunch on the floor of the aquarium in the middle of the day, I opted to make an effort to push the issues that had been plaguing me to the side and focus on fun for a change. "What did you buy?" I sat close enough that our knees touched, and he grinned as he dug into the basket.

"Well, I decided to take a chance," he said. "You seem like a relatively easy girl to please when it comes to food, so I got chicken salad and potato salad from my favorite deli. Oh, I also got cheesecake."

"I love cheesecake."

He grinned. " Me, too." He opened the basket. "Shall we?"

I nodded. "Yeah. Definitely. Oh, and if I forget to tell you by the end of our lunch, this was the best time ever."

He raised an eyebrow, surprised. "How do you know that?"

"I can just tell." And, because it was true, I could relax in the knowledge that we were going to have a great afternoon. "Now, give me the chicken salad. I'll do pretty much anything I possibly can to keep from having to pick a replacement for Renee and that includes shirking my responsibilities with mayonnaise-covered poultry."

"The faster you do that, the faster you'll be able to take off in the afternoon without feeling guilty about leaving Oliver with all the work. If there's a newbie on the premises, it will be easy, because everyone knows the new guy gets the crap shifts."

"Ah. Is that how it works in the Grimlock family?"

"No." His grin was beyond charming. "In the Grimlock family, my father picks a favorite kid every day and spoils him or her for the duration. That makes the others jealous, but they know they'll be the favorite again in a few days so they're ultimately fine with it."

"That sounds like a terrible way to raise children."

"Yeah. It's kind of fun being the favorite, though."

Twenty-Three

G etting to know Braden was easier than I thought. He seemed the type to close off when difficult questions were asked, and yet, for the most part, he willingly answered whatever I threw at him.

"Who is your favorite sibling?"

He arched an eyebrow as he finished off his potato salad. "I don't know that I have a favorite sibling. I spend time with all of them."

I didn't believe that for a second and waited, arms folded over my chest.

He sighed, the sound long and drawn out. "Redmond," he said finally.

"Why?"

"When I was a kid, he was the big brother to end all big brothers. I wanted to be like him. Then, when Aisling and Aidan came along, the three of us older ones had to entertain ourselves quite a bit. As much as my parents were used to dealing with chaos, twins were another story."

That actually made a lot of sense. "Why Redmond instead of Cillian?"

"I love Cillian," he stressed.

"I know. You love all of them."

"Cillian is the family bookworm. On winter days when we were stuck in the house, Redmond found mischief and Cillian disappeared in a book. We often had to track him down and force him to participate in games.

"He's the easiest to get along with, don't get me wrong," he continued. "I simply have more in common with Redmond."

It was a completely honest answer and it made me realize he was trying hard to be an open book for me because he thought that's what I needed. I appreciated the effort. "And Aisling is your least favorite, right?"

"Aisling is ... ." He trailed off, his brow wrinkling. "She's my sister," he said finally. "We all went out of our way to protect her when we were kids. She had a mouth like you wouldn't believe."

"I've met her."

He snickered. "When she started dating we made a game of it. Dad liked to pace when she was out, and my mother would talk him down. This was right before she died, of course. Most guys thought Aisling was hot, but they were afraid to ask her out because they thought Dad would hurt them ... and if he didn't we would."

"So, you enjoyed terrorizing your sister," I prodded. "I think that's normal in most homes. I was an only child, but I always wanted siblings. I felt alone after my parents died. You guys had each other after your mother died."

"Yeah. We've always had each other." He snagged my hand and flipped it over so he could study the lines crisscrossing my palm. "Mom was the one who told my father to chill out when Aisling was on a date. She thought his reactions were funny and was the only one who could talk him down from a ledge. When she died, my father needed something to focus on. Smothering Aisling became that thing."

"Is that why she moved out earlier than the rest of you?"

"Partially. Aisling needed air after my mother died. She was determined to stay out of the family business and wanted out from under my father's watchful eye."

"I didn't realize she wasn't always a reaper."

"She did other things before joining the fold." Braden's face lit with mirth at some memory I wasn't given access to. "She lost her job, though, and had no choice but to come back to the family business if she wanted to pay her bills. The odd thing is, she's a decent reaper ... except for her penchant for talking to the souls. She needs to stop that."

"You guys seem like you get along okay," I noted. "I keep hearing stories about how you like to crush one another with horrible words and fight until only one of you is left standing, but I haven't seen that."

"You've only seen my sister in a vulnerable state," he continued. "When you met her, she was nine months pregnant and got stuck trying to climb a fence."

Now it was my turn to smile at the memory. "Your father was hilarious when he came to retrieve her. Actually, all you guys were hilarious."

"Aisling has never enjoyed being vulnerable. The pregnancy was difficult for her. Now that she has Lily she feels even more vulnerable because Lily can't even cry out a warning if something attacks. I mean, what would've happened if Aisling had the baby before my mother came back from the dead? Would she have used the baby to force Aisling to give up her life? That's what I keep circling back to. I think that's exactly what she would've done."

I felt inexplicably bad for him. "That's not what happened," I reminded him. "She's gone. She can't hurt you again. Your sister is fine. The baby is fine. Your family will be fine."

He lifted his eyes until they met mine. "That's what I keep telling myself. Over and over, I kept telling myself that we've come out the other side. It's not always easy to remember."

"I guess not. Still, you seem to be doing okay."

His eyes gleamed. "I believe you said I was awesome last night."

"I'm pretty sure those words never exited my mouth."

"Your memory is crap because I blew your mind. It will come back once the shock recedes."

I playfully swatted at his arm, but he caught me around the waist before I could make contact and rolled both of us to the blanket and kissed me. It was a sweet and adorable moment, and I sank into it because I didn't care how schmaltzy it probably looked. It felt right. That's all that mattered. I'd given up fighting my attraction to him.

When I opened my eyes again, all I saw was his face ... so I smiled. Then the hair on the back of my neck stood on end and a chill washed over me. I gripped Braden's arms tightly and pulled my head back to scan the aquarium over his shoulder. Sure enough, the ghosts were back.

"Fire and brimstone," I muttered, pushing Braden away so I could get a better look at the twenty ethereal bodies surrounding us.

"Holy ... !" Braden lost all his color as he scanned the room. "I take it these are the ghosts you've been talking about."

"Yeah." I rubbed my sweaty palms over my knees as I faced off with Lauren. She seemed to be the leader of the group, although that was most likely my perception because she had the only face I recognized. "Hey, guys. As usual, you have the worst timing ever." I was going for levity but my words came out tight and shrill.

"What do we do?" Braden asked, looking around. "I mean ... how do we get rid of them? Should I try absorbing them with my scepter?"

"Aisling already tried that. It didn't work."

"Maybe she did it wrong."

"Is there more than one way to press the button?"

"Ugh. You sound like her." Braden dragged a hand through his dark hair and shook his head. "We can't stay exposed like this. If they attack, we're easy targets."

He wasn't wrong and still ... . "If they wanted to attack, they could've done it already. They're not here for that."

"How can you be sure?"

I extended a finger toward Lauren, who made a mournful sound through her rigid mouth and raised her hands toward me.

"Don't even think about it." Braden moved to swipe at her, but his hand merely passed through her ethereal body. "Oh, geez. I don't like this at all." In a protective move I should've seen coming, he pitched forward and made sure Lauren couldn't move any closer to me without going through him.

"She's not going to hurt me," I said gently. "I misunderstood at the spa. I thought they were trying to attack."

"Aisling said the ghost that went for her was attacking."

Actually, the more I thought about it, that was true. The teenaged ghost was clearly perplexed when he went after her. "Maybe they're like people." I licked my lips as I thought through multiple possibilities. "Maybe he was frustrated and made a mistake. Maybe he was a ghost for a very long time and lost his cool ... or maybe only for a short time and he panicked."

"And you don't see him?" Braden scanned every face. "He's not back, is he?"

I shook my head. "No. He's not back. I'm pretty sure I destroyed him."

"So, why not do the same with these guys?" He looked hopeful. "Destroy them and we can get out of here."

"I won't."

"Why?"

"They need help. Unless they're aggressive, I won't go after them. They're not hurting anybody."

"They're hurting my ego. I'm scared spitless," he admitted. "I don't like this ... and I especially don't like that." He cringed when Lauren reached through him in an effort to get to me. "Stop that!" he hissed, fury on full display. "I don't like that at all."

"You have to let it go," I admonished, frustration bubbling up. "She's trying to tell me something."

"What?"

All I could do was raise my hand and touch my fingertips to hers. Technically, there was no contact, but I put as much effort as possible into the touch all the same. Nothing happened. "I don't know. I only know that they need help. We're the only ones who can give it to them."

BRADEN INSISTED ON SPENDING THE afternoon protecting me. Even though he couldn't fight the ghosts — and they didn't make a move in my direction — he was a muttering mess as he spent the entire afternoon pacing the gate room and talking to himself.

The ghosts disappeared not long after they appeared, making me wonder if they had limited energy and burned themselves out quickly when visiting. That was pure conjecture on my part, but I couldn't push the idea out of my head.

I took the last two jobs myself and sent Oliver home early. He'd been doing the work of three people for the past few days and that wasn't fair. He flashed a smile when I suggested he surprise Brett with a special meal. I could tell he wanted to tease me, but given Braden's bad mood, he wisely waved and went on his merry way.

After finishing up, I stopped at my apartment long enough to pack an overnight bag and then joined Braden in his BMW for the drive back to Grimlock Manor. While I thought it might be more beneficial if he stayed with me for the evening, he was so keyed up about the possibility of ghosts watching us that I readily agreed to return with him.

Honestly it was for the best ... at least for now.

In typical fashion, the house was buzzing when we arrived. Braden immediately directed me toward his father's office, keeping a firm grip on my hand as we cut through the house.

"You've been gone all day," Redmond immediately started complaining. "I had to pick up two of your charges this afternoon, something you ordered me to do instead of asking."

"I bet he's not your favorite right now," I muttered under my breath, earning the first real smile Braden had managed in hours.

"Pretty much," he agreed, visibly forcing himself to unknot his nerves. "I'm sorry. I'll make it up to you and buy a round of drinks at the bar later in the week."

Redmond was petulant. "I don't think that'll be enough to make it up to me."

"Then sit there and pout," Braden snapped, causing several sets of eyebrows to hike.

"What happened with you guys?" Cormack asked from behind his desk. He had Lily asleep in his arms, and the second the conversation turned serious the baby started fretting. I found that interesting, especially since she'd been quiet up until that point.

"Well, I saw the ghosts," Braden replied. "They came out of nowhere and boxed us in."

"You're clearly all right," Cormack noted, shifting his grand-daughter and giving her an odd look. "So are you, little girl. Why are you crying? I just fed and changed you."

"Maybe she's annoyed that Braden stuck me with two of his charges," Redmond suggested. "She knows that Braden is a big poopy-head and he's annoying her."

"Oh, stuff it," Braden complained, moving behind the desk and extending his arms. "I'll take her."

Cormack studied Braden for a long beat and then acquiesced. I could read his line of thinking from across the room. His son was agitated and the baby was likely to calm him. The problem was, the second the baby landed in Braden's arms, she started fussing.

"What's this?" Braden looked momentarily panicked. "She's not going back to that crying constantly thing from a few days ago, is she?"

I moved to his side and took the baby from him. She immediately stopped crying and stared up at me with an intense set of lavender eyes.

"That's better." Braden exhaled heavily, relieved. "Why doesn't she like me any longer? I'm her favorite uncle."

"I'm her favorite uncle," Redmond fired back.

"Jerry is going to be her favorite uncle and everyone knows it," I offered, watching the baby's lips curve. If I didn't know better, I would have thought she was smiling. It was far too early for that. "I have an idea."

I abandoned the ghost discussion — at least for now — and carried Lily nearer to Redmond. He was quiet when I leaned close. Lily didn't let loose a peep. Of course, neither did Redmond. "How many extra hours did you work to cover Braden's shift?" I asked.

Redmond's scowl immediately returned. "Two. You owe me, Braden. I had big plans to hit on the girl with the bellybutton ring at that coffee shop and I missed her because I was doing your job."

Lily whimpered and started squirming.

I immediately headed over to Cillian, who was quietly reading on the couch. The second Lily was close to her quiet uncle, she stopped fretting.

"What are you doing?" Cormack asked.

"Conducting an experiment," I replied, moving Lily closer to Redmond, who was still grousing like a child who had lost a candy bar.

"You know how hot that chick is, Braden," he continued. "I think she might be the one for me. I hate it when I miss her."

"The one?" Braden rolled his eyes. "You've barely talked to her. You get all tongue-tied when you're in the same room with her."

"I do not. I am all charm, and she is putty in my hands."

Lily wailed, and when I turned to take her back to Cormack I found Griffin hovering in the doorway. He looked concerned ... and intrigued.

"What are you doing?" he asked as I bypassed him and handed the baby back to a calm Cormack. He was used to his children arguing about shifts, so he didn't say anything to quiet them. Instead, he accepted the baby and watched me for a reaction.

"Huh." I dragged a hand through my hair. "Do you have any psychics in your family?"

The question clearly caught the Grimlocks off guard.

"No," Braden answered first.

"Uncle Milton thought he was psychic, but it turned out he was just psycho," Redmond offered.

"I'm pretty sure there are no psychic reapers," Cillian replied.

"Not that I'm aware of," Cormack supplied. "Why do you ask?"

"The baby is picking up on emotions," I explained. "She gets upset when the person holding her is upset. I thought at first she was picking up on Aisling's nervousness, but it's more than that. She picked up on Cormack's agitation when we mentioned the ghosts and she picked up on Redmond's annoyance about having to cover Braden's shift."

"That's because it's pretty much the worst thing that happened all day," Redmond said.

I ignored him. "She was fine with me because I was calm. Braden was still agitated from the ghosts, so she was squirming. Cillian was calm, so she was fine with him. Cormack is used to you guys arguing so he didn't pay any attention to it and was calm again."

"What are you saying?" Cormack asked. "Is there something wrong with Lily?"

I shook my head. "No. I think she might be a touch sensitive. I mean ... she's far too young to test if she's psychic. That phenomenon doesn't usually become measurable until a child is at least five, sometimes older. I think she's just sensitive and picks up on people's emotions. It's ... interesting."

"I had an aunt like that," Griffin offered, taking everyone by surprise. "She claimed that she could feel the emotions of trees and animals as well as people. Everyone in the family called her a loon and ignored it, but ... she was serious."

"Well, maybe she's getting it from your side of the family," I mused. The thought hadn't occurred to me, but it made as much sense as anything else. "It's not the end of the word, but it is something to watch. If the entire family is upset, Lily is bound to be upset. As long as someone is calm and serene, the baby most likely will be."

"But she spent two weeks complaining," Cillian pointed out. "Someone had to be serene in her presence during that time."

"Not necessarily," I challenged. "Aisling was nervous about being a new mother. Griffin was anxious about Aisling. They were isolated for most of that time."

"And you think Lily picked up on that." Griffin moved to stand behind his father-in-law and grinned at his daughter. "Are you already doing amazing things? I knew you were going to be awesome. I mean ... how could you not be absolutely amazing?"

I could feel the love flowing from him from seven feet away.

"Of course she's amazing," Cormack said. "She's my granddaughter. She had no choice but to be amazing."

"I'm pretty sure I'm responsible for the amazing things she's doing this time," Griffin argued.

"You don't know that. Just because you had a crazy aunt doesn't mean you're responsible. I'm responsible."

Lily started whining again, causing me to arch an eyebrow. Cormack and Griffin immediately adjusted their tones.

"It doesn't matter who made her amazing," Cormack said, beaming at the tiny girl resting in his arms. "She's going to be loved beyond reason ... and spoiled rotten."

"Yeah, she's going to be a total monster," Griffin agreed, matching

Cormack's smile. "She reminds me so much of her mother sometimes it makes my heart sing."

Cormack sighed. "Me, too."

"Oh, geez." Redmond rolled his eyes. "Does no one care about my pain?"

"Shut up," everyone barked in unison.

"We're sick of hearing it, dude," Braden said. "I'll make it up to you. I promise."

"You'd better."

"We should talk about the ghosts," Cormack suggested, shuffling Lily to her father's arms. "And, I believe that means Lily should go someplace else so she doesn't read the temperature of the room."

"I think you should start testing that practice on a lot of things," I offered. "It will make handling the baby much easier."

Griffin smiled as he gave me a grateful nod. "Thank you. You have no idea how helpful this is."

"She's all kinds of helpful." Braden shot me a wink. "But back to the ghosts. We have to do something. This can't continue."

"Do you have any suggestions?" Cormack asked.

"No."

"Then we need to work together to come up with a plan because I have no idea what to do either."

And there was the conundrum.

Twenty-Four

I t didn't take long to deduce that the Grimlocks enjoyed theme meals. The fact that they had a Chinese bar — complete with the best spring rolls I'd ever eaten — was the final straw that made me realize their world revolved around food. All of them were good eaters, and Cormack often rewarded his children with specific desserts.

"You like red velvet cake," I said to Braden as we sat on the floor in the nursery with Lily later that evening. He'd volunteered to get her ready for bed, which included changing her diaper and dressing her in a lavender jumper. He then proceeded to talk to her in the most ridiculous voice I'd ever heard, asking her moronic questions she couldn't possibly answer ... and melting my heart in the process.

"What?" He cast me a sidelong look. "Did you say something?"

"Red velvet cake," I repeated, lightly smoothing the baby's hair. The night nurse had already given her a bath and she smelled like baby powder. "That's your favorite."

He stilled. "How did you know that?"

"Because your father had five different types of cake for dinner. You all went for a different choice. Maya, Jerry, Griffin and I grabbed whatever we gravitated toward from the offerings and your father took a small sliver of each cake."

"I ... are you sure?" He looked flummoxed. "I guess I never noticed it before, but you're right. My father samples multiple slices on cake night."

I couldn't stop myself from laughing at his befuddled expression. "He goes out of his way for each one of you. I don't think you realize how lucky you are to have him."

"Oh, we realize. We definitely realize." Braden wrapped Lily in a blanket and cradled her. "When my mother died, he almost killed himself trying to be everything each of us needed. He realized after weeks of exhaustion that it wasn't possible, but we all gave him credit for the attempt."

"He's a really good father."

"He is." Braden made a cooing sound. "Look! She just smiled at me. I told you I was going to be her favorite uncle. Hah!"

I didn't have the heart to tell him that was most likely gas. He could bicker with his brothers in the morning, which I was certain would be a lovely conversation, what with all the 'no, I'm going to be her favorite uncle' boasting flying around the room.

"Can I hold her for a second?"

Braden readily handed over Lily, who had heavy eyelids and looked to be ready for sleep. "She's cute. You can't keep yourself from holding her."

"She's cute," I agreed. "She looks like you."

"I don't think Aisling will agree."

"She looks like all of you," I corrected. "Poor Griffin didn't have a chance against your genes. They're obviously dominant."

"I think Griffin is fine with it. He loves my sister ... and the way she looks."

"Yeah." I swaddled the baby tightly and then lifted her so she rested her head against my shoulder. "At this age, a baby should be an open book. I've been around quite a few of them in the French Quarter. A lot of the voodoo women bring their children to market, so I learned about reading babies back then."

He furrowed his brow. "You read babies? I don't understand."

"For money. We never seemed to have enough of it. When my grandfather realized I could read minds – at least to some extent – he started hiring out my services."

"How old were you?"

"Ten."

"Geez. At ten, my father used to give us a hundred bucks to rake the leaves. I'm starting to think we had it easy."

I arched an eyebrow. "Starting? You live in a freaking castle."

"You need to let that go. It's a mansion, not a castle."

"It looks like a castle."

"Yeah, well ... continue with your story." He patted my knee before moving his hand to the baby's back. "Is she sleeping?"

"Soon. As for my story, there's not much to it. A woman came in one day. I could read a lot of happiness even though she was mourning the loss of her dog. I realized the happiness was coming from her toddler, who hated the dog, and it kind of grew from there."

"So ... you're saying you can read babies. What does Lily have to say?"

"Lily is so new she doesn't yet have a complicated thought process. She's basically happy and sad. Her emotions will grow quickly, so be prepared for that."

"Because she's picking up on our emotions?"

"Yeah. She's definitely picking up on your emotions."

"Even more than other babies, right?"

"Definitely." I rocked Lily and closed my eyes. "Give me a second."

The little girl was warm, content, and on the verge of falling asleep. That meant her mind was open to invasion, which was exactly what I wanted to attempt. When I stepped inside, I found a much smaller room than when I visited Granger's mind, and it was completely open.

In one corner, her parents sat on a couch. They boasted those wide smiles parents use when trying to make their children laugh. I had to bite back a chuckle when I saw them because I very much doubted Aisling would enjoy the way her daughter saw her.

I moved to my right and found Cormack sitting at his desk, although the office was much smaller in Lily's mind. That was to be expected. Her ability to measure space and distance was severely limited. Also in Cormack's office was Cillian, who was reading a book. They both boasted wide smiles.

A few feet away, Braden and Redmond argued with one another. I realized it was a memory from earlier in the day, though they tossed nonsense words at each other now. Lily couldn't grasp language, so her uncles were forced to yell at each other in gibberish. They weren't too loud, and I couldn't help but wonder if Lily was processing their argument, perhaps realizing that the fighting wasn't necessarily true animosity.

In another corner, Aidan and Jerry sat looking at a magazine. I figured it was supposed to be a bridal magazine, but in Lily's mind it was simply a bunch of pages that they flipped through while pointing at various items. Occasionally they lifted their heads and waved, but then they immediately went back to the magazine.

I circled twice more to make sure I'd seen everything and then retreated from the infant's brain. Braden was staring at me when I opened my eyes.

"Anything?" he asked, reaching forward to take Lily so he could put her in her bassinet.

"She's kind of funny," I admitted after a beat. "I mean ... really funny. She sees the world in a very limited way. In her mind Aisling and Griffin simply adore her, the same as Cormack. She sees Cillian with a book, which is his nature. She sees Aidan and Jerry as distracted with their wedding."

"What about me?"

"I don't know about normally, but tonight she saw you and Redmond arguing." I saw no reason to lie. "You might not want to make that the regular way she sees you."

Braden's expression darkened. "Did she say who she liked most?"

I chuckled. "No. She can't pick and choose that way yet. One day she will. By then, she'll have better defenses so it won't be so easy to just hop in her brain and look around."

"Can I ask why you did that tonight? I mean .... what did you expect to find?"

"I wanted to get an idea of what was supposed to be there when a ghost wasn't in control."

"Ah." Realization dawned on Braden's face. "You're worried about Granger."

"I think he's the key."

"So ... what do we do?"

"I don't know." That was the simple truth, and it was causing me anxiety I didn't want to share with Lily. Slowly, I stood and took a step away from her. She was down and out, dead to the world for at least a few hours. "We should let her sleep."

"Okay." Braden was agreeable. He flicked off the light, leaving the cutesy nightlight Cormack bought to cast dancing shadows on the walls. He linked his fingers with mine as we moved toward his bedroom. "Do you have any idea where to look?"

"No, and I find that frustrating."

"I bet. You like being in control."

"Is that your way of saying I'm a control freak?"

"Nope." He shook his head, his lips forming a charming smile. "I'm not an idiot. That's my way of saying there's nothing more you can do tonight so you should focus on something else."

I understood what he was getting at. "Do you have any ideas about what I should focus on?"

"I have one."

"Oh, yeah?"

"Yup." He wrapped his arms around my waist and swept me into his room. "Let me tell you about it."

"I'm guessing it's a fascinating subject."

"Oh, you have no idea."

BRADEN WAS A SNORER.

I thought for sure I would never be able to deal with someone who sounded as if he was cutting down trees with a power tool while I was trying to tune out the world, but for some reason I managed to sleep regardless. When I woke the next morning, he was still snoring – directly in my ear.

"Wow." I rubbed my forehead as I pulled back, causing him to shift. "That is loud."

He tossed an arm over his head. I didn't want to wake him — he clearly needed rest if that snore was any indication — so I carefully slid out of bed.

The urge to flee momentarily reared its ugly head again, but I pushed it aside quickly. The worst was behind us. Braden's siblings had a go at us the previous day. It was probably out of their systems. Even if it wasn't, I didn't want him to think that I'd simply abandoned him. That didn't seem a good way to build trust, and Braden was clearly the sort of guy who needed trust in a relationship. I needed trust, too, so we were a good fit.

I showered in his suite bathroom, changed into the clothes I'd packed, and found him still sleeping when I exited the bathroom. At a loss for what else to do, I took a sheet of paper from the notepad on his dresser, wrote "I'm downstairs" in big, loopy letters, and signed it with a heart. Once I finished, I frowned at the heart. It seemed a little too cutesy. Of course, writing multiple notes was worse.

I put the note on my pillow and then quietly exited the bedroom. I heard him snoring as I made my way down the hallway.

It was still early when I hit the main floor. It wasn't even eight yet. Braden had made it clear the previous day that he considered anything before eight to be an ungodly hour. If his siblings were the same, that meant they were probably still asleep. Cormack was another story.

I found him alone in his office, his head bent over his computer as he read a report. I felt out of place, slightly doltish, but I knocked on his doorframe all the same. "Um ... are you busy?"

His smile was warm and engaging. "Come in." He waved for me to join him. "I'm surprised you're up. The people in this house sleep in unless we're mired in a catastrophe."

"I noticed. All the bedroom doors are still shut."

"Yes, well, my children are spoiled, in case you haven't noticed."

"Oh, I've noticed."

"Jerry sleeps in like the rest of them. Griffin would usually be up and headed to work by now, but because he's off he's taken to getting sleep where he can. Maya is already at work, but I can't take credit for her. She's simply a go-getter."

"I didn't realize Maya spent the night again." I accepted the mug of coffee he poured from the carafe on the corner of his desk. "Do your children always converge on your house this way? I mean ... when something is happening, that is."

"Pretty much." He grinned. "Even though three of them have their own roofs to hide under, I often find them under mine."

"Which you like."

"Am I that transparent?"

"You love your children," I replied simply. "That's written on your face whenever you're in a room with them. They obviously irritate you — I'm pretty sure most of them are aware of the phenomenon and get off on it — but you still love them."

"I do indeed." He squinted one eye as he regarded me. "How are things with you and Braden?"

I wasn't expecting the question. "Oh, well ... ." I felt my cheeks flood with color.

"I wasn't asking for specifics," he said hurriedly, mortification washing over his handsome features. He was responsible for all of his children's looks, which was a good thing. "I was asking in a broad sense."

"Things are good. I ... um ... ."

"You're incredibly uncomfortable with the question," he surmised, pressing the heel of his hand to his forehead. "I didn't mean to make you feel uncomfortable. That's not fair.

"It's just ... Braden has been the one I've been worried about for months," he continued. "After Lily died a second time, well, he was the one hurting. Aisling was as well, to a certain extent, but she had the baby to focus on, and that eased her pain quite a bit."

"He's okay. I mean ... he talks about her sometimes. His mother, I mean. I don't push him. I just listen when he wants to talk."

"What does he say?"

"I can't tell you that." I made a tsking sound with my tongue. "I know you're worried, but I'm not talking behind his back. Let's just say he seems pretty good to me and leave it at that."

Cormack's smile was rueful. "I guess I can live with that." He sighed and turned back to his computer. "I've been trying to get the home office to unseal Carroll's file. They're putting up a fight. They don't seem to agree with me that his spirit is still hanging around."

"They think you're lying?"

"They think I'm misreading the signs."

"How is that different from lying?"

He chuckled. "That's a very good question. I don't have an answer. I don't believe they're going to unseal the records, though, which puts us at a disadvantage."

"Yeah." I combed my damp hair. "I've been thinking about something. I keep circling, but the more I think about it, the more sense it makes."

He steepled his fingers and offered me a grave look. "Lay it on me."

"You might think it's ridiculous."

"Aisling was attacked by a mirror monster, stumbled over zombies and managed to survive storms that made people crazy. Nothing sounds ridiculous these days."

I was intrigued. "Storms that made people crazy? Well, we're definitely coming back to that. For now, I think I know why Carroll disappeared and then suddenly came back to this area."

"You have my full attention."

"It never made sense to me that he'd want to return," I explained. "Also, why go after a teacher the way he did? Why invade a child's mind? I don't think the attacks were a choice but a necessity."

"How?"

"That's what I'm getting to. I think he's been around for a few weeks gathering strength. I think he was weak before and started feeding on people to build himself up. All the people he fed on turned into the ghosts we've been seeing.

"I'm willing to bet that if we go through the files of people who have died or gone missing in the immediate area — and only files from the past three weeks — we'll find all our ghosts," I continued. "I think he's killing them and harnessing their energy."

"You still haven't explained how."

"That I don't know. I've only figured out the part about where he was the past fifty years."

"Well, I'm officially intrigued. Where was he?"

"The library."

He stilled. "The main office library?"

"No. The library we uncovered at the aquarium. It was closed up years ago, covered so people would never know it was there. Why?"

"Well ... huh." He stroked his chin. "That's a very intriguing point. I never got an answer to my inquiries regarding the closing of the library. With Aisling giving birth, I let it fall by the wayside. Apparently I need to up the pressure."

"It's the only thing that makes sense," I admitted. "The library closed about the same time Washington disappeared. The thing is, as far as I can tell, Carroll disappeared at the same time. He was a loner, so nobody noticed until he was gone several days. They assumed he either did something to Washington or saw something happen to him and fled. Perhaps he even disappeared voluntarily. I believe whatever happened to Washington happened at the same time Carroll went missing. I think they're tied together."

"Do you have any ideas on how to prove this hunch?"

"Just one ... and it's not something we can do here."

"Why not?"

"Lily," I answered simply. "You don't want those ghosts in your house, and we need to find a way to break the spell keeping them silent. We need answers, and the ghosts are the only way to get them. That means we have to talk to them on the island, which is where they seem to be strongest."

"Well, I'm all for keeping Lily safe. What do you need?"

"A few supplies ... and Aunt Maxine."

He nodded without hesitation. "A séance. That's the plan, right?"

"That *is* the plan. I need her help ... and I'll need a few of your sons, too. I won't risk Aisling because she obviously has more important things on her mind, but I need at least three of them."

"Well, Braden is a given. Cillian should go because he might recognize some of the faces from the research he's been conducting. I'll send Redmond, too. That will keep Jerry from trying to join in."

"Thank you."

"I'll attend as well," he stressed. "We're in this together now, Izzy. We have no choice but to figure out what's going on and end it."

AMANDA M. LEE

I was glad he insisted on coming. I had no idea what I was doing and he would be a grounding force.

"Then that's the plan after breakfast. What are we having for breakfast, by the way?"

"Waffle bar."

I smirked. "Yup. Another theme. Your children are extremely food-oriented. You manipulate their behavior with food."

"Of course I do. They're like dogs sometimes. You have to give them treats to perform."

I laughed. "I'm guessing you don't want me to tell them that."

"I don't mind if you tell them. They already know. It's not exactly a secret. They were like a pack of monsters as children. It always took chocolate to rein them in."

"Well ... that's a horrifying visual you just painted."

"Just wait until you have your own pack of monsters. You'll see I'm right."

"I'll have to take your word for it."

"For now."

Twenty-Five

Aisling was agitated about being cut out of the action until her father pointed out the obvious issue with her attending.

"You're on maternity leave."

"So what?"

He realized his mistake right away and adjusted tactics.

"If you get possessed by one of these ghosts, Lily will pick up on the malevolent emotions and never stop crying," Cormack said, using a tone that I was certain he probably whipped out to placate his youngest child when she was young. "You don't want that."

Aisling's expression was so dark I figured she might never again welcome the sun. "I know what you're doing."

"What's that?"

"You're tucking me away like the lone female I am to protect me."

"It's not about being female. It's about being Lily's mother. She needs you to take care of her."

"And you don't want me there to muck things up," Aisling muttered. "I get it."

"I want you safe. More importantly, I want my granddaughter safe. That means you need to stay here, away from danger. It won't always be this way, but she's not even three weeks old yet. You're still recovering ... and I have to do what's right for you and her. You're not coming."

Aisling steadily met his gaze and then switched course faster than anyone I'd ever seen. "Can we have an ice cream bar for dinner tonight?"

He flicked the spot between her eyebrows. "Yes. We're having grilled steaks, corn on the cob and potatoes. It's going to be the first big grilling night of the season."

The corners of her lips turned up. "That doesn't sound so bad."

"No. Also, you're going to have the whole day with Griffin to do ... whatever it is you guys do. It will be relaxing."

"We can't do that for another six weeks. The doctor said so."

It took Cormack a moment to realize what she was implying. "I can't believe you just said that to your own father." His expression darkened. "Are you trying to kill me?"

"Where do you think we got that kid you're so fond of?" she fired back.

"And ... I'm done." He held up his hand and strode toward the door. "Griffin, you're in charge while I'm gone," he barked.

For his part, Griffin seemed amused by the scene. Most men would've put up a fight at the thought of their wives going off to face evil ghosts, but he didn't as much as say a word while Aisling was wheedling with her father. "I like being in charge. There's still leftover cake from last night, right?"

"Yup."

"Then I love being in charge." He held out his hand to Aisling. "Come on, baby. We'll have a cake-eating contest. That's dangerous, too, because you go crazy when you have too much sugar."

"I don't go crazy." Despite her words, Aisling followed her husband. "I want ice cream with the chocolate cake."

"I'm sure that can be arranged."

AUNT MAXINE MET US AT the aquarium's front door. She didn't put up an argument when I told her what I had planned over the phone. When I saw her in person, though, I sensed things were about to take a turn.

"I thought maybe you forgot me," she said as I unlocked the door, giving a cursory look to the four Grimlocks I had in tow. "How are you, Cormack?"

"I'm fine, Maxine." The smile he sent her was small but heartfelt. "It's good to see you."

"It is," Redmond agreed, giving her an awkward side hug as I pushed open the door. "I was going to stop in for a visit, but ... well ... things got complicated, like they always do."

Maxine's smile was warm. "I knew you would eventually stop by, Redmond. It's not your way to hold a grudge. The same with your father and Cillian."

"I'm still kind of angry," Cillian admitted. "I know you meant well, but ... you should've told us what was happening."

"I considered it," Maxine acknowledged as I led everyone into the room. "I didn't know if I could do it until I was already knee-deep in the spell. I didn't want to get your hopes up if I couldn't pull it off. Even after that, it was her idea to keep it quiet."

I stilled as I locked the door. "Mrs. Grimlock didn't want to see her family?" I found that hard to believe given everything I'd heard about the woman.

"Oh, she wanted to see her family," Maxine said. "She was desperate to see them. It was the fact that she couldn't stay that kept her from storming into the house and demanding time with each child. She went there every night to watch you through the windows. Did you know that?"

I spared a glance for Braden and found his eyes misting. Instinctively, I grabbed his hand and gave it a squeeze, a gesture that wasn't lost on my aunt.

"What did she see us doing?" Redmond asked.

"I believe there was a game of sock hockey in the foyer ... and she watched as Aisling broke into your father's desk to steal licorice."

"I knew my stash was light," Cormack muttered.

"She spent some time at the townhouses watching Aisling and Aidan," Maxine continued. "She wanted to see Griffin, of course. She was thrilled with him, thought Aisling ended up with a fine specimen of a husband."

"Did she say that?" Cormack asked.

Maxine bobbed her head. "She did. She said Aisling found the perfect man, someone who reminded her of you but who had enough patience to put up with you. She thought it was miraculous a man like that existed."

"Hey, I think it's miraculous that I didn't kill Griffin for putting his hands on my baby," Cormack shot back. "Why do I never get credit for that?"

Maxine snickered. "She also spent time watching you and said she was thrilled at the way you parented the children, that you somehow found a balance between spoiling them rotten and being a firm disciplinarian."

"He wasn't all that firm," Braden countered, his voice low. "Did she say anything about me?"

Maxine's eyes were kind when she turned to him. "Yes. She said you grew up to be handsome and brave ... and that she was most worried about you because you seemed enamored of the other her."

"The other her? Is that how she referred to ... what came back?"

"It was another part of her," Maxine pointed out as we moved toward the hallway that led to the gate room. "It was the weakest part. The strongest came back to save you."

"And she did save us," Cillian said, clapping Braden hard on the shoulder. "That's the important thing to remember. She saved us, made sure that ... thing ... couldn't take Aisling. She was our mother until the end."

Braden forced a smile. "Yeah. That's the important thing."

THE GRIMLOCKS TOOK A STEP back to allow Maxine and me to prepare for the séance. I wasn't sure who came up with the idea, but by tacit agreement the four of them spent their time marveling over the construction of the gate and holding other manly discussions about sports, hamburgers and why Ford made a mistake when it didn't add another truck to its fall vehicle lineup while we got down to the nitty-gritty in the library.

"I was starting to worry," Maxine admitted, keeping her voice low. "I hadn't heard from you in a few days. You should make more of an effort to keep in touch."

"The phone works both ways," I reminded her. "You could've called me."

"I didn't want to infringe on the new life you're building."

I sighed. "You're part of my life, Aunt Max. It's just ... what's been happening here is weird. It took me by surprise. I've been busy."

"With Braden?"

I steadfastly ignored her gaze as I chalked a pentagram on the floor. We'd decided to bolster the power we would be funneling into the séance with wards and charms in an effort to break whatever spell was keeping the ghosts from talking.

"Oh, are you not talking about him?" Amusement flitted through her eyes as she straightened. "Are you embarrassed?"

"I'm not embarrassed." My temper flashed. "Why would you think I'm embarrassed?"

"I'm simply trying to ascertain why you wouldn't want to share your good news with me."

She sounded far too amused. "It just happened."

"What just happened?"

"Aunt Max." I adopted my sternest voice as a form of warning. "I'm not trying to be difficult. No, really. It's just ... it's new. We've already been dealing with crap from his family. It would be nice if we didn't have to deal with crap from you."

"You're the only child I'll ever have." She turned solemn. "You're my niece, but I think of you as my child. Do you know what that means?"

"I'm your only chance to torture someone?"

"Exactly." She grinned as she straightened. "You need to stop taking life so seriously. If people take the time to joke with you, it's because they care. Braden's siblings run him ragged because he probably did the same to them over the years. You're a new element, but they clearly like you."

"Yeah, well ... I like them, too." The simple truth sent a pang coursing through me. "I like them a lot."

"Even Aisling?"

"Especially her. She's outspoken and tough. She's also weirdly vulnerable, especially now that she's dealing with a baby that seems to pick up on the moods of others."

"Wait ... what?" Maxine made a face. "The baby is empathic?"

"I'm not sure I'd go that far," I hedged. "The baby is absorbing the emotions of those around her. It could be normal, but it somehow feels deeper than that. We'll have to wait to see how it plays out."

"Have you spent much time with the baby?"

"Here and there. She's extremely popular when it comes to being cuddled by her parents, uncles and grandfather, so you have to fight for a chance to hold her."

Maxine snickered. "That is going to be the most spoiled child who ever walked the face of the earth. I mean ... she's the first grandchild and will probably stay that way for at least a few years. She is going to be the absolute devil."

"Right now she's just a baby who likes it when the people who hold her are calm. She had a rough go of it for a bit because Aisling was anxious. Now that Aisling has calmed down, the baby is doing the same."

"That's good. I think Aisling will be a decent mother if she gets out of her head."

"She's already a great mother ... and Griffin is a terrific father."

"Well, that's a given." Maxine dusted off her hands as she finished lighting candles and glanced around the room. "I think we're ready. It's much cleaner in here than I thought it would be. Electricity would be nice, but this isn't half bad."

"Jerry cleaned it the other day."

"How?"

"The vacuum cleaner from upstairs and lots of extension cords. Oh, and he found a Dustbuster in the maintenance closet."

Maxine chuckled. "That sounds just like him. Are you ready to get this show on the road?"

"Absolutely."

. . .

BRADEN SAT TO MY RIGHT, Cormack to my left, and Redmond and Cillian dispersed around Maxine so we could begin the ritual. It was obvious they were nervous by the way they kept glancing around at the shadows. I pushed their agitation out of my head and focused on the problem at hand.

"Let us do the talking," I warned as I lifted my chin and snagged Maxine's gaze. "We need to control the flow of magic if we're going to make this work."

"Are you sure it will work?" Redmond asked as he grabbed Maxine's hand. "I mean ... are you sure you can get these ghosts to talk?"

"No." That was the truth. "Something has been done to them. I don't know what it is, but we need to figure it out if we're going to free them. That is the ultimate goal here."

"I thought the ultimate goal was to get Carroll out of Granger," Braden countered. "That's the big worry, right?"

"Yes, but the ghosts are still a problem we need to solve. Lauren's soul never appeared. There was never a chance for anyone to absorb her. That means something else is being done to these people to absorb their souls right away. We need to figure out what that is ... and how to free them."

"Okay. I'm ready." Braden gripped my hand tightly. "Bring forth the ghosts."

I grinned at him as Cormack rolled his eyes and got comfortable. "That's the plan."

"I can't remember the last time I sat on the ground like this," Cormack complained. "It's undignified."

"You'll get used to it," Maxine admonished. "Just let us do the talking. We've got everything under control."

That was a bit of an exaggeration, but there was no reason to worry them. I cleared my mind, inhaled deeply through my nose, and held Maxine's gaze for almost a full minute. Then we started chanting in unison.

At first we called to each other, essences joining. Then we called to souls that might be lingering near us. Gathering spirits is tricky business, so we had to make sure the words were exact. At a certain point, we sped up and started speaking over each other. Our voices grew, started echoing, and there were at least four voice trails going when a pounding started in the back of the library.

"What is that?" Redmond asked, jerking to look over his shoulder. "Is that a ghost?"

"Shut up," Braden warned. "Can't you see that Izzy and Madame Maxine are in the middle of something? You're ruining it."

"I'm not ruining it," he shot back. "You're ruining it. I mean ... big time. Why can't you just shut up?"

"Why can't both of you shut up?" Cormack challenged. "I mean ... seriously. You're acting like children. If I knew you were going to behave in this manner I would've brought your sister. At least she would've been entertaining ... though she wouldn't have liked the dirt and bugs either."

"What bugs?" Cillian made a face. "I'm not a fan of bugs. You're not talking about spiders, are you? Ugh. I really hate spiders."

I tuned out their voices and focused on the whispers. *Come. Speak. Transcend.* The orders were given over and over and still the chanting continued. At one point I lost control of what I was doing and jerked my head to the ceiling. Out of the corner of my eye, in the reflection of a window pane, I could see the Bruja mask blinking as I took control of the situation.

"*Phasma,*" I intoned, the mask increasing in strength. "*Phasma. Pervenio. Phasma.*" Over and over and over. Eventually, I wasn't even sure I was saying the words out loud. There was a possibility they were trapped in my mind.

That's when Lauren appeared at the edge of the circle. She slammed into being, seemingly from another plane of existence given the twisted expression on her face, and still I repeated the words over and over again.

She opened her mouth and I was certain she would finally speak. But she made no sound. Instead, she raised her hands to her ears and shook her head, anguish rolling across the room in waves.

"Will you look at that?" Cormack was focused on the ghost. "She's really here."

"That's Lauren," Braden explained. "That's the teacher who died. Izzy pointed her out to me on our picnic yesterday."

"You had a picnic?" Redmond was incredulous. "It's not warm enough outside for a picnic."

"We had it in the aquarium."

"Oh, that is so romantic," Cillian deadpanned. "Our little Braden is turning into a real Romeo. I'm so impressed. That right there is how you keep a girl for the long haul. You have to keep doing stuff like that."

"I think it's lame," Redmond lamented. "I think Braden is already whipped and I'm never going to let him hear the end of it."

"Shut up," Cormack barked. "Don't you understand what's happening here? There's a freaking ghost right over there."

"I see her." Redmond was blasé. "She's not doing anything. In fact, she's pretty boring. Has anyone tried to see if we can simply absorb these souls with our scepters and be on our way?"

"No, Redmond, no one thought of trying that," Braden deadpanned. "You're the smartest man in the world. You clearly came up with the best solution."

Redmond ignored the sarcasm. "Thank you."

"I didn't mean it!"

I poured as much energy as I could muster into the spell, but it didn't help. Lauren simply shook her head hard and offered up a tortured expression.

"She still can't speak," Maxine noted. "We're missing something."

"I don't understand. We need to speak to her. We need ... ." I broke off, something occurring to me. "Wait a second." I released Braden's and Cormack's hands and hopped to my feet. "I have an idea."

"What are you doing?" Braden demanded, scrambling after me when I started walking toward Lauren. She'd stopped shaking her head and was now looking in my direction. "Tell me what you're doing," he prodded. "I'm serious. You're making me nervous."

"Braden, perhaps you should step back," Cormack suggested.

"I'm not stepping back. I want to know what she's doing. Izzy?"

I didn't answer. I couldn't. My attention was focused on Lauren as I closed the distance. She seemed to recognize what I was about to do, and instead of trying to dissuade me she eagerly nodded.

"Izzy?" Braden's voice sounded as if it was coming from a long distance as I stopped directly in front of the fallen teacher.

"*Communico*," I ordered, my heart pounding. "*Communico*." I held up my hands to mimic her stance and stepped directly in front of her, my head snapping straight back so I could stare at the ceiling as she funneled every image she could into my brain.

"Izzy!" Braden was desperate as he moved behind me. "Stop! Whatever you're doing, just ... stop!"

I couldn't have followed his instructions even if I wanted to. It was already too late. In fact, it was so late I thought there was a chance I would never be able to separate my consciousness from hers.

"Izzy!"

I shut my eyes as the images blurred. It was time to separate, but I lacked the strength. I'd seen everything at least three times, but I couldn't pull away.

That's when Braden took it upon himself to intervene, even if it was ridiculously dangerous.

"Enough," he barked, grabbing me by the shoulders and pulling with all his might. "That's freaking enough!"

We hit the ground hard, the muffled wind sounds I'd been engulfed in only moments before diminishing. My eyes rolled back in my head as Braden positioned himself on top of me and began to yell.

"Don't you dare pass out! I'm serious. I mean it. Don't!"

It was too late. My brain was overwhelmed and needed to be reset.

Twenty-Six

"Izzy!"

I snapped open my eyes and found Braden practically lying on top of me. He looked as if he was about to have a meltdown – and not a fun one, like when he fought with his siblings about which Batman was the best Batman – and I gasped in surprise as I tried to move him off my chest so I could breathe.

"You're cutting off my oxygen, Braden," I wheezed.

"What?" He looked so relieved when I finally spoke that he didn't fully absorb my words until I jabbed him with my elbow.

"Seriously," I growled.

"Braden, get off her." Cormack's expression was kind as he grabbed Braden around the waist and hauled him up. "You'll smother her, son."

Braden was obviously shaken. He looked between his father and me for confirmation. "Right. I ... right."

"Chill out, drama queen," Redmond ordered, clapping Braden on the shoulder as he moved closer to get a better look at me. "Do you know your face turns into a skull-like thing when you perform magic? It's completely freaky."

"I've been told," I replied, propping myself on my elbows so I could look around the room. "What happened to Lauren?"

"The ghost?" Cillian asked, arching an eyebrow. "She disappeared when Braden wrestled you away from her. It was as if she didn't have the power to stay." He hadn't moved from his spot on the floor. "That was really freaky, by the way. I hate to agree with Redmond because he's always an idiot, but the skull thing is weird. It's going to take some getting used to."

"I'm sorry."

"Don't apologize to him," Braden snapped, grabbing my hand. "The skull thing is cool. They're just jealous. I think it's totally hot."

Cormack shot his son a speculative look. "How much sugar did you eat today?"

Braden balked. "What? Why?"

"You're a little shrill. I need you to take it down a notch."

"Take it down a notch," Cillian and Redmond echoed in unison, chuckling.

Despite the serious nature of the situation, Braden cracked a smile. "Dad used to say that to us all the time when we got out of control as kids," he offered. "We started mocking him when he said it. Then, when we got older, we made it a drinking game and didn't tell him."

"They mock me all the time," Cormack agreed, sliding his arm around my back and helping me to a sitting position. "Tell me how you're feeling. Do we need to take you to a hospital?"

"No." I immediately started shaking my head. "I'm okay. I just ... saw a few things."

"I'll bet you did," Maxine said, her expression dark and foreboding. She'd been so quiet I'd almost forgotten she was in the room with us. "Do have any idea what you just did?"

I wasn't a fan of her accusatory tone. "I communicated with a ghost." I brushed my forehead with the back of my hand and found I was dripping with sweat. "She showed me something."

"What did she show you?" Cillian asked. "Do you know how she died?"

"Yeah. She was attacked by whatever ... thing ... I saw on the camera. It wasn't Granger."

"I never thought it was Granger," Cormack supplied. "The boy is too small to have broken her neck. Did she explain to you what that thing was?"

"It's Carroll."

"Well, of course it is." He was calm as he pulled a handkerchief from his pocket and used it to wipe my brow. "You're a little clammy for my liking. Are you sure we shouldn't take you to a hospital?"

"I'm fine." I was firm. "There's nothing they can do for me. I'll be back to normal in a few minutes."

"I'm not sure that's good," Redmond teased. "Is that skull face part of the 'normal' you?" He used the appropriate air quotes and got an elbow in the gut from Braden for his efforts. "I was just kidding. Geez." He rubbed his ribs. "You have zero sense of humor where she's concerned. You'd better learn to lighten up."

"Yeah, that's not going to happen." Braden smoothed my hair with shaking hands. "Just tell us what she said to you."

"Yes, tell us," Maxine echoed. The expression on her face told me something was bothering her, but I didn't ask in front of our audience. She would tell me when she worked her way around to it.

"We need to go to the casino," I replied, choosing my words carefully. "I need to talk to Oliver."

"Why?" Cormack queried. "Hasn't he helped all that he can?"

"I think he knows more than he's letting on."

"And Lauren told you that?"

"She showed me more than flashes of her death. She showed me images from Carroll's death, too."

"And Oliver was there?" Cormack didn't bother to tamp down his surprise. "I don't understand."

"That makes two of us. We definitely need to talk to him. I can't be certain what I saw. It happened far too fast."

"Then we'll talk to him." Cormack helped me to my feet, going so far as to murder a hovering Braden with a quelling look when he tried to grab my arm. "Son, do you remember what I told you when you tried to beat up the gaggle of girls who were causing trouble with your sister in middle school?"

Braden made a face. "Yes, but I don't think this is similar."

Cormack feigned patience. "What did I tell you?"

"That girls don't like being treated like girls."

"I don't believe that's exactly how I phrased it."

"That women don't like being treated like women," he automatically corrected.

"I didn't phrase it that way either."

"Oh, geez." Braden let loose an exasperated sigh. "That women don't need to be constantly protected because they can take care of themselves."

"That's better." Cormack grinned broadly. "I'm glad to see you were listening."

"I was totally listening," Braden agreed. "That's why it always struck me as weird when you said things like that and then tried to wrap Aisling in cotton to keep her safe. I even remember the time you tried explaining to her that the female brain didn't mature until it hit forty, so that's when she was allowed to pick her own dates."

Cormack's smile slipped. "You know, you don't have to remember absolutely everything I've ever said or done simply so you can throw it in my face."

"I'll keep that in mind ... on our way to see Oliver."

"Yes, Oliver." Cormack returned to the issue at hand. "Let's see what he has to say for himself. I'm dying to hear his excuse for holding back information."

That made two of us.

THE CASINO WAS A CASINO in name only. Basically it was a place for corporate events and weddings. It was a beautiful building, dated without looking old, and I was surprised by how quiet it was when we entered.

"I guess I expected something else," I muttered as I trailed behind Cormack.

"Haven't you ever been here?" Braden asked.

I shook my head. "I mean ... I guess I could've been here as a kid. I don't remember. I thought when they said casino that it would include slot machines and blackjack tables."

"You said the same thing when you were little," Oliver announced, appearing on the stairwell above us. "Good afternoon. I didn't realize we were having guests today."

"Yeah, well, we didn't realize you were withholding information regarding Ryan Carroll's death," Cormack announced, causing me to cringe. This confrontation would've been better if it had been just the two of us. Now it appeared as if I was bringing reinforcements to bully him.

"I see." Oliver's expression was neutral. "What makes you think I'm hiding information?"

Redmond jerked his thumb toward me. "She just did the Hokey Pokey with a ghost and apparently they shared brains for a bit."

That was a simplistic explanation for what happened, but he wasn't wrong. "I touched the other plane," I added. "Lauren showed me a few things, including things she wasn't present for."

"And that brought you to my doorstep?" Oliver's expression was dark. "Why?"

"I saw something." I scrubbed my cheek. "I saw you ... crying. They were tears of blood. You were in the library and there were people around you taking things off the shelves."

"In other words, you were here when the library closed," Cormack noted. "The actual moment when it was closed, I mean. You were present, but you failed to mention that."

"More than that, you lied to me." I found my courage and glared at him. "You said you didn't know why the library was closed. You said it with a straight face and I believed you."

"And you think I lied?"

"I think ... you lied," I confirmed, my heart twisting. "The thing is, I don't think you lied simply to be malicious. I think you're protecting someone."

"And who would that be?"

"Yourself," Braden automatically answered. "Everyone knows vampires only care about themselves."

Oliver showed his teeth and growled. "If that's the case, then why are you here? I may be outnumbered, but that doesn't mean I can't take the whole lot of you if it comes to it."

Sensing things were rapidly getting out of control, I took a bold step forward and held my hands out in a pleading manner. "Don't. I know you weren't protecting yourself. Dragging this out will only end in disaster. Please don't do this."

"What are you talking about?" Cormack asked. "Do you know more than you said? Do you know who he's protecting?"

"He's protecting me," a male voice announced from behind us, causing me to swivel quickly. There, walking in from the side door, was Brett Soloman. Not only was he in charge of the casino, which apparently meant booking weddings and meetings rather than the unsavory things I was imagining the past three weeks, he was Oliver's longtime boyfriend.

"You're Brett, right?" Cormack furrowed his brow. If he was worried about being trapped in a building with two vampires, he didn't show it. "I don't believe we've ever met."

"That's because I have nothing to do with the gate." Brett strode forward and extended his hand in greeting. He seemed resigned more than upset. "It's nice to meet you. I've heard good things about you over the years."

His blue eyes were heavy as they tracked to me. "And I haven't seen you in a very long time," he continued. "Of course, I've seen you since you returned. You just haven't realized it. I didn't want to approach in case I confused you."

His reaction threw me for a loop. "I don't understand. I ... do I know you?"

"You were little the last time we saw each other. You spent a lot of time with Oliver and me. We liked to spoil you." His smile was wistful. "When Oliver said you were coming back, I was excited. Then, when I realized you didn't remember us that excitement turned to trepidation. Still, you grew into a beautiful woman. I always knew you would."

I felt out of my element. "I don't understand why you've been hiding from me."

"Hiding? No. Giving you time to adjust? Yes. We wanted to be very careful that you didn't remember too much too soon. We agreed Oliver would spend some time with you first and then we would feel you out about the memories you're obviously holding back. That's a conversation for another day." He flicked his eyes to Cormack. "You're here about Ryan Carroll. You shouldn't be questioning Oliver. I killed him."

Oliver snarled and vaulted over the side of the railing. He landed next to me with an echoing thud, causing me to flinch as he took up an aggressive stance next to his boyfriend. "Don't even think you're taking him."

"I'm not interested in taking him." Cormack was matter-of-fact. "That's the furthest thing from my mind. We need to know what's going on. Carroll has taken up residence in a small child and he's controlling ghosts to the point he's prohibiting them from speaking. Izzy put herself at risk to meld with one in an effort to learn what she could."

Oliver let loose a low groan. "Geez. You always were way too curious. I hoped you'd learned to look before you leap, but apparently that hasn't happened."

"We needed answers," I replied simply. "I didn't know where else to get them. Lauren has been trying to communicate with me from the start. She whispered the first time I saw her. I just remembered that during our ... meeting of the minds. Or maybe I remembered but forgot I remembered. I don't know. It's not important.

"I couldn't make out what they were saying that first day because all the ghosts talked at once," I continued. "I was freaked out and I wanted to get away, and apparently that was a mistake because they've been silenced since. They tried to communicate that day, but Carroll somehow muted them. I think you know why."

"I don't know the specifics," Oliver cautioned, dragging a hand through his hair and swallowing hard. "I have a few ideas. As for Ryan, ... he should've been laid to rest years ago. I don't understand why he's back."

"Because you killed him?" I glanced at Brett for confirmation.

"I did." He showed no sign of remorse. "He had it coming. He was trying to kill people to prolong his own life."

"And how did that work?" Cormack asked, moving to the couch in the middle of the room and sinking down. "Why don't we all get comfortable?" he suggested. "This conversation might take some time, and there's no reason for everyone to keep eyeing each other as if we're at odds."

Braden took my hand as he steered me toward the couch, making sure I was positioned between Cormack and him as Oliver and Brett took the chairs across the way. Cillian and Redmond each grabbed wooden chairs from next to a small table by the window and dragged them to either side of the couch, making sure Aunt Max was comfortable before they sat.

"This conversation won't take all that long," Brett countered. "I thought we should tell the truth back then, but Oliver was worried. We were already dealing with stares and whispers because we were two men living together. The vampire thing was secondary, believe it or not. He didn't want more trouble heaped on us."

My heart went out to him. "You said Carroll was killing people to prolong his own life. How was he doing that?"

"The normal way," Brett replied without hesitation. "He killed people who didn't show up on his lists – at first he tried to find criminals, but that wasn't as easy as he thought so he started killing anyone who crossed his path and he thought he could hide – and then he took the souls and used them in a ritual he concocted with Peter to bolster his life."

I furrowed my brow. "I'm not sure I understand."

"It was an old ritual."

"I still don't understand."

Brett glanced at Oliver and then sighed. "Peter was a crossroads demon."

I was utterly flabbergasted. "What? I ... what?"

"He was a crossroads demon," Brett repeated. "I'm not sure how he wormed his way into being gatekeeper, but it was quite the coup. He managed to collect souls while also getting a paycheck. No one was the wiser ... except for us."

"Did you say anything?" Cormack asked, leaning forward. "Did you let the front office know what was happening?"

Oliver nodded. "I did, but only after the fact. That's on me, and I've regretted it for a very long time."

"We need to know the whole story," I prodded. "It's important."

"I know. It's just ... Brett did what had to be done. He did what I couldn't, or at least what I was unwilling to do at the time. I didn't mean for things to go as far as they did."

"That ultimately doesn't matter. We need the whole story. I know you." I spoke from the heart. "I feel as if I've known you all my life. If you felt the need to cover it up, you had a reason. There's no reason any longer. Nothing bad can happen if you tell the truth."

He looked taken aback. "Why did you just say that?"

"Because you said it to me when I was a kid," I replied without hesitation. "I was afraid of getting in trouble because I stole a piece of a candy from the gift shop and I was crying in the basement. I confided in you and that's what you said."

"You remember everything?"

I shook my head. "I remember that. I had a flash yesterday when I got a piece of hard candy from the jar on your desk. It was a quick thing. I was going to bring it up but ... I never got the chance. Between ghosts and other stuff, I've had my hands full. You told me that then, and you were right. I didn't get in trouble. Things were better after because I was no longer mired in guilt. The same can be true for you."

He let loose a sigh and then shook his head. "You always were a naïve little thing. Still, you're right. It's time." He tilted his head toward Brett. "It's your story to tell. I don't even remember most of it."

"My story," Brett agreed, licking his lips. "Okay. Well, here we go."

Twenty-Seven

"It's important to understand that I didn't spend much time around Peter," Brett started, adopting a far-off expression. "I had other things going on. The gate was never a concern for me. That was Oliver's thing. He liked working near it because he was always worried something bad would happen near it. He wanted to be on the front line to stop whatever that something was.

"Me, on the other hand, I honestly didn't care," he continued. "I didn't have many questions about death. I'm a vampire. Those questions didn't mean to me what they meant to other people. Heck, Oliver had questions, but I couldn't be bothered. I was much happier planning weddings and doing my own thing."

He dragged a hand through his dark hair and shot me a small smile. "The first time I met Carroll was on a day Oliver needed help. There were only two people monitoring the gate back then, which was a mistake. Three people are better because it means there are fewer chances for screw-ups due to fatigue."

I cast Oliver a rueful look. "I guess that's why you've been on me to find a replacement."

"That and other reasons," he acknowledged.

"Oliver had something to do for the reaper council and someone needed to monitor a surprise intake," Brett continued. "He called me to see if I could pinch hit. I agreed because I had nothing better to do and I wanted to help.

"When I got there, the room was supposed to be empty," he said. "It was quiet at first. I sat at the desk and read a book. I didn't realize I wasn't alone until I heard something in the library. I headed in that direction ... and found Peter."

"If you were called in to cover the intake, why would Peter be here?" I asked, confused. "I'm not sure I understand. Why couldn't he monitor the computer?"

Brett snickered. "Oh, you're so young ... but cute." He winked at me. "First, there were no computers back then. The intakes were more ... involved."

That hadn't occurred to me. Of course there were no computers back then. Er, wait. "There were computers back then," I argued. "They were simply bigger."

"And not something we used," Cormack said. "Early computers were expensive and the amount of memory we needed didn't exist. Back in the day, scepters had to be transported here for the transfer."

"Oh." I tried to picture that in my head. "Okay, well ... go on."

"I heard voices and was confused," Brett explained. "When scepters were dropped off, it was usually by one person. The local reapers took turns collecting them at a central location and drove them to us. We would then discharge them into a receptacle close to the gate ... and that was basically it.

"So, when I heard Peter's voice I was understandably confused," he said. "I was under the impression he was outside of the office, which is why they needed me. I headed into the library, and that's where the voices grew stronger. Peter was there ... and he wasn't alone."

"Carroll," I surmised.

He shook his head. "Ghosts. Green ghosts ... and a lot of them."

"And Peter was talking to them?" My mind was going a mile a minute. "How? Why?"

"I'm going to make a long story short because this could go on forever," Brett replied. "I asked that very question. Peter was stunned to see me. He started freaking out and demanding I leave. When I refused, he told me the whole story ... but only because I refused to let it go no matter how many times he tried to get me to give up my questions.

"It seems Carroll approached him one day when visiting the gate," he continued. "Carroll made a point to volunteer to drop off the scepters as often as possible. He wanted access to the gate, you see, and it wasn't because he was scientifically minded or curious."

"That explains how he got such easy access to the gate," Cormack mused, rubbing his chin. "I was always confused, because the gate was considered a huge secret up until about twenty years ago. No one was really supposed to talk about it, let alone visit it."

"That was the norm," Brett agreed. "I asked Peter what was going on and demanded answers. I was so worried, I showed him my teeth. I had no intention of hurting him, mind you, but I thought it was important to get answers."

Cormack nodded once. "Of course."

"Peter was a blubbering mess," Brett supplied. "He told me a fantastical story, swearing up and down that he initially joined forces with Carroll because he was curious. He said he didn't want to cheat death —which I'm not sure I believed at the time or even now — but that he was terrified of the things Carroll had been doing.

"Basically, he was drawing souls from the other side by way of a scepter he modified," he continued. "He would stand very close to the gate and try to absorb souls that were directly on the other side."

"How is that possible?" Cillian asked. "I thought once you crossed the gate you were stuck on the other side forever." He looked to his father for confirmation.

"We all believed that," Cormack said. "I know I did. Since the wraith crossed over and returned, though, I've had a few questions of my own. The home office hasn't been keen on answering them."

"Which means you suspect it's possible to cross through the gate and return, too," I mused.

He shot me a pointed look. "I don't know that I believe that," he clarified. "I would not risk it on the information we have right now. My belief system has shifted a bit in the past month. That doesn't mean I believe it's a fact. It simply means I'm curious."

"You conveniently kept that information from us," Braden muttered.

"What good would it have done?" Cormack challenged. "I'm not risking my life, or my children's lives for that matter, to cross the threshold. If you think that, you're crazier than that loon Carroll, who we've yet to hear the whole story about." He turned back to Brett. "Finish it."

"There's not much to tell. Peter said that Carroll had been collecting souls from the other side because they were stronger than the ones he could absorb here, somehow magically emboldened or something, and then basically feeding off them, using their energy to build his strength. He was determined to live forever."

"I still don't get it," I pressed. "I mean ... I understand that he wanted to live forever. Everyone who ever met him basically said the same thing. How did he feed off the energy of the dead?"

"By turning himself into a cannibal of sorts," Oliver replied, stretching out his long legs. "I've done a lot of research on this since it happened. All I can say with any degree of certainty is that Carroll turned himself into a hybrid ghoul, kind of a fancy wendigo, only this time he was feeding off supercharged souls. They sustained him ... and he enslaved them. The problem was, the ghosts couldn't go anywhere after he sucked them from the other side. They were trapped here because fractured souls can't pass over."

Braden stirred beside me. "That's not true. My mother's soul was fractured and the bigger part crossed over."

"Really?" Oliver arched an eyebrow. "Are you sure about that?"

"We're sure," Maxine replied. She'd barely said anything since we'd arrived at the casino. It was obvious she was thinking ... and hard. Still, she was involved in the conversation. "Lily's soul left a small piece behind, which was with her body. The part of her soul that crossed over was much bigger than the part left behind."

"Hmm." Oliver rubbed the back of his neck. "Carroll was feeding on souls to sustain himself. He had a plan to prolong his life. He also was making himself stronger. He got it into his head that he didn't need to steal souls from the other side, which was becoming difficult."

"You see, he didn't know when there was a soul on the other side close enough to absorb," Brett volunteered. "He could only take one every month or so when he started. He was fine with that because it was new and he got a rush every time he gnawed on a soul.

"The souls that had been on the other side were stronger, so he wanted those," he said. "He didn't have trouble murdering people for their souls, but he wanted those strong souls. He even took to taking his collected souls and releasing them at the gate only to try to capture them right away again. He thought he could fool people that way, but it didn't work. He kept getting hungrier.

"Like any other drug, he wanted more," he continued. "He started feeding every week ... and then he tried coming every day. Something or someone caught on across the gate and moved all the souls away from the opening at some point. Peter said that by the time he went two weeks without feeding he was almost without reason and frothing at the mouth."

"You have to understand, he was getting stronger," Oliver said. "Things like his bad knee improved. He had a skin rash on his elbow, something chronic, and it also healed. He thought he'd stumbled on some great elixir, a way to make life better forever for a chosen few ... and yet he ignored the ghosts who were piling up along the way."

"The ghosts don't have souls," I murmured. "That's why the reapers can't absorb them with their scepters."

"Parts of their soul remain in those green forms of theirs," Oliver corrected. "Pieces of their souls live in Carroll. Unlike Lily Grimlock, who had enough of a soul to cross over, I don't think these ghosts are in charge of the main portion of their own souls. This is where the end of the story comes in." He turned to Brett, expectant. "Tell them the rest. It's time we put everything out there."

Brett sighed and nodded. "I was frustrated with the story Peter was telling me. He painted Carroll as the bad guy. I think that was true, at least to a certain extent, but Peter knew what was going on and I found him equally evil.

"He swore up and down he was trying to stop Carroll, but I didn't believe him," he continued. "We argued ... rather loudly. Apparently Carroll heard. He was furious when he came into the library. He accused Peter of betraying him, telling his secrets.

"I could tell right away when I saw him that he was crazed," he said. "He had a wild look in his eyes. Some people say cannibals go crazy after a time. I think Carroll was a different sort of a cannibal, an energy cannibal if you will, and was going crazy, too."

"I hadn't seen him in a bit," Oliver offered. "Peter arranged the schedule so he was always here when the souls came in later in the day. He sent me home. It didn't make much sense because that was the whole reason I had a job, but he kept me away in the afternoons for two weeks. I didn't understand why until after the fact."

"I argued with Peter and he started crying," Brett explained. "Everything spewed out. He told me about Carroll's plans, the murders, all of it. Obviously I was disgusted. The ghosts left behind were shells of themselves. I was determined to find a way to free them ... except that's when Carroll showed up.

"He was crazy, like I said. He accused Peter of betraying him, trying to steal the power he'd amassed. He was a complete and total kook. I told him I was calling Oliver and stormed out of the room, leaving the two of them behind."

"Did you call him?" I asked.

"Yes, but leaving that room was a mistake." Brett was solemn. "I called Oliver from the phone in the gate room. Back then, there were no cell phones. I had to stay in one spot to make the call. I gave him a barebones explanation and he promised to get to the library as soon as possible.

"It was already too late by then, although I didn't know it," he continued. "By the time I'd finished, Carroll had killed Peter and collected his soul. He was ranting, going crazy. I couldn't believe what I was seeing. That's when the ghosts explained things."

"The ghosts talked to you?" I perked up. "But ... how? The ghosts can't seem to speak. They could that first day, but they've been muted since."

"I think that's something Carroll's shade did to them," Oliver replied. "Yeah ... I think he's a shade. My research suggests that's the case. But there's still more to the original story."

Brett made an odd throat-clearing sound. "I was upset when I realized Peter was dead. Carroll had a knife in his hand and was pacing, screaming about people betraying him. I tried talking him down, but the conversation didn't last long. When he blamed Peter for what happened, said it was his fault for going behind his back, I saw red."

"You killed him," Cormack mused, rubbing his hands over his knees. "That's why we could never find him."

"I killed him," Brett agreed. "I snapped his neck in a fit of rage. I ended it all right there. The minute he was gone, the ghosts started moving toward the gate ... as if drawn there. They crossed over when free of him. I thought it was finished, that I'd done the right thing."

"The ghosts were gone by the time I arrived," Oliver explained. "Brett told me what happened. I agreed he did the right thing. We were certain it was over ... and yet we had two bodies to deal with. We decided to dispose of them the only way we knew how ... fire."

My stomach twisted. "Lovely."

"We weren't alone," Oliver said quickly. "Edward Hatfield was here. I called him. He was a friend and the head of the home office at the time, a position now held by his son. He came right away, and when we told him what had happened he said we had to eradicate the evidence. He didn't want the story getting out in case someone else tried the same thing. It was too dangerous.

"So, he watched us burn the bodies and he helped us seal off the library," he continued. "He thought it was best to pretend the room never existed. Only a few people had been in the gate room at that point. If any of them asked, I was to tell them there was a rodent infestation that forced the closing of the room. Eventually they would stop asking ... and what happened would be part of the past."

"And yet it's not part of the past," I announced, hopping up so I could pace. "It's sitting directly in front of us. You said the ghosts were drawn to the gate. Were their souls intact when that happened?"

"I don't know," Brett replied, holding out his hands as he shrugged. "I assumed they were free when Carroll died, that their soul pieces somehow joined together."

"What about Carroll's soul?"

Brett looked lost. "I assumed he crossed over with the ghosts. Obviously I missed something."

"Carroll was too powerful by the time Brett killed him," Oliver volunteered. "I've been doing a lot of research ... I mean a lot ... and I think that Carroll's soul fragmented when Brett killed him. It was already a grotesque thing because of what he did, and when small pieces started flicking away it freed the ghosts so they could cross over.

"Carroll's spirit remained behind, though," he said. "I don't know how it remained hidden for so long, but it's back, and we need to find a way to get rid of it."

"You said it yourself. You closed off the library. He was locked in there for decades. His body was burned, but he was strong enough to keep from crossing over. Once the library was sealed, he was trapped. I'm guessing the room was warded."

Oliver arched an eyebrow. "How did you know that?"

"Because the wards were meant to keep others out, but they served a dual purpose. They kept him in. When we discovered the room a few weeks ago, we destroyed the wards that were protecting it."

"And he escaped," Cormack finished. "How did he manage to grow so strong in such a short period? He's a shade. He has no physical form."

"Except he does ... kind of." I thought of Granger and shuddered. "He's been possessing people and feeding off souls. He killed Lauren, ate her soul, and then took over Granger's body. I think he's been doing it for weeks. I think all those ghosts I saw are recent kills.

"And, since he learned his lesson with people talking and betraying him, he figured out a way to silence the ghosts," I continued. "He saw they were trying to talk to me that first day and made sure that didn't happen. He didn't want us figuring it out."

"So ... you're saying that he's a powerful ghost who can eat people and he's inside of a little kid," Redmond deduced. "Isn't that what we knew beforehand?"

"He's a shade," Oliver corrected. "That's different from a ghost. In fact, the things you call ghosts that have remained behind aren't really ghosts in the truest sense of the word. They're displaced souls ... and they can't cross over until we destroy the shade and free them."

"And we can't destroy the shade while it's inside of Granger," I added. "It will destroy the boy. That's why he's hiding in a child. We might risk it with an adult. We can't with a child."

"That means we have to get the shade to leave the boy and figure out a way to destroy him," Cillian said. "Do you have any idea how to do that? I mean ... I could do some research, but I've never dealt with a shade before. I didn't even realize they were real."

"Actually, I have dealt with a shade before," I announced, shuddering at a distasteful memory. "There was a ghoul in New Orleans after Katrina. I ... you know what? It doesn't matter. I know how to get rid of a shade. It takes a powerful spell. We also need a few specific ingredients, most of which I can get from the conservatory here. There's one, though, that I'll need help with."

"What is that?" Cormack shot me an encouraging look. "Whatever I can do to help, I'm willing to do. Tell me and I'll find the ingredient."

I pressed my lips together, uncomfortable. "It's a difficult ingredient," I said finally. "We need blood from a member of Carroll's family. The magic I'm going to work is a blood spell, so ... I need blood."

Cormack's face fell. "You need blood from Carroll's relative ... and the only living relative we're certain he has is Angelina."

"Oh, well, that should go over well," Braden said dryly. "Who wants to be the one to call her?"

"There's only one choice for that." Cormack was grim. "I guess we need to call your sister off the bench after all. She's going to get her way again."

"I don't like the sound of that," Redmond said quickly. "Why can't Cillian do it? She's still in love with him."

"Because Aisling is the one she's really drawn to," I answered for Cormack. "She may make a big deal over Cillian, but he's not the reason she keeps coming around. It's Aisling. Your father is right. She has to be the one to approach Angelina."

"That won't be a nightmare or anything," Redmond lamented. "Everyone assume crash positions."

Twenty-Eight

isling was all bluster, bravado and haughty egotism when she strolled into the aquarium. We'd moved our meeting of the minds to the building we planned to work out of, and the extra swagger in her step was a thing to behold.

"You rang," she said dryly.

Cormack's eyes lit with amusement when he saw her, while Braden made a face and Cillian smothered a laugh.

"Hey, kid." Redmond swooped in and hugged her, which I found interesting. He was the oldest brother, which meant he ragged on the males in his family and apparently doted on the lone female. "How is my favorite niece?"

"She's with her father, who is eating all our cake." Aisling's eyes bounced around the room. "I might be a little loaded up on a cake, too. I just thought I should make you aware."

"Oh, good," Braden drawled. "A sugar rush. That's exactly what we need."

"Shut it." Aisling jabbed a finger in his direction. It just happened to be a middle finger. "Don't make me come over there."

"Yeah, yeah, yeah." Braden didn't look particularly worried. "When does Angelina get here?"

"Soon." Aisling checked the clock on the wall. "I told her the island pimp was only going to wait so long to see if she was Belle Isle material, so I expect her to be prompt."

Cormack made a stern throat-clearing sound. "You didn't say that, did you? There's no way she'll show up for that."

"Oh, she'll show up. She can't help herself." Amusement danced through Aisling's lavender eyes. "She needs attention right now. I'm the only one who can give it to her."

"How do you figure?" Braden challenged. "When we saw her, she was drunk as a skunk and making an ass of herself at Woody's. She was getting plenty of attention."

"That's not the attention she wants," Aisling countered. "She wants individual attention. Even though her mother treated her poorly — that woman was a menace and a half, quite frankly — Angelina misses her. She got used to the criticism and she's struggling without it."

Cormack slid her a sidelong look. "How do you know that?"

"I know all and see all."

"How really?"

Aisling shrugged. "I saw her the night her mother died. I was the one who reaped Mrs. Davenport, if you remember."

"I remember," Cormack confirmed. "You volunteered even though you were going through something yourself. That was right after the storms, right after Griffin almost ... well, you know. I thought for sure you would hole up with him for a full week. Instead, you volunteered for a job you should've passed on."

"Oh, I wanted to pass on it. I hated the whole thing." Aisling smiled at the memory, although the expression was humorless. "Angelina's mother has always been the devil in disguise. Not even a good disguise. I was still the only one who could handle that job."

"Because you're starting to like Angelina?" I asked the question before I thought better of it. The way the Grimlocks snorted in unison told me I'd misjudged the situation.

"Oh, I'll never like Angelina," Aisling grimaced. "Never. Not even a little. Never ever."

"Then why did you volunteer to do something nice for her?" I was curious.

"Because she helped us ... kind of ... by not pressing charges during one of the storms. Her mother wanted to, even though I was trying to protect her. That's a whole big story that we'll get into later. The thing is, I had to be the one to reap Angelina's mother because I'm the only one who wouldn't feel sorry for her ... and she hates it when people pity her."

I tilted my head, considering. I wasn't sure I believed the part about her not feeling sorry for Angelina. Still, the rest of it made sense. "She held it together because she didn't want to look weak in front of you."

"Pretty much. She knew I would be the one to reap her mother's soul even though I wore my ring and she didn't see me. That knowledge was enough to allow her to keep her pride."

"Okay, let's say that makes sense," Braden said. "Why do you think Angelina is going to show up now?"

"Because she can't not show up," Aisling replied simply. "She loves a challenge ... and I challenged her to get her to come here."

"I'm almost afraid to ask," Cormack said as he shook his head. "How did you challenge her?"

"Oh, well ... ." Aisling didn't have a chance to answer because at that moment the door flew open behind her. She was standing close enough she had to hop to avoid the door hitting her, and she burst out laughing when she saw the woman storm into the room.

Angelina appeared as if she'd been in the middle of a salon appointment when Aisling made the call. Her wet hair hung lifelessly over her shoulders, and she looked absolutely furious as she peered around the room through half-cut bangs.

"This had better be good," she announced.

"You're looking as lovely as ever, Angelina," Redmond offered, grinning. "What a pleasure it is to see you."

"Stuff it, Redmond." Angelina's eyes filled with fire. "I'm here for the box full of gold you found with my great-grandfather's name on it. You said I had thirty minutes to claim it. That's the only reason I'm here."

Cormack slowly tracked his eyes to Aisling as I bit my bottom lip to keep from laughing. Oliver and Brett were far too amused to hide the fact they were having a good time and both ducked their heads together and began chortling.

"You told her there was gold waiting for her here?" Cillian asked, horrified. "Aisling, that is … ."

"I told her that pimps were waiting," Aisling corrected. "I might've thrown in the gold thing to make sure she showed up, though."

"I. Can't. Even." Cormack rubbed his forehead. "Why would you think that's a good idea?"

"Because it obviously worked," Aisling replied, grinning. "You're welcome."

"Oh, geez." Cillian slapped his hands over his eyes and fought to regroup. "Okay, well, I guess I should be the one to tell her." He tentatively took a step in the fuming woman's direction. "Angelina, I regret to inform you there is no gold. Aisling lied to get you here. I apologize for her methods, but we really are happy to see you."

"And we can rarely say that," Braden added. "The happy part, I mean. Usually when we see you people start hoping for diarrhea and heartburn to ease the agony that is your presence."

"Nice one." Aisling pumped her fist and bobbed her head at her brother. "That diarrhea part was especially inspired."

Braden saluted. "I learned from the best."

"Oh, shut up," Cormack ordered. "You guys are making things worse."

"I'll say," Angelina seethed. "Why would you trick me to come out here if there's no gold? Unless … ." She narrowed her eyes as she turned to Cillian. "Let me guess. You've finally decided to dump the boring nurse and you're ready to give it another go with me. I knew you would come around.

"Of course, I don't know why you needed to enlist your sister to help you open the avenues of conversation again," she continued. "That was a weird choice. You don't have to ask. I'm ready and willing." She held up her arms, as if waiting for a hug. "Come and get me."

"I think I just threw up in my mouth a little bit," Cillian complained.

"I'm right there with you, buddy." Redmond clapped Cillian's shoulder. "I'm kind of curious to see what will happen if you go over there.

In my head, her jaw opens like a shark and she swallows you whole. Why don't you see if I'm right?"

"Knock that off right now!" Cormack was at his limit as he glared at his sons. "This is not the time. We have a very serious situation. In fact ... ." He trailed off and sucked in a breath to calm himself. "The thing is, Angelina, we need some of your blood. I know that sounds weird, but we need a little of it to conduct a ritual."

Whatever she was expecting, that wasn't it. The face Angelina made was straight out of a horror movie. "You want my blood? What is wrong with you?" She moved to escape through the door, but Aisling smoothly stepped in to block her path.

"We can't let you leave." Aisling was grave. "We need your blood. We'll take it by force if we have to."

"By force?" Angelina's forehead wrinkled. "I can't believe I fell for your crap over the phone. I should've known you were lying when you said you'd found gold doubloons."

"Doubloons?" Cillian's eyebrows practically flew off his forehead. "You told her we found doubloons?"

"Griffin and I were watching *The Goonies*," Aisling replied, unruffled. "Pirate treasure was the first thing that popped into my head."

"There are days I want to give my children to someone else," Cormack muttered, shaking his head. "So many days."

"Well, I'm not giving you my blood." Angelina was beside herself. "I can't believe you would even ask. I knew you guys were into freaky stuff, but this is beyond the pale. I just ... hate you guys so much." She moved to push Aisling out of the way, but the youngest Grimlock was having none of it.

"I said we would take it by force and I meant it!" Aisling threw herself at Angelina, wrapping her arms around her neck as she attempted to wrestle the woman to the ground. "We need that blood and we're not allowing you to leave without it. Someone get a knife!"

"Aisling!" Cormack barked out her name as he attempted to find a way to separate her from Angelina. "Let her go right now."

"She'll run," Aisling argued. "We can't allow that. We need her blood. In fact ... Redmond, give me your pocketknife."

Obligingly, Redmond dug in his pocket until he came back with the item in question. "Where do you want me to cut her?"

"Her butt," Aisling replied. "It's so big she won't even notice a little blood going missing from that area."

"Okay."

"Knock that off!" Cormack ordered, grunting when an errant elbow hit him in the stomach. "Braden, grab your sister!"

"Oh, why do I have to be the one to grab her?" Braden was petulant as he stepped forward and wrapped his arms around Aisling's midriff. "Stop doing that, Ais! You'll kill her if you're not careful."

"Let me go," Angelina shrieked. "I will call the police if you don't stop." Her hair was a mess, almost completely covering her face when Braden finally managed to wrestle Aisling off her back. Both women were breathing heavily and glaring at one another, their chests heaving, when Cormack stepped forward with outstretched hands.

"Angelina, this is important," he pleaded. "We don't want to hurt you. We just need a vial of your blood."

"Why would I possibly give you that?" Angelina groused. "I mean ... what kind of sick freak wants someone else's blood?"

"It's about Ryan Carroll. He's ... not entirely gone. Not only that, he's hurting people. We need your blood to make sure he can't come back. I swear it won't hurt. You won't even know we've taken anything from you."

"Oh, I'll know," she growled.

"You're the only person who can help us," he pleaded, changing tactics. "Without you, this entire operation is lost."

Angelina blinked several times and then she started shaking her head. "Tough noogies. I'm not giving you my blood. You're a bunch of morons if you think that's going to happen. Now ... get out of my way." She moved to shove Braden and Aisling aside so she could make her escape. Cormack spoke before that could happen.

"Well, I tried being reasonable," he lamented. "Aisling, have it your way. Wrestle her down and take the blood by force."

I couldn't believe what I was hearing. "Seriously?"

He nodded. "There's only one way out of this. If she won't help of her own free will, we'll simply have to take what we need. Aisling, go nuts."

Aisling let loose a war whoop — apparently she wasn't lying about the sugar rush — and this time when she jumped on Angelina it was with added vigor. For her part, Angelina looked momentarily shocked ... and then started putting up a vicious fight.

"You'll never take me alive," she called out.

"Good," Aisling shot back. "Finally we agree on something."

THE WRESTLING match ended when both women were exhausted. Angelina lay spread eagle on the floor, her eyes on the ceiling, and didn't say a word when Oliver swooped in to draw a bit of blood. I wasn't even sure she noticed what was happening, but when she finally stood to leave there was an added glint in her eyes that hadn't been there before.

"Don't forget the park, Aisling," she called out. "I'll see you there in twelve days ... and you're going to be crying when I'm done with you."

"Yeah, yeah, yeah." Aisling waved her off and focused on her arm. "I think I'm going to bruise. Griffin won't like that."

"Yes, well, you can explain to Griffin that you let Angelina get the best of you and that's why you're bruised," Cormack suggested.

"Hey!" She extended a warning finger. "That is not what happened at all. I ... you ... we ... um ... I'm still getting over giving birth." She sounded petulant as she made her excuses. "It wasn't a fair fight."

"Oh, poor Aisling," Cillian cooed. "She's no longer the baddest Grimlock on the block. Now she's a mother. We should get you one of those aprons that proclaim you 'world's best mom' so people know not to pick a fight with you."

Aisling's mouth dropped open. "I can't believe you just said that to me." She groaned as she rolled to her feet. "I'm taking you down next. Just you wait."

"You're not taking anyone down," Cormack countered, snagging his daughter by the nape of the neck before she could spring into action. "In fact, your part in our current tale is finished. It's time for you to head home."

"But, no," she protested. "I need to hang around and see you take down the shade. I'm part of this."

"You are," Cormack agreed. "You also just said it yourself. You're not quite back to full strength. Before you open your mouth and start whining about that, it's not my fault. You gave birth. That makes you a hero in my book, no matter what comes next."

"Definitely a hero," Braden agreed. "I'm still in awe you managed to grow a human being and then find a way to kick it out of your body without dying. But you need to rest. It will take time to get back to your normal self."

"There's no shame in that, Aisling," Redmond offered. "You're already stronger than the rest of us."

"If I'm strong, why do I have to leave?" Aisling complained.

"Because we have no idea how the shade will react to the ritual," Cormack replied without hesitation. "We have to remove him from the boy remotely, which means he's going to be summoned to this location. The first thing he's going to do is search for a body. You might not want to hear it, but you make an enticing target because your defenses are down."

Aisling squirmed as she shifted from one foot to the other. "I still don't like this. I should be in the thick of things."

"You're here." Cormack tapped the spot above his heart and caused me to smile. "You did the hard part for us already. You got Angelina here. We have her blood. Now you have to leave, because we can't risk you."

Aisling let loose an exaggerated sigh. "I can't believe I'm missing the fun part. I want to see the bad guy go down."

"We'll tell you all about it over dinner tonight," Cormack offered. "We're having chocolate mousse with gummy worms for dessert."

Aisling brightened considerably. "That dirt cup thing that we saw in a magazine and you made the cook learn how to make." Her grin was so wide it threatened to swallow her entire face. "That's a great idea. Izzy hasn't had that one yet."

"I'm looking forward to it," I promised. "I'll tell you how everything went down while we're eating."

Aisling blew out a long breath and nodded. "Okay. I'll leave you guys to the fun part. As soon as that baby is holding up her own head, I'm going to be right back in the thick of things."

Cormack chuckled. "I expect nothing less."

Braden added, "It's not fun to fight evil without you."

"Definitely," Cillian agreed. "It won't be long until you're finding trouble again. Have a little faith. You can't seem to escape it."

"Yeah, well ... ." Aisling stopped in front of her father long enough to give him a hug. "Do what you need to do. Be careful. You might make a mistake if I'm not here to tell you what you're doing wrong."

Cormack chuckled as he gave her a hug. "We'll be careful. You text as soon as you get home. I want to know that you're safe."

"Oh, don't worry. I'll be home with my husband and baby, watching television. There's nothing safer than that."

She almost looked disappointed as she trudged toward the door.

"Have some more cake," I suggested. "The sugar can only help."

She grinned as she waved. "Now that right there is a fabulous idea."

Twenty-Nine

Maxine and I worked together to ready the spell ingredients while Oliver and Brett handled the wards. Cormack and Braden watched the action from chairs, working overtime not to get in the way, while Cillian and Redmond headed toward the Duskin School for the Deaf to verify the exact moment Granger was back to himself and safe from Carroll's machinations.

"You shouldn't have done what you did," Maxine scolded when we were close to finishing the spell ingredients. "Melding with that ghost the way you did ... ."

"It was necessary," I finished. "We needed information. That was the quickest way to get it."

"Yes, but to meld with a ghost ... ."

"They're not normal ghosts. I knew that going in. There was something off about them. Do you really think I haven't dealt with ghosts during my time in New Orleans? They're commonplace down there, although that seems to be sacrilege if you talk to the reapers up here."

"Yes, well, the Grimlocks take their job very seriously," Maxine said. "You could've lost yourself with that little exercise, my dear. I'm not one to tell you what you can and can't do, but you can't do that."

"Except I *did* do that," I reminded her, pressing the heel of my hand to my forehead. I felt a migraine brewing and my aunt was the source. "I'm fine. In case you haven't noticed, the only thing bad that happened was that I was a little slow for about ten minutes. If that's the worst that comes of it, I'll consider it a win and move on."

She made a noise halfway between a sigh and growl. "Izzy, you've always been a brave girl. Even when you were little, you jumped in headfirst and didn't care who you were taking on. That doesn't mean what you did this afternoon was right. Have you considered what could've happened if she took you over?"

"Who? Lauren?" I bit back a laugh. "She's not powerful enough to take me over."

"I'm sure people thought the same thing about Carroll at one time. Look what happened. Two vampires underestimated him. They thought his soul weak enough that death could stop him. That's not always the case."

"Yes, but in this particular instance, it was the case." It took everything I had not to explode. "I love you, Aunt Max, but I'm not a child. I've been taking care of myself for a really long time. Even when I was still technically a child, Grandpa gave me a lot of rope."

"To hang yourself?"

"To spread my wings," I corrected. "I was angry he didn't allow me to stay with you when I was a kid, but I think he did the right thing. He was strict with me, but he taught me so much. I was never worried when I crossed over with Lauren. I understood on an instinctive level that everything would be fine."

"Except you couldn't know that." Maxine refused to back down. "I don't want to dampen your enthusiasm because I think you've grown into a fantastic woman. That doesn't mean you're infallible."

"Did I say I was infallible?"

"No. I can see it in the way you carry yourself, though. You're getting a little too big for your britches, Missy."

"My britches seem to fit just fine. As for what happened with Lauren ... I'm sorry you're upset, but I found the answers we were looking for. I would do it again."

"And what happens when you're wrong one day? No one is right all the time."

I very much doubted most of the Grimlocks believed that. Now wasn't the time to mention it, though. "I guess we'll have to wait until that day comes." My temper burned hot and fast as I stood and dusted off the seat of my pants. "We're ready to call him. Do you want to stay or go? I can do this without you if necessary. We can't fight. We need to work together."

The sigh that escaped was long and drawn out. Still, she cracked a smile as she accepted the hand I extended in her direction and climbed to her feet. "I love you, Izzy girl. I always have. I don't chide you because I enjoy it. It's my job to look out for you."

"And you're doing a phenomenal job." I cracked a smile for her benefit. "It's okay. I know what I'm doing. I've dealt with a shade before. Once we draw him here and trap him in the devil's snare, all we have to do is banish him to the other side. Then he's their problem."

"You hope."

"I know. We won't make the same mistake Oliver and Brett did. They didn't realize what they were up against. We do. We'll end him this time."

Maxine didn't immediately say anything. Finally, when she did, all she could do was hold out her hands in defeat. "I'm with you until the end."

"I know. That's why you're a good aunt."

"Don't make me regret it." She wagged a finger and then motioned for the others to join us. "It's time. Is everyone in place on the other end?"

"Hold on." Cormack pulled out his phone and pushed a button. I watched as he waited for the call to connect. "Cillian, it's Dad. Are you guys ready?"

I waited for him to listen to the speaker on the other end. It seemed to be taking longer than it should have.

"Is something wrong?" I asked after he was quiet for a full minute. "Did something happen to Granger?"

He held up his hand to quiet me. "That's a lovely story, Cillian," he said after a beat. "I hope your brother gets lucky with the secretary with the big ... eyes. I don't really care that he's distracting her by flexing his muscles. I also don't care that you could flirt better but you won't because you're a good boyfriend. I care about Granger."

He was silent again as I let out the pent-up air I was holding inside. "Well, that's great. We're about to start. You know what to do once he's clear of the boy, right? Just ... be watchful. I'm doubtful Carroll will be able to return, but you need to be mindful all the same." A pause. "Yes, I definitely think you would flirt better than Redmond. Are you listening to me? Good. It will happen in a few minutes. Get ready."

He disconnected his phone and sighed. "I really wish I hadn't insisted on having five children."

I didn't believe him for a second. "Which ones would you trade?"

"Cillian and Redmond," he answered without hesitation.

"Does that mean I'm your favorite today?" Braden asked hopefully.

"Maybe. It's between you and your sister. That thing she did when she jumped on Angelina and declared it was a good day to die was kind of funny. She's edging you out just a bit."

"I guess we'll see if I can take her out by the end of the day," he offered.

"That sounds like a fabulous idea." His eyes flicked to me. "I'm ready. What do you want us to do?"

"Stand here and here." I pointed toward the pentagram. "Oliver, Brett, we need you, too." They joined us, taking aggressive stances in the circle. Oliver positioned himself to my right while Brett stood between Cormack and Braden. They separated themselves so they were at either side of the circle. If I had to guess, that was deliberate. They were acting as our protectors, which was completely unnecessary.

Still, I spared a smile for both of them. "Let's do this."

Oliver nodded as he squeezed my hand. "We'll do it right this time."

"That's the plan," I agreed, closing my eyes. "Here we go."

The ritual was part voodoo, part hoodoo, and a little standard witch thrown in for good measure. It was something I devised with several priestesses when I realized what we were up against so many years ago. I was still a teenager then, sowing my wild oats and having a good time with the adventure. Things seemed more dangerous now, the stakes higher, and I couldn't help being a little nervous.

The men waited patiently as Maxine and I began chanting in unison. I led the spell and she held on for dear life, to the point I was eventually speeding ahead and she was left behind to serve as a sentry of sorts. My grandfather taught me that magic was to be performed from the heart or not at all. That meant you had to believe in what you were doing, and that you were helping the greater good rather than working against the greater cosmic balance.

That's what dictated my actions now.

"Come to us now," I bellowed when I came to the end of the Latin chant, "Ryan Carroll."

My heart skipped a beat and I swear I heard the drums of the voodoo priestesses in my head.

"Ryan Carroll," I repeated. "Ryan Carroll. Ryan Carroll."

Maxine joined in. And then, probably because they didn't know what else to do, the men started chanting his name as well. I felt Braden's hand holding mine. It was sweaty and the anxiety he felt oozed out of him as I worked to push his fear to the back of my brain. It would do no good to worry about him now.

"Ryan Carroll!" I practically screeched his name a final time. It was necessary over the blast of wind that blew through the room with enough power that several of the books Jerry had organized days before blew off the shelves.

A whirlwind formed in the corner of the room, ectoplasm green and hatred forming a vortex. The wind spun and I heard a screamed protest as the shade was forced into our haven. The whirlwind churned through the room, traveling in our direction and spitting fury and hatred as it chewed up the distance. I recognized right away that Carroll was trapped, that he had nowhere to go. He recognized it, too, the second the devil's trap snapped to life and encased him.

"No," the creature howled, taking a ghostly form as he swiveled back and forth. His voice sounded otherworldly, as if he'd long since severed ties with his human body. That was true, so I managed to look on him as he was, serpentine and ethereal.

"Hello, Ryan," I offered, managing to keep my voice even despite the way my nerves twitched. "How are things?"

"You, wretched girl," he hissed. His tongue wasn't forked, but it was so black I had to look elsewhere to keep the bile from rising. "I warned you what would happen if you messed with me. I told you what your fate would be." He growled as he threw himself in my direction. The devil's trap managed to keep him at bay, the barrier not even shaking. "What manner of magic is this?" He lifted his hands and felt around the trap. "I don't understand."

"You can't leave," I replied simply. "We channeled you here. We trapped you here. You're done."

"I'm not done. I'm only getting started."

"Yeah, well ... you keep thinking that." I rolled my neck but kept my fingers linked with Braden and Oliver's. "How did you survive here so long without a body? Are you anchored to something? Perhaps an item of clothing or a trinket?"

"I'm not telling you." Carroll was beside himself as he continuously turned in a circle. "I will find a way out of this infernal room. I won't be trapped here again."

"We didn't realize you were trapped here the first time," Oliver offered, speaking for the first time and drawing Carroll's horrific gaze. "We thought we'd killed you."

"You put up an admirable effort," Carroll snarled. "But I'm stronger than you."

"Not so strong that you could break the wards on the library," I countered. "You were trapped here for a long time. The only reason you managed to escape at all was due to a happy accident. I'm sure that if Oliver realized you were still here he would've fought harder to keep the library a secret."

"Definitely," Oliver agreed. "You have no idea how badly I wish I'd known you were in here. I still don't understand how it happened."

"I'm just that powerful," Carroll snapped.

"No, you're just that lucky," I corrected. "You had no idea you were going to survive. Don't pretend otherwise. In fact, you probably thought you were lost when Brett killed you and disposed of your body. There was something left, of course. I'm guessing it was something small and dark that withered in the shadows while you were locked away.

"You festered in here for a long time," I continued. "There was nothing to feed on, so you floated. Time probably had no meaning. Were you even aware of what you'd lost as the years elapsed? I think that's a big, fat 'no.'

"Then, a few weeks ago, the wall between the gate room and the library crumbled," I said. "In the process — perhaps because so many people were in and out — the wards were destroyed, too. The wards weren't meant to keep you in. They were meant to keep others out, though they made an effective trap.

"When you realized you were free, you fled," I said. "That was smart. You escaped quickly, but I don't think you made it very far. The conservatory, perhaps? I know a few of the regular volunteers who are supposed to keep it up have gone missing. That's why Claire has been filling in. Someone had to take care of the plants, and she's always looking for a reason to get away from her husband."

"They're such a lovely couple," Brett drawled, earning a small smile from me.

"It was easy for you to feed on the other volunteers," I continued. "They were human and unprepared for attack, unlike Claire, who could've probably fought you off ... which is why she's still standing. I'm guessing the bodies are somewhere on the grounds ... though you obviously could've possessed them and forced the bodies to another location. Is that what you did?"

"Wouldn't you like to know?" Carroll growled, frustration pouring off him as he continuously threw himself at the edges of the devil's trap in an attempt to find a weak spot.

"I would like to know," I admitted. "If we can put those people to rest, that would be a godsend. That includes the ghost I shredded in the spa. I know who he is, by the way. I saw the missing person sign at the park welcome center. I didn't even realize what I was looking at that first day. Heck, I didn't realize what I was looking at when I zapped his soul. It was only today that the pieces started fitting together."

"Good for you."

"I think I've figured it all out," I pressed. "I know what happened with Granger. One of the ghosts tried to speak through him right before it happened. Actually, one of them managed to speak but I didn't realize what was happening. They knew and tried to warn me, perhaps because they sensed something different about me. If I'd listened, I could've stopped this. I wasn't open that day, though, and I'm sorry for it."

"Yes, we're all sorry for it," Carroll mocked "We're all sorry you're such an idiot."

"I'm not an idiot, but I have been slow. I looked in the wrong places for answers. You're a simple shade. Sure, you're a shade that can possess other people, but you're still a shade. That means you're nowhere near as strong as you think you are."

Carroll made a strangled sound as he threw himself at Brett with every ounce of energy he had. "Let me out! I won't be trapped here. Not again."

I ignored his fury and remained focused on what had to be done. "Tell me where the bodies are," I demanded.

His eyes gleamed as he faced me. "I'll tell you for my freedom."

"No."

"That's the only thing I'll deal for. There's nothing else you can offer me that will get you what you want."

My patience was wearing thin, but I held it together for the sake of those who stood with me. "If you won't tell us, then I guess those families will have to suffer. I won't let you go. I know what you're capable of, and while it will sadden me to think of those families never finding closure, I won't let you roam again. Someone else will die if that happens, and that guilt would be too much to bear."

"Let me out!" He screamed directly in my face, his eyes going a deadly red. It was easy to see that any tendril of sanity he had was severed long ago. He was barely coherent, and beyond reason. "We should probably finish this," I said to Maxine.

She nodded. "Yes. Definitely." She released Cormack's and Brett's hands and dug in the bag of ingredients on the floor. "I guess it's time for the final act." She gripped the package of powder we'd made and started sprinkling it in the center of the circle. "Ashes to ashes," she started.

"No! What is that?" Carroll made a big show of trying to shrink back against the wall of the devil's trap and make himself appear small.

It was a wasted effort. "Stop! I'll tell you where the bodies are. If you let me go, I'll tell you where the bodies are."

I felt sorry for him in a way. He was beyond redemption. He probably always had been. I also felt sick to my stomach given the things he'd done. The latter feeling was what allowed me to reach into my pocket and retrieve another bag of the same concoction Maxine spread on her side of the circle.

"Dust to dust," I intoned as I began sprinkling it on the figure.

"Stop! I'll stay locked in here! I won't bother anyone again. Just stop!" Carroll tried to climb the walls, but there was no way out.

"May this man's spirit turn to mush," Braden offered helpfully as Carroll's screams began fading.

"We should add another packet for good measure," Brett suggested. "I mean ... just to be sure this time."

I knew what he was really saying and nodded. "Here." I dug an extra packet out of my pocket and handed it over. "You should probably do the honors."

"I would enjoy that." He smiled grimly at the wasting ethereal figure in the middle of the trap. "I really wish I'd known what was happening back then. I could've saved those lives we've since lost."

I lifted my eyes to the ghosts that were rapidly appearing in the library, all of them landing with a "zip" before immediately turning their attention to the gate room. None of them stopped to witness the end of their tormentor. None of them spoke. Not even Lauren, who paused by the door long enough to wave.

I wanted to ask her if she regained the ability to speak. I wanted to ask if she thought she would find peace.

In the end, it didn't matter. I'd done all I could for the trapped ghosts. The rest was up to them. So I leaned into Braden as he slid his arm around my back and watched as the ghosts crossed the gate and disappeared into a better forever.

Finally, it was over.

Thirty

Cleanup was easy.

Given what Carroll was, there was nothing left once his essence was destroyed. No dust. No blood. No ghostly remains.

His physical remains were burned long before, so he was gone ... and there was nothing but happiness left in his wake.

"What about the ghosts?" Braden asked, brushing my hair from my face and drawing my eyes to him as we sat at one of the ancient tables littering the library. Oliver and Brett were busy circling the room to make sure he was really gone this time. No matter how many times I told them it wasn't necessary, they continued their ministrations.

"They crossed over," I replied. "You saw them."

"They didn't say anything. Do you think whatever power Carroll had over them died with him? I mean ... will they be able to communicate on the other side?"

That was a very good question. "I don't know. I hope so. There's really no way for us to check."

"Well ... then I guess we'll focus on other things." He adopted a bright expression. "For example, how do you feel about a nice seafood dinner? There's a place on the Detroit River that has excellent scallops and crab legs. I was thinking we could get dressed up and everything."

It was a surreal offer given everything that was going on. "Well ... I happen to love seafood. I'm not sure today is the day for that, though. I thought maybe we would order delivery and go to bed early ... here. I mean, unless you're desperate to spend another night playing shark games with your siblings."

Braden's smile was soft. "I think I can make that work."

"Oh, you guys are cute," Brett enthused, shooting us a smile. "I think you're just adorable."

"And I think they're going to be trouble," Oliver shot back. "We'll worry about that later, though. As far as I can tell, Carroll is gone."

"He's definitely gone," I agreed. "He didn't have the power to stand on his own. I think he only managed to survive as long as he did due to a fluke. The wards kept him in. That meant he couldn't pass through the gate. He held on ... and when the wards failed, he managed to escape.

"Somewhere on this island there are a good twenty bodies," I continued. "He killed people every chance he got to get stronger. He killed the volunteers for the conservatory, the ones who just stopped showing up.

"He killed that boy I saw at the spa, the one I shredded before I realized what was going on," I continued. "I don't know why he was on Belle Isle, but I'm convinced he was killed here."

"It's Belle Isle," Braden said "I can think of a hundred different reasons a teenager would want to hang out here. Most of them involve smoking pot."

Cormack cuffed the back of his son's head. "I don't ever want to know why you think things like that."

"That's probably for the best," Braden agreed.

"I don't think Carroll built up the strength to leave the island in his shade form," I supplied. "He was trying hard, but he was weak. He amassed an army and fed himself during the process, but he jumped into Granger that day at the aquarium. That changed things for him, allowed him to leave the island. But it limited what he could do outside of Granger."

"Why do you think that?"

"Because he didn't want to leave the boy. That much was obvious. I have a few hunches about why, but one of the biggest is that he was safe inside that small package. He had time to regroup, figure out how the world had changed, and he could hide in a small child who wasn't expected to interact with his surroundings in a regular fashion."

"I get what you're saying," Braden acknowledged. "Granger didn't talk. Carroll could be as quiet as necessary while figuring out the next leg of his plan. But you said Granger talked that first day. He warned you that 'they' were coming. Why would Carroll warn you about his own coming?"

"That wasn't Carroll." It had taken me a bit to figure out this part of the story, but I was fairly certain I was right. "That was Granger. The ghosts whispered to him, like they did to me. They might have even spoken through him. I guess that's still up for debate. They tried to warn him when they realized what was happening. They talked through Granger ... which is only part of the reason Carroll felt the need to silence them. What little power he'd managed to gather since being resurrected was spent silencing them. He never got a full foothold because he had to keep regrouping."

"You sound sure of yourself," Oliver noted. "How much of this is fact and how much is conjecture?"

I shrugged. "I saw a few things when he was flashing in and out there at the end. He was trying to cling to this world with his last breath. He couldn't shutter when that was happening, so I saw what he did ... and what he knew ... and how he planned to fulfill what he thought of as his destiny."

"And how was that?"

"Kill as many people as possible. He wasn't exactly imaginative when coming up with a plan. He wanted the powerful souls. But he needed to be close to the gate to get them, and he had no scepter.

"That meant he had to start small," I continued. "He had to bolster his strength with the volunteers at the conservatory. He also had to hide what he was doing so we wouldn't immediately come looking. He wasn't prepared to fight us because he didn't have the strength.

"He was getting stronger when he saw the tour arrive," I explained.

"He thought he might be able to get a big boost of power from them. Instead, he got something else. In his last moments, I saw what he really had planned. He wanted to hop from Granger to a reaper – maybe even one of you – and steal your scepter so it would be easier to gain access to the gate and the sort of souls he needed. He wanted to start sucking them from the other side again. He thought enough time had passed to allow him to get away with it ... at least for the time being."

"Yeah, well, at least it's over." Cormack straightened and rolled his neck. "Well, over other than a certain conversation I'll be having with the higher-ups about Carroll's sealed file. They could've helped us a great deal if they'd simply told the truth from the beginning."

"So could I," Oliver pointed out.

"Yes, but you were protecting someone you love," Cormack said. "I don't agree it was necessary – Brett did what had to be done – but I understand. The home office could've told us as much as possible without exposing the two of you. I don't understand why they didn't."

"It's over," Oliver argued. "Why push things?"

"Because they need to be pushed. We can't do our jobs if we're operating in the dark. It's that simple."

Oliver held up his hands in defeat. "Okay. I get it. You'll do what you have to do and I'll stay out of it."

"That would probably be best," Cormack agreed. "Perhaps you should focus on your job for a bit? That goes for both of you." He slid me a look. "You still need to hire a new assistant."

Ugh. I'd almost forgotten about all that. "Can't it wait? I'm sure we can make it another week or two. I'll pick someone before the end of the month."

"Oh, no." Cormack made a clucking sound with his tongue. "You'll do it tonight. You can't clock out – or go on any planned dates – until you give me a name."

That sounded like emotional blackmail. "But ... ." I looked to Braden for help.

"I can't help you." Braden shrugged. "Just do what he wants. He won't let it go until you do."

Oh, well, that was just ridiculous. With nothing better to do, I stormed through the library door and into the gate room. There, still sitting on my desk, was the stack of personnel files. Oliver had whittled it down to five names and then I'd completely forgotten about the endeavor.

"Fine." I grabbed the stack and mixed them up. I shut my eyes and picked one. I forced a smile for Cormack's benefit as I opened the file and read the name. "Paris Princeton."

Cormack was amused as he trailed me into the room. "Don't you want to put more effort into the choice than that?"

"Nope. I have a good feeling about her."

Cormack didn't look convinced. "Well, I guess it's your choice. If that's who you want, she's all yours."

"Great." I offered him a genuine smile this time. "Does that mean we can be done for the night?" I gestured toward Braden so there would be no mistake who I was talking about.

"I think you should let us off early," Braden added. "I mean ... Izzy did take out a shade and save the world."

"Save the world?" Cormack chuckled. "Don't you think that's a bit of an exaggeration?"

"Not if it gets us off work early."

I waited for Cormack to answer, but the twinkle in his eyes telegraphed his response before he even opened his mouth. "Go ahead," he said. "Have a good evening."

"Score!" Braden pumped his fist and grabbed my hand. We were almost to the door before he slowed his pace. "Wait ... does this mean I'm your favorite today?"

"Izzy is my favorite today."

"I'm fine with that."

Cormack snickered. "I figured you would be. Enjoy your night ... and have fun. It's back to the grindstone for both of you tomorrow."

"Deal." I waved at him and laughed as Braden chased me toward the stairs. "We have the whole night. What do you want to do?"

Braden turned petulant. "You said takeout and bed. I was totally looking forward to that. You can't change your mind now."

"Then takeout and bed it is. We can start figuring out the rest tomorrow."

"And what is the rest?"

"You know ... the rest. We're in a relationship now. I'm pretty sure that means there are rules."

"Ugh." Braden made a tortured face. "I hate rules."

"Something tells me you'll survive."

His smile was cheeky. "Something tells me you're right."

CPSIA information can be obtained
at www.ICGtesting.com
Printed in the USA
LVHW041809110820
662922LV00011B/1194